Scribe

to the
Pantheon
of Rome

Also by David P. Tangredi:

Journey to the Temple of Ra

T he Return" has been prophesied for millennia. The very year predicted now approaches. And **THEY** have formulated a plan...

John's serendipitous journey begins when he happens upon a small Middle Eastern village. There, he encounters a spiritually gifted family. Each offers their love, support, and wisdom. Together they foster John through an initiation, transforming his wandering into purposeful endeavor.

Follow John as he travels through the four directions. Watch as he discovers the spiritual gifts he possesses. Learn how his *Journey to the Temple of Ra* empowers him to become the *Scribe to the Pantheon of Rome*.

Scribe
to the
Pantheon
of Rome

David P. Tangredi

ISBN: 978-0-9893673-3-2

January 25, 2017 Edition

Published by:

A Fool's Inclination Publications
AFoolsInclination.com

It matters not what inspires you toward love.
Appreciate the inspiration and the love, whenever and from
wherever it comes—for from appreciation, inspiration, and love
flows the fulfillment of ALL desires.

Prologue

J ohn and Johannes left the Temple of Luxor and trudged back to the inn...dazed, partly from the intense, midday sun, but mostly from the session. They felt overwhelmed by the message John had channeled.

Are we being asked to deliver these teachings to mankind?— John wondered. *How are we supposed to do that? Ra, you didn't give us further instruction? Seth, where do we go from here?*

Ra told them that they are never alone, and yet each felt completely alone, albeit together.

How am I supposed to go back to any semblance of a normal life after that?—Johannes thought. *I am not a teacher; I am a businessman.*

One journey had indeed ended. That much was well understood. The next journey, however, was just beginning...

0 – *Zero* – **Nihil**

Zéro – Zero – Cero – Null

Zero existed before time and space, before the first second, before the first atom. At zero, there is no separation: no beginning and no end. As soon as there was an observer, there was the observed, and from the zero came the one and the two...

Zéro – Zero – Cero – Null

John carefully ran his index finger under the flap, breaking the wax seal. He pulled out the contents: a letter, as expected, but he also immediately discovered what provided the additional bulk. He placed the Egyptian currency aside and read the letter…

1 – *One* – I

Un – Uno – Uno – Eins

R a? Seth? Is anyone here with me?" John looked around, but didn't recognize anything he was seeing. "Where am I?" he wondered. Something felt odd, but he didn't know why.

Up ahead, a small cabin piqued John's interest. Actually, it looked like a miniature castle, or maybe a part of one. It was the **size** of a small cabin, but the façade was topped with a crenelated roofline, characteristic of a medieval fortress.

As John got closer, he saw the deep moat that surrounded the structure. He then asked himself, "How do I know it is deep? The water is dark and murky." The moat was too wide to jump over, and too ominous to swim in, so he decided to walk around it to see if there was a way across.

As he circled the building, each face came into view: the second, the third, and then the fourth. They all looked identical. He counted as he went along, but was never quite sure how many sides there were. Not a window or a door was found in any of them, and never a bridge across the moat.

Why does this fortress feel so familiar?

He continued a bit further until he faced the next side squarely. From that angle, he could only see the one wall. He examined it intently and could almost feel the texture of the stone as if touching it with his hands.

Where have I seen stone like that before?

John began searching his memory for clues, but was interrupted by a screech. He looked up and saw a golden hawk circling overhead. It screeched a second time and then soared toward the horizon.

John watched the bird until he could no longer make out its

shape. It simply became a black dot barely visible against the dusky sky. His eyes moved down to the horizon—to the silhouette of three pyramids that separated the dimly lit sky from the dark sandy land.

"I have to get back to Cairo! What have I done?"

Urgency took hold of him and he began running towards the pyramids, following the hawk's lead.

"Is there enough time?" John said aloud. "Please tell me there's enough time."

"You have all the time in the world; there is no reason for you to hurry."

John stopped in his tracks and spun around to see who had spoken to him. He saw nothing but sand in all directions.

"Who's there?" he called out to the emptiness.

"Do you not recognize my voice?" came the reply.

"Ra, is that you?"

"Yes my son. I am Ra."

"Ra, what is happening? I need to get back to Cairo...right now! Can you take me?" There was worry and panic in John's voice.

"I can guide you, yes, but what is your concern?" Ra said calmly.

"I don't know. I just have to get there before...before I don't know **what** happens!"

"John, do you remember what we told you about the Journey of the Fool?"

"You told me a lot about it," John said, a bit annoyed.

"The most important part is this: the Journey of the Fool is always from where you are to where you want to be."

"Yes, I remember now."

"So, you are clear where you want to be, yes?" Ra asked.

"Yes!" John said impatiently. "I need to get to Cairo and soon!"

Ra's patience was unending. "I understand, my son, but do you know where you are?"

"Well...no. I thought you could help me with that." John looked around, but saw no landmarks, no road signs.

"My son, the greater part of most journeys is figuring out where one is. That is the point—or rather the **starting** point. Ha!"

"So, does this mean you aren't going to tell me?" John lowered his head, feeling defeated.

"Dear **one**, did I not give you **two** eyes with which to see? Behold your here and now. You look, but you do not **three**!"

"**Three**!? What does **that** mean?" John voiced the question, but he somehow knew that Ra had already departed. He fell to the ground, sobbing. He covered his eyes with his hands and the world went dark. When he removed his hands, however, he still could not see.

"Ra? Ra! Where are you?" John screamed, and his voice echoed. He was no longer out in the middle of the desert. It was now dark and cold and he was inside...

Is this a cave?

The ground was no longer the soft, warm sand of the desert; rather, it was a cold, hard, stone floor. He stood and walked slowly, his hands scanning the darkness in front of him. The sound of his footsteps echoed, causing him to shiver with fright. The air around his hands was somehow cooler than the air around his face, and then he felt the cold wall in front of him. He traced his fingers along the mortar around the stone; the shape was a rectangle.

A stone wall. Am I in a prison cell?

And then John understood. He put his ear to the stone and could hear the faint sound of water flowing in the moat just beyond the wall.

"How did I get in here? More importantly, how do I get out? Ra, help! I'm trapped!"

"Look first...then see. Know where you are...and know where you want to be. Then take the first step."

Un – Uno – Uno – Eins

J ohn woke from the dream and what felt like a full day of sleep. The session at the Temple of Luxor had taken so much out of him, he had barely made it back to the room before collapsing on the bed. Now that he was awake, his sense of time was distorted.

He didn't know what part of the day it was or even which day.

After looking out of the window for clues, John finally decided it was neither early nor late, likely noon or mid-afternoon. He then scanned the room.

Johannes was not present, which didn't surprise him, but what did surprise him was that the room looked as if it had been straightened up while he was asleep. His belongings were placed neatly on a chair next to the bed and the only other evidence that the room was occupied, other than his body under the sheets, was a goblet of water on the nightstand.

Water!

Yes, that was exactly what he needed right now. The sight of it induced the strongest thirst he had felt since that fortnight walking in the desert. Back then, even after guzzling from his canteen, he still felt thirsty—a psychological trick his mind played on him due to the sun, the heat, and the sand that abounded.

As John returned the now empty goblet to the nightstand, an envelope caught his attention. His name was written on the front and in Johannes' handwriting. John reached for the envelope and saw his hand tremble. He lifted the envelope; it was sealed. His breathing became strained.

If this were a simple, "I ran out to get food," note, would Johannes have sealed it?

It was also too thick to only contain a letter.

John carefully ran his index finger under the flap, breaking the wax seal. He pulled out the contents: a letter, as he had expected, but he also immediately discovered what provided the additional bulk. He placed the Egyptian currency aside and read the letter:

Dear John,

First and foremost, I am sorry. I am sorry that you are reading these words rather than hearing them, and I am sorry you have to be receiving them at all. I am sure you have figured out by now that I have left the Inn. Who knows, looking at how tired you seem as I write this, I might even be out of the city by the time you read this. I hope you are not disappointed in me…again, and I hope you can find comfort in the fact that—this time—I am at least explaining myself.

I am not like you and these sorts of things are not easy for me. I can't do this. I can't do this 'work' and I can't pretend that everything is just fine the way it is. I know about your feelings. I know you care for me deeply and I know there is so much you wish to say. I also know that your fear—of rejection, perhaps—prevents you from doing so.

John, I am neither running away from you nor shunning you because of how you feel. These are what make you the great man that you are. These are the truest parts of you; parts that need to be let out to run free; parts that will make someone—some man—very happy.

The truth is: I am a bit intimidated by your expressiveness. You wear your heart on your sleeve and when I don't respond as you would like, you get hurt and frustrated all over again. I see how you struggle with this. I'm not as unaware as you might think.

Furthermore, this channeling work that you have discovered, these messages from…wherever—I don't know what I think about all of this. I don't disbelieve in the possibility of this being true. In fact, I have spent these past weeks wishing it were all true, wishing that I would come to believe in it as strongly as you do. But alas, I do not. What you need most is to be surrounded by others that believe in this the way you do—people who can support you wholeheartedly.

I have thus decided to return to the life and work I am comfortable with. Maybe someday down the road our paths will cross again and maybe at that time, I will be able to offer you something more. For now, I feel this is best... for both of us.

I've left you some money and paid in advance for the next two nights here at the inn. I hope this gives you enough time to work out what is next for you. I have complete faith in you, John. Your spirit and your charm shine brightly. You will not go unnoticed.

Until our journeys collide once again,

Yours,

Johannes

John's eyes stayed fixed on Johannes' signature even as it blurred, partly from the tears in his eyes and partly from the tears that soaked into the paper. Yet accompanying his feeling of loss was a strange calm.

For months, the weight of a conversation unspoken went virtually unnoticed, but now he could feel the difference. He had been afraid to broach the subject. He **was** afraid of rejection and feared driving Johannes away.

"And now Johannes is gone anyway. Would it have made a difference if I told him how I feel?"

For that matter, was John willing to admit to himself how much he loved Johannes?

Un – Uno – Uno – Eins

Johannes watched the city of Cairo as it receded to the south. It was only a few hours earlier that he had arrived.

During the first half of Johannes' trip from Luxor to Cairo, he assessed his decision. He was confident that he was not running away as much as he was doing what was best—*for everyone. Maybe there were better ways to handle the situation*—he considered, but that aside, the decision felt right.

He noticed a sense of satisfaction that came from allowing himself to simply be the man that he was. The brutal honesty of embracing one's own limitations provided a relief he never would have expected. It was as if the act of **trying** to be something he wasn't had fueled self-judgment for not being it. Once he had accepted all aspects of himself, right then and there, he began to like himself again. And the one thing he liked most about himself was being a man who knew how to enjoy what life had to offer. He then thought about the reason he traveled to Egypt in the first place. *I came here to have fun. Now what do I want to do?*

Convinced he had, in fact, made the right decision, Johannes spent the second half of the trip to Cairo exploring the myriad avenues that lay before him. He moved to the bow of the riverboat and gazed down the Nile. He began thinking of the numerous times John had spoken about his experiences in Italy. He recalled the loving family that had taken John in, the colorful descriptions of food and architecture, and the seemingly endless beauty. The Italian culture was apparently rich and inviting and Johannes was intrigued.

As if guided by the Universe itself, upon arriving in Cairo Johannes discovered that the neighboring ship was bound for Italy and imminently departing. He boarded the vessel without giving it a second thought. "Surely this is an omen," he conceded.

With Cairo's buildings now blending into the sandy-scape that surrounded it, the invisible walls around him loosened and fell away. Johannes wasn't sure where in Italy he would visit, what he would do when he got there, or even the point of the trip, but the idea excited him. *Besides, I have the entire journey across the Mediterranean to think about it.* His breathing calmed and soon he felt as relaxed as his days on the beach in Crete.

Un – Uno – Uno – Eins

L ord Ra, thank you for meeting with me. I have been wrought with anxiety. This situation…I…I could not have predicted. I am at a complete loss! John cannot channel without someone like Johannes to hold space for him. I know not how to guide him in light of this manifestation! What shall I do?"

Seth's auric colors oscillated rapidly within a wide spectrum, indicative of his stress over the unexpected turn of events.

"My dear Seth, worry not my son. The Perfection of the Universe is at play. The Wheel of Fortune has turned; we merely need to roll with it to reap what it has to offer. Johannes has exercised his free will, as he is wont to do. A new plan is already in the offing."

Seth's colors oscillated more slowly until they settled into a single hue.

"Thank you my lord. Is it appropriate for me to know of this new plan?"

"In time, my son. Trust. Allow. Follow your own inclinations. Have you forgotten that **you** create your own reality as much as John does?"

"Forgive me, my lord. I just do not wish to see John hurt again."

"I understand."

"My lord? If I may?" Seth was always nervous posing questions to Ra.

"Yes?"

"When do you think you will tell John who you really are?"

"In time, my son."

Seth lowered his head to hide his frustration. He could no longer keep track of how many times he received **that** as an answer: "In time." *For something that is an illusion, it seems to be the answer to everything!*

Un – Uno – Uno – Eins

J ohn was surprised he was taking Johannes' departure as well as he seemed to be. Overall, he felt neither hurt nor depressed. After that first time when he had first read the letter, he hadn't cried again.

Maybe I am beginning to trust the process—he thought to himself.

He did feel alone, but that was neither good nor bad.

"And that letter! Johannes' generosity was not unlike him, and would be very helpful, but the fact that he had said what he had said; that's huge!"

As a result of his optimistic perspective, rather than feel abandoned, John felt cared for. The money Johannes gave him wouldn't last forever, but it was enough to get him to the next place, *wherever that will be*.

John used up the two prepaid nights in Luxor, and then boarded a tour boat back to Cairo, which was free because the tour guide recognized him from their trip up the Nile weeks earlier. This meant that he had plenty of money to rent a room in Cairo while he figured out what to do next.

And there were many options.

What John most wanted to do, however, was channel again.

Will Ra, Seth, or Isis show up when I call on them? What will they say about Johannes' departure? Do they have a recommendation as to where I should go next? And what do they want me to do with all of the information they already provided?

All of these questions swirled around in John's mind until he asked: "I've never tried to channel by myself. Is this even possible?"

John had to find out and so he sat as he had in each of the previous sessions to see what would happen.

At first, all John experienced was calmness and quietude. He cleared his mind, but no voice came save his own. Images intermittently floated by as when meditating, but no orations of wisdom.

John then called out to Seth, Ra, and Isis: "Is anyone there?"

Silence.

"Does anyone want to talk to me today?"

Silence.

John took a deep breath, made sure he was relaxed, and tried once more, but to no avail. "I guess this doesn't work when I'm by myself."

Right.

The mental response came to John in English, even though that wasn't the language he was using. He switched to English and continued.

"Did I hear you correctly? Is that you?"

Right.

"Who's there?"

Right.

"This isn't funny."

Right.

Exasperated, John blurted, "All right! You win. I give up."

He had started hopeful, but was now irritated. Either he was playing a joke on himself, or spirit was, and in either case, he didn't like it. So he pushed the session out of his mind and started thinking about the future, *the imminent future.* Not wanting to waste too much time and money, he whispered to himself, "I need to come up with a plan!"

Un – Uno – Uno – Eins

T he calm waters between Cairo and Italy made for smooth sailing. The vessel Johannes had boarded was destined for Bari, a port city along the southeastern coast of Italy located just above the 'heel' of the 'boot'. Bari sat across the Italian peninsula

12

from Naples and across the Adriatic Sea from Albania. The complete journey would take a bit more than twice as long as the trip between Cairo and Crete.

For his days at sea, Johannes had set up his stateroom like an office. Really, this was just an exercise in perspective since there was nothing to **do** save **think** of it that way. He felt energized and invigorated and did not want to waste any more time fooling around.

"I need to come up with a plan," he said to himself as he began organizing his thoughts. His intention was to choose a location that would facilitate business advancement and personal enjoyment alike. John had spoken highly of the region surrounding the city of Naples, *but it wouldn't be right to go there*—Johannes surmised, as if it would be a betrayal of some kind.

He set his sights on completing a plan before reaching Bari— one that included an ultimate destination and purpose.

"That sounds easy enough," he decided.

Un – Uno – Uno – Eins

T he next day, John decided to go for a walk. Walking would help him think and it would allow him to burn off some of the frustration he was feeling. He left the inn and chose a direction at random. It was more important to move than it was to get somewhere.

After circling through some of the busiest sections of Cairo, John's mind started to focus. He iterated through various options for a future course of action and then narrowed the list down to three choices: he could go back to the Middle East and visit Sara and the Emperor; he could return to Italy and maybe find some work with Felizio; or he could travel to somewhere he'd never been. Heidelberg—Johannes' hometown—was clearly out of the question. And staying in Cairo, or Egypt for that matter, just didn't feel right.

Content with having at least accomplished that much, John put off a final decision and sought after a meal. By this point, he found himself literally in the middle of Cairo's busiest plaza. Two significant journeys had started there, but John's hunger kept him from thinking about either of them.

He stopped and looked around. A number of food stands were visible as well as open-air restaurants.

Do I want something quick to eat, or do I want to sit and relax for a while?

No sooner had he questioned his desires than his attention was diverted. A strong but frail looking hand took hold of his arm.

"Young man, your seeking emanates from you like an odor. Which hunger is strongest within you now? Food? Travel? **Or purpose**?"

"Excuse me," John replied. "Do I know you?"

"We have not met, young man, but I know who you are. I have seen your auric signature before, two months ago when you first entered the land of pharaohs."

"How do you know when I arrived in Egypt?"

The old woman ignored his question. "Where has your fair-haired brother run off to now?" she asked him.

Shrugging his shoulders, John replied, "Geez, you tell me. That man..."

The woman's eyes widened. "So he **has** abandoned you again."

"Well, he's run off, if that's what you mean, but he didn't abandon me, exactly. He just..."

"I see. Hmm. Yes. Oh? I understand. Yes." The old woman appeared as if she were talking to an invisible being.

"Are you seeing something? Are you getting something?" John asked.

"I believe so. You are more difficult to read now. Are you aware of this?"

John rolled his eyes. "Well, if I am, then that's a first. For the past two years I've been an open book to the spiritually endowed."

"There are two causes. For one, you are being shielded. A field has been placed around you. No, do not worry; it is not a curse. It is protective. However, the second reason is actually more...significant. The departure of your brother has...altered the flow of events. Yes! His abrupt departure was not anticipated—or at least not expected."

"So what does this mean?"

"Come with me, my boy. Let me read your cards. A message has been trying to reach you."

The old woman dragged John to her table. He was surprised by her strength. She pulled him along faster than he cared to go and her grip was firm, almost painfully so. The woman pushed John into a chair and then quickly moved into a second one on the opposite side of her small, square table. She then began shuffling her cards.

Eyeing him suspiciously, the woman said, "The cards tell me that you are familiar with them. Is this so?"

"Yes. I know the Tarot. Well, I've used them before, but I'm not proficient or anything."

The woman shuffled a bit more and then laid out four cards in a row. She flipped them over one at a time and studied them. She then began explaining each to John.

"Yes, I see. It is very clear. There has been a change in the plan. The work you expected to do can no longer be done. The river must be allowed to change course. This shift seems not to be a problem for you. The Eight of Cups suggests that you are ready to move on."

"I guess. I'm not sure I fully understood what I was supposed to do anyway. But I do feel like things have changed and that's fine with me, so long as I know where to go from here."

She pointed to the next two cards. "These indicate where you are right now: a pair of aces! Yes, indeed, a wholly new plan has been created. This—the Ace of Wands—is the new purpose slated for you. It shines brightly—so much potential, so much warmth. And here—the Ace of Swords—shows new knowledge, new communication."

"But I tried to communicate earlier and I couldn't get through."

"Are you certain?"

"Well…no…not certain. It felt like they were teasing me."

"No, no. They were not teasing. They delivered you a message. They're calling you toward a new direction."

"Direction? Oh. I did hear the word 'right', but something like 'north' or 'west' would have been more helpful."

"My boy, you did not hear 'right' as in the opposite of 'left'. For that matter, you did not hear 'right' as in the opposite of 'wrong'." The woman then pointed at the last card. "You heard '**write**' as in the opposite of '**read**'!"

"Write? They want me to write?"

"See here—the Eight of Pentacles—the apprentice uses tools to create. Yes, they want you to write: words, numbers…wisdom!"

John sat quietly, thinking about what the woman was telling him.

She went on. "My boy, in spoken communication the speaker and the listener are linked—in time and space. They must be present with each other in the here and now. This requires synchronization and resonance. With written correspondence, that is not the case. What is written can be read…**later**! The entanglement extends over time and space and thus less coherence is needed. Stop trying to speak and begin to write!"

"That sounds easy enough."

"As easy as one, two, three!"

John paid the woman for the reading. He was so satisfied with the information, he almost forgot he was hungry—at least until he neared a food cart and smelled the aroma of freshly grilled meat.

Un – Uno – Uno – Eins

J ohannes worked best when he was comfortable, and he was most comfortable within a routine. Each morning, he would rise with the sun and stroll along the main deck to fully awaken in the cool, morning air. This gave him a bit of exercise and allowed him to check in on the ship's progress. After, he would return to his stateroom and spend the rest of the morning working on his plan.

Most days, Johannes had to force himself to take a break in the afternoon. On nice days, a break might last a good few hours, but in any event, a conversation with a member of the crew or even the captain was typical. After sating himself with food and rest, Johannes would be back to work, often until retiring. If nothing else, his schedule made the days pass quickly.

The idea that he began to foster was a way to expand the family business into Italy. Klaus, Johannes' boss and father, had always preferred eastern expansion, avoiding competition from other Europeans. Johannes, on the other hand, found himself rooted in the West. He had already set up an office on the island of Crete— although possibly for no other reason than to visit regularly. Greece more or less straddled Eastern and Western Europe, so a location that was decidedly west was his preference. Italy was a fine choice.

But where? That was the question that remained to be answered.

Un – Uno – Uno – Eins

Each time John sat to write, he felt silly. *At least writing to oneself isn't as weird as talking to oneself*—he admitted.

He tried writing a story, writing as if in his journal, even writing poetry, but nothing seemed to work. Ultimately, he decided to write Ra a letter:

Dear Ra,

According to this fortuneteller woman I met a few days ago, you want me to write. But what am I supposed to write about? I have been trying for days now and I am getting nowhere. I **am** supposed to write, yes?

Right.

Right? I thought I'm supposed to write!

Right. Write!

So what do you want me to write? A letter?

No. A number.

A number? You don't want me to write a letter; you want me to write a number?

Right.

I'm confused.

Apparently.

Now we're getting somewhere. At least that word has four syllables.

You wrote a number. Good. But 'four' is not the number we have in mind.

No? Then what is the right number?

One.

One? Why one?

Can you think of a better place to start?

I guess not. But I don't understand. What do numbers have to do with anything?

Ah, that is precisely the question we wish to answer. Over these past two years, we've taught you much and now your journey continues.

We showed you the Zodiac with its twelve signs, but why are there specifically twelve? We taught you the meaning of the four elements, but why only four? We explained to you in detail the three selves, but why precisely three? And we described to you the twin flames, but why simply two?

These are not chance or random. All numbers have value and this you will come to know...and write. And, as with all else, the symbols, the models—these are merely tools for teaching wisdom from one realm to another.

So you are saying that numbers are important and a good way to teach. You want me to write about them. Then what?

Do you remember the description of the Fool given to you by the Magician?

Yes.

Would the Fool be concerned about the fourteen when he is standing next to the one?

I guess not.

For now, allow this to be your introduction. We will start the first lesson next time. Good night.

Good night. And thank you.

As always, you are very welcome.

Un – Uno – Uno – Eins

H alfway across the Mediterranean, Johannes arrived at the answer to his burning question.

Venice, he concluded, was ideal. For one, it was a significant Italian port and was geographically closest to both Budapest and Heidelberg. Two, Venice was purported to be one of the most beautiful cities in the world. It was known for its unique canals, elegant art, and classic architecture. Last, it was home to a culture more relaxed than Italy's larger cities.

Furthermore, Johannes' ship was already nearing the Adriatic Sea along the eastern coast of Italy. Bari was therefore literally en route to Venice, and this appealed to Johannes' propensity for efficiency. If he had chosen a city on the west coast, he would have to back track, sailing around the widest portion of the peninsula, extending his travel and delaying his start.

The unique combination that Venice offered thus appealed to Johannes, both for personal experience and professional advancement. He therefore decided that Venice was the perfect starting point for an exciting new venture.

Having made his decision, Johannes gave himself the rest of the day off to celebrate.

Un – Uno – Uno – Eins

With renewed faith, John was eager to write. He felt connected again and this excited him. Although it had taken a few times before he succeeded, he wasn't easily discouraged.

Un – Uno – Uno – Eins

Johannes ascended the carpeted stairway, donning his best shirt. He entered the first class dining room and was immediately greeted by the maître d'.

"Good evening, sir. How many are there in your party?"

"Just one. But give me the best table you have available and show me your finest wines. Tonight, I am celebrating."

"Congratulations sir. Please, follow me."

Johannes followed the maître d', noticing the lavish decoration. Red velvet drapes framed the floor-to-ceiling windows and white lace covered the dining tables. The silverware was actual silver and the glistening gold napkins were silk.

The maître d' pulled out a chair that faced the western horizon.

"How is this, sir?" Waving his hand out toward the scene, he said, "Your timing is perfect. The weather is ideal this evening."

"Indeed it is," Johannes replied, taking the seat offered him.

The maître d' excused himself, but hardly a moment passed before the sommelier arrived.

"Good evening, sir. As you requested, I present to you our finest wines."

Johannes glanced at the wine steward's selection, but didn't recognize any. "How is this one?" he asked pointing at an Italian red.

"The best Italy has to offer! I highly recommend it," the sommelier replied.

"Very well," Johannes said.

The sommelier then performed his rehearsed ritual: displaying the label, opening the bottle, waving the cork beneath Johannes' nose, pouring a splash into a glass, smelling it himself, and then presenting it to Johannes for him to taste.

Johannes, familiar with the routine, swirled the wine, breathed in the aroma deeply, and sipped, making sure to pause before nodding his approval. A part of him wanted to laugh, but he restrained.

While the sommelier filled Johannes' glass, completing the ritual, the waiter placed Johannes' napkin in his lap and presented the menu. He nodded silently and then left, giving Johannes time to enjoy his wine and peruse the menu at his leisure.

Now alone, Johannes sipped his wine and took in the breathtaking view. The scene centered around the brilliant orange sphere as it slowly approached the sea, turning ever more red as it descended. Wispy clouds loitered about, reflecting the orange glow, and the crescent moon smiled brightly further above.

It occurred to Johannes that this was one of his last opportunities to watch the sun set into the ocean.

He then thought about John.

Johannes couldn't decide which John liked more: basking in the warm glow of sunset or staring at the icy moon. Here he was now doing both.

Before meeting John, Johannes never thought about the luminaries. However, after spending months with his unique...friend, both the sun and the moon would forever be linked to John in his mind.

"You have to admit: that man has a way of getting under your skin," he mumbled to his glass before taking another sip.

A few moments later, the red orb touched the glassy surface of the sea. Lost in the moment, Johannes thought—*I wonder where*

John is and what he's doing right now...

Un – Uno – Uno – Eins

With the orange glow of sunset warming his face and illuminating the paper, John began to write:

The Beginning

I am Ra and I am one with THE ONE. Today, we are here not so much to speak with you about THE ONE, but to speak with you about the one. It is always fun to start at the beginning.

Numbers were initially created for counting. First you had one, and then you had two. But numbers are not merely about quantity; they have meaning in and of themselves. They carry vibration. Astrologers look to the heavens for guidance. Numerologists look to the numbers.

In your modern era, numbers are used nearly as much as words. They are useful for identification and location. Think of your inn; do you not find your room **via** its number? Letters are addressed with numbers, and time—minutes, hours, and days—are kept track through them.

All of this is what we would call the mundane value of numbers. Now allow us to introduce the **profound** value of numbers. Today we start with one.

As far as whole numbers go, one is the smallest. Its only factor is itself. It is thus indivisible. The word 'individual' is derived from the word 'indivisible'. **You** are an individual.

As man's knowledge has expanded, many things thought to be indivisible have turned out not to be. Even the atom can be split! But a man—can you divide a man? No, not physically. You can split his loyalties, but his body must remain whole to remain alive.

The most basic meaning of one is **individual**. Be it man, animal, any living **being**, or even so called inanimate objects—all are individual and **unique**.

The next basic meaning of one is **begin**. When you embark a journey, you start with an **idea**—full of potential and desire. The journey, in a sense, has already commenced before the first step. That is because the idea was **inspired**—the process set in motion in the non-physical. So one is the state of **initiation**, before action has taken place. And yet, it is also the state of being after separation. An individual exists only after having been separated from his creator. Like a child born of his mother— he is only one once the cord has been cut.

One represents **independence** and **freedom**. THE ONE created every one and then imbued each with the freedom to create for him or herself. This is not limited to humans. The beasts create in this same way, albeit beyond your awareness.

In human discussions, when there is confusion as to what is being conveyed, one might ask: "What is your **point**?" You ask this because you want to know the **root** of the **matter**. All of these words: 'point', 'root', and 'matter' pertain to the one.

First Density

In the greater fabric of being, there are densities of existence—not simply the physical and the non-physical. The first density is the realm of **matter**. Each atom in all *materia* lives in first density. Matter is simply consciousness commissioned to hold a finite amount of space for a finite amount of time. Through this the entire physical universe is constructed.

First density consciousness has task, but also purpose. It is given **existence** and is invited to learn awareness. Each atom, in time, becomes aware, and then evolves to the next stage of being. You will learn each level in turn—just as the atom does.

One in Sacred Geometry

Sacred Geometry is closely related to Numerology. They are congruent and have correlation. In Sacred Geometry, the number one is symbolized by a **point**. A point contains one simple dimension and nothing more—no length and no width. It has location, but not direction. It is a **singularity**.

The **now** is also a singularity; it is a **point in time**. Every moment is a new now, yet now is all there is. Time is possibly the single most fascinating creation of THE ONE, keeping in mind that consciousness wasn't created; it just is.

Chakra Number One

You, as a human being, have a number of energy centers called chakras. What is considered your first is the one called the **Root Chakra** or **Base Chakra**. Its purpose is to keep you physical and rooted in the physical realm. It provides for your existence. Through it, you are linked to first density and are thus able to touch and interact with matter.

And know that within the one whole body that you have, there are many ones. Each of your cells contains all of the information of your entire body's design. This is a model of THE ONE. Every one within THE ONE contains the power of THE ONE in the same way that every cell in your body contains the intelligence to construct a whole new body.

As you know from the aces in the Tarot, one represents **raw energy, raw power, raw material**. It is **pure potential**. The point in space, has not yet chosen a direction, and thus has the potential to move in all directions.

At one, you have all the time in the world, but there is no reason for you to wait. When you fully embrace the power of one, and thus the power of THE ONE, you will need nothing—from anyone—ever.

Before we go, there is one personal message we would like to convey. Do not fret over Johannes' departure. He is merely one expressing his individuality and exercising his free will. In this regard, he is living within his purpose.

2 – *Two* – II

Deux – Due – Dos – Zwei

A couple of days after making his decision, Johannes was struck by a realization. He looked at the calendar and counted the weeks: more than two months had passed since he last contacted his father.

Surely Klaus is getting a little concerned by now—Johannes reasoned. He had never gone that long without checking in, even considering his spontaneous vacationing.

He quickly fled his quarters and ascended to the main deck of the ship.

A steward, who saw him approach, greeted him: "Sir, how nice to see you up and about today. How may I be of service?"

"I am curious. How long before we arrive in Bari?"

"We have just today entered the Adriatic Sea. We shall reach the Italian shore this afternoon."

"Good. It is urgent that I send word to my father, informing him of my presence on the continent."

"Sir, if you draft and address a letter, I will make sure it accompanies our highest priority outgoing mail."

"Thank you, my good man. That will be most helpful."

Johannes returned to his stateroom and composed a letter.

Dear Klaus,

I am sure you are concerned as to my wellbeing, having not heard from me for longer than usual, but I will spare you the details of my distraction. Suffice it to say, I am happy and healthy and once again within Europe's borders.

Some time after departing Germany, I arrived in Crete,

mixing some much-needed sunshine with resourceful endeavor. I trust you have received indication of the successful business I created there? Hopefully my colleagues followed through on their promises and tied up any loose threads that may have existed.

In any event, you should also find solace in knowing that I am creating a new business plan to expand our interests into the country of Italy. I am currently nearing her southeastern coast en route to the majestic canaled city to carry out my design. By the time you receive this notice, I will have likely taken up residence in Venice and will have hopefully accomplished the least of my intentions.

Expect additional updates more frequently from now on. If you wish to send a letter before my next correspondence, address your response to the main post office near Piazza San Marco and I will look for it there.

Yours,
Johannes

P.S. By the way, John successfully located me (in Cairo…long story). He is well and is pursuing a line of work well suited to him. Give the Queen and little sister my regards.

Deux – Due – Dos – Zwei

After his first breakthrough, John was so excited he sat to write everyday. Much to his delight, the next message came through right away.

Collaboration

Welcome. I am Ares.

And I am Eros.

We are two within one.

We are two within THE ONE.

We are another manifestation of the Twin Flames.

In Greece, I am known as the God of War.

And I am known as the God of Love.

We are thought of as father and son.

And yet we are merely two sides of the same coin.

Two is a simple number, yet rich with diversity. Half of all whole numbers are divisible by two. More than any other number, two has been embedded into the words of man: two of a kind, a pair, a couple, a duo, a duet, a duel.

Much of duality has been created in twos. You have day and night, light and dark, male and female, yang and yin. Hot and cold, good and bad, on the one hand this and on the other hand that. When man views the world, he first sees in black and white. We, of course, mean this metaphorically. Duality is a classroom endowed with the greatest potential in learning!

There is a saying that goes: "All is fair in love and war."

And thus you have Eros and Ares.

Love and war, however, are not true opposites. The opposite of love is not hate. The opposite of love is fear. All things that are not born from love stem from fear. Fear is the root of all hate and so-called evil. When you learn of a man's fears, you will come to understand his motivations.

But let us not speak of extremes; let us speak of archetypes. On the one hand, there is **partnership** and on the other hand **opposition**. These are the basic meanings of two.

At first glance, 'partnership' and 'opposition' appear to be antonyms, but metaphysically they are not. Pro and con are more alike than different. Both sides come from the same place. Enemies are not opposites, merely expressions of same. Each believes his view is right. Each believes the other's view is wrong. In war, their beliefs are so strong, they are willing to fight—and willing to die. They may fight over gods or religions, lands or resources. They may fight over culture or mores, but each desires the same outcome and yet fails to see this **correlation**. They are reflections of one ideal resonating in opposition.

You cannot create peace through war or compliance through coercion. It may appear that way for a while, but the waves of aggression you send out will always return and the very things you seek to defeat will grow ever stronger.

Alas, you can only battle your fears for so long. To truly rid yourself of them, you must accept them, walk through them, let them go, and then focus on them nevermore.

Remember from your earlier teachings: "to know your intention, look to your attention." Whether you be **for** something or **against** it matters not, it is your **focus** on it that binds you. When you fight against something, your fixation on it makes it seem real. The more you push on it, the more solid it becomes.

Two contains within it **balance** and **tension**, **cooperation** and **conflict**. Win-lose is of the two, but so is win-win. The choice is yours, for **choice** is also of the two.

The number one represents a state of being; the number two represents a **situation**. You are an individual and you are living inside of duality. The two is everything around you, everything outside of you.

Second Density

And this leads us to the description of the next realm of being. Second density is the domain of plants and animals. Matter, having gained awareness, advanced. Plants and animals—down to single celled organisms—are born with **awareness** and are internally driven toward self-awareness. Each seeks to know its self!

Duality is created for this purpose. To best know one's self is to continually compare self with other—what is 'I' and what is 'NOT I'. You can see this expressed from one end to the other. Plants, for example, are not as clearly delineated from their surroundings. They cannot, generally speaking, exist outside of the soil. They are melded to their environment, and for the most part, cannot move freely.

Animals represent further development within second density. They **do** move freely. They **do** exhibit observable choice. They must forever discern whether another is prey or predator, friend or foe, foodstuff or fatal, life sustaining or life abating. They graduated from the density of existence. They still exist, but now must **act** to survive.

The work of survival serves them. By observing what surrounds them and learning how that which is outside of them affects that which is inside of them, they come to know who **they** are. They have not yet formed personalities or identities. They do not call themselves by names or categorizations. They operate primarily through instinct, at least until they learn another way.

Chakra Number Two

And this brings us to what would be considered your second chakra. The **Sacral Chakra** links you to second density. It is your center of **instinct**. It is the part of you that desires living. Your first chakra keeps you physical; your second chakra keeps you alive. Your first chakra is

31

concerned with your atoms, with your physics; your second chakra is concerned with your cells, with your biology.

Two in Sacred Geometry

There are two shapes to consider for the number two. On the one hand there is the **line** and on the other hand the **circle**.

A line is constructed by connecting two points. When two points are joined, an infinite number of points exists between them. The line represents **choosing** and illustrates **direction**.

The line is drawn by Eros...

...but is also a symbol of Ares. The sword is in the shape of a line...

...and so is the phallus.

The pure potential of the one has now been directed into function. Whatever may be the motivation, energy is now **thrust** forward—in love, in war, in purpose.

The second symbol for two, the circle, is also line: a curved line that is drawn around a center point. All parts of the circle are equidistant from the center.

It can be said that the line is a symbol of male and the circle is a symbol of female. In fact, **gender** first appears in second density, and the resulting sexuality is fueled by the energy created in your second charka.

Now, you may have noted that men and women are often viewed as opposites, but we ask you, are they really that different? Do they not both have two eyes, two ears, two arms, two legs, two hands, and two feet? Do they not desire love and abhor fear? Do they not strive for the strength to overcome weakness?

Yes, men and women are different in physical ways. Most are even different in emotional ways. Each gender has its strengths, its assets, and also its challenges. Each comes from a slightly different perspective; some of this is innate, and some of it is learned.

Another pairing that is forever linked to the vibration of two is **birth** and **death**. One marks the beginning of biological life, and the other the end of it. For birth to occur, a line must be joined with a circle. The sperm, the male gamete, which resembles a line, must penetrate and merge with the ova, the female gamete, which resembles a circle. Together they form a zygote, the two that come together to form one.

Death can be created in an analogous process. The sword, a line, pierces and penetrates the heart, a circle. In this case, the force is destructive rather than constructive. **Force** is a **vector**; it has strength and direction, and is thus another aspect of two.

What is not widely known within humanity, or at least not fully understood, is that birth and death are the same. When you are born to one reality, you die in the other. But birth and death are illusions. They create the apparent boundaries of life: the beginning and end of it. In reality, life is continuous and unending.

In the Roman numeral system, two is written as: II. Be they lovers, twins, allies, or enemies—two is forever constructed from one and one.

You are the center of your own universe, the point at the center of a circle. However, from all other points, you are **other**. And this is the basis of the Perfection of the Universe. You are here to live your purpose: to create your own reality and then experience it, and yet, what you create is also a part of another's reality. What you do influences everyone around you. You are simultaneously the **expression** of self and the **experience** of others.

For now, we break. We shall split the discourse of two into...two. Ha! Before commencing with the second half, we request from you a task. We have taught you the ways of manifestation. We have told you that the Journey of the Fool is always from where you are to where you want to be. So where do you want to be?

Ponder your preferences; discern your desires; write down your wishes. For our next communication, we will discuss a course of action for you to consider so that you can consciously create what you choose. When you are satisfied with your selection, sit and you will be joined in light, in love, in union.

Deux – Due – Dos – Zwei

W hen his ship dropped anchor in Bari, Johannes was prepared to spend a few days ashore, but that was before he learned that a passenger ship for Venice was leaving before nightfall.

He weighed the situation. *On the one hand, a couple days to explore southern Italy could be nice. On the other hand, I can be in Venice before the end of the week. Should I expend the effort to find a room and get settled for only two nights? Or should I take advantage of this opportunity and get my new life underway?*

Johannes looked out across the city, trying to get a feel for Bari…and Italy. To him, it simply looked and felt a lot like Greece. From conversations he had had with the crew, he knew Venice would be different. It was unique, after all.

It wasn't long before his mind was made up.

"Arrivederci, Southern Italy. Venice awaits me."

Deux – Due – Dos – Zwei

J ohn was torn. On the one hand, the past two sessions had gone well—much better than he had expected. With little effort, information flowed in and was fascinating. On the other hand, nothing else was going well. Life seemed a chore. He was unhappy. He felt discontent, disconnected, and unmotivated. The contrast was strange.

How can one feel such a connection in one area of life and not in any other?

John also began to feel as if he were invisible. When he walked the streets of Cairo, no one took notice of him. When he stood in line or sat at a restaurant, he wouldn't get waited on unless he specifically spoke up.

Furthermore, he was growing more nervous with the passing of time.

I need to make a decision or I'm going to squander all of Johannes' money and still not have a plan.

It was his hope to use the money to get to wherever he was going next with enough leftover to give him time to find work. Whenever John thought about it in those terms, his discontent quickly gave way to panic.

"OK. Calm down. There has to be a solution," he would tell himself.

He tried asking for help directly from Ra or Seth, Eros or Ares, or whomever else was out there, but whenever he wrote personal requests, he got nothing in response.

"How can that be?" he exclaimed. And yet, at the same time, he knew the answer. Now that he had been given an assignment, nothing would come through until he completed it. He could tell; he had tried enough times.

And yet completing the assignment wasn't a simple endeavor. Whenever he attempted to list his desires, he either felt anxious or apathetic.

Seth, of course, knew exactly what was happening. He had, after all, been John's guide from the beginning.

In the past, whenever John experienced something he had especially desired, it was too quickly and painfully taken away from him. Pleasure, in John's mind, thus always resulted in pain— connection leading ultimately to separation. No matter what transpired, he always seemed to circle back around to the same place: hurt, lonely, and longing for love.

So a part of John didn't want to call in his greatest desire for he believed his greatest fear would most certainly follow.

Apathy wasn't fun, but it was easier than pain.

Deux – Due – Dos – Zwei

T he ferryboat traveling from Bari entered *La Canale Grande*. Once the gangway was secured in place, Johannes disembarked the ship, marched directly through *Piazza San Marco*, and entered a *pensione* located on a quiet alley just off of the grand square. He carried with him nothing more than the papers he had been working on. It was his intent to secure a room first, then send for his belongings afterward.

T h e *pensione* was comfortable, well lit, and had all the amenities he needed to get his Italian life started. As soon as he was unpacked, he got to work. His primary task was to search for a location to serve as his new office.

Within days, Johannes found a space that suited his needs. The office could accommodate four employees—a bit larger than he needed, but which allowed for some much anticipated growth. Best of all, it included a modestly furnished apartment upstairs.

One space that serves two purposes: how convenient!

Johannes moved in that afternoon and began setting up shop.

Deux – Due – Dos – Zwei

F or days, John intermittently put the point of his pencil to the paper, as if to write, but nothing came—no questions, no solutions, no information. He simply felt…blank…like the sheet of paper in front of him.

One morning, while feeling lost in the middle of nowhere, John wrote the two words that bounced around in his head:

Now what?

He placed his pencil down and looked out the window. When he stood up, he jostled the desk and his pencil began to roll. He looked down, intending to catch it, but froze. The pencil continued to roll and fell to the floor. John did not move to pick it up. He blinked, but the image he saw remained and it struck him profoundly.

"Where did that come from?" he asked the room. "Did I write that?"

John looked up from the paper. He looked around the room and then absently out the window. He was deep in thought. He scanned back through his memory—second by second. He remembered writing the one frustrated question, but nothing more. And yet, in his own handwriting, a single word appeared on the paper as an answer to his question:

Cards

When John first read the word, the intended meaning did not occur to him. But then he figured it out. It was only days before that he had met the old woman who had given him a reading using her Tarot cards. And the reading **was** helpful—immensely. Even before she began the reading, John had filled with anticipation. It was as if he was a kid again. When he was young, he was always excited to play with the cards, even if he wasn't able to understand them very well.

"Cards do have a way of bridging the gap," he said out loud.

Even when one couldn't figure out the complete message, there was always something gained by reviewing the wisdom written about each one.

And so, seemingly out of the blue, John's state shifted from apathy to purpose. He now had something to strive for, something he could **do** for himself.

Deux – Due – Dos – Zwei

F inding an office was Johannes' first task. Hiring an assistant was his second. He interviewed a number of candidates, but in his mind he kept circling back to one: a young woman named Sofia.

On paper, Sofia wasn't the most appropriate choice: her English was not as good as some of the others and her experience was limited. Yet, something about her felt familiar. She was easy to talk to, had a genuine interest in Johannes' business, and didn't try to sell herself the way the others had. Johannes felt an instant rapport; he trusted her.

Johannes gave himself a week to meet and interview candidates before deciding. He told each to come back at the end of the week to hear of his decision. When the time came, selecting Sofia seemed the most natural thing to do.

Deux – Due – Dos – Zwei

W ith a skip in his step, John left the inn in search of a deck of Tarot cards that suited his liking. Little did he know, finding Tarot cards was not going to be difficult. In the first shop he visited, the clerk assured him that in Cairo they were plentiful.

"The Major Arcana of the Tarot **originated** here in Egypt after all," the man said. "The ancient Egyptians, being more visual in their expression, **drew** their stories rather than simply write them. Thus both hieroglyphics and the Tarot were born."

The shopkeeper was less certain about the Minor Arcana, but believed that the suits originated somewhere in the Middle East, likely within the ancient Sumerian civilization of Ur.

"The modern Tarot only subtly resembles the ancient drawings, however," he explained. "Medieval times influenced the designs a great deal—the names too. Europeans expanded the use of Tarot by bringing their versions to all of the places they visited. Today, even here in Egypt, the European decks are more popular."

The clerk completed his discourse by directing John to a nearby shop.

After a short walk, John located the shop he was told about. Inside, decks fashioned from near and far lined an entire bookshelf. He at first thought a deck that was decidedly Egyptian would be intriguing, but then admitted that a traditional deck would be easier for him to use.

Until I become proficient, I had better stick to this one—he thought as he selected the ever-popular Rider-Waite deck and brought it to the front counter to pay for it.

When John arrived back at his room, he spread out his new cards while ravenously chewing a kebab he had purchased on the way. He gazed at the glossy and elegant deck and then at the grease on his hands. Not wanting to soil his cards before their first use, he stuffed the remainder of the kebab in his mouth and quickly retreated to the washroom to clean up.

Upon returning, John was again torn. He wanted to take time to look through the cards and enjoy the beautiful images. At the same time, he was anxious to do a reading. He then assured himself that there would be time enough later to enjoy each and every card. So he collected the cards back up and began shuffling them.

New cards were always a bit of a challenge. They were stiff and slippery. The first time he tried to shuffle them, cards went flying in all directions.

"I guess that's one way to mix them up!" he said, laughing at himself.

John shuffled the cards one way, and then in a different manner. He spread them out en masse and collected them back up in the hopes of shuffling them some more. He was so focused on randomizing the cards, he did not contemplate a specific question or topic.

Without giving it a thought, he deemed the cards ready. He cut the deck in half and laid out five cards in the form of a cross, following what he had remembered from long ago.

The card in the center, which represented the current situation, illustrated a despondent scene. One meaning was poverty—another was desolation. In each case, the downtrodden were separated from what they needed. The card to the left, the past affecting the present, showed a heart: pierced by three swords and bleeding. It didn't take an expert to figure out what that one meant. The card at the top of the cross represented his greatest strength and was The High Priestess. The card at the bottom of the cross, the greatest challenge, was The Devil.

"Heaven and Hell," he mumbled to himself.

As John looked at the symbols that surrounded the images, he pulled out the booklet that accompanied the deck. Descriptions were given for each card, but the following resonated with him the most.

For the High Priestess, he read:

The High Priestess represents the occult, the unseen, and highlights our connection to spirit in all of its subtle and unexplained ways.

And then for the Devil, he read:

The Devil card is not about that which is evil, merely that which is of the earth realm. We are captivated by riches and drama alike. We fear pain and desire pleasure. In various ways, we get ensnarled in the webs of life. Are you overly enticed by some aspect of physical existence? Is responsibility weighing heavily upon you?

"Look at that? The cards **do** know what's going on!"

As John considered what he had read, understanding grew. Yes, his connection to spirit was strong—first the visions, then the channelings, and now the writing. It ebbed and flowed, but had grown over time and remained with him.

At the same time, he felt lost in the physical world. Now that Johannes was gone, he was unsure where to go or even what he wanted to do. And he **was** supposed to be compiling a list of his desires.

It's bad when you have desires that are unmet, but it is worse when you can't connect to desire at all. I guess it's time for me to do a little soul searching, eh?

As if answering his own question, John then looked at the last card on the right side of the cross. It was the guide card and depicted the King of Cups. Instantly John was reminded of Felizio and in that moment, he wished his jolly friend were sitting beside him.

"Felizio always had a way of making me feel better about anything that was happening in my life."

In a flash, he was ready to start his list. He pulled out a fresh sheet of paper and, at the top, wrote:

I wish I could be more like Felizio.

Deux – Due – Dos – Zwei

As the week went on, John kept adding to his list. Each day, the items grew more heartfelt. When John reached what he believed to be a description of his greatest desire, he sat with anticipation to write once again.

The Journey

In many ways, zero exists outside of Numerology. That is because you can never arrive at zero from any other number. Zero represents the absolute, where nothing is separate—with no beginning and no end. Once you move to the one, you also have the two because in order to have an **observer**, you must also have **that which is observed**.

In actuality, all numbers, words, symbols, signs, religions, and philosophies are dualistic (rather than absolute) because they represent mere pieces and parts of the whole. The absolute is beyond description. Nevertheless, symbols, and thus numbers, are valuable for conveying knowledge.

We've asked you to contemplate those desires you wish fulfilled. Have you done this?

Yes.

Good. Now as we continue, we wish for you to keep these desires in mind, thus this teaching need not be merely theory but application.

Manifestation, the bringing of an idea into physical form, can be likened to the journey from the one to the two. One represents the individual. Two represents anything and everything outside of that individual: be it a situation, an experience, an object, or another person. To personalize this discussion, tell us of a desire that you included in your list. In fact, tell us the greatest of them.

Without a doubt, my greatest desire is a romantic partnership. Through my experiences with Johannes, I know how fulfilling a meaningful relationship can be. So that is what I desire, first and foremost.

Well done and well stated. Your desire is clear. You understand what you want, and why. And how coincident that your desired experience is quintessentially of the vibration of two.

You are one sitting here contemplating the experience of partnership. You are not just contemplating partnership generically, but seeking a partner specifically with which to experience it. From our perspective, you are one seeking another one.

Yet from your vantage, you are one seeking to connect with something—someone—outside of yourself and thus a one seeking a two. Remember the symbolism of the circle and the line. At this moment, you are a point at the center of your own circle 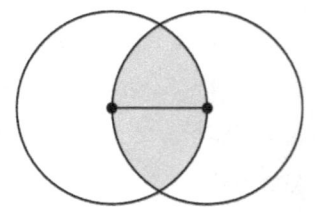 seeking to connect with another point at the center of his. Once your desire has been made manifest, your center point will connect with his, as if with a line, and your circles will overlap in shared experience and creation.

For the sake of completeness, it matters not what is desired. It may be an object, an experience, a feeling, or a state of being. The fact that one perceives that it is missing is the starting point.

Remember, the Journey of the Fool, in this case manifestation, is from where you are to where you want to be. You perceive that an appropriate partner is missing from your life and you believe that in order for you to experience what you desire, you have to find him, to meet him, to connect with him, and to be chosen by him.

Another way to look at one and two is **oneself** and **other**. Notice that all of these words contain the letter 'o'. This is a hint of the zero—the absolute—which is the no thing hidden within everything.

In the absolute, there is neither time nor space; there is no separation. On some level beyond your awareness **you** exist outside of time and space, forever united with Source and thus connected to THE ONE. In this perspective, you **already have** what you desire, here and now, and in all of the colorful details that you imagine. In fact, even as we discuss this, your Higher Self is experiencing all that you described.

Yet you, a lonely one, are not experiencing this pleasure. You neither see your partner nor know his name. You cannot caress his skin, hear the timber of his voice, or stare deeply into the glistening eyes within his handsome face. You cannot make love to the **idea** of him, and thus you yearn for a touch, for a kiss—for all of the exquisite expressions of love. You want nothing less than an Adonis to call your own. Have we surprised you by revealing the intimate details of your desire?

A little.

John, I did not introduce myself to you when we started, and that was on purpose. My name is Aphrodite and I am thought of as the Goddess of Love. I am, in a sense, the female counterpart to Eros. Your Higher Self knows your greatest desire. He (if we may assign gender purely for discussion) selected me to accompany you in this exercise. I have access to him and he has energetically described to me the experience that you desire. You created it through your imagination. The manifestation for him is instantaneous. As soon as **you** desire it, **he** experiences it.

So the question becomes: how can **you** perceive and experience your desire? This is the beginning of the journey.

The answer is simply that you must utilize the power of the one.

You are an individual one, yet simultaneously a part of THE ONE. You are thus forever connected to the absolute. However, as long as you keep looking at a desired experience as something you don't have (or can't have), you will not be able to reach it. Your eyes deceive you, and in believing solely what you see, you continue to hold yourself away from the experience you so desire.

So how does one rectify the situation? How does one shift out of limited perception?

One approach is to contemplate all of the aspects of one until you find what is missing. For example, maybe you do not feel worthy of partnership. Maybe you believe you need to be someone else in order to have what you desire. Maybe you even look to specific others and desire to be **them** in order to have what **they** have. In all of these cases, where is your attention? Your <u>at</u>tention (and thus <u>in</u>tention) is on what you are not! Your desire and intention are therefore not aligned; they are not in line; they are not connected. And if your intention is not connected with your desire, then your experience cannot be connected to your desire either.

So, the journey from the one to the two is not a journey at all. You need only be the one that you are to have what you desire. In fact, it is paramount that you be who you specifically are because your desire was born from it! **You** desire what you desire and thus the fulfillment of that desire is linked to **you**! You created it and therefore it is yours. If you try to be someone else, then you will never meet up with the desire **you** created!

Now, let us apply another perspective. So you are one who desires a relationship with another. Why? You, of course, have already stated this. You have experienced what it **feels** like to be in a partnership—albeit a limited one—and now you desire a greater partnership so that you can **feel** that way **more**. So, truth be told, what you really desire is a feeling. Do you realize that this is **always** the case? No matter what is desired, the underlying aspect of the desire is always a feeling. And in fact, **feeling** that feeling is the fastest way to gain access to the desired outcome.

You, John, specifically desire the **expression** of love. You desire loving another, even more than being loved in return. You most enjoy the feeling of love radiating out of your heart center. Of course, you are also afraid of this very experience. You have mistakenly associated future pain with present joy—and so when you experience joy, you wait for the other shoe to drop. This is another piece that is missing. An errant belief is keeping you from truth. Your fear of pain has you closing doors presented to you, thus denying opportunities to experience the expression of love that you desire.

Now let me ask of you this. Right now, in this very moment, think about Johannes. Think about him in all the delectable details you can visualize. Think about the best of times you shared with him. Think about all that you respect in him; all that he possesses that is beautiful to you. Think about how much you love him. And **feel** it. Feel that love for him as it pours out of your pores. Feel your heart open. Feel your unique expression of love emanate from who you really are. Can you feel your love for him?

Yes.

Can you feel the difference between your love for him, and the pain you feel from not having him?

Yes.

The pain and love are clearly different, but you have linked them together and thus feel them both simultaneously. As you allow yourself to feel your love for Johannes, you also feel pain. Believe it or not, this is very common among humans. One often says, "love hurts," but it is not love that hurts, it is loss. "Loss hurts." They need to rewrite all of those songs—ha!

Now, for the moment, let us focus on the love you feel. It is energy, yes? It is light. It is sound. It is music! It is vibration! Like heat, love can be felt by those around you, even if it is not directed toward them. Have you noticed that a person **in love** is often sought by many others? That is because the love that emanates from them **is** accessible to all who listen. A person who emanates love thus becomes a very **attractive** person.

The experience of expressing love is with you—even now! The feeling you desire is accessible to you even though Johannes is not present, even though he has not chosen the partnership you offered him. The message here is this:

You do not need a partner's cooperation to experience what you desire.

You can love Johannes as much as you care to, right here, right now. In fact, you can fall in love with anyone and anything—everyone and everything—if you so choose. Then you would forever experience love emanating from your heart. You are capable of every feeling that you desire. You need not objects, experiences, or people. In absolute reality, you are all that you need.

Yet, it **is** easier when one shows up in physical form to inspire, accept, and reflect your love. It is far more fun to play, to touch, to look upon the object of your desire and tell him and show him how much you love him. That is why you are **here** in physical form after all!

One purpose that is common among all pieces of THE ONE immersed in physical form is to **experience**. THE ONE experiences All-That-Is through all of us. And thus, all desired experience is supported by THE ONE.

When you count, you start with the number one. It is the first step within any endeavor. It is also you. You are the one thing that you always take with you. That's why the first step toward anything desired is always **self**.

The Journey of the Fool is always from where you are to where you want to be. These are the most important things to be aware of: **where you are** and **where you want to be**. That's as simple as one and two.

Now let us play with some math. Within every instance of two, there is one. In fact, every number contains one and is divisible by one. And from one, all other numbers are created.

Let us illustrate this for you. Here is a sequence created by adding one:

1, 2, 3, 4, 5, 6, 7, 8, 9, 10, 11, 12, 13, 14, 15, 16, 17, 18...

In numerology, all numbers larger than nine are reduced by adding the digits together iteratively until arriving at a single digit number. Thus ten reduces to one like so: 1+0=1. The numerological version of the above thus produces this:

<u>1, 2, 3, 4, 5, 6, 7, 8, 9,</u> 1, 2, 3, 4, 5, 6, 7, 8, 9...

Notice that the second nine positions repeat the first nine.

So, from one, we can create any number: one through nine. It works this way because the one was created in the image and likeness of THE ONE. Every one has the power to create and then experience all the other vibrations.

There is nothing one can't do!

Now, look at a sequence created by adding two:

2, 4, 6, 8, 10, 12, 14, 16, 18, 20, 22, 24, 26, 28, 30, 32, 34, 36...

Numerological reduction yields:

<u>2, 4, 6, 8, 1, 3, 5, 7, 9,</u> 2, 4, 6, 8, 1, 3, 5, 7, 9...

From two, all of the other numbers are created as well! The order is different, but nothing is added and nothing is removed. In nine iterations, we reach each number one through nine—same as with one—and then the cycle repeats.

Math is revealing, but also deceiving. In math, 2>1, but in reality, two is not greater than one; it is not less than it either.

The greatest gift bestowed upon you is choice. You can seek through one or you can seek through two, and in either case, you can arrive at all experiences equally—just as easily, just as difficultly. That is because two is merely the reflection of one and is created from one. Everything you see **out there** is created from everything you think and feel **in here**.

Do you wish to experience a marriage or a sacred marriage, a truce or an alliance, a pairing or a partnership? Are you trying to create a whole from two halves, or are you seeking the experience of wholeness to then share with another?

The lesson in this exercise is this: seek anything outside of yourself that you desire, but do not seek to complete who you are through it. You are an individual—a whole one. Nothing outside of you will change that. Nothing outside of you will make you greater than you already are. An experience may inspire the best of you, but you created the experience in the first place, so the potential was always there.

Achievements will not make you a greater man, but through expressing your greatness, you will achieve whatever you intend. Relationships will not make you whole, but through embracing the whole, beautiful, and unique expression of God that you are, you will attract cherished relationships of all forms.

Desire all aspects of two that you wish—that is why you are here—however you must always return to the one inside in order to meet it. Twos will come and go: partnerships and oppositions, projects and accomplishments, relationships and reflections. Within and underneath all of them, the one remains. You will always be; you will always express; you will always create. Keep that in mind with all that you seek. **Be the one!**

Deux – Due – Dos – Zwei

I t didn't take long for Johannes and Sofia to settle into a comfortable routine. Sofia was a fast learner and proved to be an ideal office mate. It was the little things. She was considerate and attentive—as skilled at caring for people as tending to business matters.

For example, most mornings Sofia took it upon herself to reheat the water and refresh Johannes' cup of tea. It took Johannes days to realize that she did this solely for him. He at first thought she was fixing herself a cup too, only later realizing that she didn't drink tea in the office...or coffee for that matter.

And then came the delicious lunches. Johannes, being especially focused on his work, often skipped the midday meal. Once Sofia noticed the pattern, she began ordering food for him, or bringing something back when she went out. Without saying a word, she would place the meal on his desk, which kept his hunger from causing too much distraction.

Johannes typically failed to acknowledge the gesture explicitly, but hummed with delight between delicious spoonfuls. As it turned out, that was all the encouragement Sofia needed.

Deux – Due – Dos – Zwei

E ncouraged by Aphrodite's message, John decided that he needed to lighten up. He had become too serious…and too somber.

"Life is meant to be lived," he told himself. He thus made an effort to get out more.

Some evenings, John indulged in a glass of wine in the downstairs bar at the inn. Other evenings, he strolled through the city just to see what would catch his interest. As he opened up to the world around him, the world responded in kind.

Soon he didn't feel invisible any longer.

3 – *Three* – III

Trois – Tre – Tres – Drei

O ne Friday evening, a few weeks later, Sofia approached Johannes' desk and cleared her throat to get his attention.

"*Signore* Müller, if I may?"

"Yes?" Johannes responded, but kept his eyes on his paperwork.

"I am about to leave for the weekend and I…*Signore?*"

"Yes, Sofia."

"You are aware that this is Italy, *Signore. Sì?*"

Johannes looked up questioningly. "Yes, Sofia. Of course I know this is Italy."

Sofia held Johannes' eye for a moment, then looked down demurely.

"Well, *Signore*, your work ethic is beyond that of any Italian I have ever met. In Italy, one's time relaxing and enjoying *famiglia ed amici* is held in high regard. Aren't you concerned that you will burn yourself out?"

"Sofia, thank you for your concern. I know myself and this is well within my capabilities. I am German, after all. I will be fine. Once I get the business up and running, I will take time to enjoy this beautiful city you have been blessed with."

"*Signore*, as long as you are here, you have been blessed with it as well. Don't forget that!"

"Thank you, Sofia. *Grazie Mille!* Please, go enjoy your weekend and I will see you on Monday—late I hope!"

"*Grazie, Signore. Buon Weekend* to you as well! *Buona Notte.*"

Johannes watched as Sofia disappeared beyond the doorway and returned his attention to his work. However, not a minute later, he felt eyes staring at him and he looked up again.

"*Signore*, I'm sorry to disturb you, but, seeing as you'll be working all weekend, would you care to finish for today and join my friend and I for *un bicchiere di vino?* Victoria is visiting from London. She's been traveling throughout Italy for a couple of months now and I'm guessing she's craving a rich and lengthy conversation in English. I'm sure she would appreciate someone more fluent than I am. I'm afraid she'll exhaust my abilities in no time. Besides, she can share with you her perspective on the places she's visited, since you've not seen much of Italy."

Johannes thought for a moment and deemed this an opportunity not to be missed. He was curious about other parts of Italy, yet found the Italians' perspective of their own country a bit… biased…since every inch of Italy was simply described as, *"molta bella!"*

"Sofia, you have convinced me. After all, this work will still be here in the morning. Please, after you."

Sofia hugged her boss in a brief moment of excitement and led them out of the building. The *caffè* where she planned to meet Victoria was about a twenty-minute walk from the office. Uncharacteristically, Sofia rambled on the whole time, primarily telling Johannes all about her friend.

For a moment, Johannes began to wonder if the meeting was meant as a setup.

"…and I told Victoria all about you…and…this work. I'm not sure I've said this, but I very much enjoy working for you, *Signore*."

"Please Sofia, if we are going to be social, you must call me Johannes. I can't be more than five years older than you anyway!"

"Sorry *Signore*…I mean…Johannes."

Sofia then giggled in the most adorable way.

Trois – Tre – Tres – Drei

One evening, John stumbled upon an open-air tavern. It featured a triangular shaped patio nestled between three buildings. The scenery combined with the warm evening air created an ambiance that was too inviting to pass up.

Although it was early for the dinner crowd, the place wasn't exactly empty either. John decided it was just the right amount of activity to suit his mood. He selected a table in the corner, then ordered a glass of wine from the waiter. A couple of sips later, he felt himself relax considerably.

After finishing the majority of a first glass of wine, John found himself staring blankly ahead and in the general direction of an attractive woman. He only realized this when she waved to him.

"¡Hola! ¿Quieres un poco de mi vino? ¡Es muy rico!"

"Che?" John was confused because although he understood what the woman asked him, he knew she wasn't speaking Italian. He then thought to ask, *"Parli italiano? O francese o inglese?"*

"¡Sí! Puedo hablar francés." The beautiful woman then switched to French and added, "I was asking if you would like some of my wine. It is very good!"

"I actually understood you, but I'm not sure why."

"Oh. Spanish and Italian are similar—enough to be understood much of the time anyway."

"Ah. You are from Spain?"

*"Claro. Cataluña. Cerca de Barcelona—*I mean—close to Barcelona. My name is Maria. What is your name?"

"I am John. It's a pleasure to meet you."

"Igualmente, Juan. So you've not been to Spain, eh?"

"No, but how did you... Oh forget it. I guess it's obvious."

"Juan, you are very cute. Sit with me and let's drink wine together and talk. I ordered a bottle. I don't know what I was thinking."

"I would like that. Thank you."

John sat and Maria lifted the wine bottle, but when John held out his glass she pulled the bottle back.

"You're glass is not empty," she chided. "When trying a new kind of wine, one should always start with a clear glass. Finish what you have and rinse out your glass with some water. Then I'll pour you some of mine."

John froze. He was stunned. Maria, in her own words, echoed something Felizio had said months earlier. John could almost hear his friend's voice as he recalled when Felizio compared love to wine.

Amico mio, to open up to love, it is imperative to clear out anything that is old. It is only the empty chalice that can receive and retain the full *bellezza* and *piacere* of love. There are thousands of varieties of wine out there and many eager to pour you some. Make it your goal to be the empty vessel. By all means, fill your glass with a little of this wine and a little of that. Taste the Chianti and the Pinot Grigio alike. Give yourself time to determine exactly what wine best suits you, but in between, be sure to empty out your glass every time. Keep yourself clear, and that will allow you to sample the true essence of whatever wine is given. Then, when another drinks from your cup, they will taste your true love and have the best opportunity to choose or not what you have to offer.

"That's it!" John whispered. *That's why I've been struggling. My glass isn't empty! Why hadn't I thought of that?*

Maria placed her hand gently on his. "Is everything OK, *Juan?*"

John pulled himself out of his thoughts and quickly drank the last of his wine. He rinsed out his glass as Maria had instructed and said, "Yes. Sorry. Something you said reminded me of a friend and got me thinking. He loves wine. What am I saying—he loves **life**!"

"And you? Do you not **love** life?"

"Well, I didn't…what I meant was…oh, forget it. You're right. I've been having a tough time lately. It seems whenever I turn around, everything's changed and it takes me a while to figure it out again."

"Sounds like you're thinking too much."

"God—I love a woman's perspective! Sorry. I…I miss being around women. I haven't been…" John suddenly turned red as he realized how his words could be misconstrued.

"*No te preocupes.* Don't you worry." Maria reached over again and patted John's hand. She then mumbled to herself in Spanish, "A little young, but **very** cute…"

John wasn't sure he caught what she had said, but blushed further nevertheless.

"*Juan.* I have decided. You are going to share the rest of this bottle with me. After, we will have dinner and then go dancing. There is nothing like *musica y bailando* to lift one's spirits!"

Trois – Tre – Tres – Drei

J ohannes and Sofia neared the *caffè* and were spotted by Victoria immediately. She caught their attention by exuberantly waving them over. Before either of them spoke, Victoria grabbed Johannes' hand and introduced herself. She then hugged Sofia and started talking as if she'd been waiting all afternoon for them.

Victoria told them about her day and then quickly segued into the next subject. She asked questions, but didn't wait for answers, and then began speaking of her adventures in one small Italian village after the next. Her descriptions were colorful and her details numerous. Had her stories not been so entertaining, they would have been tedious.

Johannes wondered if the incessant monologue would become tiresome, but for the time being, he was enjoying himself. Since she was doing all of the talking, he got to sit back and relax, taking it all in.

Sofia, for the most part, remained quiet as well. After all, Victoria hardly let her squeeze in a word edge-wise. And since Johannes' attention was primarily on Victoria, she got to steal long glances at her handsome boss.

At times, she found herself wishing she didn't work for him because she found him surprisingly different than any man she'd ever met. Handsome men were plentiful in Italy, and even a blond haired, blue-eyed one could be easily found, but in Johannes was something that was vastly different. For one, he didn't ogle at or hit on attractive woman. That was refreshing.

But as long as he's my boss, he's off limits—she found herself thinking. She didn't know where that rule came from, but neither questioned nor challenged it.

At one point, while Victoria was especially engrossed in her discourse, Johannes glanced over at Sofia. She was looking at him, toward him, or maybe past him. She was clearly deep in thought and did not react or acknowledge his eye contact. And in that moment, she looked different. Johannes couldn't tell if it was the warm sunlight on her face, or the way the Venetian breeze played with her hair, but for the first time since he'd met her, he didn't see Sofia as merely a person, but saw her as a woman—a beautiful woman.

And then Victoria's exuberance and laughter drew both of the others out of their thoughts and back into her storytelling.

Sofia and Johannes caught each other's eye for a moment before returning their attention to Victoria.

Trois – Tre – Tres – Drei

J ohn and Maria drank wine, ate, talked, danced, and drank more wine. Maria set the pace and John tried his best to keep up. Throughout the evening, John revealed more and more of the events of the past few months, albeit superficially. Little by little, Maria filled in the blanks. Finally, late into the night, or rather early in the morning, Maria questioned John outright.

"So, *Juan*, are you in love with this Johannes you speak so much of?"

"Well...yeah...I...guess. Not that it has made my life any easier." John held his head down and avoided eye contact. "He's not interested..."

"I'm sorry to hear that," she consoled.

John continued to avoid eye contact until Maria grabbed his hand.

She looked him directly in the eye and said, "Well, it's his loss. And mine, of course!" She then laughed heartily and tugged on John's arm until he began to laugh with her.

Trois – Tre – Tres – Drei

56

T hree hours and two locations later, Victoria paused for longer than usual. She turned to the others and announced that she was ready to retire for the evening. She then stood and looked at them as if questioning their hesitation.

Johannes looked at Sofia, shrugged his shoulders subtly, and they both stood simultaneously.

The three walked back to Victoria's *pensione* in the most luxurious quiet that Johannes had experienced in a while. Well, not really, but it felt that way in comparison. Once they reached their first destination, it was Sofia that broke the silence.

"Victoria. It has been a pleasure. Sleep well. *Buona notte.*" She then kissed Victoria on each cheek.

"Victoria, so nice to have met you. I hope the rest of your stay in Venice is lovely, and do stop by the office if you find yourself in the neighborhood." Johannes awkwardly moved in to shake Victoria's hand or give her a hug—unsure which was more appropriate.

Victoria grabbed Johannes' hand and shook it vigorously, then hugged him firmly but briefly. "Thank you both for such a wonderful evening. I'm sure I'll see you, Johannes, again before I leave, and Sofia, we must do this again soon. Good night."

Without hesitation, Victoria turned on her heels and entered the inn.

Johannes and Sofia glanced at each other, and then Johannes held out his hand as if to say, "After you." Without verbally agreeing to do so, it was understood between them that Johannes was walking Sofia home.

Trois – Tre – Tres – Drei

J ohn walked Maria back to her home and hugged her goodnight. Maria relaxed into his arms and enjoyed the affection fully. After the hug, Maria kissed John on each cheek, then a third time.

"There might not be any passionate love making in our futures —at least not together—but that doesn't mean I can't treat you to another of my many talents." Maria winked and smiled as she said this, and then more seriously went on to say, "Come back Sunday, shortly after sunset, and I will serve you the best *Paella* you will ever have—at least as good as I can make in this country."

John accepted the invitation, hugged Maria again, and then set off back to his inn.

Maria watched him walk away and noticed a skip to his step. If she hadn't known better, she would have thought that she had gotten to him. *That man! He is going to be the bane of many a woman's existence...some men too!* She then smiled despite the thought and entered the apartment feeling surprisingly content.

Trois – Tre – Tres – Drei

J ohannes felt something lingering between them, but was unsure what **it** was. As they walked in silence, he reviewed the evening for clues. There were many, albeit subtle ones.

In the end, he drew no conclusions as to what would happen next. He was still unsure how much of this was simply the way Italian women were, and how much was an actual indication of attraction.

Interestingly, Johannes never stopped to consider what **he** felt or what **he** wanted.

Meanwhile, Sofia basked in the intimacy. Johannes walked with his hands in his pockets and she slipped an arm through his as if it were the most natural thing to do. In Italy, public affection was enjoyed abundantly. It didn't have to mean anything deep or presumptuous. For Sofia, it was simply what she wanted to do.

To Johannes, the display was exciting, stimulating, and... different. Women he'd been with in Germany were passionate behind closed doors, but cool and distant in public. Here, affection was the norm, and he wondered if this was a reason everyone loved Italy. He then remembered what John had said—how in Italy, even affection between men was accepted more than anywhere else he'd been.

Then, without intending to do so, Johannes felt John's presence.

He remembered when John held onto him that night in Germany and how it felt similar but different to the way Sofia held onto him now. And in that moment, Johannes surprised himself. He was surprised to think of John at a time like that, but was even more surprised that it was neither disturbing nor unpleasant. He didn't regret the experience they had had and yet it neither increased a general attraction towards men nor affected his relationships with women in the slightest.

A moment later, Sofia moved in a little closer and this caught the entirety of his attention. The air had grown chilly and Sofia sought comfort in the warmth between them.

Johannes would have been content to walk like this for a while longer, but they had reached Sofia's apartment and the awaited moment of truth was upon them. So little was said that evening, one directly to the other, and yet the non-verbal conversation was immense.

Johannes kept his hands in pockets as he turned to face Sofia.

Sofia uncurled her arm from his, but kept a hold of him with her hand. She then reached for his other arm with her free hand and looked him in the eye. After a nice long gaze, Sofia reached for Johannes' face and placed her lips on one cheek, then the next, and back to the first. The last kiss lingered for just a moment before she pulled away.

"Johannes, I hope you got to see a different side of Venice this evening. I am very happy that you came along."

"I am too, and yes, I think I've seen a different side of a lot of things tonight," he admitted.

"*Buona notte,*" she whispered, as she drew her arms around him.

Johannes pulled his hands out of his pockets and placed them gently around Sofia's back. As the hug lingered, he moved his awareness to all of the places her body met his. He could feel the softness of her cheek, the firmness in the way she held onto him with her hands, and the lightness of touch: her leg to his. Before his thoughts traveled into the more intimate, she let go of him.

Sofia opened her door and Johannes watched. She walked in and turned to look at him one last time. She just couldn't help but admit how beautiful a man he really was. And then, before she became tempted, she waved and shut the door.

Trois – Tre – Tres – Drei

J ohn climbed into bed and was fast asleep. The affects of the wine and dance helped. Yet before the sun rose, he was awake again.

He was surprised to be up before daylight considering how late he had retired, yet something unseen moved him out of bed and over to his desk. It was unlike him to write in the middle of the night, but he didn't exactly feel in control of his actions. He watched himself light a candle and pull out some paper.

Not a moment later, he was writing:

The Trinity

Good Morning, John. I am Jeshua—better known by the English version of my name: Jesus. I have been observing you and awaiting my turn in line, so to speak. It is a joyous occasion to commune with you tonight.

I am sorry to have woken you after such little sleep, but truth be told, it was more the affects of the wine than my presence. I have partaken a glass or two in my lesser and greater lifetimes, so I am familiar with its affects on the body.

I am here to begin the next of your numerical inscriptions. I requested this homily specifically because the number three is so very dear to me. If you were to study those writings that originated from my most well known lifetime, you would find numerous references to the three. No, I did not speak numerologically of three; instead I spoke of the Holy Trinity: God the Father, God the Son, and God the Holy Spirit.

Three is indeed holy. It is magical. It is the first of three numbers that

60

have special properties. All numbers are significant, but three of them hold a place on their own; and the first of them is three. For this discourse, I will refer to THE ONE as 'God' and use the English word as it is comprised of three letters. I could just as easily use the words 'I AM', for they are equally as appropriate and also written with three letters.

When God **created** this realm, He did so via the three. Evidence exists all around you. Notice there are three dimensions of space (axial, lateral, and vertical) and three aspects of time (past, present, and future). Later, you will see examples of the three hidden within other numbers.

Also notice how rarely you find threes in nature. Creatures have two legs, four legs, or many. You find ones, twos, fours, fives, and sixes, but rarely threes. And yet everyone has noticed that strange happenings **occur** in threes.

The secret is this: three is about **creating**, but not about what is created.

In the previous discourse, you were shown how one and two both create each of the other numbers. This works for all save the three special numbers. Watch what happens when we create a sequence by adding three:

3, 6, 9, 12, 15, 18, 21, 24, 27…

…and then reduce numerologically:

<u>3, 6, 9</u>, 3, 6, 9, 3, 6, 9 …

The three only produces the three, the six, and the nine. Any guess as to what the other special numbers might be?

Allow me to introduce to you my friend, Joseph. He was my father once and was a carpenter and an artisan. He knows quite a bit about the special attributes of three.

John's candle flickered a few times. It nearly went out, but then stabilized.

Greetings, my friend. The number three brings with it the gift of **creating**, as in **constructing**, but also **creativity**, as in **artistry**. Any good carpenter knows that one without the other is significantly lacking.

Both builders and artisans employ special (and sacred) geometry to design, construct, and beautify their creations. Tonight, I would like to discuss with you one such tool: the triangle.

A triangle is drawn by connecting three points with three lines and once formed contains three angles. There are different ways to classify triangles. In our first method, triangles are categorized by their largest angle. We have **acute** triangles (where the largest angle is less than 90°), **right** triangles (where the largest angle is exactly 90°), and **obtuse** triangles (whose largest angle is greater than 90°).

In a second method, we categorize triangles by the number of sides of equal length. Thus we have **equilateral** triangles (all three sides are the same), **isosceles** triangles (which have two equal sides), and **irregular** triangles (where all side are different).

Notice that in both of these categorizations, the three repeats within itself.

The right triangle is the most special triangle, bar none. Not surprisingly, there are three right triangles that are most notable.

The first right triangle that is special is one that is derived from a square. If you draw a square and bisect it from one corner to the opposite, you will have formed a pair of isosceles right triangles. We call them 45-45-90 since they have two angles of 45° and one of 90°. If we draw an additional line connecting the remaining two corners of the square, we form four 45-45-90 triangles. Notice that the right angles move from the outer corners to the center. Interesting, don't you think?

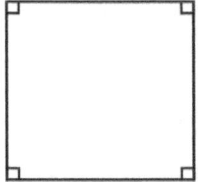 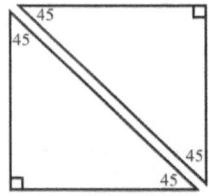 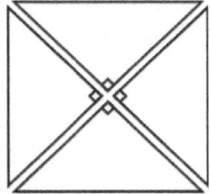

The second right triangle that is of special interest is derived from the equilateral triangle. In this case, we bisect the equilateral triangle from one vertex to the middle of its opposite side. In so doing, we form two 30-60-90 right triangles. Notice the 3-6-9 pattern that we saw above. When we draw similar lines from the other two vertices, we create six 30-60-90 right triangles. How intriguing!

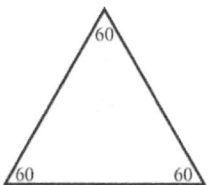 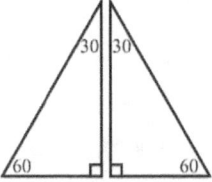 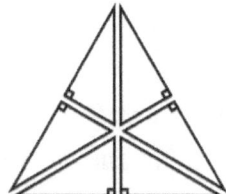

And finally, a right triangle that was of highest interest to builders like the ancient Egyptians is the 3-4-5 right triangle.

1: Take a cord twelve segments long.

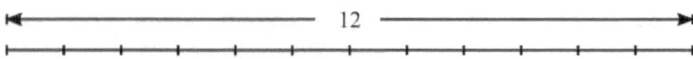

2: Bend it three segments from one end and four from the other.

3: Then bring the ends together.

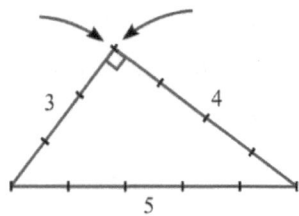

You will always form a right angle where the two ends meet! How useful this was to the ancient architects! It didn't matter whether a segment be an inch, a foot, or a yard, this always works.

All in all, the right triangle is so special, it has spawned a science of its own called trigonometry.

Before I give you back to Jeshua, I would like to walk you through a derivation I think you will enjoy.

1: Draw an equilateral triangle and bisect it by drawing a line from the top vertex to the center of the base.

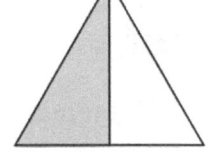

2: Rearrange the right triangles to form a rectangle.

3: Rotate the rectangle onto its longer side.

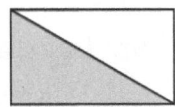

4: Now, bisect the rectangle a different way by drawing a line from the center of the top to the center of the bottom.

5: Bisect each half-rectangle by drawing a diagonal line from the upper middle corner to the bottom outside corner.

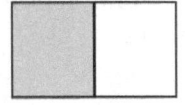

6: Isolate the resulting triangle.

In step one, when we divided the equilateral triangle in half, we created two 30-60-90 right triangles as before. These are also known as **Golden Triangles** because the ratio of the two shorter legs is what is called the **Golden Mean**.

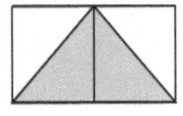

The rectangle in part two has the same area as the equilateral triangle as it is constructed from the same two 30-60-90 triangles. It is called a **Golden Rectangle** because the ratio between the short side and the long side is again the Golden Mean.

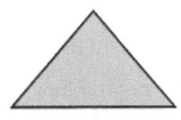

In part five, we created four identical right triangles. Each contains one quarter of the total area. The final triangle thus contains half of the total area of the Golden Rectangle, half of the total area of the equilateral triangle, and the same area as the Golden Triangle. This resulting triangle is an isosceles triangle. Its height and width are the same as the Golden Rectangle, thus the ratio between them is again the Golden Mean. In a sense, this last triangle is another type of Golden Triangle. When you look at it, what comes to mind?

It reminds me of the pyramids in Egypt.

Indeed! The faces of the Great Pyramids are, in fact, triangles of this form.

From this exercise, you see that the Golden Mean is hidden inside the equilateral triangle and relates to the 3-6-9. The Egyptians used the Golden Mean in many of their constructions, not just the pyramids.

Alas, you will learn more about the Golden Mean, but much later. For now, I will spare you more geometry so early in the morning and give you back to Jeshua.

John stared at the candle. It shifted left and right, but did not flicker.

Dearest John. The number three is intriguing and mysterious. Were it not, you would never look beyond the two.

Consider this, if something unusual happens twice in a short period of time, one often shrugs it off as coincidence. Yet, when it happens a third time, all take notice and often say, "Isn't that **odd**."

The human experience of romantic love is of the three. When two love each other, something unseen moves in between them. Even outsiders can sense and feel this mysterious aura.

With the creation of human life, two come together to produce a third: 1+2=3. This is what we call **co-creation**. Whenever two connect, it is natural for co-creation to occur.

Go back to sleep. There is more to come and plenty of time with which to receive it. Blessings to you my brother and may you always feel the Holy Spirit that surrounds you.

The candle flickered wildly and this time went out. To John's amazement, it took an additional few moments before the light drained out of the room.

The strangest things happen in the middle of the night.

John climbed back into bed, closed his eyes, and saw numbers and shapes floating in his mind. As he watched, he could begin to see how the numbers were in fact different from each other. The one, the two, and the three **felt** different.

And then when they are combined...

That was more or less the last lucid thought John had before drifting back into the realm of sleep.

Trois – Tre – Tres – Drei

J ohannes sat at his desk and gazed out the window. He had woken later than normal, but not as late as one would expect considering the night before. Following his normal routine, he had fixed himself a cup of tea and had immediately descended the stairs to his office.

It was convenient living above the office, but now he wondered if a bit too convenient. Most would find distraction having his or her home so close to their office, but for Johannes, it was the other way around. It was easier to go to work than find other ways to entertain himself.

This particular morning, he simply could not focus on the paperwork before him. He kept thinking about the evening before and most specifically the last part of it. He found himself wondering what Sofia had planned for her weekend and then wished it were Monday morning already—when she would be on her way in.

"I guess you got to me, Italy. You win. I'm taking the weekend off and will find something else to do."

Johannes laughed. He never talked to himself out loud. But John had all the time. *It's funny how you pick up another's habits when spending a lot of time with them.*

After considering various options, Johannes decided that some shopping was in order. His modestly furnished apartment contained everything he needed, but little more. Any woman would deem it a "bachelor pad" at best: functionally adequate but lacking creativity.

The office, on the other hand, had ambiance. That was because he had put Sofia in charge of the decorating. Johannes ran his fingers along the curved lines of his Baroque desk, gazed at the Classical painting on the wall, and admired the statuette on Sofia's desk. The small details **did** make a difference.

"It's time to turn my house into a home."

Up until then, Johannes hadn't given his apartment much thought, but now he wanted it to be nice regardless. He thus set out to find and purchase artistic touches to improve the décor. He was living in Venice, after all, where the artistic standards were higher than most places. Here, art was not an afterthought; it was considered from the very start. It was a way of life.

Trois – Tre – Tres – Drei

S unday evening, John arrived at Maria's apartment just after sunset. When Maria answered the door, John pulled her out of the building.

"Look at the sky! Isn't it beautiful?"

Wispy clouds lingered along the horizon providing a rich array of texture and color. Further up, the sky transitioned through pink, lilac, aqua, and ultimately a deep ocean blue to the east.

"El cielo es muy lindo. ¡Tu también!" Maria looped her arm in John's and watched the sky with him. He clearly wanted to wait until the display dissipated before heading inside. Luckily, the Paella was simmering on the stove and didn't need her attention.

As John watched the sky with Maria at his arm, he thought about how different this relationship was for him. Sara had felt like a sister. Lorita, the Queen of Heidelberg, and some others were motherly figures. But his rapport with Maria was unlike either of those. He kept looking for a role model relationship to compare to, but could not come up with one.

He then imagined what it must be like to have her as a wife. *She briefly mentioned her husband once. I wonder where he is. Surely he appreciates how amazing she is. How could he not?*

A few moments later, the clouds no longer caught sunlight and morphed into a dark almost dingy gray. A tiny bit of pink hovered just above the horizon, but otherwise only deep shades of blue remained.

"We can go in now. Thanks for enjoying this with me."

"*¡Claro!* Thank you for dragging me out for it. It was a treat."

John followed Maria into the kitchen and was struck by the delicious aroma. He watched as she inspected and stirred the contents of her stew.

Maria, deciding the *Paella* was done, turned off the stove and returned her attention to her guest.

"I'm going to let that cool some," she said. "Do you want a tour in the mean time?"

"I would love one," John replied.

As John followed Maria through the house, he could clearly tell the foreign influence. The majority of art and décor were clearly not Egyptian. There were some pieces of locally made furniture that had been added, similar to things John had seen in other places in Cairo. Interestingly, they did not distract from the overall feel that John assumed to be Spanish.

Maria took John through the rooms one by one. Although the apartment had a woman's touch, John could detect evidence of a distinctly male influence, which he assumed to be her husband. And yet, one of the rooms must have been—*for a son?*

"And this is Carlos' room. Did I mention that I have a son? He is off studying at university now, back in Spain. My boy—he has more of his mother in him than his father. He would rather be home in Spain than anywhere else in the world."

John started to ask Maria about the men in her life, but hesitated. The evening was just getting started and he thought it would be better to wait until she offered on her own.

Maria ended the tour back in the kitchen, reached into the cupboard for a couple of bowls, and asked John to place them on the table. She then grabbed water and wine glasses and handed them to him when he returned.

"Would you be a dear and open up a bottle of wine?" she asked him. "I have already selected one appropriate for tonight's meal. It is that one over there."

Helping out with the preparations made John feel even more comfortable than he had to begin with. By the time they sat to eat, he felt as if they had done this dozens of times already. The food, the location, and the host were all foreign to him, and yet John felt completely at home.

Trois – Tre – Tres – Drei

S unday afternoon, Johannes returned from the market and directed the deliverymen up to his apartment. They carted the majority of his purchases. In his hands were the rest: three bouquets for the office.

Earlier, Johannes had stopped at the flower stand with the intention of purchasing a single bouquet for Sofia. In a moment of panic, he opted on buying three instead. He would place one on Sofia's desk, as planned, and place the others elsewhere in the office.

This way, it won't be so obvious what I am up to—he reasoned.

Johannes could feel a new connection forming between them, but he didn't want to be presumptuous.

In the last of the daylight that remained, Johannes unpacked and arranged his new belongings in his apartment. Once it got dark, he went down to the office to arrange flowers by candlelight.

Sofia rarely beats me to the office in the morning—he considered, as he added one last rose to Sofia's bouquet—*but I don't want to take any chances.* Taking a few steps back to admire his work, he said softly, "I want it to look nice as soon as she walks in."

Trois – Tre – Tres – Drei

D inner was amazing, and the conversation pleasant, however Maria asked all of the questions and didn't offer many details of her own life. So while John's stomach was satiated, his curiosity was not. Before he could muster the nerve to ask questions, Maria segued the conversation in a new direction.

"John. I'm curious about this…thing that you do. What did you call it? Channeling? Do you think you can do that for me right now?"

Sudden panic flowed over John.

"Well…I…I never channeled in…I…I think it would be difficult for me to do that right now. I haven't been able to channel since Johannes left, except when I am writing." Composing himself, John then said, "but I have an idea. How about a reading instead?"

"A reading?"

"Yes, with Tarot cards. I have them in my bag. I'm not an expert by any means, but I think it'll be fun."

"OK. A girlfriend of mine had a reading once, back in Spain. We were out for an afternoon walk and happened upon a street reader. My friend was moved to get one. I wasn't impressed enough to get one myself, but I think she got something out of it. What do we do?"

John fetched the cards from his satchel, which was sitting by the door, and began shuffling the cards on his way back to the dining table.

"I haven't done a reading for anyone but me, at least not since I was a kid. But I don't think there is a right or a wrong way to do it. Here, shuffle the cards, and then when they feel right, hand them back to me."

Maria shuffled the cards pensively. As she did so, John wondered what she was thinking. It was a first to see Maria quiet and contemplative. So far, any time a thought crossed her mind, she voiced it immediately. Even though she hadn't shared many details about her life, it never seemed as if she was holding anything back either.

A few moments later, she handed John the cards. He held them for a moment, removed the top card for some unknown reason, and placed it face down to the side. He then laid out ten cards in the

Celtic Cross pattern he'd been practicing recently.

"For fun, I'm just going to tell you what I see, you know, first impression. If something isn't clear, we can consult the booklet to see if there is more information. OK?"

"You're the reader!"

"Hmm. It appears that you have been reminiscing. You have been visiting the past in your thoughts. Remembering happier times perhaps? And I would say that you've been thinking about two men—your son and husband maybe? Whatever you've been thinking about, it has led up to a decision, a dilemma perhaps? Have you been contemplating something? Do you have to make a choice between two options?"

"Go on. I want to hear all that you have to say first, and then I'll tell you what this is about."

"OK. Hmm…this card—here—it seems to me that while you've been thinking about good times in the past, it appears that you're also missing something that's been lost. As I tune into it, I feel strong sadness—grief maybe?"

John looked at Maria and detected a shift in her expression. He could see that he touched upon something. There **was** sadness underneath the cheerful, fun loving expression that he had only seen up to now. He went on.

"The future. Let's see... This first card shows another man. I distinctly feel like he's going to be of help. This may sound weird, but I think this card represents me. Well, it's signified me before… a few times. Anyway, the card after that shows movement, literal movement. Could be a trip…could be a move. Do you have a trip planned?

"Oh, and look at this! All remaining cards are the same color. They are yellow, sunny, and warm. This one shows water in the background. Whatever potential this is showing, it is going to feel good. I keep getting drawn into that one. Wherever that is, I want to go! It looks beautiful!

"So…what do you think? Does it apply to your life at all?"

Maria sat for a moment and stared at the cards. She looked up at John and then back down. She then took a deep breath and began to tell John her story.

"John. Let me start by telling you how I ended up in Cairo. My husband, Fernando, is an archeologist—he was. He died six weeks ago. Anyway, he was always a bit of an Egyptologist. He was fascinated by the pyramids and dreamt of finding clues as to their origin.

"A number of years ago, he heard talk of a discovery. An ancient city, buried under layers of sand had been exposed. The crew here in Egypt needed all the help they could get to unearth it. Fernando jumped at the opportunity.

"And so the three of us moved here. Carlos was not exactly excited about leaving all of his friends, but Fernando convinced him that time in a foreign country was important to his development. Fernando was clear that Carlos didn't have a choice; he just wanted him to know that it would be good for all of us.

"And it was. Carlos adjusted rather quickly, and actually enjoyed his time here. When he graduated, he decided to go back to Spain for university, as I mentioned.

"As much as I missed having my boy near me, it was nice having it back to just Fernando and me. It was like when we were young and first married. He was well into his routine at the dig, and kept regular hours. He even took time off now and again so we could enjoy what the city had to offer.

"And that leads up to about two months ago. The dig up north made a…discovery. Something they found in the temple showed the way to a—well—Fernando called it 'buried treasure'. This was the most excited he'd been in years. The possibility of being a part of a team that exhumed a treasure of this magnitude was nearly more than he could handle. In the end, it took his life."

"What happened?" John asked with a look of shock on his face.

"You see—word got out about the possibility of treasure, and one day, the dig was raided. Fernando tried to convince the robbers that nothing had been found, but an altercation ensued and he was badly wounded. His team got him back to Cairo, which enabled me to see him one last time, but he died later that night. It is sad; I so loved that man. But he died pursuing his dream, and what more can any man ask for?"

John reached out and placed his hand on Maria's.

"So…this is my dilemma: Carlos does not know yet. I can't

send a notice to him; I must tell him myself, in person. So a trip **is** forthcoming. The choice is whether to move back to Spain or just visit. Truth be told, **that** decision has already been made. I **will** move back to Spain. I think the **real** question is whether to simply move back right now, or travel there first to see Carlos and then come back for all of my belongings. I am not looking forward to delivering such bad news to Carlos, but I am also not looking forward to moving a houseful of belongings all by myself. I thought that I could bring Carlos back here to help me. He might miss a semester of school, but I'm sure he would want to go through his father's possessions before I got rid of anything. Details, details, details..."

"What if I help you?" John said this without thinking. "Ever since Johannes left, I've been unable to decide what to do or where to go. I've simply been stalling."

And then he was silent. The uneasy feeling that started halfway through Maria's talk grew. The dig, the discovery, the buried treasure—too many pieces fit. John was afraid of the answer he might get, but he had to ask.

"Maria. What was the name of the ancient city where they were digging?"

"It has three names. The only one I can remember is Heliopolis; 'City of the Sun' is what it means."

A pang of guilt collected in John's stomach. It felt like a pool of acid burning his gut. Was he responsible for this? Was it not the message he channeled that led to Fernando's death? The Archeologist he had met at the temple was not Spanish, so it couldn't have been Fernando, but he must have been brought in as a result.

"Maria. I feel really bad. I feel responsible."

Maria looked at John and shrugged her shoulders. She then gently rubbed his arm and said, "John, these things happen."

"No, you don't understand! I mean I really **am** responsible. I told you about the channeled messages, but I didn't give you details. Johannes and I were in Heliopolis a few months ago. I channeled a message to an archeologist there. In that message, they spoke of buried treasure. It has to be the treasure that Fernando was sent in search of; I'm sure of it! If I had never come to Egypt, Fernando would still be alive!"

John held his head in regret and Maria again reached over to him.

"John, don't think like that. You couldn't have known what would happen. Besides, you said yourself that you never knew what information would come through beforehand. How could you be responsible?" Maria then looked off to the side and added, "And yet, at the same time, what a coincidence it is: us sitting across from each other right now. John, **this** isn't an accident." She waved her finger between them. "Fernando's death was an accident, but this, right here, right now, cannot be."

"Maria, I don't get it. This is just like I was saying the other night. As soon as I regain my balance after a chain of events, I get surprised with something else."

"John, that's life. I've been around a little longer than you have and stuff like this does not surprise me any longer. Life is a mystery. How boring it would be if it were not."

"I would still feel a lot better if I could be useful. I am serious. I would like to help you move back to Spain. I've traveled a lot these past few years and I've learned some things."

"Well, John, I think it has been decided then. I will send word to my sister and tell her that I am coming home. When I get to Spain, I'll leave my belongings with her until I find a new home. She lives outside of Barcelona and has plenty of space. I'll visit Carlos first thing and tell him the dreaded news. And then I will work on starting over."

"I still feel bad about all of this, but it is a consolation knowing that I'll be of help."

"So John. What will you do when you get to Spain?"

"Who knows? Thirty minutes ago, I didn't even know I was going!"

Trois – Tre – Tres – Drei

L ater that evening, John sat, taking in all of what the day had brought. Intermittent waves of guilt lingered as he tried to sort out everything he discovered. The more he thought about it, the more questions he came up with. At the same time, he now knew whole-heartedly that he and Maria were karmically connected, and this consoled him.

He then thought about the upcoming trip. He was excited about that. He looked forward to getting to know Maria better, and it was nice finally having a plan. He felt useful again and was more than ready to put Cairo and Egypt behind him.

Yet still more questions came. For example, what would he do once he got to Spain? In the hope that answers would also come, he reached for some paper.

Creation

I AM that I AM. I am not one. I am not all. Like the three, I am that which joins the one and the two in Holy Communion. I am unnamed—I am beyond naming. And yet there are many names that have been associated with me. I am most commonly referred to as the Divine Feminine.

In the realms beyond yours, there is deity and divinity. Deity is that which is named, with voice and personality. Divinity is unnamed; it is pure essence. It is blended. It is vast and yet subtle. I am only able to speak to you in words thanks to Quan Yin. In a sense, it is really she who is channeling to you from the essence that I AM.

That which is truly of the Divine Feminine is unpolarized. It is neither male nor female. And yet the qualities of the Divine Feminine **are** more accepted by women than men. And so, within your realm, I am spoken of in these terms.

Jeshua, when on Earth, was a male vastly imbued with the Divine Feminine. He began this discussion and now we continue it. Jeshua introduced you to the Trinity and Joseph spoke to you about the triangle.

When you visualize the trinity, you can think of each piece as the point of an equilateral triangle. Each is connected to the others, draws support from the others, and offers service to the others as well. Resist viewing this triangle as a hierarchy; it is not. The three points are equally as significant and participatory.

The Christian Trinity that Jeshua spoke of is not the only example of the holy three. The maiden, the mother, and the crone depict a decidedly feminine variation. These can be viewed as the three stages of a woman's life, be it that she chooses to bear children or not. Mothering, you see, need not be specifically birthing.

The maiden years are a time of absorption. Those are the years of a person's life when she most embodies the one. It is in this phase that she forms herself from that which surrounds her. She learns from her mother, her tutor, her priestess, and her clan. She must continually absorb and decipher, choose and discern. This is not restricted to women, wouldn't you say?

In those years that she bleeds, a woman is within her maternal phase and capable of bearing young. During this time, she is naturally inclined towards another, be it child or mate. In this part of her life, she most resonates with the vibration of two. Self is no longer her obvious focus, but instead other. The one within her is fed by her service to another. As wife, as mother, as artist, as performer, as businesswoman, as teacher— the emphasis is typically toward that which is outside of herself. Again, I ask you, is this decidedly female? Do not men often follow a similar pattern?

Through the natural course of evolution, each person progresses, and may proceed to the phase represented by the crone, matriarch, queen, or medicine woman. With her children grown and her priorities shifted, her focus evolves. In this stage, if she chooses, she begins to embody the essence of the High Priestess and moves toward the vibration of three. That is because she has now more fully accepted the Divine Feminine within her. She invites the essence that I AM to enter her body, promote her purpose, and guide her work. As such, she is no longer merely concerned with the two or the one. Instead, she has reached a wholeness of three that contains within it the two **and** the one. She is now in service to all. If she serves only other and denounces her self, she is off track.

In this phase, she can be mistakenly seen as a bitter crone. There are times when a strong slap teaches more effectively than a gentle caress. There are times when a single tsunami more effectively initiates fulfillment of a thousand requests. Thus, in many a lore, be it Kali or Eris, Sekhmet or Athena, war and destruction are attributed to the Goddess. Men start wars with each other, but natural disaster is always blamed on Mother Nature.

Truth be told, the realm of duality requires both creation **and** destruction. They're really one and the same, a single force that acts within both parts of the cycle. As with birth and death, they are inseparable. In the Tarot that you play with, there is the Three of Cups **and** the Three of Swords. At the Three of Cups, you celebrate gain. At the Three of Swords, you mourn loss. With gratitude, you anticipate what is desired, and with regret you begrudgingly offer up what does not serve you.

Earlier this evening, you witnessed this at play. A single event resulted in both pleasure and pain. A message you brought forth has been shown as the apparent cause of gain **and** loss. Fernando's death resulted, but so will the birth of a new child. You will be happy to know that the tour guide's wife is already pregnant. He followed the guidance you brought forth and will soon reap the benefits.

My son, you are woven into the fabric of creation and destruction. You can find yourself responsible for both, if you choose to look at it that way, and yet you will only feed the ego in doing so.

The plant and animal alike employ chemistry for survival. Molecules are broken down in one part of the cycle, and reassembled in another. Altogether, the cycles are completed in nature and remain in balance, yet one that is ever changing and evolving.

The difference between destruction and creation is nothing more than perspective. You do not see the destruction of the nighttime when the sun rises. You do not see destruction of ignorance when learning occurs. You do not see destruction of solitude when a dear friend visits.

With every breath you take, there is the destruction of one form and the creation of another. It is all simply the flow of energy. From the perspective of your scientists, they would say that energy is neither created nor destroyed. They follow it as it changes states, sometimes potential, other times kinetic. Ebb and flow, when considered together, comprise the cycles of life and existence. Three is that which joins all apparent opposites together.

Allow this to be the second of three discourses on three. Until we meet again, know that I am ever-present within the cycles of your existence. Blessed be.

Trois – Tre – Tres – Drei

When dawn broke, Johannes was instantly wide-awake. It was still dark in his apartment even though the sky was aglow. Between the pending sunrise and his eyes adjusting, the room began to emerge out of the darkness.

Johannes turned to look at the elegant hand made clock he had purchased the day before. The man that sold it to him set the proper time and gave it a good wind before wrapping it. Johannes could tell he was the one who actually made it by the care he had given it within the transaction.

A few minutes after staring at the clock, Johannes finally noticed the time displayed and guessed that he had just enough time to get ready and get to the office before Sofia got in. At first he couldn't remember what time Sofia usually arrived, but then he remembered what she had said the week before about the timing of sunrise and the onset of spring. He had only been half listening since he had been concentrating on whatever was in front of him.

Come to think of it, that's normally the case. I think Sofia is right. I am a bit too focused on work most of the time.

Johannes showered and then selected clothes for the day with a little more intention than usual. Again, he was trying not to appear too obvious, but didn't want to just throw anything on.

He made himself a cup of tea and headed downstairs. While he sipped his tea, mostly waiting for it to cool, he stood near the front door and inspected the office. A part of him evaluated his flower-arranging skills. The bouquet on Sofia's desk was most prominent, but the others were also conspicuous.

He then looked around in a way that he could only attribute to John's influence. He thought about how much had been accomplished in such little time. The office really did look as if it had been in use for years. And it suited all of his needs—for now and the foreseeable future.

John, of course, would have looked at Johannes' manifestational progress more esoterically than Johannes did, but that's another story.

To Johannes, what lay before him was simply the result of focused effort. He did have to admit, though, that it never felt like work. Ever since he left Cairo, he had been invigorated once again. There wasn't a single moment when he had to push himself into anything. He had had his playtime, and was now motivated to get things accomplished.

John often told him how nice it was that he was self-motivated. John himself was, at times, but it all depended on his mood. When he was happy, he was content to do just about anything, help nearly anyone, and never complained. But when he was unhappy, he wanted nothing more than to mope and be on his own.

Well, he wouldn't necessarily admit that, but that's how it seemed to me—Johannes thought.

And yet, John did manage to get himself out of his emotional bouts one way or the other.

I think John has taught me how to be comfortable around another person's emotions—Johannes admitted to himself.

Johannes thought back. He remembered how uncomfortable he became when a girlfriend got too emotional in his presence. He usually offered suggestions, but that just seemed to make matters worse.

"Stop trying to fix things and just listen to me." How many times had he heard that?

John, being an emotional guy, but a guy nonetheless, never **said** that to him—in words. Instead, he would simply clam up and avoid interaction, even if standing right next to him.

Johannes was amazed at how John could be right in front of him, and yet miles away at the same time. He was like that when he was upset, but he was also like that when "tuning in," as he would call it.

Although in that pensive moment Johannes almost missed John, he was also happy to not have him around right then. He just wasn't sure how well John would handle the current situation with Sofia, *assuming there is a situation...*

Right on cue, Johannes heard the sound of footsteps outside the door. He quickly moved over to his desk, sat down, and found something to feign attention on.

Sofia walked through the door and paused.

Johannes didn't want to look up, but rather relied on his peripheral vision to investigate. Sure enough, Sofia had noticed the flowers right away. He could see her look around the room, at him, and then back at her desk.

Without saying a word, she walked up to him, kissed him on the cheek, and then walked over to her desk.

Johannes looked up and watched as she walked away, unable to hold back a subtle smile. Before she next looked over to him from her desk, he put his eyes back down to his paperwork.

Sofia saw the subtle smile on Johannes' face and could tell that he was being coy, which in total warmed her heart.

So Friday night wasn't just a dream—she thought.

4 – *Four* – IV

Quatre – Quattro – Cuatro – Vier

Maria and John met in the early afternoon to start putting together a plan. By that time, Maria had already written a letter to her sister and posted it. She had also written to Carlos to tell him that she would be coming for a visit. She had gone back and forth on that one a few times, but ultimately decided on sending it.

Maria let John in and escorted him straight to the kitchen where she had set out sandwiches. As they ate, she started in on the first order of business.

"It may take us a few weeks to get everything arranged and packed for this trip. I was thinking—there's really no reason for you to continue renting a room at the inn. I have plenty of space here. Why don't you stay in Carlos' room for the remainder of our time in Cairo?"

"That would be great! Johannes was very generous with the money he left me, but it will be nice to not have to spend any more of it on the room. I was tallying some figures this morning. I have what's needed to get to Spain and should have enough left over for the first few weeks. Hopefully I'll find work by then."

"And that brings me to my next thought. I am paying for your ticket to Spain. We're going to have to take a freight ship there and I am heading to the port this afternoon to work out the details."

John opened his mouth to say something, but Maria cut him off.

"John. No arguing. First, I don't expect that our tickets will cost much compared to the fee for the cargo. And second, Fernando is paying for all of this. He's the one who left and set all of this in motion. Luckily, he had made sure I would be taken care of. And I am. Furthermore, his company has offered additional payment, since his death was a result of injuries he attained while working. So don't you worry your handsome little head. Besides, I am putting you to work! Think of this as a job, if you must."

John smiled at Maria's feistiness, but was also grateful.

"Now, after we finish lunch, I'm going to head to the port. There's no point in you accompanying me. I shouldn't be long. Besides, I have a task that I would like for you to do...and it will probably take you a few days. No point in putting it off. I would like you to box up my husband's personal belongings. I just can't be distracted with the emotions it will conjure if I do it. I'll go through them with Carlos when we're in Spain. It'll be better for you to deal with them now. I can't tell you what a help that will be for me."

After lunch, Maria cleared the table and then gave John further instruction to get him started. She then gathered a few of her things and departed.

Quatre – Quattro – Cuatro – Vier

E ach day, John spent at least half of his time sorting and packing Fernando's belongings. At first, the thought of going through someone else's personal things felt strange to him, but then he reminded himself that, for now, this was his job. As he thought about it more, he realized that, in a way, it was appropriate; it was his penance—a way to repay the karmic debt. Then, soon enough, he let go of the idea that Fernando's death was partly his fault.

After that, the task became fun, as if he were putting together a puzzle that when completed would show John what Fernando was like. To start, John decided he would collect and sort everything first, and then pack it all afterward. Four days later, he found things that Fernando likely hadn't touched in months. They had gathered dust, and so John took to cleaning them as part of the process. Some of the items appeared to be artifacts, likely from one dig or another, and so John gingerly wiped each down and organized them.

84

At various times, and without thinking much about it, John began to form a mental image of Fernando—not so much what he looked like for there were pictures of him among the items, but what he felt like, what kind of man he was, and what his personality might have been. Oddly, he felt a connection forming with the man he would never meet. In fact, on an occasion or two, he even talked to Fernando while he worked.

Then one day, while not paying close enough attention to what he was doing, he dropped a figurine on the floor and it shattered. As he gathered the pieces together, he berated himself audibly, "Damn it, John. Pay attention to what you are doing. I'm so sorry Fernando."

No te preocupes, mi amigo.

John looked around the room and felt goose bumps on his skin. It was one thing for unknown non-physical beings to contact him, but it was a little eerie for a recently deceased man to do so.

"Fernando? Is that you?" he asked to the room.

Sí.

"I'm sorry I broke the statue."

Do not worry, my friend. It would not be good for Maria to take that to Spain. It is better for it to remain here in Egypt, even if in pieces.

"Really? Well, I'm sorry—sorry about **everything**."

Amigo, do not be. All is well! Maria knows this and Carlos will too—in time.

"Are you sure?"

¡Claro que sí! My friend, if you could only see what it looks like from this side, you would know. Alas, for now you will have to take my word for it.

"I guess I'll just have to trust you. Is there anything I can do for you—any messages I can convey to Maria or any special requests for your belongings?"

Actually, yes—there are other objects that must not leave Egypt. It would be nice to not have to break all of them to keep them here, ha! I will guide you as you pack. If you feel inclined to set something aside, do so knowing that it is my resolve. Place those items in a special box and tell Maria to give them to my colleagues. They will know what to do with them.

"Your wish is my command!"

John felt giddy. The task had become even more exciting now that he knew he wasn't exactly doing it alone.

Quatre – Quattro – Cuatro – Vier

F or the rest of that first week and all of the next, Johannes and Sofia performed a dance that was primarily non-verbal. Each day, Sofia's subtle affections grew. She set the pace and Johannes happily followed. For example, when they worked on a task side by side, Sofia would occasionally place a hand on Johannes' arm, briefly at first and then for a bit longer as time went on. Her touch was soft and exciting, enough to convey her feelings, but never to tease or entice him.

Because Johannes got to see Sofia all day, he was content with the way things were developing. He wasn't sure how increased intimacy would affect their working relationship, and thus kept a wait-and-see attitude.

One day, when his confidence peaked, Johannes decided a more obvious gesture was in order. At the end of the workday, he set out to find an appropriate gift.

When it came to gift shops, in Venice one wanted for nothing. The city was populated with artisans who created beautiful items. Glass figurines and ornate masks were the most plentiful. And nearly everything the Italians created brought with it a touch of romance. *Amore* went into—and thus oozed out of—everything they created.

Johannes entered a shop at random and was quickly convinced he would find the perfect gift there. Initially, Johannes found himself continually coming back to a gorgeous heart-shaped paperweight made of glass. The paperweight was translucent, so one could see all the way to the rich crimson center. The outer layers of glass were less colored, but contained flecks of silver. The affect was amazing.

Ultimately, Johannes decided it was not the right time for a gift like that. They hadn't even officially been on a date after all. Instead, he settled on a crystal star unlike anything he'd seen before. The star was carved from a piece of rose quartz, rather than blown of glass like the majority of items. And the pink color would suit Sofia's taste, from what he had observed.

One thing that struck Johannes as a little strange, though, was the way the clerk eyed him when he brought the star to the counter. The man seemed surprised that Johannes wanted that specific item and was almost reluctant to sell it to him. He kept asking Johannes why he was buying it and what he planned to do with it.

Johannes was reticent to address the man's prying, and simply said that it was for a special woman. That seemed to quell the clerk's curiosity.

After Johannes exited the shop, he quickly turned and walked back in. He couldn't take the chance that the glass heart would be sold before he was ready for it. He would simply hold onto it until the time was right, *hopefully not too far in the future*.

It was expensive, but that didn't dissuade him.

Quatre – Quattro – Cuatro – Vier

S eth sat back, took a virtual deep breath, and felt more at ease than he had in weeks. It was clear to him now that a wholly new timeline had formed to replace the one he'd been having a hard time letting go of. **He** could go visit the original timeline and thus see how it **could have** unfolded, but doing so did nothing to help him with the new one. And, of course, time spent over there simply left him more frustrated.

All of that potential gone to waste!

It was only in that very moment that Seth started to admit to himself that the new timeline was working out despite his failed attempts to redirect it. In fact, the more he had tried to manipulate the flow of circumstances, the more karmic everything became—especially for him.

*And that Horus is no help either. He and Johannes are having a blast with this new timeline. Sure, **they** are happy. Look at what's developing on their side!*

And yet, Seth reminded himself, things **were** going well for John as well. John was content—happy even—although not exactly falling in love.

And the communications!

Entities were coming out of the woodwork to talk to John and John was happily connecting to each without Seth's help. It seemed everyone was on board the new timeline save him.

Seth had started to feel like he wasn't being a very good spirit guide and so, with strong intent, he set out to change that.

Quatre – Quattro – Cuatro – Vier

T he day John completed his assignment, he heard a knock at the door. Men had arrived bringing crates Maria had requested for her belongings. After several bustling moments, John heard nothing more. He almost thought Maria had departed with the men until he heard a subtle stirring in the kitchen.

Shortly before dinnertime, John emerged from the back bedroom with the last box of Fernando's items. The artifacts were left unwrapped, slated to remain in Egypt. He placed them in the living room, but didn't say anything about them right away.

John could see that Maria was nearing completion of dinner and took it upon himself to set the table. Intermittently, Maria delegated a task by handing him an item; he carried it out with full understanding. The two worked in silence, knowing full well that conversation would ensue once they sat for the meal.

In watching the way they interacted, it was clear that a comfortable rhythm had developed between them.

Partnerships are as unique as the individuals paired. Some couples laugh the entire time they are together. Others carry on lengthy, intellectually stimulating conversations. Some duos love to compete, while others work well as a team.

John and Maria's relationship was diverse, yet uncomplicated— rich, yet easy. Some would call it a mutual admiration society. Others might say it was Venusian. The love and affection each felt for the other was grand, yet free of the encumbrances of sexual attraction. Conversation flowed readily from the start, yet long periods of quietude passed just as comfortably. Because each felt indebted to the other, both continually strived to reciprocate.

Furthermore, the connection between them did not take away from either's independence. For example, when John retreated due to an emotional need for solitude, it was met without the slightest resistance from Maria. She was well accustomed to domestic partnerships and although required almost no alone time, was happy to give John as much space as he needed. She was simply thankful to have him there in her home and in her life for as long as it would last.

John had struggles he had to face alone, and Maria did as well. Underneath her calm, pleasant exterior, she felt trepidation. She expected the trip to transpire without issue, but was less confident about the rebuilding of her life, even in Spain. She knew she had been putting off tears that had to come sometime. Would they come as a gentle shower or a torrential downpour? And then, of course, there was that dreaded conversation with Carlos that weighed heavily upon her. Her grief, she could manage, but his too?

The two enjoyed the conversation and companionship of the meal, while holding back some thoughts of their own. After they cleared the table and cleaned the kitchen, John excused himself earlier than usual. He was fatigued from packing up the last of Fernando's belongings, but was also in the mood to write a bit before retiring.

Foundation

Master John, I am Metatron, master architect from the realm of Archangels. I am mathematician, engineer, and numerologist, and I am here to share with you some of my knowledge.

I would like to begin by discussing the number four. Yes, you are correct in noting that we have not completed the number three. Oh how nice life would be if everything simply proceeded in order. But it does not and I shan't either.

Four is the number that I am most fond of...I think. Well, yes, after eons of time, I am still uncertain. Just when I believe I have learned all there is to know on the subject, the Universe shows me more. This is because THE ONE is creating faster than IT is understanding.

Ponder with me for a moment. Imagine, if you may, what a fourth dimension of space would be like. Can you? Where would it be? Challenging, is it not? No matter what direction you look in, there you have what simply lies within three dimensions.

And yet, in this reality you are so accustomed to, there are fours everywhere. Take for example the four directions: north, south, east, and west—and the four elements: earth, fire, air, and water.

Four in Sacred Geometry

Earlier, Jeshua, Joseph, and the Divine Feminine spoke to you about the Trinity and the triangle. Being a specialist in Sacred Geometry, I now introduce you to more geometry of interest. To begin, note that the four is decidedly represented by the square. Each of its four sides is of equal length, and all of its corners are at right angles. And yet, where do you most often see a square? As the face of a cube, of course! No matter which side you look at, a cube always looks like a square when viewed face on.

Notice that both of these terms are used in mathematics. When you multiple a number by itself, you **square** it, and if you multiply it by itself again, you **cube** it. In a sense, four is our first square: $2^2 = 4$. That is, of course, because we do not count zero and one. No matter how many times you multiply zero and one by itself, the result will always be zero and one respectively.

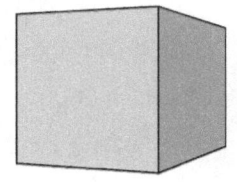

The cube looks like a four, but is not created from four. In fact, it is a product of the three. It is one of our first two sacred solids. Before we continue, let me give you a little more background.

In Sacred Geometry, there are figures and solids. Figures are two-dimensional, and thus flat. Solids are three-dimensional, and have volume. All of the solids we will discuss with you have flat faces, with one exception. The surface of a sphere is two-dimensional, but curved. You'll have to wait a while to hear more on that one.

For all other sacred solids, a minimum of four faces must exist and each is represented by multiple numbers. Take for example the tetrahedron. It is named as such (tetra-hedron) because it has **four** identical **faces** and yet each face is an equilateral **triangle**. It thus connects the three and the four.

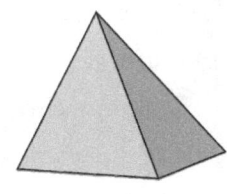

The tetrahedron is a pyramid, but is not the same as the pyramids here in Egypt. Those pyramids have four triangular faces and a square base. With the tetrahedron, no matter which way you turn it, it will always look the same. You will not see many tetrahedrons in the man-created world, and practically never in nature, but let me assure you that energetically they are everywhere.

The The very planet you walk upon is, in fact, held together via a pair of them! When two identical tetrahedrons overlap in opposite orientation, they create what is called a **Merkaba**—an exquisite three-dimensional star. Use your third eye and look upon the image I am sending you.

Now let us get back to the cube. The cube contains an axis for each of the three dimensions of your realm, which can be drawn by connecting the centers of opposing faces. And as we've already discussed, the cube's faces are perfect squares.

The boxes you've been working with resemble cubes, and so does this room. If you were to describe the room to me, you would likely say that is has four walls, a ceiling, and a floor. That is because, within your three-dimensional experience, the lateral and axial dimensions are interchangeable, while the vertical is never mistaken for the other two. I can spin you around and around and yet you would still be able to tell me which way is up. That is simply because gravity has its way with you—with all of you residing within the planetary realms.

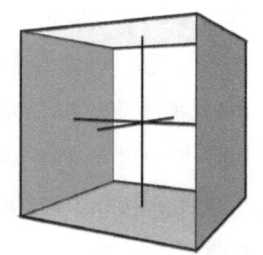

Back to the room; look at how many features show up in fours. As we said, there are four walls surrounding you. Your chair, your table, and your bed all sit upon four legs: a configuration of **stability**. Bring your attention to the rectangular door and windows. Although they are not perfect squares, they do contain four sides and four corners like a square. And as you look up toward the ceiling, you will see four corners likely gathering spiders.

Speaking of animals, notice how the majority of your beasts are four-legged. Not so in the insect kingdom, or among the birds, but with mammals, reptiles, and amphibians, four legs prevail. That is because the vibration of four is primarily concerned with **support** and **stability**. Four is the **foundation** upon which the other numbers reside. The only reason matter exists for any length of time is because it has been rooted into the physical via the resonance of four.

You were told earlier that there are three aspects of time, and yet four is also timely. Notice how humanity sections off time into fours—the four seasons: winter, spring, summer, and autumn—and the four times of the day: morning, afternoon, evening, and night. Four is what keeps your life resembling in the morning what it was the night before.

Another important aspect of four is **rest** and **reprieve**. When one learns to rest and enjoy one's creations before creating anew, he or she reaches a true joy and proficiency of being. Go now and rejuvenate yourself with a full night of rest. There will be more to come soon my friend...

Quatre – Quattro – Cuatro – Vier

During the first half of the next day, the crystal star remained hidden within the top drawer of Johannes' desk. It was nestled inside of a decorative box—content and anticipatory. After the midday meal, Johannes kept opening the drawer and fingering the box, unsure when to present it. He finally opted to arrange for an evening meal one night during the weekend.

Yes, that's perfect. Not in the office, where's the romance in that?

"Sofia, can I ask you a question?"

"Certo, Signore!" Sofia now called Johannes 'Signore' as a joke and he was beginning to like it simply for that reason.

"Do you have plans this weekend? What I mean is—are you free for dinner one of the next few nights?"

"Yes. In fact, I do not have any plans. I am free all weekend!" Sofia, having anticipating an imminent dinner invitation, had kept her social calendar clear. Now she was enjoying having caught him a little off guard. Feigning ignorance, she said, "Why do you ask, *Signore?*"

"Well, I would like to know if you would be interested in having dinner with me—as my guest of course. I was hoping that you could select a nice *trattoria*, something a little upscale. I haven't been to any of Venice's finer establishments yet."

"Absolutely, *Signore*. For which night were you thinking?"

"Well, since you are free, how about this evening? The weather is quite nice, don't you think?"

"I expect it will be a splendidly pleasant evening tonight." Sofia selected her words carefully. "And I know just the place," which she had decided upon days before. "Why don't we meet at my apartment at 8:00. We can take a gondola from there."

Gondola! Why hadn't I thought of that? Johannes then admitted to himself that this was **her** hometown after all, so he couldn't be expected to outthink her in the romantic idea department.

"It's a date!" Johannes said this more excitedly than he had planned, but didn't care by that point. And luckily he had waited until late in the afternoon to broach the subject, because now both of them sat quietly, minds racing, but with no thoughts of work.

After a few moments, Johannes said, "I have an idea. It has been a good week—I mean productive. We've made so much progress, let's quit early and then I'll see you at 8:00 this evening."

"Thank you, *Signore*. I do have some personal business I can attend to. Until 8:00..." Sofia quickly arranged a few things on her desk, grabbed her bag, and kissed Johannes on both cheeks on her way out. Johannes was almost disappointed because he knew that a single kiss was more intimate than a kiss on each cheek, but the night was young...

As soon as Sofia departed, Johannes took the gift out of the drawer and set it on the desk. He admired the cubic box and the intricate designs drawn upon it.

Quatre – Quattro – Cuatro – Vier

H ey Seth!" Horus had learned much in the past few months. In fact, he had grown so comfortable within the light realms he stopped thinking in terms of location. Whenever he wanted to visit with someone, he simply called out to them, rather than **travel** to them. It was so much easier.

"Horus. How are you? Or am I going to regret asking?" Seth was still feeling a bit down on himself.

"Seth, you should be happy! Sorry, I shouldn't '**should**' you, but you know what I mean. Things are good! Look how well everyone is doing!"

"You're right, Horus. In fact, you've been right about a lot of things lately! That's fine; I'm man enough to admit it."

"'Man enough'? Seth, you don't sound like yourself."

"Very funny, Horus! So—you called? What's on your mind?"

"Actually, I'm surprised you didn't call me! Haven't you noticed what's happening?"

"I'm not sure I know what you're talking about."

"Well, hmm, maybe you haven't noticed. You have been awfully focused lately. Here's the thing. Whenever Johannes thinks about John, I get to see what John's doing in that moment. It's actually pretty cool. Johannes doesn't **see** anything, but he does **connect** to John when he thinks of him much in the way we do— he's just not aware of it. Anyway, this has happened a few times and as a result, I've gotten to **listen in** on a few of John's... communications. Quite interesting stuff, don't you think?"

"Absolutely!" Seth now felt proud, even though he was not responsible for John's success.

"I've noticed that, although Johannes doesn't **hear** the communications, they **are** affecting him. Just yesterday, he bought a crystal in the shape of a Merkaba! He was simply drawn to it when he saw it. At first I thought it was a coincidence, but then today Johannes started thinking about the cube-shaped box it's in. I was, of course, observing his thoughts and could swear I saw a shimmer of Metatron's communication among them!"

"That **is** pretty fascinating, Horus! I wonder why this is happening?"

"I don't know, but pay attention and let me know if you notice anything."

"*Certo, Signore!*" A moment after Seth said this, he couldn't keep from laughing. He, at first didn't want Horus to know that he had been **eavesdropping**, but the temptation to tease him was simply overwhelming.

"Very cute! Well, 'don't you worry your handsome little head' about what's happening over here!" Horus retorted. "It's all working out just fine!" With that, the two of them broke out in full laughter, more than either had in a while.

From the distance, their twinkling auras grew so bright, a number of others took notice.

Quatre – Quattro – Cuatro – Vier

J ohannes reached Sofia's flat about fifteen minutes early and had to walk around the block to kill some time. When he knocked on the door, Sofia opened it just a tad sooner than he would have expected. *Hmm, maybe she was ready a little early too.*

The two caught a gondola and rode more or less in silence. Johannes nearly hovered above the water because Sofia had looped her arm in his as before. He considered the situation—*It is still mild, so she can't possibly be cold.* He then chuckled to himself for analyzing well beyond the need to do so.

The gondola ride ended too quickly for either of them. Soon after, they were seated in the restaurant. Johannes, without conferring with Sofia, ordered a bottle of French wine. He didn't know Italian wines just yet, but knew French wines well, and thus ordered something especially delightful.

Sofia, following his lead, quickly ordered *l'antipasto* and then eyed Johannes as if to say, *"Touché!"*

Johannes caught on immediately. *She's enjoying this game— almost too much!* He thus decided that once they ordered their entrées, he would present the gift. He was beginning to wonder if she suspected, but then pushed the thought from his mind.

The waiter returned with the bottle of wine, conducted the ceremonial tasting, and then asked what they desired for *i primi e secondi piatti*. After he walked away, Johannes looked over his shoulder to make sure he would not be disturbed. He then reached into his jacket pocket. When he pulled out the box and placed it on the table between them, Sofia's eyes widened momentarily. *Ah, so my gift is indeed a surprise*—he surmised. *Good!*

Johannes pushed the box toward her and spoke: "Sofia, I want to say this is a 'thank you' gift, but it's more than that. A friend of mine told me once that even more powerful than gratitude is anticipation. This gift is thus gratitude for what's been **and** anticipation of what's to come. I am happy that you are here seated across from me and I am anticipating whatever is in store for the future."

Sofia quickly diverted her stare from Johannes' intense eyes and looked at the box. She couldn't look at him with any hope of holding back the tears that welled up.

Much the way he had done earlier, she admired the box and the decorations upon it. She had seen many like it, but each was unique, so she examined it carefully. At the same time she was stalling to gain composure.

After her emotions calmed, she glanced back at Johannes for a brief moment and picked up the box. The top rested snugly upon the base. She thought it was glued in place until it finally eased off. Once opened, she at first saw only tissue paper. She gingerly pulled at the paper until it was separated and then peeked at the stone. The candlelight was dim, yet reflected off of the crystal. However, it wasn't until she lifted it out of the box that she fully understood what it was, and even then, it was unlike anything she'd ever seen before.

Sofia recognized the stone, and knew of its supposed properties. She then wondered if Johannes knew. However, the shape she was not familiar with and she wondered if it had special properties as well.

The crystal warmed up in her hand and a shiver ran through her. She could no longer hold back a tear, but luckily shed only the one. She had suspected that the night would be special, but even this exceeded her expectation.

While continuing to hold the star with one hand, she reached over and held Johannes' hand with the other. Then, with all of her might, she burned the moment into her memory, for this was possibly the happiest she'd felt in her whole life.

Quatre – Quattro – Cuatro – Vier

Chakra Number Four

Greetings Master John. I am Ra. The fourth chakra, the **Heart Chakra**, is the middle of the seven energy centers. It is the foundation of light. All that exists below it reaches down toward the earth, and all above it reaches for the heavens. The fourth chakra, in one sense, is the most important, for if one's heart is open, all else will flow to and through him. However, if one opens all chakras except the fourth, though his experiences may amaze and stimulate, they will never satisfy. You see, a man cannot find fulfillment save with an open heart. Wisdom, knowledge, expression, love, power, pleasure, and existence will feel like naught without an open heart with which to receive it.

Fourth Density

We jumped ahead to four before completing three. That is because you are currently within third density, yet imminently awaiting the fourth. In fourth density, all will see without eyes, hear without ears, and feel without fingers. That is because your **clair-** senses will be fully activated: clairvoyance, clairaudience, clairsentience, etc. This does not mean that you will lose sight, hearing, or touch; you will simply have access to more.

In fourth density, all will be telepathic and empathic. You will better know when someone is lying or telling the truth. You will feel when they are truly happy or feigning. There will still be things hidden from you, but far less. And this is because in fourth density, you will have new purpose. Your study of love will have reached a level of understanding that will propel you into purpose. Then nearly all of your physical experience will be to express love in wonderfully delightful ways.

Many claim that they live for love now, but they do not see the truth. In third density, individuals focus more on the expression of **self** and the attainment of **power** even within the context of their so-called loving relationships. There is no judgment here, for this is natural within third density. Let us now return to the three and cover what was skipped.

Chakra Number Three

The third chakra, the **Solar Plexus**, is your center of **power** and **will**. It is what separates you from the animals. Yes, you have experienced some willful beasts indeed, but those specific creatures have already pierced the boundary between the second and third densities. They exhibit will because they observe and imitate you!

As we have said before, second density is about achieving self-awareness—in third density, you have most certainly arrived. You are all quite aware of yourselves, even if you are lacking awareness of everything else. You **know** what you want, and you want it badly. You enjoy feeling powerful, and hunger for more. You treat the majority of your interaction with others as a battle to be won.

Third Density

In earlier times, when you were closer to second density, you fought in more obvious ways. Your brawls were personal and your clashes frequently ended in death. As time progressed, you have fought less and your expression has shifted. Most of you are no longer fighting for survival, even if you are struggling with a whole set of other things. Your greatest desires these days are centered on fulfillment! You wish to make a name for yourself. You wish others to see and appreciate your art! You wish to **create**, not just survive or exist.

The chakra for third density has been your subconscious focus. You have sought and have gained—again and again—the power of self. You are coming to understand that power **of** self is not the same as power **over** self or power over **others.**

You are learning to utilize your upper charkas more, but still place emphasis on the third. Notice how the majority of conflicts in your realm are simply battles of will.

In fourth density, the wars will end, at least in the version of fourth density you are destined for. Since your goal and the goal of all others around you will be to exercise all expressions of love and learn fathoms more wisdom than you can currently imagine, you will be protected from life forms that exist only to feed upon the energy of others.

Suffice it to say: lessons will not end. There is so much more to learn; so much more to create; so much more to experience. You will create your own reality as you already do; yet you will have vastly more awareness of this. You will better see which creations are yours and which are others. You will continue to have choice, and yet the question you will ask most often is, "How can I best express my love in light of this situation?" You **are** love and will come to **know** this.

In third density, you've been looking for love in all the wrong places. In fourth density, you'll be hunting high and low for places to give it away.

We love you beyond the extent that you will feel or know for many years to come, but we tell you anyway, we show you anyway, because we are here to fulfill our purpose, and that purpose contains all of what fourth density is about and more.

5 – *Five* – V

Cinq – Cinque – Cinco – Füne

J ohn and Maria's departure day arrived and John was more than ready for it. Maria, on the other hand, was less eager.

At the start of their preparations, John and Maria had fallen quickly into a comfortable and easy routine, which then held steady throughout their final weeks in Egypt. Maria found solace within the constancy. Waking each morning, knowing, for the most part, what the day ahead would contain allowed serenity to set in. And the busy work, which was not the least bit taxing, but which resulted in consistent and visible progress was rewarding. Now that there was nothing left to **do**, Maria wondered whether her idle hands would start to wring.

John saw things differently. To him, when one's efforts were solely focused toward a specific goal, there was nothing quite as satisfying as reaching it. His anticipation flowed too easily into impatience. He was content having tasks at hand to fill his day, most especially with a soul mate at his side, but he grew ever more impatient with each passing day. Knowing his time in Egypt was nearing its end, he was anxious to get on with it.

Despite the difference in perspective, the budding kinship brought nothing but joy to both of them. Although the circumstances surrounding them were about to change, they were happy to know that they were venturing off together. Yes, they both knew that once they reached their destination they would part ways, but neither of them focused that far ahead.

Early that morning, the majority of Maria's belongings left the apartment. Men from the ship had carted it all away. These items would remain unseen to her until they disembarked in Spain—more than a month in the future.

John looked around the empty apartment and Maria did the same. They silently took inventory—of all they had accomplished, but also of their entire time in Cairo. Maria had years' worth of memories in Cairo, and yet John's memories were significant nonetheless. He was acutely aware that he was not simply leaving Cairo, but leaving all of Egypt, and it was in Egypt where his relationship with Johannes had been at its best. It may not have been in the form he had hoped for, but it had been fun, comfortable, and consistent.

And then John grew emotional. Maybe the pending departure was getting to him after all. Maybe it caused him to think about Johannes in a way he hadn't allowed since the man left. He often craved change, yet was still challenged by it when it arrived.

While John choked on his Egyptian memories, Maria pondered her own with no regret. Like John, the man she loved was gone, except he left the earth and not just the city. And unlike John, she'd experienced more than twenty-five years of partnership with him. She had satisfied all of her desires because growing old together was not one of them. *Old*, that was something she never wanted to become. *Fernando, you left before we got old!*

And so Maria did not conjure up very many of her memories; instead she simply eyed the apartment knowing this would be the last time she would do so. The apartment no longer held her. She could not connect to its bare walls. Her belongings were gone, and for all intents and purposes, she was too. Nothing of her remained save her physical presence.

Maria took a deep breath, looked over at John, and reached for his hand. She then walked to the door and pulled him behind her. With the preparations completed, and the journey still hours away, all that was left was to enjoy one last afternoon in the city.

"Let's go out and have some fun," she said, "and say goodbye to Cairo in style!"

Cinq – Cinque – Cinco – Füne

B y midmorning the next day, their ship entered the waters of the Mediterranean Ocean. All the night before, they had sailed down the west fork of the Nile.

John and Maria stood at the stern and watched the Egyptian coastline recede southward. The temperature on the open sea was already vastly different than in the city. The winds were strong and the surface choppy. John, at first too focused within his thoughts to notice, soon realized that the motion of the boat was nauseating him. He excused himself and retreated to the stateroom.

As soon as John walked away, a member of the crew approached Maria.

"Madame Jamerez, good afternoon. Has your trip been pleasant thus far?"

"Good day, Officer Myklos. Yes, it has been quite pleasant."

"And your stateroom? Are you satisfied with it? Is there anything that you need?"

"My fine man, at the moment, I am in need of nothing."

"Very well. I wanted to inform you of the latest from the captain. He's estimated that we'll arrive in Rome in two weeks. Your connection to Spain is not due to depart until a week after that. Even if we hit unpleasant weather and have to divert or slow down, you'll still not be in jeopardy of missing it."

"Thank you, Officer Myklos. Do keep me apprised of any changes."

"As you wish, Madame."

Cinq – Cinque – Cinco – Füne

J ohn took a sip of water and then reached for a ginger beer to settle his stomach. He considered lying down, but then thought it would be worse and decided to sit at the desk instead. He knew thinking about his stomach would add to the problem, so he struggled to find something else to focus on.

On the desk, a pile of stationary caught his attention. As he stared at it, the inclination to write grew. He rummaged through the desk drawer in search of a pen or a pencil to write with and quickly found what he was looking for.

A Rogue Wave

Greetings. I am Poseidon to the Greeks, Neptune to the Romans. The ocean is my domain and as you have already witnessed, the winds beat upon her relentlessly. The combination of wind and water makes for unpredictable change. Smooth seas give way to the rough with nary a moment in between. Even when in the calmest of waters a rouge wave can wreak havoc seemingly out of nowhere.

Appropriately so, we will now flow back into your lessons and dive into the vibration of five. Five is very much like a rouge wave. It is, more often than not, the bringer of the unexpected. Five is a departure from the linear progression of the one, two, three, four.

Five in Sacred Geometry

There are two ways to look at the five, and thus two geometric figures to illustrate it. In one view, there is the pentagram, and in the other, the pentagon. Let us draw them for you...

Look upon them. Can you **feel** how different they are? Notice that the pentagram looks ominous, while the pentagon seems innocuous.

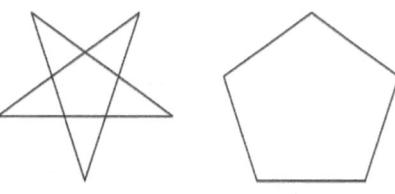

The pentagram's shape highlights its five points. They jut out sharply and appear painful to the touch. Contrastingly, the pentagon highlights its five sides; the obtuse corners turning more smoothly from one side to the next. With the pentagon, we are at our first approximation of the circle. A pentagon can be made to roll, unlike the square and triangle that precede it.

In both visualizations, movement is apparent. Lore has often described a star as a beacon of light guiding one forward—the five-pointed pentagram being the simplest of them. You can draw a pentagram in five simple strokes and without picking up your pencil. The pentagram draws you forward; yet, it is only through the pentagon that one is able to get there. It may be a bumpy ride, but it does roll.

As you may have already guessed, the primary vibration of five is **change**. At the four, things feel solid and constant. However, when reaching the five, change becomes evident; It is undeniable and often abrupt. This change had been in the works already; via the five, it is made manifest.

When considering the evolutionary journey, keep in mind that four was never meant to be an end. If you view it that way, when you encounter the five it will be as with the pentagram—its sharp protrusions bringing pain and suffering with each turn.

When this happens, strive to move from the pentagram to the pentagon. **Roll** with the changes. Keep watch as to where they lead you. Traveling can be a challenge, but it **is** required to reach new lands!

Chakra Number Five

The fifth energy center is the **Throat Chakra** and is the place from which you speak your truth. Note, however, that no matter how eloquent you may be, your words can still be misconstrued. That is because the vibration of five is about **expression**, not results.

The Perfection of the Universe is always at play. THE ONE at any time will employ you to participate in the perfection that is. So your expression, albeit precise and clear and specifically what you intend, can yet be dramatically misunderstood by another resulting in chaos and fear for them. The other is wont to hear what they hear, and it is their right to do so.

Fifth Density

In fourth density, beings desire most to express their love and learn wisdom. At fifth density, having expressed love and gained wisdom, one will then begin the effort of unifying the two. All of fifth density exists for this purpose. Many a guide to those in third density resides in fifth. They are still in loving service, as with fourth density beings, but through the close observation and guidance of specific others, they learn to meld love and wisdom together.

Within fifth density, one is still individual, yet observably beginning the journey back to unity. At the same time, the movement in fifth density—the vibration—is faster; so much so, it is no longer what you would consider physical. Matter doesn't exist in the same way—or rather it is not experienced as it is in the earlier densities. Fifth density resembles your dream realms: objects often morph into other objects; gravity no longer keeps you on the ground; and time ceases to be linear. In fifth density, your body is composed of light, and is thus as changeable as your aura.

In five, expect the unexpected and remember the lessons of the sea. You cannot control the waves. Roll **with** them lest you get tossed overboard **by** them!

After John finished writing that last sentence, he **had** to stop. The seas started rolling worse than before and he was sure he was going to get sick. The whole time he sailed with Felizio, he had never experienced anything like this, nor when he was on his own. He drank the rest of his ginger beer, more from a fear that it would spill than from any hope it would calm his stomach. He then moved over to the bed—with the trash bucket near by. As he lied there, he tried to picture in his mind a more pleasant scene, but with his eyes opened. When he shut them, he felt worse.

Maria walked into the room and spotted John suffering through the motion. She wasn't affected other than having to hold on to keep from falling. She fetched a moist washcloth and laid it over John's forehead and later his eyes. She then placed her hand on his chest. By that time, John was able to keep his eyes shut.

Maria's hand on him seemed to help, but little did he or she know what was really happening.

John then lifted the washcloth and peeked at Maria.

"Any word as to how long this will last?" he asked her.

"Officer Myklos said swells like these are not uncommon this time of year. Spring always brings the roughest seas, apparently. So, while they are not likely to go away completely, they ought to calm down a bit once we're further from the coast."

"Well I hope I get used to them. I wouldn't want to spend the entire trip in bed—or worse yet, the head."

John made it through the afternoon and luckily the seas calmed in time for dinner. He had been forced to skip the midday meal and was hungry. By the next day, John felt his sea legs (and stomach) returning. The worst was over, or so he hoped.

The ship was large and provided a number of places to explore and plenty of people to observe. This kept John from getting bored. He guessed the sea would look pretty much the same everyday and soon stopped noticing it altogether. It was for this reason that he was quite surprised to see land approaching before two full weeks had passed.

John had estimated on his own that Spain would be at least a month-long journey. He didn't know of any islands that lay directly en route and thus figured they wouldn't see land until reaching their destination. So on that day he first saw coastline, he ran up to Officer Myklos and asked him about it.

"Master John, that's the southern shore of *Calabria*. From here, it should take no more than two days to reach *Civitavecchia*."

"Civitavecchia?"

"Yes, Sir. *Roma* does not sit on the Mediterranean. We port in *Civitavecchia* just outside of *Roma* to unload and reload before returning to Cairo."

"But…I don't understand…I thought we were going to Spain?!"

"Master John, **you** are going to Spain indeed, but **we** are not. You must take a different ship to Spain from Italy. Did Madame

Jamerez not tell you this?"

"No, she most certainly did not! Thank you for the information." And just before Officer Myklos walked away, John asked, "Oh—one more question. Do you happen to know when the ship to Spain leaves?"

"I don't know exactly, but I believe about a week after we port. If I'm not mistaken, Madame Jamerez is planning on visiting *Roma* for a few days in between."

John was simultaneously excited, confused, and annoyed. "Why did Maria not tell me we're going to Italy?" he mumbled to himself. "And for a week no less!"

He then questioned how close *Civitavecchia* was to *Napoli*. Was it possible he could visit the Nuotos while he was there?

And then thoughts wandered into his mind that got him reeling. *Should I stay in Italy?*—he considered. *Maria's belongings are taken care of. She doesn't really need me for the remainder of the trip.*

John hadn't thought about Italy since those first few days after Johannes left. And once he decided to accompany Maria on this trip, he thought of nothing but Spain. He never could have imagined they would be going to Italy on the way! Could he resist the temptation to stay in Italy once reaching her shore?

"I must talk to Maria," he mumbled to himself. "I have to find out why she didn't tell me about this."

John had loved that the ship was large, but that was before he needed to **find** someone. Maria wasn't in their cabin, and he didn't find her in the dining hall either. She wasn't on the main deck earlier, the first place he had looked, and now that he was back, she was still nowhere in sight.

Where is she?

Of course, it was quite possible she had been in all of those places, just not at the same time he was. So many hallways and stairways snaked around the ship; he could have gone one way while she went another. He then decided to circle back around and check the stateroom once again. This time, when he entered the room, he saw Maria sitting at the desk as if she'd been there all day.

"Where have you been?!?" he blurted out at her.

"Well good morning to you too, John. I am having a lovely day. Thanks for asking."

Maria's sarcasm slowed John down for a moment. It, however, did not quell him completely.

"Sorry. It's…well…I…I just found out that we're approaching the southern coast of Italy! You didn't tell me that we were going to Rome!"

"I didn't? Hmm. I guess it slipped my mind and then I thought I had mentioned it. I intended to tell you the day I bought our tickets. I was told that no ships sail between Spain and Cairo this time of year, and that traveling to Rome was the best alternative, since there are a number of options to get to Spain from there. So I set it all up that morning and didn't give it a second thought. Why are you so animated about this?"

John didn't know what to say. He couldn't exactly share with Maria his thoughts about staying in Italy.

"I'm…I'm just surprised; that's all."

Maria could tell there was something he wasn't saying, but she let it go for the time being.

"We have nearly a week to explore Rome," she offered. "I thought that would be fun!"

John realized that he was being bratty and ungrateful and adjusted his attitude accordingly.

"I'm sorry, Maria. Rome will be lots of fun, I'm sure. The whole thing just caught me off guard. I did tell you that I have friends in Italy, didn't I?"

"You did. They are in Sorrento; is that right?"

"Yes, just outside of Naples."

"Oh." Maria paused for a moment. She did not know that Sorrento was near Naples. Naples was another port mentioned where they could have made a connection to Spain. She simply chose Rome because it sounded more interesting. She, of course, could not mention this to John now, lest she upset him again.

"Do you know how far Naples is from Rome?" John asked her.

"I don't believe they are close; if that's what you're wondering."

"Oh. I guess I feel bad because I said I would write to Felizio and Lorita, but I haven't yet."

"Well, why don't you write to them now and mail it from Rome. I'm sure it won't take but a few days to get to them from there."

"That's a great idea! Why hadn't I thought of that? And I'll tell them to send a response to Barcelona! That way I can hear how everyone is doing!"

John's mood appeared to have transformed completely and Maria smiled proudly to herself. She had not only avoided further ado, but also managed to coax John into a better mood. She then reminded herself that it usually didn't take her long to cheer someone up, especially him.

Cinq – Cinque – Cinco – Füne

J ohannes and Sofia's relationship started off special and got sweeter from there. Sofia set the pace, but one that consistently brought Johannes more and more into her life. The next big step was introducing him to her mother.

Tomasina, Sofia's mother, hounded her about it weekly. "Why haven't I seen this young man who has stolen your heart?" she would often say.

Yet Sofia was hesitant. For one, she neglected to tell her mother that Johannes was not Italian. That alone could cause a stir. Then there was the fact that she…happened…to work for him—another faux pas. Lastly, he wasn't a *good Catholic boy*. That's three strikes against him.

Little did Sofia know, however, her mother was fully prepared to accept this man into the family regardless. Tomasina was ever so grateful that the family curse didn't seem to be affecting her daughter.

Tomasina came from a line primarily of women. A boy was born only once every three or four generations. The most recent male birth occurred twenty years earlier, so no boys were expected for a while. But that wasn't the curse.

Tomasina, like her daughter, was an only child. This was something she had struggled with all of her life. In Italy, nearly everyone had brothers and sisters. Whenever someone spoke of his or her siblings, Tomasina felt that old sting of longing. And yet that too was not the curse. Her mother had a sister, and her aunt had three daughters. The oldest of Tomasina's cousins had two children, one being the only living male born into the family. So although Tomasina didn't expect a grandson, she did expect a granddaughter or two; she just didn't expect them any time soon. And **that** was because of the curse.

The curse was basically this: no woman in the family found true love the first time around. Some remained unmarried for far longer than normal. The rest had had at least one failed relationship to start. In many cases, the one failed marriage was all there was. Tomasina's eldest cousin was the only one she could think of who managed to find true love the second time around.

Truth be told, the curse wasn't really about **true** love. It was about **long-lasting** love. For example, Tomasina's mother **had** loved her father; he just didn't stick around very long. The family often said how difficult he was to get along with. When he was killed at an early age, no one was surprised. He had created so much trouble by then; it was simply a matter of time before it caught up with him.

With Tomasina's uncle, well that was a different story. Everybody had loved *Zio Giacomo*…and *Zio Giacomo* loved everyone, but **that** was the problem. *Giacomo* was simply not cut out for marriage. His libido was too strong. After a while, he couldn't hide his trysts any longer, which resulted in a lot of pain for Tomasina's aunt. In the end, nearly everyone went from loving *Giacomo*, to hating him, at least in words.

Luckily, Tomasina's cousins didn't seem to be hurt by their father's actions. *Giacomo* may have been a terrible husband, but he was a good father. He loved his girls demonstrably, and so far there had only been one failed marriage among them. Furthermore, Tomasina's cousin's second marriage was a complete success. Her cousin by marriage was now the most respected male in the whole clan.

Tomasina therefore held strong hope for this boy, who her daughter loved demonstrably. She teased Sofia about meeting him, but was happy to wait as long as it took. Sofia's pace was a good thing. Had Tomasina known that Sofia was fretting over her supposed opinion, she would have rectified the situation immediately.

And so, although Sofia's fears loomed, they would not be realized. When she finally extended an invitation to her mother, it was met with complete joy.

Sofia, however, still had more to worry about. She was presenting her beau to her mother, but she was also **cooking** for them. This was not her first meal, of course, but would be the first time cooking for Johannes **and** the first time cooking for her mother. She didn't know which she was more concerned about. Certainly Johannes wouldn't judge her by her cooking since he clearly loved her, *but an Italian woman is* **expected** *to be a good cook*—she kept thinking to herself. And it would be an insult to her mother if the meal didn't come out right. *A daughter's cooking is a reflection of her mother's*—Sofia conjectured. They had cooked together often, but Tomasina was always there to make sure everything proceeded smoothly.

After giving it some thought, Sofia deemed it best to choose a meal she could prepare ahead of time. She therefore selected her grandmother's recipe for lasagna, a unique and creative version she'd never seen anywhere else. All the work could be done the night before and the entire meal, save the *pane ed insalata,* would be served in one bowl.

To ensure that all went well, Sofia kept her Saturday free. She used the morning to buy all of the ingredients—*fresh of course*—and then spent the afternoon putting everything together. Sunday, she would simply bake the lasagna and toss the salad. *Surely I can't mess **that** up!*

Sofia did commend herself for one exploit. Earlier that week, in an astute moment, she asked Johannes to bring the wine. First, this would be one less thing for her to worry about, and second, it would provide an opportunity for Johannes to impress her mother.

"Johannes is quite knowledgeable of wine and has never selected anything but the best," she asserted. "Mother will certainly notice."

She now added, "Hopefully, that will compensate for his

German, non-Catholic upbringing."

Cinq – Cinque – Cinco – Füne

Having adjusted to the new itinerary, John could now enjoy the change of view it offered. The remainder of the voyage to *Civitavecchia* would be along the Italian coast, which would be quite picturesque.

The Strait of Messina was the first of many beautiful scenes. The liner, having navigated around the southwest corner of the Italian peninsula, traveled due north with Sicily to the west and the 'toe' of *Calabria* to the east.

John recalled the last time he was there. He and Paolo pretended they could touch each side with their outstretched arms. Now, John had to race back and forth—port to starboard. On a vessel that size, it wasn't as easy to see in both directions at once and he couldn't decide which view was better.

John marveled at how different everything looked traveling north. Last time, as they neared the narrow opening of the strait, it seemed as if they were entering the mouth of a river. Of course, as they sailed south, that 'river' grew wider and wider. This time, as they traveled north and hugged the coast of *Calabria*, it seemed as if Sicily drifted ever closer.

In his mind, John tried to visualize the coastline from above. He then remembered that a map of the entire Mediterranean hung on the wall in the ship's library. With curiosity, he set out to investigate. He wanted to get a lay of the land—and sea, but he also wanted to see exactly how far Rome and *Calabria* were in relation to Naples.

From across the library, John noticed that the ship's course had been indicated on the map. When he got closer, however, he found himself upset again. From the Strait of Messina, their route had them traveling directly toward Naples, then veering northwest along the coast to *Civitavecchia*. This meant that Sorrento and Capri would be within sight off of the starboard side of the ship.

As if the previous exercise were just a practice run, John's emotions reeled even more than before. He had accepted that Naples was far from Rome, but he didn't expect *to sail right past it!* Clearly, he was frustrated being near, but unable to visit Felizio and the Nuotos, *but why am I so attached to the idea?*

"If only I could yell out to them as we sail by," he whispered to himself. He then pictured waving to them from the ship as they passed, which calmed his anxiety.

Ra often says that time and space are illusions, so I'm not really separated from anyone? I guess I can greet Lorita and Felizio with my thoughts?

John decided that when the ship was closest to Sorrento, he would *reach out* to Felizio with his thoughts and send a hello vibrationally. The distance, of course, shouldn't matter, but the idea made him feel better.

But then John noticed something more. The approximate sail times had been written on the map.

"Darn it! We're going to be passing Naples in the middle of the night!" he groaned. Now he was disappointed all over again, and this irritated him. The ups and downs of his emotions were getting the best of him.

John threw up his hands and retreated to the stateroom. The walk placated him. When he reached the room, he tried his hand at some writing.

"Maybe someone will cheer me up with a good message."

A Mercurial Exchange

Ciao, amico mio. I am Mercury of Rome and soon you will be traveling on roads I helped inspire. I am known as the god of trade and commerce and many a thoroughfare was built for those purposes.

My dear boy, you have mostly certainly noticed the pentagrams inscribed on the pentacles of your beloved Tarot, yes?

As you know, the suit of Pentacles represents earth. However, based on all that you've been taught thus far, wouldn't you say that the number **four** is what most resembles the element of earth? So why would the pentacle be the chosen symbol?

A pentacle is a coin and therefore represents money. The element of earth exhibits the vibration of four, but money, which is used to **move** earth, is of the vibration of five.

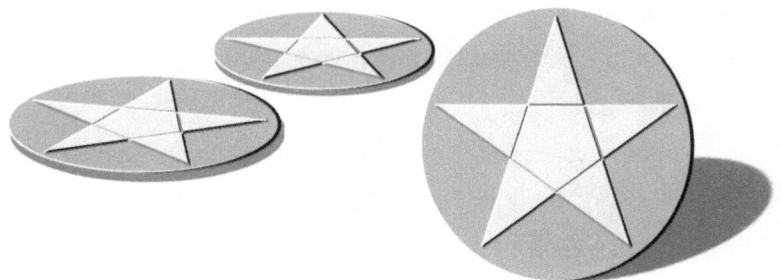

Think of it this way, money only has **value** when it is **exchanged** for something. You could sit upon a veritable fortune, but if you were not permitted to spend any of it, you would be as poor as the next man.

You cannot **eat** gold. When it comes right down to it, gold is only as valuable as the useful things it can buy.

This universe is vibrational. It exists through movement, for that's what vibration is. The stability of matter, and thus the number four, is an illusion. Nothing remains the same for very long. Change is all there is.

Keep in mind, however, that through love and wisdom, one can **direct** change, **inspire** change, and manifest **desired** change! And consider this: what do you call a pile of coins in your pocket? **Change!**

Those who live on the streets beg for change because subconsciously, that is what they seek. They desire a change in their circumstances and believe that "spare change" will get them there.

It has been brought to my attention that you wish to send a message to your friends who live within the former empire of Rome. Take heed, messages too are within my domain. You see, those roads built under Roman command were not just constructed for the trade of merchandise, but also the exchange of messages. What, say you, is the difference? Nothing I say! Information is as valuable as gold and, in fact, many a gold piece has been exchanged for it!

Send messages to your friends, vibrationally **and** in written form. Make use of your fifth chakra. Hesitate not and fret even less. They know you are safe, and feel it in their hearts, but your written words will bring them added joy.

You have voice; use it I say! Are you not writing upon paper at this very moment? Write to them! Thoughts are real, misunderstand me not, but words and actions are real too!

Set the wheels in motions and behold what follows!

"Wow! I guess that message was clear!" John said out loud.

Heeding the advice given, he quickly pulled out a second sheet of paper and began composing a letter:

Ciao Felizio e Lorita,

How are you? I think of you often. Sorry I haven't written before now. How are Paolo's studies going? And Carina—is she keeping up with her French?

Believe it or not, as I write this I am sailing through the Tyrrhenian Sea and will soon be in the vicinity of Sorrento! Unfortunately, we will not drop anchor there. I am helping a woman named Maria move back to her home country of Spain. I only recently learned that we are stopping in Roma on the way. I will mail this letter from there.

You will be glad to know that I made it to Cairo! And you'll never believe this, but I ran into Johannes my first day there—while climbing the pyramids no less! Things between us were better than expected, although not exactly what I had wished for. We traveled together for over a month, but then, he left. I wonder if I'll ever see him again.

*More news: I channeled again…a few times! In fact, the messages that came through had us visiting one temple and then another. A couple times, I even had an audience! There really **was** a reason for me to go to Egypt, and it wasn't just about Johannes. I learned and experienced so much.*

*Unfortunately, I haven't been able to channel since Johannes departed, at least not with my voice. But I **can** bring through messages when writing. I think they want me to create a book. We'll see what comes of it.*

My heart misses you terribly, most especially now that bella italia is within sight. I wish I was able to visit, but alas, not this time. I will come back soon, I promise.

Should you wish to reply, address a letter to the main post office in Barcelona. We'll head there after a few days in Roma. I look forward to hearing from you and, of course, seeing you soon!

Ciao, ciao e tanti baci,

Yours, Gianni

In writing the letter, John was now able to finally calm the part of him that fretted over being close, but unable to visit. He knew they would receive the letter a few short days after he reached Rome and he knew that Mercury was right; it would bring them joy to hear from him.

He also hoped they would write back to him…

6 – *Six* – VI

Six – Sei – Seis – Sechs

The ship dropped anchor in the port of *Civitavecchia* earlier than expected. Favorable currents, light winds, and clear skies all helped. With bags in hand, John and Maria clambered ashore and immediately boarded a coach to Rome.

The first half of the three-hour trip into the city was pleasant, albeit less than scenic. The bare hills offered less beauty than a more typical Italian landscape. However, once the cityscape came into view, the beauty abounded. The classical architecture was breathtaking.

Furthermore, the weather was ideal. Rome was just far enough from the coast to temper the ocean breezes. From the looks of things, John wondered if it was the first warm day of spring there; it seemed as if every Roman citizen was out of his or her home and roaming the streets.

Intermittently, John shared a few words with a young Italian woman seated next to him. He asked if she was visiting Rome, but discovered that she was returning home from a holiday in Sardinia. John initially spoke with her to practice his Italian, but soon realized that an opportunity had presented itself. He thus began interrogating her for recommendations of sites to visit during their stay. The list included: *Il Colosseo, La Fontana di Trevi, Il Pantheon, e la città nella città—Il Vaticano.*

John turned to Maria and whispered, "I'm glad we're here for six days!"

After listing sights popular with the tourists, the young woman spoke of places native Romans enjoyed visiting: *musei, piazze, parchi, giardini, e ristoranti.* Fortunately, John's journal was handy; he took notes furiously. There wasn't enough time to translate for Maria, but he did make a quick comment to her under his breath every now and again.

"John, ask her about hotels," Maria interjected, "preferably near the center of Rome."

"Have you been following the discussion?" he asked her.

"I can understand enough," she confessed. "You're doing well! I like listening to the two of you speak in Italian!"

As requested, John asked the young lady about hotels and then jotted down her suggestions.

At that point in the conversation, the coach crossed over *Il Tevere*, the Tiber River, and entered central Rome. John, satiated with the information he obtained, allowed the conversation to ebb and flow naturally. Intermittently, the young Italian woman pointed out an interesting sight as they rode by, but otherwise remained silent.

The coach reached its destination of *Piazza di San Giovanni in Laterano* and came to a full stop. The driver opened the door to the passenger compartment and announced their arrival. John disembarked first and helped each of the women step down. The driver, meanwhile, pulled bags off of the back of the coach and set them on the curb.

John looked around and took in the entirety of the square, focusing primarily on the surrounding buildings and boulevards. Maria then tapped him on the shoulder and pointed up and behind him. Towering directly over them was Rome's tallest obelisk.

John dropped his gear...and his mouth fell open. Symbols he had seen all over Egypt decorated the full height of the obelisk. Near the top sat the most familiar of them, none other than Horus depicted as a falcon and adorned with his characteristic double crown. John's knees started to buckle and he felt as if he would fall over—partly from looking up at a steep angle and partly from the object that now consumed all of his attention.

It then hit him. He **recognized** the obelisk, but not from having seen it before. It was, in fact, the missing twin of the tallest obelisk in Egypt.

"Maria! I...I know this obelisk. I mean...I know where it once stood in Egypt. I've seen its twin. Together, they straddled the entrance of the temple in Karnak. The abandoned twin looks blatantly askew without its partner. The Egyptians are still upset at the Romans for stealing this. I...I can't believe... H...how did this... I...I'm flabbergasted! I never would have imagined that I would run into this one. I didn't know it was in Rome! I simply figured it was somewhere in Europe."

Maria observed John's amazement and could easily picture the adorable young boy he must have been. She then giggled discreetly to herself. She'd seen John worked up before, but this was the first time she'd witnessed him completely beside himself. She realized that, in this regard, he was similar to Fernando. If Fernando were standing there with them, he would react to this Egyptian artifact in the same way. He too would find its presence in Rome appalling.

Italians streamed by, hardly noticing the visitors, and John and Maria didn't pay them much attention either. Maria kept watching John, and he continued to scrutinize the obelisk, agape and silent, his mind racing in six directions at once.

Maria allowed John another few minutes before pulling him out of his fixation. "John. We need to find a hotel. You can always come back later and gaze at this some more."

John begrudgingly agreed and allowed Maria to lead them away from the piazza, looking over his shoulder repeatedly.

By the time Maria and John located a hotel with vacancy for the five nights they required, they were out of time and energy for sightseeing. They decided to rest briefly before heading out for their first Italian supper.

"I'm so excited!" John exclaimed. "For six days, we get to eat the best food in all of Europe!"

Maria considered contesting, but then acquiesced. *He's right—* she thought to herself. *No one in Europe can compete with the Italians when it comes to food.*

Six – Sei – Seis – Sechs

T he day of reckoning arrived. With the lasagna bubbling in the oven and the salad tossed, it was only a matter of minutes before there came a knock at the door. Sofia expected her mother to arrive first, a little early as usual. Johannes, she anticipated, would be punctual.

Surprisingly, Johannes was the first to show up and with flowers in hand. He specifically came early to arrange the bouquet before Sofia's mother arrived.

No sooner had Johannes placed the arrangement on the table than Tomasina arrived rapping lightly at the door. Johannes made as if to let her in, but Sofia quickly waved him off. She didn't think it would look right for Johannes to meet his mother at the door.

Sofia greeted her mother with a hug and two kisses, and then escorted her into the apartment. Before she had a chance to introduce Johannes, Tomasina caught sight of him and made straight for him. She chattered away in Italian about how nice it was to meet him—all wasted since Johannes didn't understand hardly any of it. She then threw her arms around him and gave him a warmer welcome than he expected. She kissed him on both cheeks, gave him one more kiss, and then held him at arm's length to look him over.

"Mama, this is Johannes. I'm sorry, Mama, but Johannes doesn't understand very much Italian. He has been learning, but since he works so much, his progress is slow." In English, she said to Johannes, "This is my Mama, Tomasina. Earlier she was saying how nice it is to **finally** meet you." With that, Sofia rolled her eyes almost imperceptibly.

"Mama. Johannes is German and is a successful businessman. He works in his father's company, but is mostly his own boss. He came here to expand the family business into Italy. So far, things are going well."

Sofia took a deep breath to gear up for the evening. She had been so concerned about the preparations, she had forgotten that she would be translating all evening.

It'll be so nice when Johannes learns Italian—she thought to herself.

Six – Sei – Seis – Sechs

W hile Maria rested, John considered what he could do to pass the time. He wasn't tired enough to rest, but didn't feel like wandering around on his own. He ultimately decided to sit at the desk and write. Secretly, he hoped he would get information about the obelisk from Karnak or maybe the reason he was in Rome.

Harmonious Experience

Master John, we encouraged you to ride the waves of change brought on by the five. You have experienced ups and downs as a result of unexpected turns, yet despite feeling completely off course, here you are in a place wrought with meaning for you. The unexpected shifts of the five, rough as they may be, will carry you to harmonious shores in time... if you let them.

I am Saturn, god of the Romans and known as the bringer of abundance and peace. I am here to begin a discussion of the number six, fittingly so as the sixth planet of your solar system is named after me.

Recall how the three produced only the 3-6-9. Now watch what happens with the six. This sequence:

6, 12, 18, 24, 30, 36, 42, 48, 54...

yields:

<u>6, 3, 9</u>, 6, 3, 9, 6, 3, 9 ...

The three and the six are intrinsically connected. In reality, the six is simply the three **experienced**. Allow me to illustrate this to you.

First, let us revisit the cube. Recall that it contains a single axis in each of the three dimensions: axial, lateral, and vertical. When you look directly at a face, you see a square, which is imbued with the vibration of four. But note how many faces there are. The cube has **six** identical faces and, for this reason, is also called a hexahedron.

When you place yourself at the center of a cube, notice how the **three** dimensions of space become **six** directions: forward and backward, left and right, up and down. The three is thus experienced as six. Your realm of duality doubles the effect. Now can you begin to see how special the cube really is? It is created from three, projects a four in each direction, and yet is experienced as a six from the inside looking out.

The realm in which you reside is not simply a realm of space, but a realm of space-time. There is the here...and now. Time is required to move from one place to another. It is therefore the **passing of time** that allows the three to be experienced.

You create by exploiting the power of three, which occurs in an instant. Yet, in order for you to fully experience creation, you must surrender to the whims of time. It takes time for your desires to manifest, which may frustrate you; however, you also get to spend time enjoying them, which delights you.

Space is a product of three. Time is a product of six. Believe me not? Then consider the way you mark off time. Do you not count 60 seconds in each minute and 60 minutes in each hour? Your day comprises 24 hours: which is 4×6. There are six hours within each segment: morning, afternoon, evening, and night. You divide a year into twelve months: which is 2×6. For six months the daylight lengthens, and during the remaining six months, it shortens.

Let us, for a moment, talk about outer space. Your Astronomers long ago noted that the planets travel within what is now known as the galactic plane. When viewed from Earth, this plane appears as a circle of constellations. Mathematicians divide a circle into 360 degrees: which is 6×60. The Astrologer's use this system as well. Their Zodiac consists of 12 signs, each containing 30 degrees. But consider this: looking up to the heavens from the surface of the Earth, there are always six constellations above the horizon, and six below it. Furthermore, only six of your planets are visible to you with the naked eye: Mercury, Venus, Mars, Jupiter, Saturn, and of course, Earth.

Your solar system, for all intents and purposes, is a three-dimensional clock. The position of the planets—in space—denotes a specific moment —in time. This is another example of the three creating the six. Fascinating, wouldn't you say?

The Romans call me Saturn. The Greeks call me Cronos. Coincidentally, there is another god whose name sounds the same as mine. He is Chronos and is commonly referred to as 'Father Time'. He and I together represent space and time: space-time.

Getting back to the cube once more, notice that when you gaze directly at a corner, the three-dimensional hexahedron projects the two-dimensional hexagon.

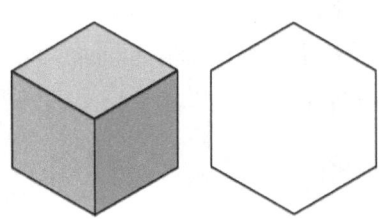

The six is **derived** from the three. In space-time, you have three dimension of space and three aspects of time (past, present, and future). So one way to look at six is three and three.

The most elegant visualization of three is the equilateral triangle. Watch as we create images of six from images of three:

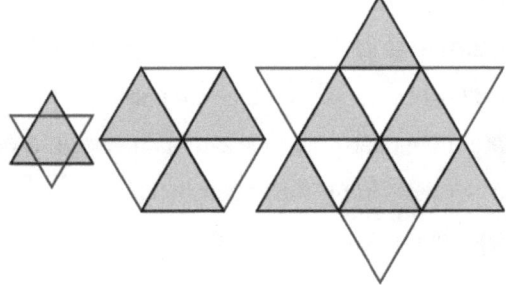

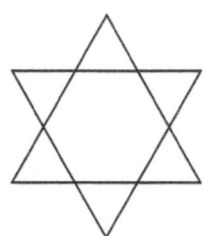

The equilateral triangle represents the Holy Trinity. The six-pointed star is another deeply religious symbol. The Star of David, as it is called, is the most recognized symbol of Judaism.

This pictograph encodes within it a number of vibrationally six concepts. Firstly, there is **as above, so below**. Of the original two triangles, the one pointing up represents man looking up to God and the heavens, and the one pointing down represents the flow of God's energy and love unto man.

Additionally, these same two triangles represent man (the triangle pointing up) and woman (the triangle pointing down). In this way, at six, we have the **harmonious** blending of supposed opposites: man and woman, yang and yin, masculine and feminine. It is only within three-dimensional space-time reality that gender is created to begin with. Thus it is only in this realm that they can be wed and yet still remain discrete. In the higher realms, one experiences itself as both male **and** female simultaneously. And at that level, when one interacts with another, there isn't merely an exchange, but also a **melding**.

Sixth Density

This brings us to the next density of experience. It is in sixth density where separation ceases to exist. In its place, collectives form. The infinite connectedness of All-That-Is becomes apparent to everyone. 'I' and '**you**' begin to fade, increasingly replaced with '**we**'. You primarily experience yourself as an individual—separate from those around you. We primarily experience ourselves more like music. Our individual notes are unique, yet are continually harmonized with those around us. Our tune is not separated from the cacophony of All-That-Is. This Universe is a symphony in which we all play a part.

My boy, have you ever witnessed scientists arguing over the true nature of light? Some insist it is composed of discrete quanta of energy called photons and have devised experiments to prove this. And yet, the other side of the argument has also been **proven** to be true, that light exists as a continuous wave. We say it is all merely **experience**.

Surely you've heard of a prism, yes? You've witnessed how the white light of the sun is split into the colors of the rainbow. And yet, when you observe the light of the sun, you don't see it separated; you see it whole. The red and the green, the blue and the yellow are all present. This is another analogy for you to ponder. You experience yourself as a narrow band of color. We, in sixth density, experience ourselves as a unified light.

Chakra Number Six

And speaking of light, let us talk of the eyes, not just the left and the right, but the middle as well. Your sixth chakra is called the **Third Eye**—no surprise that those numbers would again be related. However, do you realize that your third eye is an actual physical organ? You know your heart is real, but so is your third eye. The pineal gland nestled within your brain is an actual eye and perceives light! But from where does that light come, pray tell?

When you reach sixth density, this and many other mysteries will be revealed to you. However, before you are quick to lust after life in the higher realms, understand that the greatest of your desires can be seen right where you are. You came here to experience separation and connection, tension and harmony. You desire it all. Do not wish it away so quickly.

Maria, unaware that John had been writing, interrupted him and suggested they head out to dinner.

"It will be better for us to look for a restaurant while there is still light," she said. "Don't you think?"

John agreed and thus set his writing aside. However, the whole time they walked, a feeling of incompleteness distracted him. He knew that Saturn had more to say. In fact, he was so preoccupied by it, he didn't hear a word Maria had said.

"John! You are not listening to me!" she chided.

"Sorry Maria. When you suggested dinner, I had been writing and I don't think they were done. I guess I'm not fully…here."

"You should have said something. We could have waited a bit longer."

"It's fine. I just need to focus. Now, what were you saying?"

"I was asking what you think of that restaurant over there. Shall we go look at the menu?"

"Yes. Let's do that. It looks lovely from here!"

John and Maria crossed the street, glanced at the menu hanging in the window, and agreed to stay. After they were seated and Maria more thoroughly inspected the menu, she told John what she wanted. She could have ordered by herself, since she had figured out some of the translations between Spanish and Italian, but it was more fun for her to listen to John speak. His accent was quite good and it was obvious that he enjoyed the language.

Throughout dinner, John and Maria discussed sightseeing options for the next day, but interrupted each other often to hum with delight at the deliciousness of the food. Both of them were confident that their time in Rome would be a complete pleasure indeed.

Six – Sei – Seis – Sechs

A fter the main course was completed, Sofia cleared the table and retreated to the kitchen. She needed to brew the espresso and warm the honey for dessert. Both Johannes and Tomasina offered assistance, but Sofia assured them.

"It is no trouble at all," she insisted. "Relax and enjoy the last of the wine."

In reality, Sofia needed a few minutes to catch her breath.

Johannes watched Sofia walk out of the room and took a deep breath. An opportunity had presented itself and if he was going to act, it had to be now. He got up, walked over to Tomasina's side of the table, and sat beside her. He held her hand in his and then braced himself to say the few phrases in Italian he had been rehearsing for days.

Johannes didn't know much about Sofia's family other than that she and her mother were both without siblings. He knew her father was absent, but didn't know whether the man was dead or alive. Sofia simply never talked about him and Johannes, by choice, never asked. As far as Johannes was concerned, Tomasina was the head of the family, even if it was just the two of them. What he had to say therefore needed to be said to her.

Although Johannes was prepared to proceed, he had not yet convinced himself it was the right time. Yes, he needed to speak with Tomasina first, and yes, he preferred to do so when Sofia was not present, *but on our first meeting?* Yet the opportunity had presented itself and to him, that was a good sign. Besides, it felt right and that was more important than anything.

"*Signora Giogia,* your daughter is very special. It has not taken me long to know this. With your permission, I would like to ask her to be my fiancée."

Tomasina looked down at her hand held in both of his, and then looked up at Johannes' handsome face. She was surprised that this had come so soon, although not surprised altogether. She could see in her daughter a glow that told her all that she needed to know about this man that only today she'd laid eyes on. As she took in the entirety of the evening, she couldn't deny Johannes what he asked.

And yet, she was at a disadvantage. She could not say more than 'yes' or 'no', lest he not fully understand. *Alas*—she resigned to herself. *I will have to save my motherly advice for my daughter.* So she simply placed her free hand on top of his and said, "Yes. I give you my permission." And in saying this, her eyes began to tear.

Johannes lifted Tomasina's hand and kissed it, thanking her repeatedly. He then retreated to his original place at the table before Sofia returned. He wanted her to be completely surprised, as this would provide him a most genuine reaction.

Six – Sei – Seis – Sechs

A fter completing the main course, John perused the dessert menu and his eyes lit up.

"Maria, they have *zeppole!*" he exclaimed excitedly. "We **have** to get them!"

"What are *zeppole?*" Maria asked, raising an eyebrow.

"I first had them with the Nuotos. Lorita makes them from scratch. She mostly called them *pizza frita*—fried dough."

"Sounds…decadent."

John ordered the *zeppole*, but when they arrived, he had a puzzled look in his face.

"What's the matter?" Maria asked.

"These don't look anything like Lorita's," John replied.

The first three *zeppole* were covered in sugar and filled with cream. The other three were lathered in honey and sprinkled with cinnamon and nuts.

John took a bite of the first kind and smiled with pleasure. "Wow! This one is delicious!" He broke off a piece of the second kind, popped it into his mouth, and then licked his fingers repeatedly. Tilting his head, he said, "This one reminds me of Athens. The Greeks put honey on **everything**!" He then went into a discourse of all the desserts they had had in Greece.

After dinner, John and Maria walked back to the hotel via an alternate route, partly for a change in scenery and partly to extend the journey. Once they were back in the room and John lit the lamp at the desk, Saturn made it known that he was ready to complete their discussion. As if no time had passed, the discourse continued.

The Hexagonal Lattice

We now wish to more fully discuss the six-sided polygon called the hexagon. Visit the keepers of the bees who produced the honey for your dessert, and they will tell you all about the hexagonal honeycomb. Bees and wasps, both of which have six legs, innately understand the strength and perfection of six.

Hexagonal lattices can be expanded in all directions within a plane while always remaining stable and efficient. It is for this reason that the hexagon is one of the most significant building blocks in nature. Outside of the hive and well beyond your vision, the hexagonal configuration is abundantly found all around you. If you ask a chemist, for example, to illustrate sugar molecules or the flavonoid molecules in honey, he or she will draw hexagons to show how the atoms are linked together.

Hexagonal lattices are embedded deep within organic matter and are necessary for biological life. The carbon atom is at the center of it all. Carbon, which has an atomic number of six, is the physical manifestation of the vibration of six.

One form of pure carbon is the graphite in the center of your the pencil. In this case, the carbon atoms are arranged in flat hexagonal lattices that are loosely attached to each other. It is for this reason that your pencil writes so well; each sheet falls away from the others and then attaches itself to the paper.

Consider the lamp emitting light and heat into the room. It is fueled by kerosene, which is one of the many hydrocarbons utilized by man. Molecules comprised of carbon and hydrogen atoms are excellent devices for storing energy. The harmonious configuration enables adequate stability, while also allowing a smooth and controlled release of energy over time when burned. Were it not for the many splendid characteristics of six, you would not be able to write at this time!

Water is another substance, which is essential to your form of biological life. Each molecule contains three atoms, two of hydrogen and one of oxygen. In winter when water freezes in the air and flurries down upon you, those flakes of snow crystallize hexagonally. If you could only see the magnificent beauty of these structures, you would be awed by them.

Hydrogen, oxygen, and carbon: three atomic elements that when harmoniously bonded, and therefore imbued with the vibration of six, form the basis of life as you know it on this, the third planet from the sun. From flakes of snow to grains of sugar, from sweet globs of honey to smoothly burning fuels, the hexagon is a pattern richly in support of life.

John paused to consider what he was being told. There was so much more to life than he had ever imagined. He began to put the paper away, but then heard more coming...

Six – Sei – Seis – Sechs

S ofia returned from the kitchen with a pot of espresso and a bowl of *strufoli*. Misunderstanding the look on Johannes' face, she explained: "These are small balls of fried dough coated with honey and sugar sprinkles—a traditional Neapolitan dessert. It is typically served at Christmas time, but I was in the mood for it."

Johannes looked at her blankly, struggling to contain and conceal the emotions swimming inside of him.

Sofia, still unaware of the new energy in the room, went back into the kitchen and returned with coffee cups, dessert plates, and fresh silverware. She placed a plate in front of her mother, a second in front of Johannes, and then… *What is this?* Sofia picked up the box that sat on the table in front of her chair and replaced it with the third plate. She looked questioningly at Johannes, then to her mother, and back at Johannes.

"What is this?" she asked him.

Continuing the effort to not give anything away, Johannes held back a smile while Tomasina held back tears. Neither of them said a word.

Sofia stared pensively at the box in her hands. She knew Johannes enjoyed giving gifts, so this wasn't that unusual. First there was the rose quartz star, and then the beautiful glass heart. This box, however, was smaller than the other two. *What has he done now?*

"Open it," Johannes implored. "But first, sit down."

Sofia sat, as instructed, then untied the ribbon that was wrapped around the box. As she did so, Johannes moved his chair closer to hers.

With anticipation, Tomasina's mouth fell open. She quickly placed a hand over it to keep silent.

Just as Sofia opened the box, Johannes moved out of his chair and knelt beside her. Tears began streaming down her face as he proposed to her: in Italian, in front of her mother, and while kissing and caressing her hand.

It was a good thing indeed that she was seated.

Six – Sei – Seis – Sechs

I t took John a moment to re-center himself, but then Saturn continued.

Before we end, there is one last substance we would like for you to consider. One of the most fascinating materials known to man is made of pure carbon. It is both precious and strong. Crystallized carbon is so hard, it is used to cut all other materials, and yet, at the same time, it is the most desired gem worn throughout the globe. Crystallized carbon is what you call diamond, an element so sturdy and stable, the saying 'diamonds are forever' was born.

Do not underestimate the power, the function, the beauty, and the strength of the six when it is nurtured into its greatest harmonic configuration.

Six – Sei – Seis – Sechs

A fter dessert, and once Sofia was composed enough to stand again, it was decided that the three would go out for a walk. The intention was to enjoy a pleasant evening's stroll and to escort Tomasina home. It was early evening and a number of other families were out walking along the canals. Once they reached Tomasina's apartment, she turned to the others and broke the silence.

"Johannes. It is so nice to meet you. I hope we'll be seeing each other a bit more often from now on." Tomasina said this using the little English she had. She then turned to her daughter and continued in Italian. "Sofia. I've been meaning to ask. Could you come by one night this week? I have some things I can use your help with. Plan on staying for dinner."

Despite the fact that Johannes would not understand much of what was said, Tomasina spoke in code nonetheless. The reasoning for the invitation was a complete front. As she spoke, she eyed her daughter in a way that conveyed her true desire and it was clear to Sofia what that was; Tomasina wanted to talk privately about the engagement.

Sofia, of course, feared the worse. She questioned whether her mother truly approved or if she was just being nice in front of Johannes—and she was afraid to find out.

She thought quickly. *Tomorrow is too soon. I'm not ready for this. But if I make her wait until next weekend, she'll know that I'm holding her off.*

Sofia took a deep breath and responded, "Of course, Mama. Is Thursday evening acceptable? I can come by right after work."

"Yes dear, that's fine," Tomasina replied. She then hugged her daughter warmly and finished by saying, "Sofia. I am happy for you."

Sofia looked at her mother and felt a bit of relief wash over her. She then grew emotional all over again and a few tears ran down her face.

Her mother wiped her cheeks and kissed them. She then retreated through her door.

Six – Sei – Seis – Sechs

T he next day, John and Maria started their sightseeing in earnest. They both decided that the oldest part of Rome was the logical place to begin. In the morning, they made their way to *Il Colosseo*, the Roman Colosseum, which was possibly the most recognizable landmark in all of Rome. And yet, as beautiful and unique as the ancient structure was, John felt a stronger draw toward *Il Arco di Costantino,* which was situated just west of the Colosseum.

Pointing at the structure, John said, "Maria. When you look at that, does it remind you of something?"

"You mean the Arch of Constantine? Um—no, I can't say that it does."

John circled the structure and then rejoined Maria, who was patiently waiting for him to finish his inspection.

"Hmm. There is something about it. It feels familiar somehow. But I know I've never seen anything like it before. Humph."

"Well, there is another one over there," Maria pointed further into the Forum, "Let's go."

A short distance later, they arrived at a second arch. Maria looked at the placard placed on it. "It says, '*Arcus Titi'*. It's the Arch dedicated to the Roman emperor Titus."

"It's beautiful, but it doesn't affect me like the other one. I'm not sure why though."

John started to wander off and then stopped to look at Maria who hadn't moved but was staring at him.

Maria laughed observing how decisive John was with his interests. When something intrigued him, he didn't want to leave it, but when it didn't affect him, he quickly moved on.

The two descended further into *Il Foro Romano* and John couldn't help thinking that it felt as if they were walking through a cemetery of ancient Roman buildings. Hardly more than the skeletal remains of what once was still stood. *And if these old columns could talk, what would they say?* John no sooner had that thought and then quickly reneged, remembering what happened in Athens at the Temple of Olympian Zeus. *I take it back. I don't need to know!*

"John, look. There's another arch—similar to the Arch of Constantine."

"Yeah and I'm getting that weird feeling again. Can we get a closer look?" The two walked over to the third arch. John read the first part of the plaque, and then said, "*Arco di Settimio Severo.* Hmm. Never heard of him. Have you?"

"No. Can't say that I have."

He went on. "It says the arch was erected to commemorate the victories of Emperor *Septimius Severus* and his two sons in the Parthian war." John read a bit more to himself and then said, "Well, at least I know why there are so many triumphal arches here in the Forum. Apparently the ancient Romans were the first to create them. There used to be more of them here, but the others didn't survive." John stepped back to get a better look at the arch. "I still don't get why this arch and the Arch of Constantine affect me, but the Arch of Titus does not."

"Do you think it has to do with the design? The Arch of Titus has only one passage way, while the others have three."

"You know, I think that's it. There **is** something about the way the three arches sit inside of the square frame. Hey, that reminds me of a message I got a little while back."

"Yes?"

"Yeah. I'll have to show it to you when we're back at the room. And speaking of my writings, I just heard from Saturn." The two had left the arch and now approached the *Templum Saturni.* "Ever since we approached Rome, I've been hearing from the Roman gods."

"Really? What did Saturn have to say?"

"Well, he's teaching me about the significance of the number six. Apparently, it is important to biological life—you know—chemistry and all that."

"Not exactly what one would expect a Roman god to talk about, eh?"

"I know! But it **is** fascinating information."

The two circled around Saturn's temple and ascended the backside of the Capitoline Hill. Upon entering *Piazza del Campidoglio,* they found themselves surrounded by three *palazzi,* which housed the *Musei Capitolini.* In the first museum they visited they saw a painting depicting the ancient version of the Capitoline Hill and the majestic Temple of Jupiter Optimus Maximus.

"John, look at that!" Maria said excitedly. "Can you imagine what it would have been like to be here back then?"

John looked at the painting, and couldn't help but think how similar it was to the Acropolis. He thought of the visions he had had there and what they had felt like.

"Actually," he replied, "I **can** imagine what it was like."

"What do you mean?"

"Last year I went to Athens and visited the Acropolis. It's quite similar to this painting. The ruins of the buildings are still there. Enough remains for you to get a feel for it. Of course, then there were my visions."

"Your visions?"

"Yeah, that's when they started—in Athens. Whenever I walked through ruins, I kept seeing, hearing, and feeling what it was like in ancient Greece. It was as if I was actually there! I saw the buildings as they had been in their prime, and I saw people mulling about them, dressed as they would have been back then."

"Wow. That must have been amazing."

"It would have been except I kept experiencing a great earthquake over and over again. **That** I didn't like so much. It kind of spoiled the whole experience."

"How long did all of that last?"

"Pretty much until I got to Egypt. That's when I started channeling. I think the visions were just an interim phase because once the channelings started, the visions stopped."

"You haven't had any visions **here**, have you?"

"No, just the odd feeling with those arches. You know, I think if I weren't writing the way that I have been, I might start having visions again. It's almost as if the visions are caused by pent up information that wants to come through one way or another."

"That makes sense."

"I will say this: being here makes me miss Paolo—Felizio's son. He would **so** love to be here with us. He's studying to be an architect. He knows about some of the buildings of Rome, but I'm not sure if he's been here yet."

"Living in this country? I can see why he would want to be an architect! The architecture here is amazing!"

"Yes it is! And you know what? I helped him figure out what he wanted to do." John felt proud, but then tempered himself. "Well, actually, it was a message I channeled—from his guides I think. That was the first time I ever channeled. I thought it was just a fluke—happened the first time I met him."

John suddenly grew quiet and Maria could tell that he was feeling nostalgic. She silently grabbed his arm and led him to the next exhibit in the museum. Soon, he was back in the present moment, marveling over the pieces of art displayed there.

Six – Sei – Seis – Sechs

Monday was not a productive day for Sofia—at least not as far as work was concerned. She spent one third of the time staring at her ring, another third staring at her fiancé, and the last third daydreaming about her wedding day.

Johannes was, of course, aware of this and had expected it. He therefore asked nothing of her. He felt her stare from time to time, and when she wasn't looking his way, he stole long adoring glances at her. Otherwise, he kept himself as busy as possible.

Unlike Sofia, **he** didn't want to think about the future, the wedding, or even what had just happened. He had acted on impulse, and now that his rational side was in control again, he did not want to consider the situation lest he challenge his decision. He knew better than that. Just like in all other areas of his life, when he made a decision, that was it. It wasn't productive to second guess.

At the same time, he did love this beautiful woman who sat there staring at the ring on her finger. He **did** want to be with her—now and...*on going. Who knows what forever is like anyway?*—he asked himself.

After a bit more introspection, Johannes concluded that the only source of concern was that one little word: 'forever'. Women seemed to love it, but men? They'd just as soon forget the word ever existed. It brought no comfort and was simply a source of stress. *'Today and on going'—that feels so much better than 'forever'!*

Six – Sei – Seis – Sechs

O ver the next few days, John and Maria visited additional sights popular with tourists. They saw fountains, churches, museums, and palaces. They, of course, spent one full day at the Vatican: Saint Peter's Square, Saint Peter's Basilica, and nearly half of the day at the Sistine Chapel. Those days were productive, but tiring. Each evening, after dinner, both retired early and fell fast asleep.

Their last full day in Rome thus arrived, and John wanted it to be special. So that morning, he offered a suggestion.

"Maria. What do you think about spending some time like the locals do—you know—'When in Rome...' and all that? We can visit a park, walk through some gardens, and surround ourselves with a little greenery. What do you think?"

"That sounds like a splendid idea. I hear *Villa Borghese* is a nice park with plenty to see. It's not too far from here and *Piazza di Spagna* is on the way. You can't let a Spanish girl leave Rome without sitting on the Spanish Steps now could you?"

"That sounds perfect. Let's do it!"

A short while later, John and Maria reached *Piazza di Spagna*. The grand staircase worked its way up to the church of the *Santissima Trinità dei Monti*, which featured a prominent obelisk directly in front.

"Well John, I wasn't going to make you **climb** the staircase, but since there is an obelisk up there, I guess we have to, eh?"

"You bet. Let's go."

The two ascended the stairs and were glad they did. Even though about a hundred other tourists surrounded them, they were blessed with another spectacular view within the city.

"Hey Maria. You know, this obelisk doesn't feel right. Look at it. Does it feel like an Egyptian obelisk to you?"

"Well, it certainly looks like one; it's covered in hieroglyphics."

"Yeah, but it doesn't **feel** like the others. So far, we've seen the obelisk in *Piazza di San Giovanni in Laterano,* which is from Karnak and the one in St. Peter's Square, which is from Alexandria. They both felt good to me. But this one doesn't."

"Well, look, there's a plaque. Let's read what it has to say." Maria read the plaque and John looked over her shoulder. "John. You're right. This one is not from Egypt."

"Yeah. Says here it's a copy of one in *Piazza del Popolo*. Isn't that one of the entrances of *Villa Borghese?"*

"It is. In fact, if we go back down to *Piazza di Spagna*, we can take *Via del Babuino* directly to it. There are a few churches dedicated to *Santa Maria* up there I've been curious about."

"Well, I guess today is all about you then! First the Spanish Steps, and then *Santa Maria!"*

"Not so fast young man. You're the one who's interested in all of the obelisks. So it's not just about me!"

"You're right. Today is all about **us!**"

John and Maria descended the staircase and turned right, heading north along *Via del Babuino*. It didn't take long before they could see the obelisk situated at the end of the boulevard. As soon as John saw it, he quivered with anticipation.

A number of blocks later, John and Maria reached the end of the street where the wall of buildings gave way to the wide-open square. In the center of it all was the tall obelisk. Resisting the temptation to run, John led Maria further into the open space where Romans and tourists ambled about.

The **square** was actually oval shaped with a rectangular section that jutted out toward the south just next to where they had entered. Once they moved further into the center of the *piazza* and looked around, it became clear why it was designed that way. The rectangular section sat in front of a pair of churches, transforming them into a gateway.

"Maria. You mentioned that there were churches here that you wanted to see. Are those two among them?"

"What I was reading described two of the churches dedicated to *Santa Maria* as 'twins'—quoted because they are not really identical, but closely resemble each other. So those must be the two. There is supposed to be a third one, but I don't see it." Maria looked around as she said this.

John looked around as well and noticed a woman holding up a flag the way a tour guide does to attract attention.

"Maria. I think that woman is about to give a tour. Do you want to check it out?"

"Yes, of course."

As John and Maria approached the woman, John realized that she was holding up a French flag.

"Maria! How fortunate. She is giving the tour in French!"

A few moments later, the woman began waving people toward her.

"*Mesdames, Messieurs. S'il vous plaît.* If you wish to be a part of the tour, please gather round."

As she waited for the group to come together, John and Maria grew eager. They looked at each other, acknowledging that they both felt it. For some unknown reason, they knew this tour was going to be exciting.

"*Mesdames, Messieurs.* Welcome to *Piazza del Popolo,* the People's Square. This is the largest *piazza* in Rome and home to its third tallest obelisk.

"What you will see here, not unlike much of Rome, is a mix of architectural styles, having been created during different time periods and inspired by varying religious beliefs. This square has had a number of configurations over the years, but it has always been significant. We will begin at the north entrance. Please, follow me."

The tour guide directed the group north, away from the churches, past the obelisk, and toward a small street that led directly to...

"Maria! Look at that! I didn't notice it when we first got here. The top is different, but look; it has three arches, a larger one in the middle and smaller ones on the sides—just like the Arch of Constantine and the arch of that other guy!"

"*Septimius Severus.*"

"Yeah, him." John spoke excitedly, but made an effort to keep his voice down.

The tour guide began to speak again: "*Mesdames, Messieurs.* What you see here is the *Porta del Popolo.* In ancient Rome, it was called *Porta Flaminia* and was one of the 18 main gates through the Aurelian Walls into early Rome. At that time, nothing but wilderness lay beyond this gate—that and *Via Flaminia*, of course. *Via Flaminia* was an ancient Roman road that led to *Ariminum* on the Adriatic coast, which today is the city of *Rimini.*

"As you can imagine, this was quite a significant location in ancient Rome. All traveling from the north would enter the city through this gateway. In fact, that street directly across the square between the twin churches was the continuation of the original *Via Flaminia* and leads directly to the Capitoline Hill: the center of ancient Rome and one of the original seven hills. To this day, we continue to use the word 'capitol' as a result of it.

"In modern Rome, that street is called *Via del Corso* and ends at *Piazza Venezia* at the base of the Capitoline Hill. That square, in a sense, is appropriately named. Does anyone know why?"

The tour guided waited to see if anyone knew the answer. When no one spoke up, she continued.

"Many do not realized this because of the slanted orientation of the peninsula of Italy, but almost exactly due north of Rome is the city of Venice.

"And there is more. Look at the *Porta* again. What does it

resemble—can someone tell me?"

John excitedly raised his hand and caught the tour guide's attention.

"I was just telling my friend that it looks like the Arch of Constantine," he said.

"Yes, it does. In fact the triumphal arch is most characteristic of ancient Roman architecture. But does anyone know the connection of this design to Venice?"

Again the tour guide paused before continuing.

"Have you heard of the famous Italian architected named *Andrea Palladio?"* she asked everyone.

Some nodded and others shook their heads.

"Palladio is an architect known for his work in Venice. A most characteristic motif of his is what is known as the Palladian Arch or Palladian Window. It consists of three open spaces much like this. The center is a true arch, however the side openings are squared off, like modern doorways. The overall effect is similar. In fact, Andrea's design was inspired by his visits to Rome.

"The Palladian Window is also known as the Serlian Window, as it was also employed by *Sebastiano Serlio.* Most today simply refer to it as the Venetian Window since many of Palladio's designs are found there. If you wish to see a grand and elegant example of the Palladian Arch here in Rome, visit *Villa Giulia* not far from here in the Northwest corner of *Villa Borghese."*

The tour guide raised her flag and began directing the crowd back toward the center of the plaza.

"Now, please, let us take in the entirety of the square from this vantage. Immediately on your left, here, is *Santa Maria del Popolo.* Across the way are *Santa Maria dei Miracoli* and *Santa Maria in Montesanto.* These are three of twenty-six churches in Rome dedicated to the Virgin Mary. In fact, all three of these churches predate the current design of the square. *Giuseppe Valadier* did an excellent job incorporating the churches into his design.

"Now, please, look to the right. That is the *Fontana del Nettuno.* Surely all of you know Neptune, or Poseidon as the Greeks called him!"

John nudged Maria and pointed, clearly astounded, yet

remaining mute, eager to hear what the tour guide would say next.

"The fountain was placed in this location because it is the terminus of the relatively modern Roman aqueduct called *Acqua Vergine Nuovo*.

"Now, for those of you interested in numbers, let me point out a few aspects of this *piazza*. What is Neptune most known for?"

A number of people yelled out, "His trident!"

"Precisely. Just look at him. Neptune is always depicted with a trident in hand. The word 'trident' is derived from the Latin word *'tridentis'* meaning 'three teeth'.

"So Neptune holds his trident, but is also shown with two of his sons, which are mermen and called Tritons. Thus the fountain contains **three** figures. We already discussed how the *Porta di Popolo* contains **three** arches, and that **three** churches dedicated to St. Mary surround the square. Now notice this. Standing here and looking south, **three** streets branch off of the square. In fact, these three boulevards intentionally resemble the three tines of a trident and are known locally as *Il Tridente Romano*. So this *piazza* contains many threes, yet no one knows why."

As the tour guide paused, Maria looked at John and saw precisely as she had expected. His mouth was agape and his eyes were glazed over in wonderment. She was sure that once the tour was over, he would be babbling about it for hours!

"To complete our tour of the square, we arrive at its center. This here, as I said earlier, is the **third** tallest obelisk in Rome. It is one of eight ancient Egyptian obelisks brought here from Egypt. This one is from the city of Heliopolis where five of the eight originated. There are five additional obelisks here that were created specifically for Romans. Some were built in Egypt during the Roman Empire while the rest were built here as copies of the ancient originals.

"This particular obelisk was originally built for the Egyptian Pharaoh Seti I and later erected by his son Ramses II. The Pharaoh Seti's name, by the way, literally means 'man of Seth' as that was the Egyptian god he was devoted to. Three other obelisks here in Rome were made by Ramses II. The one that accompanied this one now resides in *Piazza di Montecitorio*. The last two are from the

Temple of Ra—*Macuteo* is in *Piazza della Rotondo* and *Matteiano* is in *Villa Celimontana.*

"All in all, Rome is home to more obelisks than any other city in the world. Not surprising when you remember that this was once the center of the Western World!

"That completes our tour. If you wish to visit *Piazza di Spanga,* follow the road on the left. If you wish to visit the Vatican, follow the road on the right. The Forum and old Rome can be reached via the center road. And for those who wish to spend a day in lovely *Villa Borghese*, take those stairs over there." She pointed to her left. "Thank you for attending and have a splendid afternoon!"

The tour ended and the attendees scattered—except for John and Maria. By this point they were both wonderstruck and stared at the obelisk in front of them.

"John, I know what you are thinking and yes, all things considered, we have to go see at least one of the obelisks from the Temple of Ra. After all, that temple has significance for both of us."

John just looked at Maria, but wasn't yet able to speak.

"The tour guide said *Piazza della Rotonda.* Isn't that where the Pantheon is located?" she asked him.

John nodded in response.

"That's on the way back to the hotel. So we'll go there later. I still want to see the park."

John, finally able to speak said, "Can we visit *Villa Giulia?*"

"Yes, I think that's fine. We'll enter the park here and exit there. Then we'll head to the Pantheon. That's all we'll have time for. Since today is our last day, does that plan work for you?"

John nodded and then followed Maria toward the stairs that led to the park.

Six – Sei – Seis – Sechs

T hursday arrived and as the day went on, Sofia grew increasingly nervous. All week, she avoided thinking about the meeting with her mother. Now that mere hours remained, she began to fret. *I hope Mama is not upset about the engagement*—she silently prayed.

Despite not saying anything about it, Sofia's body language gave away her trepidation. Johannes knew that the imminent discussion with her mother weighed heavily on her. He decided to try and help with a little distraction therapy. He walked over to her desk, presented her with a task, and placed his arm around her as he did so.

Typically, he refrained from affection while they worked, since it was a huge distraction for both of them, but in this case, distraction **was** the point. He distracted her with work and affection and hoped that she'd forget all about her concerns, at least for a few more hours. That was the best he could do for her. Once the evening came, she was going to have to face her mother whether she wanted to or not.

Six – Sei – Seis – Sechs

T he city clamored all around the park; however, within the periphery of tall trees, it was calm and serene. The locals strewn about were lounging on blankets, soaking up rays of sunshine, and enjoying a peaceful, romantic lunch. The abundant greenery filtered out most of the urban din and held in the serenade of Roman fowl.

When John first entered the park, his mind thrashed with names, histories, and images of ancient Rome. He was furiously trying to piece it all together. Despite his efforts, he could not even imagine where **he** fit in.

Luckily, *Villa Borghese* worked its charms and tempered his chaotic churning. The slow, meandering stroll cleared John's head and left him feeling refreshed and rejuvenated.

As they approached the northern boundary of the park, they began casually looking for signs telling them how to get to *Villa Giulia*. However, they found themselves back within the concrete jungle before finding any.

"I thought it would be right here," John said as he looked up and down the bustling boulevard.

Maria, spotting a street sign and then pointing to it said, "This street is called *Via di Villa Giulia.* It must be just around the bend."

The grand boulevard banked to the right and disappeared behind the mass of trees that formed the northern edge of the park. Not a block later, they caught sight of the building. The sizable front lawn was meticulously maintained, yet John hardly noticed it. Instead, he focused solely on the building itself.

From the street, *Villa Giulia* resembled a more or less typical Roman museum. The main body of the building was two stories tall and twice as wide. Wings that were only a single story stepped back from the front façade and extended out laterally.

John immediately noticed a repeating pattern of three. First, there was the main body of the building and the two wings that flanked it. Next, the front façade of the two-story section was itself divided into three. The left side reflected the right side and an ornate section sat between them. Last, the middle was itself partitioned into three: a unique and wider central arch between two others. The arrangement of the ground floor was repeated on the top floor, except in a slightly different style.

Although John was excited by what he saw, he was not yet satisfied. The triple-arch pattern only hinted at the Venetian design. It was not a true Palladian Window.

John and Maria walked up to the entryway, which sat within the main arch on the ground floor. After passing through it, Maria noticed a map of the property, and pointed it out to John. It illustrated the layout of the complex as seen from above. The front section, where John and Maria stood, was called the Casino. John had expected the building to be at least as deep as it was wide, but was intrigued to find that a semicircular section was essentially cut out of the middle. He could not imagine what that would look like and so quickly grabbed Maria's hand to check it out.

The two exited the rear of the Casino and began crossing the central courtyard. The entire building curved around them. The ground floor of the semicircular façade featured an arcade that varied as it went along. The center portion was the most interesting. It contained another triple-arch pattern, but one that more closely resembled the nearby *Porta del Popolo*—the central arch being both wider and taller than those that flanked it. The entire design was elegant and beautiful and brought together a number of typical Roman architectural motifs. It, however, was still not the Palladian Arch John came to see.

Across the courtyard from the back of the Casino was a building called the *Nymphaeum*. According to the floor plan, an enclosed garden sat beyond it. From where they stood, it appeared to be a single story. However, after passing through the front foyer, they found themselves on a porch three stories up. Curved stairs descend on both sides and one level down, a balcony circumnavigated the lowest level. From the porch, John and Maria could see nearly all of it. Only the section directly below them was out of view.

John pointed at the far side and sighed as if to say, "Finally!" Another porch sat directly across from them. **It** was designed in the Palladian style; the central opening was a true arch, while the shorter side windows were squared off at the top.

The level below contained a second Palladian Window. The columns on that level were thicker than those above, and square rather than cylindrical. The side windows were thus much narrower than their counterparts above.

John then noticed an interesting detail. The balcony floor in front of the second story Palladian Window mirrored the window itself. Rather than being straight across, a semicircular section was cut out of it.

After John's gaze moved to the lowest level, he turned to Maria and said, "Now I know why they call this the *Nymphaeum*." The four columns that supported the semicircular section of the balcony were created as beautiful nymph statues. John could just barely make out the wall further back and saw additional nymphs carved in relief.

"This building is amazing. Whoever designed it was ingenious! I'm so glad we came!" John allowed himself to get lost in the beauty for a moment. He then said, "You know, Maria, one day I'm going to go to Venice, if for no other reason than to see the buildings Palladio created."

"John, I'm sure the opportunity will arise when the time is

right" she replied.

Maria then put her hand on his shoulder, indicating that it was time for them to leave.

Six – Sei – Seis – Sechs

S ofia approached her mother's door and paused to take a deep breath.

"Here goes nothing," she whispered.

She knocked on the door and waited what felt like an hour before her mother unlocked the door. After their typical greeting, the women walked into the parlor and sat down.

Tomasina commenced the discussion: "So…how does it feel to be engaged?"

Sofia wasn't expecting that sort of question and was caught off guard. The tension, which had built throughout the day, broke and she burst into tears.

"Mama, I'm scared," she said with her hands over her face.

Tomasina placed her arms around her daughter. "Oh, Baby Girl, it's going to be all right. You love him, don't you?"

"Yes I do. I've never felt like this before."

"Well, then, what are you worried about? He clearly loves you —it's written all over his handsome face!"

Sofia wiped her eyes, looked up at Tomasina, and said, "Mama, I know he loves me. I've been worried about **you**!"

"**Me**! Why?"

"At first I was afraid that you wouldn't like Johannes for one reason or another. Then he proposes the first time he meets you, and I got worried you would think things were going too fast. And Mama, I have a confession." Sofia looked down at her hands. "There's something I haven't told you."

Tomasina's eyes widened. *Oh dear*—she thought to herself. *What have you gotten yourself into, Baby Girl?* Tomasina **hadn't** been concerned about things moving too fast…until now!

Masking her concern, she said as calmly as she could, "Now, honey. You can tell me anything."

"Well...I... You, of course, know about my job. What I didn't tell you is that I'm working for Johannes."

Suddenly Tomasina felt relief. "Dear, I know that. I figured it out well before last Sunday. Are you telling me you thought I would disapprove of **that**?"

"Well, isn't that a bad thing—to date someone you work with?"

"My Dear, you have nothing to worry about. I don't recommend it for too long. It might be difficult for the two of you to spend all day and night together, but for now it's fine."

"And you don't think we're moving too fast?"

"Well, you're engaged, but you haven't set a date yet, have you?"

"No. We're just enjoying this for now. Well, actually, I don't know what Johannes is thinking; I haven't asked him."

"Good. An early engagement is fine, provided it is a long one. Especially when it's the man's idea. My Dear, let me tell you something about our family I've never told you before."

Tomasina started in on their family history. She told Sofia what her fears had been and why she was happy to see things progressing the way they were. She then ended the discourse by saying, "And so, let's put all of these fears behind us. My baby girl is engaged and I am going to write my cousins to tell them. You're all right with me sharing your news, aren't you?"

"Yes, Mama. Of course!"

"Good. I am going to write a letter to Cousin Lorita and ask her to tell Alessandra and Cassandra."

"Mama, it makes me so happy that you approve of Johannes."

"Baby Girl, there are so few good men in our family. I can tell that Johannes is a fine young man. I am happy he found you!"

Tomasina made to get up and then hesitated. She had one more thing on her mind.

"Sofia, I don't want you to be anxious about the wedding, but I do have a suggestion for you to think about. Since most of the family is in *Napoli* and Sorrento, what would you think about getting married on the island of Capri?"

"Mama! You're planning my wedding already?!?"

Sofia smiled wider than she had all day and threw her arms

around her mother. The greatest of her fears were now behind her and she had a beautiful wedding to look forward to, even if it was a ways down the road.

Six – Sei – Seis – Sechs

A fter a long walk, John and Maria arrived at *Piazza della Rotonda*. Unlike *Piazza del Popolo*, they weren't able to see the obelisk until they'd entered the square itself.

"I guess, in some ways, it is perfect to end our touring here," John said, staring at the obelisk from Heliopolis. "Maybe the whole reason we needed to be in Rome was to behold one of the obelisks that I've seen so many times in my visions and dreams. I expected it to be a lot taller, though."

A few moments later, John glanced over to the Pantheon. "You know, I think it's fitting that an obelisk from the Temple of Ra would be placed in front of the Pantheon."

"Why is that?" Maria asked.

"Well, '*Pantheon*' is the word the Romans used for their entire collection of gods. Ra was **the** sun god of the Egyptians—at least at one time. He isn't a part of the Roman Pantheon, but it's as if he sits outside of it to keep an eye on the others!" John then started laughing and soon Maria was laughing with him.

The two sat on the ground next to the obelisk. It was nearing the end of a long day at the end of a long week. They both looked at the grand portico of the Pantheon, but couldn't muster the energy to walk over to it just yet.

A few moments later, John sighed deeply, turned to Maria, and said, "Well, we can't sit here in front of the Pantheon and not venture inside…at least for a few minutes. Are you ready to move again?"

"I guess…if we have to. I don't think the Roman police would take too kindly to us sleeping right here, do you?"

John stood and helped Maria up, and then the two visited the last site of their Roman holiday.

Six – Sei – Seis – Sechs

T he next morning, John and Maria ate breakfast, packed the last of their belongings, and returned to *Piazza di San Giovanni in Laterano* where it all began. While they waited for the coach to arrive, John kept himself busy inspecting the tall obelisk one last time. To their surprise, a number of others gathered around them with bags in hand. At first John worried that they wouldn't all fit, but this time, what arrived was a larger coach with plenty of room for everyone.

The driver first directed everyone to place their luggage into the rear compartment. He then helped the women and children onto the coach and invited the men aboard. Before driving off, he entered the passenger compartment to make an announcement.

"Signore e Signori, do we have any visitors to Rome on board today?"

John, Maria, and a few others nodded.

"In case you are not aware, before heading to *Civitavecchia*, we will take a slight diversion into *Fiumicino*. Since some of you are tourists, let me tell you a little bit about our charming port town. Today, *Fiumicino* is the larger of two towns straddling the mouth of the *Tevere*, but that wasn't always the case.

"In ancient times, the main port of Rome was *Ostia* located on the coast just south of the Tiber. However, as the Roman Empire grew, so did its trade, and so did the size of ships bringing goods into Rome. The larger ships couldn't enter the river because of the sand bars in front of the mouth. Thus Claudius, the Emperor at that time, began construction of a new harbor. This harbor was then connected to the *Tevere* via two canals.

"Later, Claudius' harbor was deemed too vulnerable, so a second harbor was constructed further inland. This was commissioned by Emperor Trajan and was thus called *Portus Traiani*. The entire area came to be known simply as *Portus*, but was also called *Portus Romae*.

"By the Middle Ages, the northern canal, *Via Portuensis,* no longer existed, but *Fossa Traiani* remained. At that time, the Tiber itself was called *Fiumara Grande*—the big river, and thus *Fossa*

Traiani was known as *Fiumicino*—the little river. That's how the town received its name."

The driver paused for a moment. He then turned to a boy sitting near the door and said, "*Scuzzi, rigazzo mio.* May I borrow your soccer ball?" The boy handed him the ball and then the driver augmented his discourse.

"The harbor that Trajan constructed is most unique—unlike any harbor anywhere in the world. It was designed in the shape of a hexagon—like the white pieces on this soccer ball. The southern edge was opened just enough for ships to pass and yet protected the harbor otherwise. Warehouses lined each of the remaining sides for efficient processing of goods destined for Rome. The hexagonal shape is evident today, however it is no longer a harbor, merely a lake. It is called *Lago di Traiano.* I will point it out to you as we pass by." The driver finished in earnest and handed the soccer ball to its owner.

John kept staring at the soccer ball until the boy noticed.

"Can I look at your ball for a moment?" John asked him.

"*Certo, Signore,*" the boy replied, handing John the ball.

John rotated the soccer ball in his hands and inspected the white hexagonal pieces of leather. He ran his fingers along the stitch lines and marveled at how the arrangement of shapes perfectly approximated a sphere. He then took notice of the black pieces and realized they were a different shape he was familiar with. Rather than six sides, they only had five. They were, in fact, perfect pentagons.

Somehow, John had never noticed that the black pieces and white pieces were different shapes. He had seen soccer balls many times before, even played soccer when he was young, but he never noticed that the shapes were different.

John ran his hands over the ball a bit longer before noticing that the boy eyed him queerly. He then felt self-conscious and handed the ball back to him saying, "*Tanti Grazie, amico mio.*"

The entire way to *Fiumicino*, John stole glances at the soccer ball when the boy wasn't looking, and thought about the way the shapes fit so perfectly together. The boy and his parents disembarked in *Fiumicino*, so for the rest of the journey, John merely stared out of the window and let his mind drift.

After they reached *Civitavecchia*, and boarded their ship to Spain, John ascended to the main deck and looked out over the harbor. He reflected on his time in Rome and how unexpectedly special it had been. He wasn't sure when he would visit Italy next and felt a twinge of sadness leaving it behind once more.

Maria joined him just as the ship set sail and remained with him until the Italian coast blended into the eastern horizon. She then sought out a crew-member to discuss the journey.

After the last of Italy receded into the ocean, John decided to head back to the room. He hadn't written a word since that first night in Rome and figured it was as good a time as any.

Despite the time that had passed, he was surprised to find inspiration return so quickly.

The Perfection of Imperfection

I am Jupiter, the god of thunder and the father of gods. I am the leader of the Pantheon of Rome and as with Ra, we are now a collective. In fact, this is the way of sixth density. We are now, forever and always, joined with those we love...in common service and collective purpose.

Ah Rome. Even with all that has changed and the years that have gone by, Rome still holds a warm place in our hearts. There is no place on Earth where we were loved more than in Rome. Rome has evolved significantly, and yet much of its history is evident still. As you have seen, there is a strong connection between Rome and Egypt. That is why it was imperative for you to return.

After writing the word 'return', John was struck with a vision. An ancient version of Rome lay before him. The scene centered on the recently completed Pantheon; a moderate size crowd of citizens had gathered in front of it. Beneath John's hands was a scroll, upon which he furiously wrote.

Yes, my boy, you have been here before. You have done this work before. This is not the first time you've been a scribe to the Pantheon of Rome. How does it feel to be back among the Seven Hills? Six beautiful days in Rome is just a taste, but it was delicious, wouldn't you say? In fact, as we scan your mind, we find the word 'perfect' hovering there.

My dear boy, it is so much easier for those in human form to see the perfection of perfection. It is much harder for you to see the perfection of **imperfection**. Such is the challenge of life in three-dimensional space-time reality. You can only walk the path one step at a time and thus do not often trust what you cannot see.

Many of you compare the passing of time with the flowing of a river. But consider this: rivers do not form straight lines. They zig and they zag and yet they always find the ocean. Rivers are **perfectly imperfect**.

Consider another example. Recall the object you held in your hands this very morning. Yes, we are speaking of the soccer ball constructed of

swatches of leather, cut in the shape of sacred polygons, and sewn together. You noticed that the white pieces are hexagons and the black pieces are pentagons and you marveled.

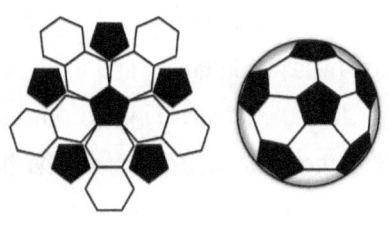

As we stated earlier, hexagons nested together form an optimal lattice. The bees know; the wasps know. Even the snakes know. You may never get close enough to study its skin, but if you did, you would find its scales fit together in a hexagonal lattice. Build a lattice from any other shape and you will find suboptimal characteristics.

However, as ideal as it may be, the hexagonal lattice employs all of its assets in only two dimensions. That is why you can draw it on a piece of paper. This lattice can grow in all directions within a plane, but never leaves it. And yet, with the inclusion of perfect imperfection, a flat plane can be fashioned into a sphere.

Have you ever tried to wrap paper around a ball? It is not easy; is it? The paper folds and crinkles haphazardly. Yet, by cutting the pieces into hexagons and pentagons, and placing the pentagons at the center of five hexagons, you bend the plane just so. As you saw with the soccer ball, they fit perfectly together to approximate a sphere.

This is an example of the perfection of imperfection and there is a message here.

Six is the **experience of creation**. Consciousness, namely human consciousness, strives for perfection, yet even when apparent perfection is obtained, the five will roll through and show itself eventually.

Five is disharmonious—a break from the rectilinear motion of the four and the six. However, it is exactly what's required for depth to be experienced. In a way, five forces you to keep creating. When you create something beautiful and then withdraw your attention from it, the earth will reclaim it in time—and that is the work of the five.

If you lived solely in two dimensions, you would not need the five, but then your life would be flat and boring. By accepting what five brings, your life takes shape and has depth, just like the soccer ball.

The trick is to know how to fit the fives within the sixes. The Universe will do this for you; you need only allow it. And that is the perfection of imperfection.

7 – *Seven* – VII

Sept – Sette – Siete – Sieben

C arina hopped up and down and pulled at her father's hand, saying, *"Papino! Papino!"*. She was always excited when Felizio came home; today, she was more exuberant than usual.

"Papino, come look. You and Mama got letters on the same day! Yours is from *Roma.* Mama's is from *Venezia!* She opened hers; it was from *Cugina* Tomasina. Open yours; I bet it is more exciting news!"

Felizio picked up his daughter, kissed her cheeks repeatedly, and said, "So much excitement all at once!" He then placed her back on the ground and accepted the letter she handed him.

"Hmm…who do I know in *Roma?*" he asked himself as he examined the front of the envelope for clues. He then flipped it over to see if anything had been written on the back.

Carina wrung her hands with anticipation. *"Papà,* who do you think it's from?"

"I don't know, my sweet. I guess I'll have to look inside to find out."

Before Felizio opened the letter, he spotted his wife standing in the doorway to the kitchen. She had heard all of the excitement and came out to catch the end of Carina's plea. He walked over to her and greeted her properly.

"Lorita, my love. How are you?" he asked as he held her in his arms. "I hear you got a letter from your cousin—good news, according to Carina."

"Yes, Sofia got engaged! Tomasina is very excited. She said it happened rather quickly, but she approves of the man nonetheless. She, of course, said, 'He's no Feliciano,' but then no one is."

Lorita smiled and gave Felizio his welcome home kisses.

Carina, despite her efforts, could not wait any longer. In a fit of impatience, she grabbed the letter out of her father's hand. "*Papino,* let me open this for you," she said to him.

Before Felizio could object, Carina wedged open the envelope and pulled out the letter. She was tempted to simply begin reading it, but she knew better. She handed the single sheet of paper to her father while trying to decipher the signature on the back.

Felizio turned the letter over, saw that it was from John, and then started reading from the beginning. Without taking his eyes off of the paper, he made his way over to the table, pulled out a chair, and sat.

Lorita fetched Felizio *una birra* and sat across from him.

Carina half sat, half stood, and continued to bounce at her place at the table.

Felizio uttered, "Well I'll be," but when Carina made to ask for details, he simply raised a finger and continued reading. Once he was done, he placed the letter on the table and summarized: "Well, it's from John. He was here in *Italia*—in *Roma*—en route to Spain. He said he didn't realize they would be passing through or he would have tried to arrange a visit.

"And this is the best part: he met up with Johannes. He didn't find him in Crete, but rather ran into him at the pyramids in Giza! I'll let you read the details, but apparently Johannes ran off again and didn't say where he was going. John is now traveling to Barcelona with a Spanish woman named Maria."

Lorita read the letter and then handed it to Carina who grabbed it immediately and began analyzing each sentence. Lorita glanced down at the letter from Tomasina, which was lying on the table in front of her, and sighed heavily.

"Feliciano," she said tentatively, "there's something I need to mention about Sofia's engagement."

"Yes, my love."

"I know this could simply be a coincidence, but given John's letter, I…I don't know what to think."

"Out with it woman! What's happened?"

Lorita took a deep breath, to stall for a moment longer, then said, "Sofia is engaged…to a **Johannes from Germany**! Is that a common name there?"

"I don't know. I haven't been to Germany."

"Even if it is **very** common, what are the odds that another Johannes—from Germany—would be expanding his father's business—in Italy—after having been…to **Egypt**?"

"Hmm—not likely. I see what you mean."

Felizio remained silent as he considered the facts before him. *It has to be the same man*—he concluded.

He looked up at his wife and said, "What do we do? John said to send a response to him in Barcelona. We should write to him right away in case he moves on from there. Do we tell him this news? As you said, it could all be mere coincidence, although it doesn't look that way."

"Feliciano, I've been thinking about this all afternoon. I didn't know the letter you received was from John, but we knew he was going to Egypt and it wouldn't be that much of a stretch for Johannes to have traveled to Egypt himself. Now we know for sure that Johannes was there. This has to be the same man!"

"I agree. Chances are, it is. We'll know eventually if he's going to marry into the family. And it's clear that John wants to come back here some day. He's family now and he knows that. He's going to find out one way or another. If I know John, he'll have a hard time at first, but he'll work through it. I think we should tell him."

Sept – Sette – Siete – Sieben

Depth

I am Pluto and it is now time to begin your initiation into the depths of the number seven.

It has been said that "one is the loneliest number," however seven feels far lonelier. At one, you are individual and raring to go. You feel independent and free. With seven, right in the midst of enjoying the harmony of six, you get yanked away from the others. You feel abandoned, isolated, imprisoned...

I am Pluto, the god of the underworld. I am known as Hades to the Greeks—a name that has since come to be associated with the gates of Hell. Seven is the most misunderstood of the single digit numbers just as I am the most misunderstood of gods.

In reality, seven has noble purpose—and so do I. We are both here to escort you to the depths of your soul; it is only a hellacious undertaking if you make it so.

I ask you, how can you correct the greatest of misconceptions in your beliefs if you are not willing to delve down to their source? How can you cure your deepest fears lest you walk through them? How can you discover your truest self without stripping away every cloak you've put on?

Many, when they first learn of numbers, have come to believe that seven is nothing more than abject suffering and wretched misery—a dark night of the soul.

Take heed, I beseech you. I am here to tell you that seven is not only important—to the initiate, it is the most significant single-digit number. It is only through the seven that mysteries are revealed and secrets told. The instantaneous quantum leap of eight can only occur after the least seen restraints have been severed by the seven.

As you have learned, the five rolls through, disrupting the stability of four. Similarly, when the seven comes, it shifts one quickly out of the apparent harmony of six. It doesn't do this merely for growth; it does this for nothing short of **transformation**.

Consider this: if the caterpillar's life were left uninterrupted, its abundant feasting would result in nothing but size. It would continue to grow larger, but would never learn to fly. It is only through its retreat into the chrysalis that the butterfly's wings are created.

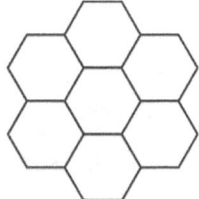

For a moment, let us return once again to the hexagonal lattice. Draw a hexagon and notice how six others fit perfectly around it. Ah, but now you have seven!

More interestingly, notice that this works with circles as well. Take a coin of any size and place six more around it and see how they fit perfectly together. The shape produced—it resembles a flower, wouldn't you say? What you behold here is a seven constructed from one and six. Notice how it retains the overall shape of the hexagon. There is a secret in this, which we will reveal in a moment.

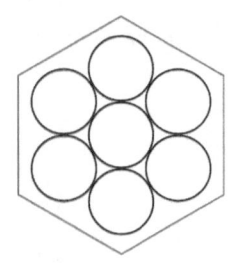

Seven can be created from one and six, but also via three and four. Remember how both the tetrahedron and the cube are related to the three and the four?

Behold! Watch what can be done with our seven circles:

Connecting the center of four circles one way illustrates a tetrahedron.

Connecting all of the center points another way illustrates a cube.

There is another way to draw seven circles together. Bring the ring of six in towards the center of the seventh until they touch. In this way, you create what is called the **Seed of Life**.

Continue the pattern outward to produce the **Flower of Life** and then notice that our original seven-circle configuration is present within it. Throughout, the hexagonal shape remains.

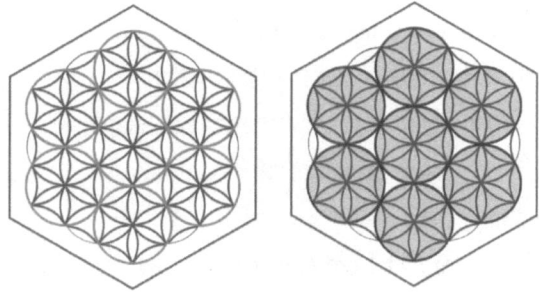

The secret wisdom is this: hidden inside of the apparent six is always a seventh. The one is what's hidden inside. Three is the **creation** of All-That-Is. Six is the **experience** of that which is created. And yet, inside, at the center of it all, is **you**. **You** are the one. All-That-Is, without one to observe and experience it, is meaningless. It is **you** that gives it meaning. You are the center point of the three-dimensional cube that extends out in six directions.

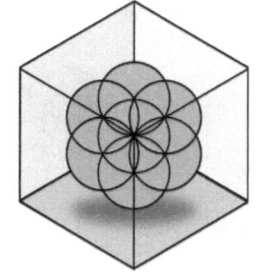

But do not confuse the box for reality! Everything that you see around you is an illusion, a projection, a creation. Your body and your experiences are part of that box. They too are created by you, but they are not **who you really are**. The challenge, symbolized by the journey of the seven, is to seek that which is within. That's where you will find who you really are. That's where you will find all of the answers.

Let us consider the Tarot. Major Arcana card number XIII is called Death. It does not portend actual death, but indicates transformation. Seven steps (or cards) after Death, we find card number XX— Judgment, which is sometimes called Resurrection. At Death, you begin the journey downward, underground, to the depth of your soul. At Resurrection, you rise again, you are reborn anew—you are freer, lighter, and more whole.

Whenever you harbor a fear of dying, remind yourself that 'death' is merely an alternate spelling of 'depth'. Be it an actual death or a bout of near-death—experienced in first person or witnessed in second person —these incidents bring you deeper into yourself, helping you reach further into who you really are. They are life-changing.

Every 'life' ends in 'death', where all of the illusions of the six are laid aside, and where only the one inside remains.

Go now. Allow the forces of nature to have their way with you. Your trip down the rabbit's hole will not be for naught. The fearful rabbit must descend into darkness and travel the full journey of seven in order to ascend out of the other side and be reborn.

"Rabbit's hole?!? Forces of nature?!? Have their way with me?!? What are you trying to tell me?"

John voiced his questions aloud, but got nothing in response. He felt the energy of Pluto retreat as quickly as it had come. *I hate when they do that. I'll never understand their comings and goings.*

Before John had too long to brew in his frustration, Maria entered the stateroom and interrupted him.

"*¡Hola! ¿Tienes hambre?* Are you ready for dinner?" Maria, preparing John for his time in Spain, began speaking to him increasingly in Spanish.

"Sure. I was writing, but…"

"I'm sorry. Did I interrupt you?"

"No—not at all. It stopped before you arrived. I got a cryptic message at the end...and then nothing. They do that every now and then. I don't like it—it makes me feel like they know something is coming, but don't want to tell me about it. Look. What do you think?"

Maria read the last few lines and then responded. "You're right. It sounds...symbolic. It does almost feel like a warning, but then again, they aren't telling you to run away from it—quite the opposite—so it mustn't be bad. They wouldn't let something hurt you, would they?"

John opened his mouth to reply, but then hesitated. Maria's question touched on something he had never thought before. *Would they let something bad happen to me?*—he asked himself. And yet, 'bad' things had happened to him in the past, **they** just never saw it that way. Some time later, they would help him better understand it all.

John pulled himself out of his thoughts and said, "You know, I'm glad we have two weeks before we arrive in Spain. I think I'm tired and a little cranky. I can't think straight any longer. Let's go eat."

Sept – Sette – Siete – Sieben

T he next two days, John spent much of his time on the lookout. He knew they had to pass through the Strait of *Bonifacio* and he didn't want to miss it. Luckily, they sailed between the islands of Sardinia and Corsica in the middle of the day.

As they approached, John thought back to the year before. He and Felizio were just getting to know each other then and had spent many a day at sea sharing stories.

He then thought back further. His mind drifted all the way back to the Middle Eastern village where his spiritual journey had begun. For the first time in months, he thought about the Magician and the High Priestess, Sara and the Emperor—his first spiritual family. *I wonder if Sara and the Emperor have started building a family of their own...*

John nostalgically watched the islands float by, realizing that the year before, when he traveled in the opposite direction, he was doing the same thing. It was almost as if the feelings of nostalgia were related to that particular location somehow. And, just as before, in exiting the strait, John's focus shifted from nostalgia to anticipation.

The year before, John was looking forward to seeing Italy for the first time. He was, of course, also excited to meet Felizio's family. Now, he was once again approaching a new land, however, this time, he didn't expect to meet Maria's son or sister and he wasn't in pursuit of anyone or anything.

Between then and now, John had sought after Johannes and had found him. The fears he had harbored were not realized, but his greater hopes weren't realized either.

"So what are my hopes and fears now?" he wondered.

John had offered to go to Spain with Maria simply because it felt like the right thing to do. Since then, he hadn't thought about it that much...at least not what the trip meant for him personally. He thus, in that moment of reflection, decided to begin meditating again, and to think about what he hoped to experience in Spain.

However, before John had an opportunity to put his intention into practice, he found himself with more idle time than he had wanted. A light drizzle had created slippery conditions, and John, distracted by thoughts of the past and the future, wasn't being careful. A misplaced step caused him to tumble down a flight of stairs. He twisted his ankle, which kept him off of his feet for the remainder of the trip.

John's physical condition naturally affected his emotions, however, instead of being frustrated, he found his hours alone cathartic. He drifted further into himself and even when Maria was present, the two didn't connect they way they had been.

Maria felt the distance that moved in between them. It was clear to her that John was preparing himself for their inevitable separation. With the end of their journey just days away, so was the end of their time together. She gave him his space, but didn't let him drift too far away while they still had time to enjoy. And yet, she too needed to prepare herself for all that loomed before her. Once she reached her homeland, there would be much to do.

Sept – Sette – Siete – Sieben

J ohn's ankle healed within a few days, which was timely. Their ship made its approach into Barcelona, which was a sight to behold. Soon John would be on his feet, hiking her hills and strolling her streets.

Although Maria had opted to remain in the room to finish her preparation, John did not want to miss the event. He squeezed in along the crowded railing to catch the display. The morning air was chilly, but the skies were clear. The sun rising up behind them reflected off of windows creating the appearance of torchlights littered throughout the city.

As soon as the ship came to rest against the wharf, the crowd began to thin; the panoramic view was now mostly obscured. John decided to stay a bit longer and watched the dockworkers below. They secured the ship and then began unloading crates from the bowels of the hull.

One worker, more handsome than the others, caught John's interest. His strength was evident. John watched with awe as the man effortlessly tossed large bags of rice from a crate to a cart. When the man stopped for a moment to wipe his brow, he looked up at the ship and noticed John staring down at him. Despite the distance, John could tell that the man's eyes were as dark as his hair. The man held eye contact for a moment, which caused John to wonder what he was thinking. He then returned to his laboring.

John could have easily spent more time watching the handsome man and the others work, but he too had responsibilities to attend to. Their journey was complete, and like it or not, it was time to leave the ship.

John made his way to the stateroom, navigating a flurry of activity. Men were collecting passengers' luggage for disembarkation, and the passengers themselves traversed the hallways en route to terra firma.

Silently, John and Maria allowed themselves to be swept up in the tide that carried them ashore. Only when they reached the passenger terminal did the pandemonium dissipate. The dreaded moment was now upon them. All that remained was goodbye.

Maria looked down at John's leg to stall a bit longer. "You seem to be just about back to normal," she said to him. "How does your ankle feel?"

"I don't think I'm ready to play soccer just yet, but it doesn't hurt any longer. And not a day too soon since I'll be doing plenty of walking from this point on, I suspect."

"Well, **do** take it easy," Maria implored. "There is plenty to see in Barcelona, but you don't have to do it all in one day. If your ankle gets sore or swollen, rest it! OK?"

"OK."

"Promise?"

"I promise. After all, I no longer have a beautiful Spanish woman to take care of me. Maria, thank you. I really appreciate everything you've done for me."

"Oh John—thank **you**! I don't know how I would have fared without you. I'm going to miss you, you know." With that, Maria threw her arms around him and hugged him firmly. They both took a deep breath and relaxed into each other's arms.

To keep from shedding tears, John thought of nothing but the energy between them. It had been there from the very beginning. He remembered feeling it those first days in Cairo. And although it didn't exactly make sense to him, it was nice. An invisible cord connected them—and the separation of time and distance would not change that; he was sure of it.

Sept – Sette – Siete – Sieben

I t took John most of the day to find an inn that was both comfortable and within his budget. Once he got settled, he decided to take a break and try his hand with some writing.

Deep Introspection

Good day! I am Kuthumi and before we burrow further into the realm of seven, we wish to bring your attention to the all of the numbers that came before. The two, the four, and the six are even, stable, and balanced. Four specifically means stability. With two, note that partnerships and oppositions are often long lasting. And the harmony of six does thankfully last a while.

The odd numbers imply motion. At three, we have creation, and thus the direction is outward. With five, unexpected change is brought on from the outside, askew and often orthogonal. At seven, we now have movement that is decidedly inward. Whatever may be happening on the surface, the underlying objective is for you to look deep within yourself for the answers.

When you consider the Journey of the Fool, one through four represents linear growth; however, it is the five that initiates the process of evolution. Watch how geometry illustrates this. At the five, we encountered our first star: the five-pointed figure called the pentagram. With six, we showed you the six-pointed Star of David. And now at seven, we show you the seven-pointed star that is a symbol associated with the Akashic Records. Notice that there is a more basic seven-pointed star within it.

Look closely at the basic stars having five, six, and seven spires respectively:

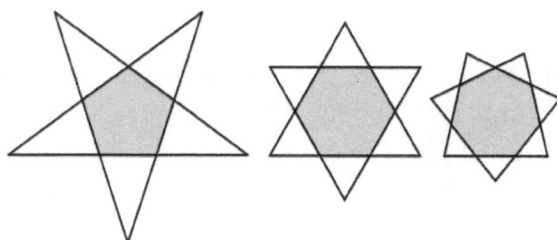

In each case, the center of the star is a polygon. Within the pentagram is the pentagon; at the center of the Star of David is a hexagon; and inside the seven-pointed star is a heptagon. This pattern continues infinitum; no matter how many spires a star may have, deep within it is a polygon with the same number of sides.

At the five, Neptune suggested that you strive for movement from the pentagram to the pentagon in order to roll with the changes that are brought upon you. Now you see that in order to do so, you must move **inward**. That is the lesson of the seven. The winds of change inspired movement, but it is only through the deep introspection of the seven that you can hope to complete the transformation. And yet, the seven is not the end of the journey either, merely a more significant beginning.

Chakra Number Seven

The seventh chakra is what is known as the **Crown Chakra** and is the last of the well-known energy centers. It is said to be your connection to heaven **above**: to God, Goddess, and All-That-Is—to Source, Spirit, the Universe, and THE ONE. As humans in third density, you view this connection as **up**, yet what seven is here to tell you is that the truer direction for this connection is **in**.

Do you recall when Metatron invited you to look for a fourth dimension of space? He asked you to look around you and then asserted that you couldn't find it out there. That is because the fourth dimension reaches **in**, and exists within each cell, within each molecule, within each atom.

Ra told you that THE ONE is all there is, and everything is of THE ONE. Well, this is how it is all banded together. At the center of every piece of All-That-Is is a link to every other piece. By going in, you are able to reach everything you desire. You can find answers to all of your questions; you can contact everyone you know; you can receive love from all sources; and you can draw to you every experience that you desire. It is all right there inside of you!

In reaching seven, the specific two-dimensional figures becomes less the point. From five onward, we simply have stars and the polygons hidden within them. In reaching seven, the shapes become increasingly difficult to distinguish. Soon our stars begin to resemble the sun and the polygons begin to approximate a true and perfect circle.

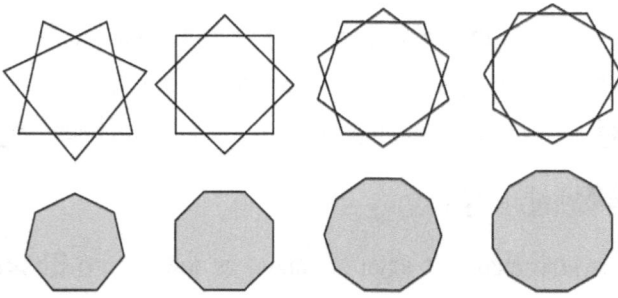

Notice, in fact, that in Astrology, the symbol for the sun **is** a circle. That is because, given enough spires, the inner polygon and the outer star become the same, thus the inside is revealed on the outside. A star with infinite spires and a polygon with infinite sides both become simply a circle with infinite points along its circumference. Isn't **that** enlightening!

Seventh Density

In reaching seven, we also arrive at the last density we can speak of. With seventh density, one's individual expression is virtually extinguished within the infinite and abundant light of THE ONE. The boundary between self and other no longer exists. Inside and outside have no meaning and nothing is seen or experienced as a separate piece of All-That-Is. Even we, within sixth density, can hardly ponder what lies ahead.

It continues to be a challenge within our vast perspective to truly imagine what complete unity is like.

Know that you are forever connected to all else. You are never alone. All that you need and desire is within your grasp; simply remember to reach inward to find it.

Sept – Sette – Siete – Sieben

With renewed energy, John ventured out to investigate Barcelona's robust nightlife. The *pensión* he now called home was situated just blocks from *La Rambla*, one of the main pedestrian boulevards that sliced through the central part of the city. Maria had listed it among the many places for him to explore. Under the circumstances, it was a fine place to start. Without any specific destination intended, John wandered up and down the promenade, taking frequent breaks to people watch.

It didn't take John long to figure out that the Spanish people were beautiful. The average height was shorter than in other places he'd been, but that didn't in any way distract from the beauty. And the Barcelonians were quite chic. Clothing shops could be found on every block and just about everyone was dressed up. It was the weekend and many were out on the town for a romantic date.

In thinking of romance, John was happy to see that public affection was as common in Barcelona as it was in parts of Italy. One could easily pick out the couples because they were always touching or holding hands. In some cases, a woman looped her arm through her beau's. In other cases, a man draped his arm over his date's shoulder.

At that hour, nearly all of the shops were closed. The multitude of cafés, bars, and eateries, however, were bustling. Although it was late in the evening, most were just sitting down for dinner, while others enjoyed a glass of wine. *The weather in Barcelona must be pleasant year round*—John reasoned, because many of the establishments had outside seating, often right in the middle of the esplanade.

After an hour of meandering, John was content to call it a night. Instead of returning to the inn the way he had come, he decided to walk along a parallel street—a decision he quickly questioned. *La Rambla* was heavily populated and well lit, but the streets to either side were neither. Despite feeling nervous, John stuck to his chosen path since he didn't have far to go.

And then he heard music in the distance and grew curious.

John was already traveling in the direction of the music, but once he reached the next intersection, he had to turn down an alley to reach its source. Halfway down the block, the music poured out from a pub.

John stepped into the doorway and paused. The front room was well lit, but was thinly populated. A counter ran along one wall and had a mirror behind it, making the room look bigger than it was. The bartender attended to his space while no one required his attention. In the far corner, a pair of men sat in a booth, smoking cigars while passionately discussing sports and politics. In another booth, a couple had just finished arguing; the man reached across the table, but the woman, with her arms crossed, shunned him.

John entered the room, but no one took notice of him. He could tell the music was coming from just beyond an arched doorway to the right. He crossed the room, walked through the archway, then down a narrow hall toward the back. At the end of the hall, a wooden door was propped open, giving access to the back patio. John poked his head through and took in the scene.

The outside patio was easily twice as large as the front room. Directly ahead and under the canopy of a large tree, a trio of men played music with drums and stringed instruments. To John's left and along the back of the building was a long wooden table. A bucket of ice was situated at one end; a large jug and glasses sat at the other end. A man, similar to the one inside, tended the makeshift bar.

John approached the table and the bartender raised his chin as if to say, "What'll you have?" John asked him, "What's good?" and without another word exchanged, was poured a glass of sangria from the jug.

With drink in hand, John took inventory of the empty seats

strewn about. The tables nearest the stage were unoccupied, but he didn't want to be that close to the music. He also didn't want to sit right next to anyone else. He ultimately decided to sit at a table along the back wall of the building. That spot afforded a panoramic view of the entire area.

As John sipped his sangria, he noticed that nearly all of the patrons were paired up save him and one other man. He then noticed that the lone man appeared to be looking in his direction.

The man eyed John a bit longer, then slowly turned to face the musicians. This afforded John the opportunity to observe him further. The stranger was handsome in that more or less typical Spanish way. But unlike the majority, he was tall and well built. John guessed he was a workman or possibly an athlete given his broad shoulders and muscled arms. Rather than sit, the man stood next to his table and leaned against a fence, his elbows resting on the top rail, his boot braced against the bottom rail. His body language exuded both confidence and ease simultaneously.

Perhaps sensing John's attention, the man turned back toward him and made direct eye contact. He then smiled in the slightest way.

John couldn't fully interpret the expression and diverted his eyes self-consciously. However, curiosity pulled at him and when he looked back in the man's direction, he saw that the man was still staring at him, and more intensely than before. The half smile returned and then the man nodded subtly as a greeting.

Well, at least he's being friendly—John thought. Not really knowing what to do, John nodded back—less subtly—and then turned to watch the musicians, again feeling self-conscious. He could see the man out of the corner of his eye and could tell that the man continued to watch him.

A few minutes later, the man walked over to the bar and ordered another beer. He then moved over to the doorway and leaned against the inside of the frame. From there, he too had a view of the entire area, but was nearly out of John's periphery. John now had to turn conspicuously to look at him. Again, curiosity got the best of him. When he finally did look at the handsome stranger directly, he found that the man had been watching him all along.

The man half-smiled briefly, then took a seat at the table that split the distance between them. He turned back toward the stage and intermittently drank his beverage.

Although John was unfamiliar with the game that ensued, instinct took over and his heart began to beat a little faster.

The man finished his beer, looked directly into John's eyes, gestured with his head for John to follow, and then stood up. Without waiting for a reaction, he walked through the door and headed into the building.

John panicked. *Am I supposed to just follow him? Is that what he meant? Maybe he just wants to talk inside?*

John's mind raced, and then he considered that maybe discretion was just the way it was between men in Barcelona. So he calmed his fears and decided to go inside. He walked down the hallway and paused in the archway. He scanned the front room, but the man was not there. He hadn't just come inside; he left altogether. *Now what do I do?*

John's curiosity egged him on. He walked through the pub and out the front door. At first he didn't see anyone, but after looking up and down the alley a couple of times, he spotted the man leaning against the wall of the adjacent building.

The man didn't look in John's direction, but once he was sure that John caught sight of him, he turned and started down the alley.

I guess he wants me to follow him. John then questioned how far he would go along with the charade without a word exchanged between them.

The man's pace was neither fast nor slow. He wanted John to follow, but didn't seem to want him to catch up. So John matched his pace and remained a number of steps behind. When the man reached the next street, he disappeared behind the corner.

John resisted the urge to run. A part of him didn't want to lose the man, but another questioned whether he should take the opportunity to head back to the hotel. He simply kept walking. When he reached the corner, he expected to see the man up ahead, but the man wasn't in sight.

John scratched his head. He looked across the way and then down the street, but saw no one. Then a subtle movement caught his attention and he could make out the tall stranger standing in the shadows, leaning against the building. This time the man looked at John directly.

John walked toward the man, except a little slower. He needed time to decide what to do before ending up at the mysterious man's side. Again instinct took over and John found himself walking past the man, and then aping his stance adjacent to him. Instead of making eye contact, John simply looked straight ahead, taking his turn at playing coy.

This pleased the man and for the first time, his half smile turned into a full grin. *"¿Cómo te llamas?"* he asked.

With the silence broken, the game changed. John turned toward the man and acted more himself. *"Me llamo* John."

The man did not introduce himself. *"¿De dónde vienes?"* he asked.

John hesitated, uncertain how to respond—not because he didn't understand the question, but because he wasn't sure of the answer. He didn't want to say he was from Egypt, where he last came from, and yet it didn't feel right or even safe for him to mention the Middle East. Plus he really didn't have enough vocabulary in Spanish to explain anything complex. He decided to ignore the question and simply said, *"Llegué a Barcelona hoy. Disculpame. Puedo hablar solomente un poco español."*

"¿Verdad? Venga conmigo. Mi casa está cerca."

"¿Qué quieres hacer?" John asked.

"Sabes," the man said with a half smile.

I know?—John asked himself—*I know…what?*

The man invited John to his home, assuming that John understood his intentions.

John did not. He was nervous, but the man's rare handsomeness cast a spell over him. The game was completely foreign to him, yet somehow the anonymity of being in a new city seemed to make a difference. John thus nodded to the man and followed him to his apartment.

The man unlocked and opened the door, gestured for John to enter, and then shut and locked the door behind them. There was just enough light filtering in through the windows for John to see into the flat. The man walked around the room lighting candles and then sat on the far end of the sofa. John just stood near the door and watched until the man gestured him over by patting the cushion next to him.

John sat, but left a bit of space between them. He was so out of his element that his mind did not attempt to figure out what would happen next. He then thought to ask the man, *"¿Hablas otras idiomas? ¿Frances, italiano, o inglés?"*

"Disculpa. No." came the man's reply.

Now what?—John thought to himself, understanding that he was nearly at the end of what he could communicate in Spanish.

The man reached over, grabbed John's hand, and moved it over to his own leg. He then said in English, "Strong like bull!" He followed that with, *"Soy torero,"* and then again in English, "I am strong like bull because I fight bulls." The man obviously knew a phrase or two in English.

John hardly noticed. His attention was now solely on the muscular thigh beneath his fingers.

The man had at first let go of John's arm, but unsatisfied with the lack of movement, he grabbed John's wrist again and moved it up and down his thigh to encourage John's participation. John was apprehensive, but also excited and thus explored the muscles in the man's leg as he was implored to do. Satisfied with John's compliance, the man moved his hand over to John's opposite shoulder and pulled him closer.

Although nervous, John enjoyed the exploration. The musculature of this man was incomparable to both Johannes and Rafi, the only men he had ever shared affection with. In fact, John had never been near a man this muscular before, let alone **touching** one. He was wonderstruck and the man could tell.

The bullfighter stretched and flexed his leg to further impress John with his muscles. Meanwhile, he kept his arm around John and massaged his shoulder firmly. He then placed his arm on the back of the sofa and slid down into a more reclined and relaxed position. Finally, he placed both hands behind his neck and rested his head upon them.

John moved his gaze from the man's leg to his face. The man's eyes were closed and a smug variation of his half-smile returned as if he could see that John was looking at him. John guessed it was all right and continued his exploration. He placed his left hand where his right hand had been, and moved his right hand up to the man's shoulder. John's left hand simply held onto the man's thigh while his right hand explored the muscles in the man's arm.

In response, the Spaniard slid down a bit further and pressed his leg against John. The whole time, he kept his eyes closed.

The situation enticed John in an entirely different way than his first two encounters. Rafi wooed John. He was considerate, romantic, and attentive. He was the first man to show interest in John and John had been flattered. If they had had more time together, who knows what would have come of it.

Then, of course, there was Johannes. Superficially, this exploration resembled that intoxicated night with Johannes, but the similarity ended there. Rather than the pent up desire that had urged him on that night, this time John was being prodded forward and nearly beyond his own comfort. Johannes was receptive at best, yet this man clearly desired John's touch…and would settle for nothing less.

Not surprisingly, John hadn't been thinking about any of this. He simply focused on what he was doing. He thought to himself that he could run his hands over this man's impressive muscles all night long.

The man passively accepted John's innocent explorations a bit longer before reaching for John's lower hand. The man grabbed John's wrist and slowly moved John's hand up his thigh until it rested upon another part of his body he was proud of.

John froze. His breathing stopped and his eyes widened. He was now completely intimidated, as this man was clearly big and firm **everywhere**. John did not move his hand, rather the man moved it for him, forcibly pressing it into himself.

The man's grip on John's wrist was disconcerting. It nearly hurt. And any time John stopped complying, the man squeezed his hand more firmly. So John did as he was non-verbally instructed, hoping things would go no further. He didn't know how far the man wanted to go and as of yet, was not allowing John to back down. John tried a couple of times to pull his hand away, but each time, the man's strong grip prevented him from doing so.

John considered pulling his hand away more vigorously, but

177

then the man let go of him. At first, John was unsure what to do and didn't move. His right hand was still on the man's arm, but now his left hand hovered above the man's lap.

Before John acted further, the Spaniard swiftly unbuttoned his trousers. John thought he was just simply making room for himself, but grew nervous again when the man freed himself completely. Then, before John imagined what would happen next, the man's left hand found John's neck and he wrapped his fingers around it.

John's body tensed, but the man did nothing. He remained motionless and quiet. This caused John to relax slightly, but as soon as the man felt this, his grip on John's neck tightened and he pulled John down into his lap.

John didn't know what to do. He, of course, knew what the man **wanted** him to do, but he was scared and didn't want to. It was clear by the man's grip that he was not going to let John go easily.

And then John's imagination reeled. *If I don't comply, he might get angry. He could beat me terribly...or do something even worse!*

John was clearly no match for the man's strength and with the door locked, running away was not an option either. So in that moment, John made the only choice he felt he could make and gave the man what he wanted.

John wasn't skilled, but got clear signals from the man as to what he liked and what he didn't like. And John did his best. He was not motivated by any desire of his own. He simply wanted to finish the job so he could be free of it, hoping and praying the man wanted nothing more.

Luckily for John, the bullfighter was not difficult to please. His orgasm came quickly, albeit lasting longer than John expected. Once it subsided, the Spanish man let go of John's neck and relaxed completely—smug and basking in the satiated feeling of release.

John, afraid to move, looked back and forth between the door and the man. He questioned whether he was free or if the 'game' would somehow continue. He stood and cautiously made his way over to the door, repeatedly checking to see if the man reacted. In the dark, it took John a moment to figure out the lock, but when he heard the familiar click, he knew he had gotten it open.

As John opened the door, the *torero* spoke for the first time in minutes. *"Gracias, amigo,"* he said. *"¡Bienvenido a Barcelona!"* He then chuckled, but did not move.

John dashed out the door and shut it behind him. Without looking to see if he was followed, he sprinted all the way back to his hotel without stopping.

Sept – Sette – Siete – Sieben

S ofia sat at her bistro table and stared at the garden just beyond the kitchen window. Steam wafted off of the freshly prepared *caffè latte* in front of her. For the past few months, Sofia's coffee would often grow cold while she scurried around the apartment getting ready for her day. Now that it was mid-spring, she woke early enough to relax and wait for it to cool.

As Sofia tested the warmth of her cup, Johannes' face popped into her mind. She sipped cautiously and pictured the man she loved more this morning than the night before. And then her mind wandered into thoughts of the future. It was similar to those days, late in the school year, when she entertained fantasies of her future house, husband, and children. These days, her aspirations were clearer than ever.

She took another sip and Johannes' face flash into her mind again, almost abruptly, interrupting the scene she was pondering. Suddenly, she felt a twinge of trepidation. *I hope nothing has happened!*

Before Sofia's imagination could conjure up possibilities, a knock at the door startled her into the present. Her hands clutched her cup protectively while she sat, frozen, trying to figure out who it could be at that hour. Her mind raced for what felt like minutes until a louder wrap forced her into action. Absently, she took another sip, almost as if she wouldn't be allowed to finish her coffee, then headed toward the door.

Sofia cracked the door until she saw Johannes standing there, then opened it completely. Instead of throwing her arms around him as she had done the last time he stood there, a subtle panic washed over her. She simply knew that for him to show up at that hour meant something must have occurred.

"Johannes, what's wrong?" she asked him. "What has happened?"

"I...I don't know, Sofia. Something is not right, but I don't know what it is."

"Well come in. Let's talk about it inside."

Sofia grabbed Johannes' hand and led him straight to the kitchen. In an Italian home, the most serious conversations happened there. She placed Johannes in her seat facing the window and lit the stove to make him some tea. From behind, she could see the tension in his posture. As she waited for the water to boil, she placed her hands on his shoulders and gently massaged them to console him. A moment later the pot whistled. She prepared and presented his tea and then sat next to him, placing her hand in his.

Johannes had been staring out of the window. He remained mute for he didn't really know what to say. Her touch drew his attention out of his thoughts. He sighed deeply and then spoke. "I...I'm not sure what's going on, Sofia."

"Well, start by telling me what you **do** know."

"That's just it. I know nothing...absolutely nothing. At the same time, I just know something is not right. I can feel it...as dread, or maybe grief. I am sure someone has been hurt. I'm afraid it could be my father."

"Has something like this ever happened to you before? I mean, have you ever had a feeling like this before?"

"No! You know me: if I can't see it and touch it, it doesn't exist...at least I've been accused of being like that. Now John—he was the intuitive one. This sort of thing happened to him all of the time. He was also a worrier...but not me. For me to feel this way must mean that something has gone wrong. Don't you think?"

"When did this...feeling...start?"

"In the middle of the night. It woke me out of a dream. The foreboding had nothing to do with the dream. Now that I think about it, I can actually remember it coming in from...

somewhere…and interrupting it. I'm sorry, this…this must sound absurd."

"Johannes. No. This is not absurd. I can feel that this is real. In fact, before you knocked at the door, I sensed something myself. What are you going to do?"

"There is only one thing I **can** do. I must return to Germany. I cannot wait for correspondence to travel back and forth. I cannot feel this way and go on as if nothing has happened. I must go to Klaus to make sure he is OK. Besides, if something **has** happened to him, I might have to take care of him…or help with things in the company. I'll have to make sure that all of his responsibilities are allotted to the appropriate men. Sofia, I came here this morning because I needed to see you, to hold your hands and look into your eyes, but I also came here to tell you that I must leave at once! I…I just **have to!**"

Sept – Sette – Siete – Sieben

T he next day, John woke with sunlight on his face. The bright luminary had already climbed above the adjacent buildings. Warm air flowed in through the open window and brought with it the clamor from down below. It was a typical day in the city.

John rolled over and looked at the clock on the wall. Instead of focusing on the dial, he saw only the pendulum swinging back and forth. He stared for what felt like minutes before catching himself. *I mustn't be awake yet*—he conceded.

He turned away from the clock and studied his clothes, which had been draped over the back of the chair. He recalled neither taking them off nor placing them there. Pieces of the night before flickered in his mind, but only those moments early in the evening when he had been alone. None of the memories felt real—rather more akin to the surreal images of a dream. John glanced out of the window expecting to see the open ocean, but then remembered that he was no longer on a ship.

John kicked off the covers and inspected his ankle. It was still a bit swollen and discolored. It was sore to the touch, but when he swung his feet over the edge of the bed and stood, he felt no pain. A memory from two years earlier flashed through his mind. It had been his first week in Asia and he had sprained his ankle then too. It was, in fact the same one. "I guess you are my Achilles ankle," he said to his leg, and then laughed audibly at the literal analogy.

He glanced at the pool of sunlight now shining on the floor and questioned the time. He then remembered that he had already looked at the clock, but did not registered what it displayed. He looked at it again and thought—*One o'clock? How can it be that late?* As if assuring him, his stomach growled.

John grabbed his pants from the night before. Without bringing them to his face, he could smell smoke wafting off of them. He thus hung them on the windowsill and rummaged through his bag for a fresh pair. Details of the night before continued to elude him. Instead, he thought of the various eateries he had seen in the early evening.

"Where should I go for lunch?" he asked himself, but as soon as he voiced the question, he forgot all about it as if he had never thought it in the first place. He tied his shoes with his mind as blank as when he had stared at the pendulum of the clock.

Another image appeared in his mind—this one from much earlier in the day. On his way from the ship, he had spotted signs pointing the way to the main post office and had made a mental note to visit it at a more convenient time. "Well, there's no time like the present," he avowed. He left the room without his jacket, but only thought about it when he exited the building. It was warm enough anyway, he reasoned, and thus continued on.

A part of John knew where to go; the rest of him simply watched the scenery drift by. The architecture was reminiscent of other European cities he had visited, but he did not make comparisons. He simply observed and walked.

Unlike the evening before, John didn't notice the people wandering up and down the boulevard. He avoided all eye contact and focused only on the street signs, which were written in both Spanish and Catalan. Without translating, he knew what most of them said. Written Spanish resembled Italian and Catalan was similar to French. Between the two languages, he could understand them easily.

Without trying too hard, John found one of the signs he had seen the day before. Having completely forgotten about his hunger, he headed directly to the main post office.

S ofia had consoled Johannes as best she could. She held his hand, caressed his arm, and let him ramble as much as he needed. When his exasperations were finally exhausted, she placed her arms around him and held him firmly. She then guided him into his business mindset so they could begin devising a plan.

The first undertaking, in her mind, was to convince Johannes to give the world time to catch up to him. She reminded him that he was in Italy, a country not known for efficient transportation. In her opinion, it would be better for him to setup proper conveyance than simply choose the first thing available. And in order for her to help him discern what would be best, she needed to consult with acquaintances, who were more knowledgeable.

Sofia then compiled a list of tasks for Johannes to work on himself. She had to keep him busy lest he stress himself further, which would cause her more consternation.

"Once Johannes leaves," she said to herself, "he'll have to take care of himself. After that, I'll have to put all of my concerns into the hands of God."

T he main post office was located on *Plaça d'Antonio López* near the northern end of the port and about half of a dozen blocks from *La Rambla*. John, in his semi-lucid state, walked the streets as if he had lived there for years. When he reached the post office, he paused to admire the architecture before ascending the main steps—the only characteristic thing he'd done all morning.

The midday rush had ended, so there were no lines at any of the windows. John found a teller unoccupied and walked up to him. Without hesitating, he addressed the clerk in a mix of French and Spanish. The teller, used to that sort of thing, understood John's request. He asked John to give him a moment while he checked in the back. When the clerk returned, he handed John an envelope addressed to him.

"Would you like stamps for—say—postcards?" the postal worker added, knowing that John was a visitor.

John shook his head in response and walked away from the window as absent as when he arrived.

One observing John with no understanding of his inner workings would surely question the entire morning. John was certainly not acting like himself. Nonetheless, those who **were** observing John knew. They saw the colors of his aura and they listened in on his subconscious thoughts. They understood that a large part of John had retreated deep inside a shell of protection. John had created that shell after his parents died and had fortified it over time. It was the only place he could hide from his abusive uncle. It did not save his body from the beatings, but it did protect his heart.

A few years after John ran away, the fortress remained intact but appeared unused. Yet both Ra and Seth knew better. They were aware of a small piece of John that remained locked inside. They couldn't set that part of John free; he had to.

In the words of Ra:

If one opens all chakras except the fourth, though his experiences may amaze and stimulate, they will never satisfy. You see, a man cannot find fulfillment save with an open heart. Wisdom, knowledge, expression, love, power, pleasure, and existence will feel like naught without an open heart with which to receive it.

But John needed to **know** that something was missing in order to go looking for it. He could feel love and joy, but nothing compared to his potential.

The challenge of opening up a wounded heart is the pain one will surely feel at the start.

In those moments when the younger John was beaten, he poured his hurt into cups and stored them on a shelf in his heart. He was too afraid to feel and express the agony while it was happening. Over time, quite a bit of that dark liquid accumulated. In fact, John's pain now filled the moat around his castle. The moat and the fortress together helped keep people out—abusers and lovers alike. They also kept a piece of John locked inside. Like Ra had said once before, a bastion of protection simultaneously serves as a prison cell. It cannot be one without being the other. In sheltering a colt for safekeeping, he was locking away a stallion that longed to be free.

The observers knew that from time to time, John's consciousness visited the small castle. He would walk around it and inspect its integrity, but he rarely entered it. In those visits, a part of him simply wanted to be sure that his fortress was still impenetrable should he ever need it again. A threat had never lasted long enough to cause him to recoil into its protection…at least until now.

And so, on this day, for the first time in a decade, the larger part of John's consciousness retracted into the stronghold he so meticulously constructed in his youth. And yet, within observable reality, he operated with ease and grace.

John left the post office and wandered. He felt no inclination to open the letter; he simply placed it in his back pocket and forgot all about it. Like a chore scratched off of the top of an agenda, he considered it done and moved on to the next endeavor, which entailed finding food to quell the returning pangs of hunger.

Sept – Sette – Siete – Sieben

J ohannes. I have a suggestion." The idea had just occurred to Sofia. "Why don't you compose letters to your father, the Queen, and maybe a significant colleague or two? If you send them today, they just might get to Germany before you do. In this way your arrival will be anticipated."

"Sofia. That's an excellent idea. Thank you. I'll do that now."

"Good. I will pass by the post office later and drop them off for you. By the time I return, I'll have your travel itinerary arranged..." *...and hopefully you will not have to depart until tomorrow, so I can at least savor one last night before you leave.*

When Sofia considered Johannes' extended absence, panic welled up inside of her. Before it became all-consuming, she pulled herself out of it. *It is not the right time to think about me. Johannes needs me now. I'll just have to wait until later...and then cry on Mama's shoulder.*

Sept – Sette – Siete – Sieben

H ours later, John returned to the hotel. He entered the room and placed a bag of groceries on the desk. One by one, he pulled items out of the bag. He had eaten before arriving at the hotel, and was therefore not temped by any of the food items he had purchased.

John kicked off his shoes without untying them and pulled off his shirt. Just before taking off his trousers, he checked his pockets and found the letter he had all but forgotten. He placed it on the nightstand, finished undressing, and then picked it up and sat on the bed. The window adjacent to the bed, which he had left open from the morning, now let in a soft, cool breeze. The street below was quieter than it had been and just enough light filtered in for him to read the letter.

Caro Gianni;

What a treat to have received your letter. It is unfortunate that your boat did not stop in Napoli; we would have loved to see you. Perhaps next time the gods will be kinder.

Tutto è bene qui. Paolo is enjoying his studies and has

already made an impression with his *professori*. He's excited for summer break because he was selected for an internship at an architectural firm in *Napoli*. He is beside himself with anticipation as you can well imagine.

Carina and Lorita are sitting next to me, staring—both telling me at the same time to send their regards. Having done this, I am now sending them off to find more constructive things to do than watch me write.

Ah, *pace*. You now get to hear from me—your dear friend Felizio who misses you. Did you think about last year when you sailed through the Strait of Bonifacio? All the memories…it is so nice to have you among them.

My boy, I am happy to hear that your trip to Egypt was fruitful. From the tone of your letter, it sounds as if it wasn't the worst it could have been, even if not the best either. I look forward to hearing of the many details when I see you.

Before I go on, there is family news that I am hesitant to share with you. The workings of the Universe are mysterious indeed. After much discussion, Lorita and I have decided to tell you the news and let you draw your own conclusions. I am reticent still, but here goes.

My dear Lorita has a cousin Tomasina, who lives in beautiful *Venezia*. Tomasina's daughter, Sofia, is about your age. Coincidental as it may be, Lorita received a letter from Tomasina the very same day we received yours, and in it was news of Sofia's engagement. The stranger part is this: Sofia is engaged to a man named Johannes from Germany, who only recently moved to *Venezia* after having *spent some time in Egypt. He is setting up a new office for his father's company.*

My boy, on the off chance this is the very same Johannes, we thought you would want to know. You have friends in high places that you can ask, no?

We hope this finds you well and enjoying Barcelona. You must promise to visit us soon, va bene? You are loved and missed.

Un abbraccio forte,

Felizio et al

John stared at the single sheet of paper in his hands. Tears streamed down his face and sobs tore through his body. He let go of the letter, wrapped his arms around his chest, and fell to the floor and curled up into a ball. The sobbing took hold of him stronger still—a burning pain in his stomach followed a piercing pain in his heart. As the walls of his protective fortress crumbled, John felt as if his chest and abdomen were ripped open. He cried unlike any time since that night, two weeks after his parents died, when his drunken uncle first beat him.

Over the next two hours, sobs washed over him in waves. In between, he was quiet and still. His inner child sought cover, but found none. The protective fortress lay in ruins; there was nowhere left to hide.

A part of John now realized that he had been holding on to the illusion that Johannes was not lost to him. Things had gone well between them, and so he remained hopeful. Johannes never said anything definite, and John had always been too afraid to ask. And thus the illusion lived on. But now the fantasy was over; the last of John's hopes crushed and strewn on the floor. Johannes was to be married. He had moved on and was happy. *And look at me*—John thought to himself. *I'm all alone in a strange city, no further along in life than when I met him.* With that, he began to sob all over again.

The next time calmness came, John picked himself off of the floor and climbed into bed. He rolled onto his side, covered himself with the blanket, and clutched the pillow next to him. Images flashed in his mind of the days he and Johannes had spent together in Egypt. Intermittently, that one night in Germany was among them. The memory of the physical experience with Johannes morphed into what had transpired the night before and then John felt those meaty fingers firmly gripping his neck. Both experiences now held deep pain for him, and the awareness of this reverberated in his soul.

Self-deprecating thoughts berated him. He questioning whether this was the most his life would ever amount to: no man ever to return his love. He could steal brief moments of intimacy, but would then be required to pay for them. Surely what happened the night before was the karmic cost of wanting and pursuing a man that did not want him back…

A final wave of sobs commenced and drained the last of John's energy from his body. The compassionate solace of sleep came for him and carried him away from the pain and suffering…if only for a while.

Sept – Sette – Siete – Sieben

S ofia watched Johannes' coach depart and felt the separation widen by the second. The concern she experienced over the past 24 hours was nothing compared to the separation anxiety she now felt. She tried to talk herself out of it by assuring herself that he would return, but she could not be certain.

What if something has happened to his father? What if his new responsibilities require him to stay in Germany indefinitely? Will he call on me? Will he come for me? Or will he forget about all about me?

The fear grew too strong for Sofia to bear and tears came in response. Johannes was now out of sight and would be beyond the borders of Italy in a day or two. Without hesitation, Sofia headed directly to her mother's house. She managed to contain herself for the duration of the walk, but as soon as Tomasina opened the door, she fell into her mother's arms and sobbed.

Tomasina held her daughter for a few minutes, then guided Sofia into the house and onto the sofa. Once Sofia's sobs subsided, Tomasina used her sleeve to dry her daughter's eyes. She started to speak, but then paused, suspecting the worst. She took a deep breath and started again.

"Baby Girl, what has happened? Is it something with Johannes? Is he OK?"

"Mama, he's gone. He's on his way back to Germany."

"Oh dear. What happened? Things were going so well. Did the two of you have an argument?"

"No, nothing like that. In fact, after these past two days, I love him more than ever! But I'm afraid I'll never see him again. What if he never comes back?"

"Baby Girl, don't talk like that. So, things are still good between you, right? Tell me what's happened. Tell me about the last two days."

Sofia wiped her eyes and blew her nose on a tissue her mother had handed her. Once she regained her composure, she went on.

"Johannes woke the other night with an acute feeling of dread. He thinks something may have happened to his father. First thing yesterday morning, he came knocking at my door, threatening to leave that very second! Thankfully I was able to calm him. I convinced him to give us some time to arrange his travel. I just saw him off this evening."

"So, does he know that something has happened? I'm not sure I understand."

"He doesn't know anything for sure. It's just a feeling. But he's never experienced that before. Mama, you know how it is when you just **know** that something is not right?"

"Yes, I do."

"It's like that. I felt it too…just before he knocked on my door. I really do think something has happened, but what if it keeps him in Germany? Mama, this hurts. I don't want to be away from him."

"And he didn't ask you to go with him?" As soon as Tomasina said this, she realized that she had made a grave mistake. Sofia looked at her with a terrified expression, and then broke down, sobbing even harder than before.

Tomasina wrapped her arms around her daughter. She felt awful —worse than the moment before. She so regretted what she had said. She felt sorry for her daughter's pain and at the same time struggled to hold off her own fears. Thoughts of the family curse floated by intermittently.

And then her maternal instincts took over. She had to be strong for her daughter. With resolve, she brushed aside all of her own fears. She patted Sofia's shoulder as if telling her to sit tight, then retreated to Sofia's old bedroom to get it ready for use. As she turned down the sheets and fluffed the pillows, she thought of all of the women in her family. She looked at the pictures on the wall of her mother and grandmother and said, as if to them, "It might take us a while to get through this, but we **will** get through this. We always do."

Sept – Sette – Siete – Sieben

M aria sat on the bed next to her son and wrapped her arms around his shoulders. Nearly as many tears streamed down her face as his. The news of his father's death had hit Carlos more brutally than she had expected. The wailing he displayed was authentic and pure, but was oh so difficult to behold. Now that the worst had passed, she could breathe again.

Maria felt Carlos' grief empathically. And although hers was different than his, she could no longer hold any of it back. Her tears flowed freely and would likely for days to come.

"*Dios mios*, comfort us in our pain," she prayed.

Sept – Sette – Siete – Sieben

L orita quickly sat herself down on the sofa. All was quiet in the house. Her son and her daughter were in their respective bedrooms, and Feliciano was in his office. She listened carefully, but sensed nothing wrong with any of them. She placed one hand on her heart to calm the racing and the other on her forehead to lessen the dizziness.

"What in the heavens just happened?" she asked the ominous silence in the room.

Sept – Sette – Siete – Sieben

T he Queen of Heidelberg stood on her balcony and looked out over the city she ruled. A screech overhead caught her attention. She turned just in time to see the hawk soar by almost within reach.

The hawk turned its head to keep an eye on her, screeched a second time, and then continued toward the horizon and the rising moon.

The Queen solemnly accepted the omen and contemplated what the message might be. *Hawks see great distances, measured in miles and days*—she thought to herself. *I am sure news will arrive soon enough. I had better prepare.*

Sept – Sette – Siete – Sieben

S ara panted as instructed, comforted only by the firm grip of her husband.

The Emperor smiled at her, brimming with anticipation of the birth of his first child. He then winced and grimaced once again when Sara's agonizing screams returned in response to the next contraction. They were getting quite close now and in those moments they were active, he felt more helplessness than he could ever remember.

The severity of the pain Sara felt grew poignant enough to throw her consciousness temporarily out of her body. As if within a dream she saw John's face and the pained expression upon it. In that moment, she forgot all about of her own pain and looked questioningly into his eyes.

She then felt the presence of three women, which caused her to lose sight of John. The younger women stood close while the eldest looked on from a distance. Sara was simultaneously awed by their beauty and calmed by their loving expression. When she opened her mouth to question them, the one nearest brought a finger to her lips.

The next contraction quickly brought Sara back into her body, but things had certainly changed. Although her labor grew stronger, her tolerance of the pain was now so much greater than it had been.

Sept – Sette – Siete – Sieben

In the middle of the night, John became aware of Seth's presence. This did not wake him, but did cause him to become lucid within his dreaming.

"How are you doing, kiddo?" Seth asked compassionately.

John shrugged his shoulders. A single tear escaped his eye and flowed down his cheek.

"I'm sorry you feel bad. You are going to get through this…I promise. I know there is nothing I can say to make you feel better right now, but I do want to share something with you to help you understand."

Seth put an arm around John's shoulder and guided him down a footpath through a lush and serene forest.

"First, let's start with a little math," Seth began. "As you will recall, five is about change…and is often unexpected. The stimulus it brings induces a shift. It is the start of a new journey…away from the four…onward and upward. Seven, you've been told, is about transformation. It is not simply growth, as in one-two-three-four; it is evolution. What you probably haven't yet figured out is that the five and the seven are related.

"In English, we spell seven: s-e-v-e-n. Notice that right in the middle of it is V—the Roman numeral five. The rest of the letters spell 'seen'. When the significance of a five is **seen**, seven is the result; thus seemingly random change can bring on a journey of transformation. Seven is, in fact, the higher octave of five. In other words, it is five to a higher power. Watch:

> Roman numeral seven is written: VII
> It contains Roman numerals five and two: V, II
> This illustrates that five plus two equals seven: 5+2=7
> Five squared is written as five to the power of two: 5^2
> Five squared equals twenty-five: $5^2=25$
> Twenty-five reduces to seven: 25/7

Up ahead, the density of trees thinned. John could see the glistening blue ocean beyond them.

"John, do you feel ashamed about what happened with the Spanish man?"

The shame John felt was so strong, he could not respond. He could not look at Seth either.

Observing John's reaction, Seth pulled him closer and hugged him more firmly.

"John, shame—if I dare say—is the greatest disease to mankind. Through shame, men and women hurt and harm themselves first and others next. Shame is too easily passed on from one to another, and it is very hard to cure. For example, let's compare hate and shame. When one hates another, that energy leaves the first, but must **travel** to reach the other. The second can shield or evade the hate. Healers and energy workers can intervene, and of course, spirit guides like me can aid and assist. In the case of shame, the hatred is directed inward. It never leaves the one. The hater and hated are the same. We, in the spirit realm, cannot temper the damage because we cannot interfere with a person's free will.

"Although we cannot prevent you from hurting yourself, we **can** help you see what is happening. We can guide you from the five to the seven and eventually the eight and the nine. We can shower you with light and love to the greatest of our ability. And we can tell you, over and over again, that we are right here with you...always."

The trail came to an end at the edge of a cliff. A sandy beach could be seen below them and nothing but waves all the way to the horizon lay before them.

John took a deep breath. There was heaviness in his lungs, but the ocean air felt refreshing.

The two sat, dangling their feet over the ledge. For hours, they silently watched the sun cross the sky and then dip below the horizon. Before it was completely dark, John was once again sound asleep…and Seth continued to hold him.

Sept – Sette – Siete – Sieben

T he next morning, Sofia woke feeling a bit more neutral. She had to admit to herself that sleeping in her old bed and having her mother in the next room were comforting to her. Since there really was no reason to rush into the office with Johannes away, she allowed herself to lie there and entertain the thoughts that rolled through her mind.

Just as a particularly strange notion occurred to her, a gentle knock at the door pulled her away from it.

"Sofia dear. Are you awake?"

"Yes, Mama. Come in."

Tomasina entered the room quietly and sat on the bed next to her daughter. She brush hair away from her daughter's face and stroked her cheek lightly.

"How are you doing this morning?" she asked. "Were you able to sleep?"

"It was a little hard at first, but once I fell asleep, I stayed asleep until about 30 minutes ago. I think the past two days really wore me out in a way I hadn't noticed."

"I'm sure they did. How were things left with work? Do you still need to go into the office?"

"Johannes did leave me a list of things to do, but there's no rush. I'm sure it will be a couple of weeks before I hear from him, and what he left for me shouldn't take but a week to accomplish. I might go in later, or just wait until tomorrow."

"I'm glad to hear that, dear. You've been through a lot. Some rest can only help."

"Mama? Can I ask you a question?"

"Yes, Baby Girl. You can ask me anything!"

"Do you think it's a little odd that Johannes never talks about old girlfriends?"

Tomasina was taken aback by the question. "Well...talking too much about old girlfriends is definitely a bad sign. He doesn't mention any at all?"

"Well, I know he's had girlfriends back in Germany because it came up once. I can't quite remember, but I think I had asked. Other than that one time, he's never mentioned anything more."

"I'm sure it's nothing."

"But—well—there is something else."

"Yes?"

"There is...**one** person he talks about...intermittently. And it's always with..."

"What, my dear?"

"Well—I can't quite put my finger on it, but whenever he does, he seems—I don't know—almost nostalgic."

"Is it someone from his childhood?"

"No. That's just it. It's the one he was traveling with in Egypt before coming to Italy."

"A lifelong friend?"

"No. They only met maybe a year ago or so—in Nepal. Johannes hired him and they traveled to Germany together. Then they were in Egypt. I get the impression that there was some... time...in between, but Johannes never seemed to want to talk about the details. Any time I ask, he changes the subject."

"So far nothing seems too strange. So why do you ask?"

"Well, I just remembered something that happened yesterday, just before he left. You see, he typically refers to his father by his first name: Klaus. I thought that was odd at first, but then I figured it was a German thing. Anyway, yesterday, he's talking about Klaus and then at one point slipped."

"How so?"

"This is what he said: 'I have to make sure he is OK. Once I

196

arrive and am assured of his health and safety, I'll contact you.' And then as he was hugging me goodbye, he said, 'I really hope nothing bad has happened to **John**, but if something has, I need to take care of him.' That's a little odd; don't you think, especially considering the circumstance?"

Tomasina tilted her head pensively, considering all she'd been told.

"Mama? You don't think I have a reason to be concerned, do you?"

Tomasina hugged her daughter and continued to ponder the situation. She remained quiet, not wanting to make things worse in any way.

8 – *Eight* – VIII

Huit – Otto – Ocho – Acht

For eight days, John did not leave his room except to get food, and he only needed to do that every third day. When in the room, he was usually in bed. Early in the week he intermittently cried uncontrollably; otherwise, his eyes remained dry in the daytime and his pillow got soaked each night before he fell asleep.

After a while, John stopped revisiting the struggles he had endured; he stopped seeing the future as a continuation of his painful past; and he stopped wasting his days feeling sorry for himself. Soon, he began having moments thinking nothing at all— not the clean, clear stillness of meditation, rather the void left behind when all of the tears have been shed. Within that abyss was held an absence of pain, an absence of sorrow, and an absence of pity. It just was. **He** just was. Misfortunes had transpired, and yet he survived them all.

He had wallowed in his misery enough and now allowed a transition to take place. Before John realized any of this consciously, he experienced it. He approached new perspectives without seeking them; he simply happened upon them.

Huit – Otto – Ocho – Acht

Sofia created a new routine for herself, which made being away from Johannes easier. Most of the work that needed to be done could be carried out anywhere; she continued to go into the office nevertheless. This way she created a consistency between her past with Johannes, her present without him, and her desired future with him back.

During those moments she missed him the most, she climbed the stairs to his apartment and talked to his plants. They talked back to her, but she didn't hear them.

Huit – Otto – Ocho – Acht

B efore Johannes reached the vicinity of Heidelberg, he encountered a band of the Queen's men. The lead guard immediately addressed him: "Herr Müller, we have come to escort you home. Your arrival has been anticipated."

"The Queen received my letter then?" Johannes asked.

In response, the guard looked at Johannes with no discernible expression and said nothing.

"Is my father well? Have you heard word of him?"

The guard again looked at Johannes blankly, but then said, "Herr Müller is in Spain. He is not due to return for a few weeks."

"So, there has been no word from him since he's been away?" Johannes asked.

"It is my understanding, Sir, that the Queen receives correspondence regularly."

"Hmm, I wonder what is going on..." Johannes mumbled to himself.

"Sorry, Sir?" the guard asked.

"Oh, it's nothing. Shall we continue on to Heidelberg then?"

Huit – Otto – Ocho – Acht

O ne morning, an oversized butterfly flew in through John's window. The wings were completely black and as large as John's palms. Having never seen anything quite like it, John keenly observed the insect, but with disbelief. "Are you real?" he asked the visitor.

The insect fluttered above his desk, and then flew high above his bed. It zigzagged over to the nightstand, and then circled the

200

room. Ultimately, it came to rest on John's satchel. It pulled in its wings and became perfectly still.

John turned away from the butterfly and glanced out the window. For the first time, he noticed that he could see a bit of the Mediterranean between buildings. He returned his gaze to the satchel and half expected the butterfly to be gone, but it was still there.

As he stared, he became aware of all of the sound flowing into the room. It was as if he'd just regained hearing after a week of deafness. Before, noise had been as absent as joy; now it sought all of his attention.

As if in response to his mental chatter, the butterfly slowly opened and shut its wings—once and then twice.

John tilted his head, intrigued. He contemplated whether the butterfly was a sentient being, rather than merely an insect, and then wondered what it thought of the condition of his life.

Again the visitor responded by slowly flapping its wings twice.

And then the butterfly did something unusual; it lifted up and then dropped into the opening of his bag. It couldn't fit all the way in, but made the appearance of rummaging through it. At times, all John could see were the tips of its wings, fluttering as it bobbed up and down. Finally, as if satisfied, it glided over to the desk and landed on the stack of paper there. It opened and closed its wings twice, then remained still. A moment later, it lifted up and darted through the window.

John jumped up from the bed and stuck his head outside. He looked all around until he found the subtle black fluttering heading straight for the sea. Once out of sight, he watched a bit longer and then pulled his head back into the room.

His awareness moved to his body and the stiffness he felt within it. The lack of activity for a full week had taken a toll on him. He stretched, yawned, and declared to himself that a walk was in order. In his mind, he pictured following the butterfly's path to the ocean. He could feel the sun on his face, which egged him on. He grabbed clothes randomly, dressed, and shot out the door.

From the hotel, John crisscrossed his way through the city until he reached the harbor and then trekked north. A short while later, he encountered a beach. He kicked off his shoes and massaged his feet in the warm sand. The constant breeze was salty and just a bit cool, but refreshingly so. After a brief rest, he strolled further north along the beach, carrying his shoes in his hands. He walked as far as he could go before encountering a jetty. He put his shoes back on, climbed up onto the jetty, and followed it out toward the water.

At the end of the jetty, John sat and scanned the horizon. It occurred to him that Barcelona was the furthest west he had ever been. This meant that the entirety of his life was lived in the direction he now faced. Symbolically, his complete history lay before him with nothing to show for it except waves on the sea.

And yet, after examining the scene more closely, he **could** see ships heading into Barcelona and away. He thought back to what it was like aboard one of those ships and then declared out loud, "I don't ever have to go back."

When he made the statement, 'back' meant 'back east'—to any of the lands in that direction. Hearing his own words, it occurred to him that 'back' also meant 'back in time'—to any of the painful memories of his past. He decided that he didn't have to go back there either and the realization caused a shiver to run through him.

A moment later, the sound of a splash caught John's attention; it was a seal. He watched with delight as the animal approached the end of the jetty. When nearest, the seal gazed at John briefly, then propelled itself further along and floated away.

John returned to the mulling of his mind and then realized something more. The seal 'passed' the end of the jetty, but that was a moment ago and thus in the 'past'. *Two words, spelled differently yet pronounced the same, one denoting space and the other time.*

He thought of a third example. *A 'wait' uses up a chunk of time, and a 'weight' takes up a chunk of space. Again, a pair of words pronounced the same, one concerning time and the other space.*

"Intriguing!" he said out loud. "We experience time and space differently, and yet refer to them nearly the same! We move 'forward' in time and 'forward' in space, and in so doing encounter what's just 'ahead'. And all that we've 'passed' moves into our 'past', and is then 'behind' us. Within our thoughts there is no difference between time and space. Memories are simply accessed as images and thoughts."

As the epiphany continued to unfold, John surmised that his thoughts were limited by neither time nor space; it only **felt** that way. In his mind he could visit any place he knew of or recall any experience he could remember. And he could imagine places he would visit or fantasize about experiences yet to come.

"And if my mind is not limited by time and space, then why should my future be doomed to repeat what happened in the past? Maybe there is hope for me. Maybe things can change. Maybe it is possible for me to find love and happiness after all."

In arriving at that resolution, John decided that he **could** go back to the places he had been, while, at the same time, experiencing them **anew**.

Huit – Otto – Ocho – Acht

When the work started to run out, Sofia decided that she needed something else to occupy her time. In a flash of insight, she opted on an eight-month old kitten. She told her friends it was a gift for Johannes for when he returned. She told everyone that the cat needed a home. The truth was **she** needed something to touch and cuddle and love while she waited for her betrothed to come home.

Huit – Otto – Ocho – Acht

Johannes' initial conversation with the Queen was brief and did not console him. He paced each day, waiting to hear word from his father. *Surely I did not imagine those ill feelings*—he thought to himself. *Do I even feel them anymore? Was this whole trip for naught?*

Johannes decided a longer conversation with the Queen was in order and set out to arrange it.

Huit – Otto – Ocho – Acht

The Many Sides of Eight

Consider the following:

One is nothing more than one: $1+0=1$.

Two is always and simply one and one: $1+1=2$.

Creating is as simple as one, two, three: $1+2=3$.

Four is constructed from one and three: $1+3=4$, and most stable when formed via two and two: $2+2=4$.

Adding one to four turns it into five: $1+4=5$, but two and three also make five: $2+3=5$.

Six is the next step beyond five: $1+5=6$; is two balanced atop four: $2+4=6$; and is most harmoniously created when three joins three: $3+3=6$.

One hidden within six makes seven: $1+6=7$. Two iterations past five is seven: $2+5=7$. When three and four intermingle, they again produce seven: $3+4=7$.

In reaching eight, we now have four combinations: $1+7=8$, $2+6=8$, $3+5=8$, and $4+4=8$. Eight can be created in more ways than the numbers before it.

In its most basic meaning, eight is the **quantum leap** also known as a **leap of faith**. As you may have already guessed, there are a number of ways to achieve this.

The Octahedron

An eight created from four and four is best illustrated by the octahedron, which has four triangular faces pointing up and four more pointing down. And yet, the octahedron also relates to the two and the six as it forms two four-sided pyramids, which resemble the ones in Egypt, and has six vertices in total.

Now look at this. When you place an octahedron inside of a perfectly sized cube, each vertex touches the center of a face on the cube!

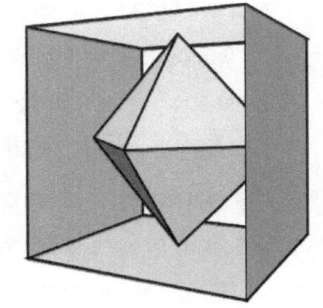

From this you can see that the hexahedron and the octahedron are related. They are Twin Flames—two manifestations with one shared purpose. In fact both of these shapes are found in nature. Dig into the earth for crystals, and you will find some that resemble cubes and others that resemble octahedrons. And yet these are just two of many crystalline configurations. Let us visit the other combinations that form eight.

The Five and the Three

We now wish to take some time to discuss a variation of eight that you find yourself in. To begin, fetch your Tarot deck and turn over the top card. Tell us what you find there.

The top card is the Eight of Cups.

Describe it to us.

In the foreground, eight cups are stacked together. Further back can be seen a man or a woman walking away from them. In the distance, we see a rocky horizon and an old moon suspended in the sky.

Do you remember what this card means?

I believe it is about letting go.

Exactly. The old moon indicates the end of a cycle—in this case, one that did not seemingly produce desired results.

Notice that when we write the number eight in Roman notation: VIII, it is always five and three. The artist reflects this subtly within the stacks—five cups on the left and three on the right. We needn't remind you of the challenges that five brings. And yet, through the process of letting go, one is able to **create** anew, and that is the three.

Let us for a moment compare romantic love to an orange—its juice deliciously sweet, its pulp appetizing. The color is bright, vibrant, cheerful, and alive. There's no better way to start your day. The pleasure of romantic love is the single most desired experience on your planet. More than half of all humans crave it, while the others pray that it will not leave their side.

Yet, when your relationships do not go the way you had hoped, is it not like getting a lemon instead of an orange? What happens when you squeeze a lemon? Will not even the slightest sip of its juice cause you to grimace? Hasn't all of the sweetness been replaced by the sour?

So one might say that the five is when life gave you a lemon. Pray as you might, it will never turn orange. Does this mean that you are destined to never experience an orange? Does it mean that the orange is **forbidden fruit**?

No! It simply means that this time around, you picked a lemon—and a lemon is a lemon and will never be an orange. Your experience is what it is and it only takes one taste to know the difference between the lemon and the orange.

We say choose again! Pick another fruit and taste again. But know that picking from the **same tree** will not correct your mistake. Lemons grow on lemon trees. If the love that you seek is likened to an orange, then you must find a tree that can produce it. To find one, you must leave the lemon tree and look for another.

And thus comes the Eight of Cups. It is the moment you stop wishing the lemon tree would produce oranges. You've tried enough times and picked enough fruit. You have now accepted the lemon tree for what it is; by letting it go you are able to move on.

Take note of the words we use. We didn't say to let it '**be**'. We said to let it '**go**'. When you let something go, you let it **pass** you by. You let it **move** into your **past**. And that's when things begin to flow.

The Journey of the Fool always begins from where you are. It says nothing about how you got there or how long it took you. It matters not whether you traveled the high road or trudged the low road; sped through the direct route or meandered the detour; whether you enjoyed the ride or fretted the whole way. Your journey is from **here** forward, from **now** forward. If it consoles you to think of it this way, consider all that occurred before to be practice and preparation for the journey ahead. The past is nothing but a dream. You have awakened; a new day beckons.

Lemon trees will show up in your life, but you needn't pick from them. Orange trees will show up too! However, if your hands are full of lemons, you will not be able to reach for an orange. Let go of the lemon trees and let go of your lemons. Just because you picked them, doesn't mean you need to carry them ever more. Lighten your load; free your hands; learn from your past and pick with greater care the next time.

And by all means, keep the lemon juice out of your eyes! You have cried enough. Once you see that the fruit you picked is a lemon, look elsewhere.

Huit – Otto – Ocho – Acht

A fter a full week of tears, an afternoon on the beach, an evening of writing, and a sound night of sleep, John picked himself up and moved on. He let go of the fantasy of a relationship with the man he had loved like no other, simply because it was the only choice available to him. In so doing, he admitted to himself that he wasn't losing anything he had to begin with. He walked beside Johannes for a while, had even slept next to him once, but they had never been 'together'. Before John got himself upset for the hundredth time, he pushed the whole subject out of his head.

With renewed intention, he focused on Barcelona. Here he was, more than a week into his stay, and he hadn't seen much of the city yet. When Maria had listed all the places he should visit, he had been ripe with anticipation. He was now ready to start exploring.

After John dressed, but before he left the room, he sat for a moment to consider a plan. He didn't have a map, and didn't know in which direction any of the sights were. The few times he had ventured out, he'd always traveled along *La Rambla*, but then it occurred to him that he had only taken the promenade southeast toward the water. He therefore decided to start there again, but this time head in the opposite direction.

In following his plan, John reached *Plaça Catalunya*, except without encountering anything particularly of interest. He thus decided to cross through the center of the plaza and continue onward. He found himself walking along *Passeig de Gràcia* and soon reached the intersection with *Gran Via de les Corts Catalanes*. Both streets were wide, tree-lined, and congested. The intersection was designed as a roundabout. A fountain sat in the center. Activity entered and exited the eddy in all directions; despite the potential for chaos, it weaved and flowed gracefully.

John watched the circular motion for a while and then peered down the boulevards in each direction. The city climbed a gradual slope to the northwest, which was the only thing that piqued his curiosity. He couldn't quite tell if it was a hill or the beginning of a mountain. He thus allowed the intrigue to propel him forward.

Three blocks later, something unusual caught his attention; it was the oddest building he'd ever seen. It looked as if it were made of wax and melting in the midday sun. The second floor windows resembled cave openings and the columns looked like those that form when stalactites and stalagmites meet. John was so entranced by the design he at first failed to notice the crowd forming around him. Once he became aware of them, he realized they were inspecting the same building he was. From what he could tell, everyone seemed to have a strong opinion one way or the other.

John began to listen in on the conversations around him and soon focused on one in particular. The man read from a book—out loud and in French. The building, John learned, was called *Casa Batlló* and was designed by an architect named *Antoni Gaudí*. The Frenchman then told his wife about another of *Gaudí's* creations: a building located three blocks further and on the other side of the street. Since John was headed in that direction anyway, he discreetly followed the French couple to see what else he could learn.

Much of the crowd traveled with them. All around him people spoke in different languages, discussing the one architect and his buildings. *This guy's work is quite the attraction around here it seems*—John thought to himself.

As the group ambled up the street, John kept close to the Frenchman and his wife. The next building was called *Casa Milà* and although it was created at about the same time as the other, it was purported to be much larger. John kept searching down the boulevard for it, which proved fruitless due to the trees. Only in reaching the end of the third block was John able to see it.

Casa Milà **was** huge. It extended halfway down the intersecting block. As with the first, its walls undulated like those of a cave. However, this building looked more like a cake coated with icing than one fashioned from wax.

John moved away from the crowd. He crossed *Passeig de Gràcia* to get a more panoramic view. From that side of the street, he could see sections of the building that jutted up above the roofline. These convinced him that a wedding cake was indeed *Gaudí's* inspiration.

Satisfied with the view from afar, John crossed both streets and rejoined the crowd. He sought out the French couple once more and reached them just as they entered the structure.

The inside of the building was as interesting as the outside.

Unexpectedly, an atrium opened up to the sky. The effect of being completely surrounded by *Gaudí's* unique artistry transported John to another time and place—strictly within his imagination. In a dreamlike state, he gazed all around...until someone bumped into him.

"Je suis désolé," apologized the Frenchman.

"De rien," responded John automatically. This, of course, caught the man's attention.

"Monsieur, parlez-vous français?" the man asked.

"Oui. Je peux parler français," replied John.

Unable to place John's accent, the man said, "Are you **from** France?"

"No," John explained, "but my father was. Where are you from?"

"We live in Lyon. Do you know of it?" This time, the man's wife spoke.

"Yes. I was there about a year and a half ago. It's a lovely city."

"Thank you. We think so too." The Frenchman said. "This is my wife, Micheline and my name is Bernard."

"Enchanté. My name is John."

"So, John, what do you think of *Casa Milà*?" Micheline asked.

"Intriguing! From the outside, it looks like a wedding cake."

Micheline smiled proudly. "Thank you, John. That's what I said, but Bernard simply dismissed it because...well...you just met us, but we are here on our honeymoon. We've been married for only eight days now!" It was apparent from the way Micheline said this that she was happy.

"Congratulations! It's good to know that these past eight days have been good for **someone**."

"Have you not been enjoying your time here in Barcelona? That is—assuming you have been here the whole time."

"Actually, I think it was just about eight days ago that I arrived —maybe nine. No, Barcelona is a wonderful city. I just received some...difficult news when I arrived."

"Family?" she inquired.

"Micheline!" her husband interjected, "Leave the man alone. We don't even know him."

"Oh, that's fine," John assured them. "You are free to ask. Maybe we'll discuss it another time, though. Let's talk about **your** time here—you know—happy stuff."

"Well, John, we only arrived yesterday," Micheline went on. "We worked our way over from France gradually, stopping a few times along the way. Bernard is a bit fascinated with *Antoni Gaudí*, so we're spending the day visiting his creations. Surely you're doing the same—you and everyone else!" she said, gesturing around them.

"To be honest, I stumbled upon the tour accidentally. And to make a confession, I've been eavesdropping on your husband. I've never heard of *Gaudí* before." John suddenly felt a bit self-conscious.

"Well, man, if you're going to listen in, you might as well come along. We are newly married, but we've been together for a long time." As Bernard said this, he looked at his wife half expecting a reaction, but got none.

John looked from one to the other and said, "I would love to join you then. Where are you heading next?"

"From here, we're going to visit the temple of *L a Sagrada Familia* and then on to *Parc Guell*—up there." The three had exited the building and Bernard pointed toward the hill that John had noticed earlier. "We'll walk to the church, but then take a coach to the park; it's a bit too far to walk and, of course, it's all up hill."

Micheline jumped in and said, "We're going to eat first. Are you hungry?"

As soon as Micheline said this, John felt pangs in his stomach. "Actually," he said, "I haven't eaten yet today. Lunch sounds delightful!"

The three walked up the street until they found a restaurant that looked appetizing. Throughout the meal, they spoke casually, getting to know each other better.

"John. It sounds like you've had a fascinating life—what—with all the people you've met and the places you've been. Barcelona is the furthest from home that **I've** ever been."

Hearing Micheline's perspective, John had to admit that his life **did** sound fascinating. "I've only been traveling for the past two years. I've loved nearly every place I've been, but it is sometimes a little difficult getting acclimated after each move."

Micheline noticed a subtle shift in John's mood and figured that he was thinking about his difficulties once again. She reach over, patted his hand, and said, "I can imagine you've seen and experienced a lot in a short amount of time."

Huit – Otto – Ocho – Acht

S ofia's cat was as black as the night and had the most adorable yellow-green eyes. He stared at her with the same look he gave her that first day, which had pierced straight through to the center of her heart.

Recalling that moment, Sofia said to him, "So this is what they call love at first sight!" She then lifted him up from her lap and kissed both his cheeks and the top of his head.

Notte, as she called him, squirmed, trying to escape. He was irresistibly lovable…and impossibly willful.

"I think a cat is worse than a man!" Sofia said to him. "Am I training you, or are you training me?" She kissed him on the nose and he playfully swatted at her in response.

Notte stared at her with his large, soulful eyes; he tilted his head and meowed. Having distracted her with his charm, he then quickly leapt from her arms.

Sofia had sought after something to occupy her time and her attention. In that regard, Notte had exactly fit the bill. Despite an occasional scratch on her arm, she regretted the decision not even a trace.

Huit – Otto – Ocho – Acht

J ohannes! Please come in." The Queen stepped aside and welcomed him into her quarters.

"Your Majesty, I'm sorry to bother you." Despite the fact that

Johannes' father had been married to the Queen for more than a decade, Johannes still felt uncomfortable in her presence.

"Johannes, you are never a bother. Please, unburden yourself. Take a seat and speak to me of your concerns."

"As you know, I came to Heidelberg to check on my father…" Johannes paused to compose his thoughts.

"Yes. I am aware of this," the Queen said.

"Well…his most recent correspondence has still not arrived! Right?"

"Yes, that is true."

"Aren't you concerned?" Johannes' fret caused him to speak more informally than he had intended.

The Queen did not react to Johannes' emotion. "When Klaus travels abroad, his correspondences are intermittent at best. It is not unusual for weeks to go by between one and the next. I am therefore not concerned in the slightest."

"And…you do not sense that anything is amiss?" he asked her.

The Queen eyed Johannes queerly. His questioning was completely uncharacteristic of him. "Johannes, historically, you and I have not discussed personal endeavors. However, given your question, I **am** going to share something with you that is a bit more intimate. Days before you arrived, I received an omen that caught my attention. After some contemplation, I discerned it was actually about **you**!"

"**Me**?!?" Johannes asked excitedly.

"Yes. It came to me that you were upset. Your arrival confirmed my suspicions. It had never occurred to me that something might have happened to Klaus until you first spoke of it. Since, I have gained no further insight. As you know, it is not in my nature to worry."

"Nor mine!" Johannes said this a tad louder and higher in pitch than he intended. "That's what makes this so unusual."

"All right, let us, for a moment, assume something is awry. By way of exploration, tell me what has been happening in your life."

Johannes hesitated, but then shared a brief synopsis of the events that transpired since he left Heidelberg the year before right after Oktoberfest.

"So you are to be married!" The Queen was genuinely

surprised. "That is splendid!"

"Yes it is," Johannes said, somewhat unconvincingly.

"I hope you are more excited about it than you seem," the Queen chided him.

"I'm sorry. I am wholeheartedly excited. I love Sofia very much. I am just...distracted by the lack of understanding and this concern."

"Do you **still** feel that something is wrong?"

"I am not sure. As soon as I arrived in Heidelberg, the ominous feeling dissipated. Now I am not sure **what** I'm sensing."

"Give me a moment." The Queen stood and walked over to her door. She motioned for Johannes to follower her out onto the balcony. Silently, she scanned the horizon, admiring the beauty of the city and the forest that surrounded it. Intuitively, she kept watch of Johannes. She looked for clues as to what was going on inside of him: mentally and emotionally. And then a notion developed within her. Johannes, she observed, peered continually in the direction of his apartment, the place he had lived for a number of years. This gave her insight.

"Johannes," she ventured, "maybe getting married is a bigger step than you realize. I do not doubt the sincerity of your feelings, but I question if you have completed your...journey to the altar, as they say. Maybe you have been guided here because there is something left for you to do...or understand."

Johannes considered what the Queen was saying, but nothing came to mind.

"Tell me this," she went on. "You mentioned running into John in Egypt. How did that go?" The Queen treaded cautiously.

"Things between John and I were...fine."

"He was not upset that you abandoned him?"

"I gathered that he **had been** upset before we ran into each other. But he never brought it up while we were together."

"And how did you leave things then?"

Johannes grew quiet as guilt washed over him.

The Queen felt it and exclaimed, "Ah, so you abandoned him again!"

Johannes quickly defended himself. "I...I didn't **abandon** him.

214

I…I left him a note and some money. That's not the same."

"I'm sorry, Johannes. I didn't mean to be accusatory."

"I do feel…bad about it, though. I don't regret leaving; it was time for me to go, but I'm afraid I may have upset him again."

"What could you have done differently?"

"I guess it would have been better if I had talked to him."

The Queen, ever brave, then asked, "Have the two of you ever discussed John's feelings for you?"

Shock showed on Johannes' face. He had no idea that the Queen knew…or anyone else for that matter.

The Queen saw the look on Johannes' face and said, "Johannes, many think that I, as Queen of this city, live a privileged and sheltered life. They believe that I reside in an ivory tower unaware of the workings of life on the ground. I assure you, this is not the case. Be it as it may, John's feelings were evident, from a distance if you asked me. Nevertheless, we had a few discussions before he ventured after you."

"He **told** you?" Again Johannes' voice rose in pitch and volume.

"Not in so many words, no," the Queen responded calmly. "Be clear, I know nothing of what transpired between the two of you. It is none of my business in any case. And I harbor no judgment whatsoever. I merely question if there is something you need to resolve around that chapter in your life."

Johannes looked down as he attempted to absorb her counsel.

"Do you know where John is now?" she asked him.

"No."

"Then you will have to make amends within yourself. If I may ask, how is the communication between you and Sofia? Are you more forthcoming with her?"

"I…" Suddenly, Johannes realized that he had neglected to write to her. He had promised that he would as soon as he arrived. "I was going to say 'yes'", he went on, "but now it occurs to me that I have yet to write to her, assuring her that I arrived safely."

"I am going to say to you the same thing I said to John many moons ago: do not judge yourself harshly. However, before you plod forward unconsciously, maybe you should check in on your responsibilities…to the people who love you."

"Your Highness, thank you for your guidance and direction. I appreciate it."

"You're welcome." After a long pause, the Queen added, "And do say hello to your father when you see him."

The Queen caught Johannes by surprise once more. He hadn't yet decided to go in search of his father, yet she knew that he would. As Johannes sat there, silent and agape, the Queen smiled proudly.

Huit – Otto – Ocho – Acht

J ohn, Micheline, and Bernard finished lunch and resumed their tour.

"So, how far is the temple?" John asked Bernard.

"Maybe eight or nine blocks from here," Bernard replied. "This street, *Carrer de Provença,* will take us straight to it. Once we cross *Avinguda Diagonal*, it'll be six blocks more."

During the walk, conversation waned for the first time since it started. Bernard kept looking at the map and John kept looking for the temple. Micheline simply enjoyed the whole scene.

Because *Carrer de Provença* was narrow and lined with two and three story buildings, they couldn't see the church until they were just more than a block away. In rounding the last corner, there it stood, towering over the city park that lay before it.

As they approached the front of the building, John was struck by how different the temple looked compared to any shrine he had seen anywhere. In some ways, it didn't look real, and most certainly not like a place of worship. Its four spires, visible high above the trees, reminded John of corncobs—after all of the ears had been eaten. Then, a moment later he thought—*hornets' nests… they look like elongated hornets' nests!* Odd as the building was, the more he studied it, the more beautiful it became. Having adjusted to the incongruity, he began to appreciate the intricacy.

From the edge of the park, the three gained an unobstructed view of the entrance. John quickly recognized the molten look present in *Gaudí's* other two buildings. He then saw it differently. Architecturally, the columns supported the weight of the portico, pushing up from below; yet visually they appeared to be pulling it down, as if keeping the church from flying away. Instead of wax, John was reminded of pizza dough.

The trio drew closer and then paused directly in front of the church to admire the intricate detail. Dozens of saintly characters, including Jesus Christ himself, occupied niches above and to either side of the doors. The figurines' style juxtaposed that of the façade. The building undulated with soft curves, while the statues donned hard lines. *Gaudí* took edges away from the areas one would expect them and placed them where one did not expect them. Although surreal, the sculptures were some of the most beautiful John had ever seen.

Bernard placed his hand lightly on John's shoulder to indicate that he and Micheline were heading in. Reluctantly, John followed them. The crowd of tourists was dense and John thought it best for them to stick together. Besides, his curiosity was growing. Somehow he knew he would be surprised a dozen times more inside.

And he wasn't disappointed. However, one surprise he hadn't expectedly was the plethora of scaffolding. While tourists ambled about below, masons continued their work up above.

Seeing John eye the workers, Bernard said, "Do you realize that it will take more than a hundred years to finish this building? It looks done on the outside, but there are additional sections yet to be started. Micheline, we'll just have to come back again and again, maybe on our anniversaries." Bernard, half joking, studied his wife for a reaction.

"I might have to come back myself," John added. "This place is simply bizarre and beautiful at the same time."

John looked around and inspected the details he could see. The ceiling was quite tall and he strained his neck to look at it. He then began to share his thoughts with the others.

"You know what this space makes me think of—the home of a giant spider! Look at those—the round, flower-like stained glass windows. They resemble individual spider webs. And the columns look like gigantic threads, especially the way they attach to the ceiling. Even the coffers look like places spiders would hide."

"Who knows what inspired *Gaudí's* design," Bernard offered.

"The man certainly had an active imagination. Spider webs could easily have been what inspired him with this one."

The three investigated as much of the ground floor of the church as they could, and then ascended a turret that was open to the public. From high above, they were treated to views of the city through the small openings John had noticed from outside.

"That's where we're going next: *Parc Guell*." Bernard once again directed John's attention toward the hill to the west. "It's very different than what we've seen thus far."

"What do you mean?" John asked.

"Just wait. You'll see," was all Bernard offered in response.

Huit – Otto – Ocho – Acht

J ohannes left the Queen's chambers not knowing what to make of her parting statement. Was she telling him to go in search of his father? Did she know what he would decide to do? Or was she simply teasing him? Regardless, he had to write to Sofia at once. He couldn't change how he had handled things with John, but he certainly didn't want to make the same mistakes with Sofia.

Huit – Otto – Ocho – Acht

N otte rested on Sofia's lap and purred in response to her caressing. For the moment, he was content and compliant.

Sofia paused to take a sip of her *caffè latte* and held it pensively. She was deep in thought.

Dissatisfied that the petting had stopped, Notte nudged her hand with his head to ask for more. This caused Sofia to spill coffee on her dress. Given her startled reaction, Notte figured he had done something wrong and leapt from her lap to escape repercussion.

While Sofia dabbed at her clothes, Notte sought entertainment. He investigated the floor around the table, but because Sofia was quite tidy, he didn't find much there. He looked around and pondered his next move. He then caught sight of a subtle stirring. His pupils widened and he lifted his butt into the air. With a single pounce, he captured the object of his interest.

Sofia gave up on the coffee stain and lifted Notte off of the ground. She intended to reprimand him in her loving way, but when she looked at him squarely, she saw that he held something in his mouth.

"Notte, what have you gotten into now?" she asked him.

The young cat beamed at his mama with pride, but was unwilling to give up his loot. However, after excessive insistence, he gifted her his prize. Besides, he was already growing bored of it. He then fled in search of new adventure.

Sofia examined the dark thread Notte dropped in her lap, wondering where he had found it. She hadn't been sewing for weeks and rarely wore black that time of year. However just as she reached for it, it sprung to life. Startled no end, Sofia screamed formidably and jumped up to fetch her broom.

Notte, figuring he was in trouble...**again**...ran for cover. He knew just where to hide.

Scrambling for survival, the spider scurried under the table and out of sight. He too was safe, at least for the time being.

Sofia returned with her broom in hand, but could not find the spider. Before she had an opportunity to search for it, a crash from the other room distracted her.

"Notte!" she yelled across the house. "Where are you and what have you done **now**?"

Huit – Otto – Ocho – Acht

A fter enjoying the view adequately, the three descended the turret and extricated themselves from the crowded church in order to find a vacant coach heading toward the park. The ride, while it lasted, was a welcomed break from walking and climbing. However, since it dropped them off one steep block away from the park, they were back to walking and climbing afterward.

The park above them was terraced along the steep hillside. The lowest section was supported by a substantial retaining wall. From the street below, one could not see other than the tops of the tallest trees.

A staircase cut through the wall and formed the eastern entrance of the park. Along either side, brightly colored designs showed prominently against the whitewashed mortar. The mosaic displays reminded John of the Middle East, even though the patterns were different.

Further into the park, John understood what Bernard had been referring to. "Bernard, you're right," he said. "This is very different. I never would have guessed that this park was designed by *Gaudí*."

And yet, after saying that, John began to see subtle hints. The undulating façades weren't as obvious, yet flat walls and squared off corners were still missing or at least sparse. The childlike appearance, reminiscent of the first two buildings, simply seemed appropriate in a park populated with children.

The three meandered, then found a quiet nook to sit and enjoy the view of the city. From the park, they could see all the way to the Mediterranean. *La Sagrada Familia* conspicuously popped out of the skyline, but so did a number of other buildings. John considered asking Bernard about them, but decided to enjoy the serenity of the moment instead.

The lofty perch and the panoramic view took John back to that day he sat looking out over the city of Lyon, and this he could not keep to himself.

"Bernard, Micheline, I just had a flashback I wanted to share with you. This right here reminds me of when I was in Lyon looking out over the city from the basilica on *Fourvière* hill."

"*La Basilique Notre-Dame de Fourvière,*" Bernard stated. "I love that church! And the view from there **is** amazing! I'm glad our city has had a lasting impression on you."

"Let's just say it was an especially introspective time for me."

"Well, I certainly hope you come visit us in Lyon," Micheline added. "This time you'll get a proper taste of the city as only the natives can show you."

"You know, I just might take you up on that," John warned,

with a smile.

"So, John, how long are you staying in Barcelona?" Bernard asked. "And where are you going after this?"

"Those are two very good questions," John replied. "When I first left Egypt, I hardly thought about what I would do when I got here. I guess I was just thinking about the trip itself. After leaving Rome, I figured that it wouldn't hurt to make a plan, but then I twisted my ankle and forgot all about it. One would think that I would have taken advantage of all of that time lying in bed, but for whatever reason, I didn't."

"Well, I hope you spend more time with us while we're here," Micheline said.

Then Bernard added, "Yeah. In fact, why don't you come with us to the *Monasterio de Montserrat* up in the mountains? It'll take a day to get there and another to get back, so we're planning for four days total. We're leaving the day after tomorrow."

"And tomorrow we'll visit more of the city," Micheline added. "You're welcome to join us then too."

"Well, like I said, I don't have a plan and I really enjoy hanging out with the two of you. Are you sure?" John looked at one and then the other. "You're not going to mind a tagalong?"

"John, like we said, Micheline and I have been together for a long time. We just decided to get married officially. You are welcome to come along—we **want** you to!"

Micheline's face confirmed her agreement.

"OK. You've convinced me," John concluded. "I'm all yours for the next five days!"

Huit – Otto – Ocho – Acht

The Web of Attraction

Kawula my son, I am Anansi and am known by few outside the tribes of West Africa. I am most revered by the Ashanti people of Ghana, a country that lies directly to the south of your present location. Traverse the Strait of Gibraltar and then cross nearly all of West Africa and you will arrive there.

Many a tale has been spun using my name. In spite of this, I am not here to tell you stories. Instead, I wish to convey wisdom—to offer shrewd advice that is not often heeded by the masses.

If you were to happen upon me in my native form, you would likely become overwrought with fear; a spider of human proportion would certainly terrify the bravest of you. Yes, I am the keeper of the arachnids and watch over the spiders and the scorpions alike. Before you cringe with fright, worry not; I will not show myself to you.

Many despise spiders and abhor their webs, expending much effort in their attempts to eradicate both from their homes. They recognize neither the mundane nor the profound value of them. Were it not for spiders, your world would soon become overrun with insects. There are neither enough birds in the sky nor critters in the dirt to keep their swarms in check.

Metatron noted that it is common for mammals to ambulate on four legs. Saturn mentioned the bees and the wasps—two among the many species of insect, which crawl around on six. However, it is only the arachnids that walk on eight. The additional legs help them clamber upon their finest creations. Surely you've seen them glistening in the early morning dew.

When you gaze upon one, what do you see? Is it not resemblant of concentric octagons? When you admired the ornate windows of *La Sagrada Familia*, is this not what you imagined?

222

The point we are making is that the wisdom of the spider is also that of the eight. A spider has eight legs and an octagon has eight sides. An octet contains eight musicians and an octave spans eight notes. The spider and the octagon are related via the web, and the octet and the octave are related through music. But what is the relationship between webs and songs I ask you? Strings! Spiders weave webs with strings of silk and musicians play music with strings of wire. Pluck a string and it vibrates. In fact, it is precisely a vibrating string that tells the spider when dinner has arrived. So the magic of eight is like the knitting of fiber: through skillful weaving beauty manifestations are created.

Spiders spin threads and musicians pluck strings for the sheer pleasure of creating. And yet, each benefits in more ways than that. Through their creating they receive items sought. Spiders don't hunt. They don't search for food. They spin their webs and wait for dinner to come to them! Musicians likewise earn their living doing what they love.

It is melodic vibrations that draw listeners to the symphony and vibrations of **wellbeing** that draw fortune to those seeking grace. To attract what you desire, love it. Sing about it. Create a net of intention and then allow the universe to bring it to you. You need only listen for the subtle resonance that lets you know when the object of your desire has landed in your web.

Use discretion, my boy, and crochet with care. If you knit a web with fear, then what you catch will not be so appetizing. Choosing the right

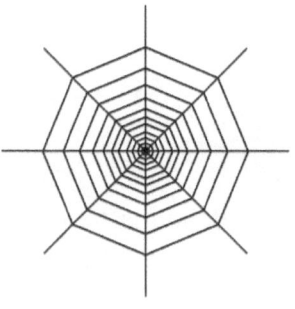

vibrations when spinning a web is just as important as choosing the right notes when playing a song. Pour into it love, excitement, and anticipation. A well-made web will not only catch what you desire, but will allow it to **stick** in your life! A web is a sticky place indeed and for this reason, it is far too easy to get entangled within it. Better to build a proper one from the start than require extricating yourself from an unwanted one down the road. We needn't remind you how difficult it can be to disentangle yourself once you've been caught.

You weave with your wants and lace with your likes; you knit with your knowing and sew with your saying. Thoughts are like threads, yearnings like yarn, darn with your desires for all is entwined with your emotions.

No one asks for misfortune, but many obsess upon it. To the universe, these actions are one and the same. You call forth what you focus on. Listen to the words that emanate from your vocal cords. Karma is nothing more than hearing your own song. If you don't like how it sounds, play a new tune. But do not fret! Even the greatest of bards can sing a bit off key. It is only by listening to the notes projected from the lips that one can perfect his serenading. Your journey is no different. Your day in the limelight awaits you.

Magnificent creatures crawl, and then walk, before they learn to run and then fly. Rest when you need, review when you must, then lift yourself back up, and venture further. You're doing fine. Much better than you know. You hear echoes of old songs, but these are not the tunes you are singing in the here and now. New harmonies will catch up to you. At this point, it is more in the ear than in the voice. Tune in and listen for the sweeter sounds that you now sing and soon the dissonant noise will fade to the background.

Huit – Otto – Ocho – Acht

T he next morning, John met Bernard and Micheline halfway between his hotel and theirs. They spent the day touring, but less purposeful than the day before. Since everyone needed time to prepare for the journey, they made it an early night and then got off to an early start the next morning.

The trip to *Montserrat* was via a full day's ride on a coach shared with others. That day, the concrete jungle warmed up quickly, but soon the buildings thinned and once they started ascending, a cool breeze blew down from above.

The monastery was nestled inside of a narrow pass that cut through the mountains. The further they climbed, the narrower the gap became, and the steeper the road. By mid afternoon they were within sight of the structure, but proceeding more slowly than earlier. John didn't mind because the view up into the mountains was simply spectacular. The monastery itself was designed to blend in with the landscape and resembled the many boulders jutting out from the greenery.

John was filled with anticipation; something he hadn't felt since Rome. Micheline could tell by the look on his face and smiled at him without saying a word. John looked away self-consciously, but then noticed the view down towards the city.

"Wow! Look at that you guys!" he said to them.

"Amazing," Bernard responded. "The monks certainly had the right idea. I could live with a view like this everyday!" He then chuckled to himself at the thought of being a monk.

By the time the coach reached the Monastery gate, the sun had already moved behind the mountaintops above and to the west. The tours of the monastery were done for the day and there was just enough time for them to get settled into their rooms before dinner. The public lodging was a building adjacent to the Monastery and fashioned after it. Even the dining hall was made to resemble the one the monks used. The biggest difference, they were told, was that in the public version, people were allowed to converse openly. The truth was, there were a number more differences left unsaid.

Huit – Otto – Ocho – Acht

I n the morning, John, Micheline, and Bernard ate breakfast in the dinning hall and then made their way over to the monastery. They arrived about thirty minutes before the next tour began and wandered around the reception hall to pass the time. When John's eyes fully adjusted to the darkness, he was struck with recognition.

John turned toward Bernard and said, "Bernal, I think we've been here before."

"What did you call me?" Bernard said, taken aback.

"Bernard..." John replied.

"No you didn't. You said **Bernal**."

"Bernal? I said Bernal?"

"Yeah. Where have you heard that name before?"

John tilted his head. "I don't know. I don't think I know that as a name."

Micheline, only listening up to this point, interjected. "John, the reason Bernard is reacting like this is because he's had a number of dreams where he was called by that name."

"Were you, by chance, a monk in those dreams?" John asked Bernard.

"As a matter of fact, I was. How did you know?"

"As I was saying, I believe we've been here before. I just had a flash—sort of like a dream, sort of like a memory. I am positive you were there...I mean here. We all were, even you Micheline, but you were called Miquel—spelled with a 'q', as in m-i-q-u-e-l."

Micheline did not react in any way John could detect.

Bernard, however, was visibly disturbed. "John, what are you insinuating?"

"Where do I begin? It...um...hadn't come up so I didn't mention it before now. Let's just say that I sometimes have flashes of other times...ancient times. It happened quite a bit when I was in Athens. I kept seeing Greece just before and during a gigantic volcanic eruption, earthquake, and tsunami. It turns out that there is historical evidence that my visions are accurate. Anyway, I just experienced something similar and this time the three of us were here. We **lived** here, as monks—I'm sure of it. And the two of you fell in love then too, but since we were sworn to chastity—and you were both men—it would have been nothing less than scandalous for you to do anything about it!"

Micheline finally spoke. "Well, John, as unimaginable as this sounds, it certainly explains some things." She then looked at Bernard deeply.

"I...I just don't know what to think," Bernard said, averting his eyes from both of them. "I am not religious and I do not believe in reincarnation, so the thought that I lived before...here...as a monk, is simply preposterous." Bernard then returned Micheline's penetrating stare and added, more to her than to John, "but if one **were** to accept reincarnation as a belief, it **would** explain some things."

John knew better than to pry into their personal matters and instead scanned the room trying to recall more details of that lifetime.

The monk, who was leading the next tour, showed up a few minutes later. Anxious guests began asking him questions, but he deferred them to the tour itself. When it looked as if no others were joining them, he gathered everyone around.

The monk started his discourse with an introduction of the Benedictine Order. He spoke in detail about the *Rule of St. Benedict*, which was written by Benedict of *Nursia*. He then gave a brief history as to how the monastery came to be constructed. After that, the monk began the tour in earnest and described various aspects of monastic life as they went along—most of which, he stated, had changed little over the years.

The pace of the tour was relaxed. When they entered a new room, the monk directed everyone's attention to specific details and then allowed ample time for everyone to investigate. John enjoyed this as it enabled him to share his thoughts with the others. It also gave him time to examine more closely the things that drew his attention and which sometimes sparked recollection.

In the first half of the tour, the guide took them through the common areas of the monastery such as the chapel, the reading room, and the great hall—each of which could accommodate the entire community at once. He then directed them down a hallway that led to samples of the monks' quarters. The rooms in this part of the monastery were unoccupied during the tourist season for this specific purpose. The first room they peered into was unfurnished. It was being restored, which exposed some of the architectural features of the building that would be hidden otherwise.

John whispered to the others. "I can see a version of this room as it would have been. There are two beds, but instead of being directly across from each other, they are in opposite corners—one there, and the other there." John pointed as he said this. He described a few more details and then quietly looked around.

Bernard listened with an open mind, but didn't believe that John's vision had anything to do with him.

Micheline, accepting John's belief more readily, tried to visualize it herself. *How does one go about remembering a past life?*—she found herself thinking.

The monk spoke up again and invited the guests to visit rooms further down the hall. Some of the rooms, he mentioned, were setup like those currently occupied, while others were staged to resemble earlier times.

Since the boys began discussing the architecture of the building, Micheline decided to wander down the hall on her own. When she peered into the next room, she was immediately struck by how it was arranged—namely, exactly as John had described. A little excited, she ran back to tell the others.

"Bernard, John, you have to come see this," she said to them.

"What is it?" Bernard asked.

"Just come look."

The boys followed Micheline into the other room and John smiled. The room looked exactly like the one in his vision. Bernard stared silently with his mouth half open.

"So John, is this what you were seeing?" Micheline asked him.

"Yes, exactly. What I didn't mention was that I was seeing **my room**—well—Bernard's and mine. This was my bed; that one was his. You know Bernard, I think we were brothers—literal brothers. The part that doesn't make sense to me though, is that I can now see us as boys. We couldn't have been much older than twelve."

The monk leading the tour passed by catching the last part of John's statement. He wasn't fluent in French, but understood some of what John had said. Speaking to them in English, he explained:

"*Señores*, forgive me, but I overheard a bit of what you were saying. I thought you might want to know that there have been times in the past when young boys were schooled here. Some were reared into the Order, while others were simply trained for choir— in Gregorian chant, for example. So, during those times, boys of age twelve would have been present."

John thanked the monk for his input and was happy to have more aspects of his vision validated. "I bet we were in the choir," he said.

Micheline smiled, enjoying the whole experience, while Bernard furrowed his brow.

At the end of the tour, the monk finished by describing additional features of the monastery worth visiting, such as the museum and the printing press. Micheline mentioned her interest in visiting the museum, and John declared his interest in the press. Since they expected there would be more to see in the museum, they saved that for the next day.

The three exited the monastery and had to squint and shield their eyes from the bright afternoon light. The morning clouds had long since burned off and the sun beat down on them. Bernard looked around and said, "In Spain, you can really tell that the summer solstice is near. There's hardly any shade. Look how high the sun is now."

John looked around but said nothing. Rome and Barcelona were at nearly the same latitude, so the sunlight didn't seem that different to him. He thought back to when he had been further north and recalled how the shadows had been longer. Of course, he was there in the fall and winter, which also made the shadows much longer.

Bernard said nothing more and John's mind drifted until Micheline pointed to the print house up ahead.

The press was set up as a self-guided tour. Signs were posted along the way, explaining the history of the facilities. This printing press, they read, was one of the oldest still in operation. The machines, of course had been updated over time.

At first John was disappointed to see that the machine room was off limits to tourists. He was then excited to learn that they could look down into the room through arched openings from the floor above. The few machines in use created a rhythmic beat that was both soothing and hypnotic.

"I can see why monks would be drawn to this work," John said to the others. "Operating these machines must be like a moving meditation. And since many of them are well read, books have to be a significant part of their lives."

After they completed the self-guided tour, they rounded out the afternoon with a late lunch/early dinner and parted ways. Micheline and Bernard wandered the grounds to enjoy the romantic beauty, while John headed back to his room to get in a little writing. The monastery, the visions, and the press all inspired him in subtly different ways; he didn't want to waste the opportunity. As always, he hoped for something personal as well.

Huit – Otto – Ocho – Acht

Notte! Where are you?" Sofia searched the perimeter of her garden...a second time, but could not find her little boy anywhere. He was not hiding under any of the bushes, she was sure of that now. *But where could he be?*

Sometime earlier, Notte had escaped through the kitchen window. Sofia, while baking, had opened the window to let in some of the cool evening air. It had never occurred to her that he might sneak out. Since she didn't see him leave, she didn't know how long he'd been gone.

"Little Notte! You are going to make your mama fret with worry —it'll be dark soon!"

Sofia tried to peer over the fence that separated her yard from the next, but she was not tall enough. "Hmm, what could I use to prop myself up?" she mumbled to herself as she looked around her for ideas. "I know...I'll use my cleaning bucket." She wasn't upset...yet...but if she didn't find Notte soon, she was going to be.

As she retreated into the kitchen to retrieve her bucket, she echoed a variation of childhood prayer: "Oh St. Anthony, come around, someone's lost and can't be found..."

J ohannes climbed down from the coach to get a better look at the collection of signs. Given the number of men traveling with him, they didn't have to stop often. He, nonetheless, wanted to be sure they were traveling in the right direction.

The signs were written in both French and German, being along the border of the two countries. Johannes looked back and forth between his map and the signs and spoke half to himself and half to his driver: "Lyon is 400 kilometers from here. Montpellier is 300 kilometers further, and the boarder of Spain is 200 kilometers from there. That's 900 kilometers total…funny how the numbers work out, eh?"

Disregarding Johannes' last statement, the driver replied, "It should take us about ten days or so, Sir. We will be taxing our horses, but can swap them out every couple of days. We have a number of places along the way where we can do that. Is that pace agreeable to you?"

"It has to be…not like we can go any faster, eh?" Johannes smiled and tried to get the driver to smile back at him.

"No, Sir. Even that pace is pushing it," the driver said stoically.

Ten days to get to Spain—Johannes thought to himself. *Then what?*

Johannes knew that his father had been destined for Spain, but knew little more. *We must stay alert lest we pass right by him on the way*—he thought with consternation.

But then Johannes reminded himself that he was familiar enough with his father's preferences to know along which roads he would travel and in which towns he would rest. With renewed confidence, he reinstated the journey and looked forward.

The One and the Seven

Good Evening, my brother. I am *San Benedetto da Norcia* and I welcome you to one of the many abbeys erected in accordance to the Benedictine tradition. To begin this evening, please, once again retrieve your deck of Tarot cards and select the bottommost card. Tell us what you find there.

The bottom card is The Star.

And what number, pray tell, is written upon it?

The Star is card number XVII—seventeen.

Given what you have learned about numerology thus far, what number does seventeen reduce to?

Eight.

Exactly. Earlier you were shown the significance of an eight created from the five and the three; now you will learn another way to reach the graces of eight. In fact, the most powerful combination for eight is via the one and the seven. It symbolizes the path of the druid and the shaman, the priest and the priestess, the monk and the hermit. It is through 17/8 that a neophyte becomes a master.

Tell us what you know about this card called The Star. Don't look up its meaning; just tell us what comes to mind.

Well, it reminds me of the story of the Three Wise Men, who, in following the Star of Bethlehem, found Jesus.

Interesting. Go on.

The Star also makes me think about what Isis said last year about connecting with the Higher Self.

Good. That is sufficient. Now look at the card and describe the image.

I see a bunch of stars. The one in the center is big and there are…let's see…seven smaller ones around it. Oh, look at that —one big star and seven small ones. That's like 17/8!

Very good! This is precisely why it was drawn that way. The artist was following guidance. What else do you notice?

The star in the middle has…eight spires. Come to think of it, they all have eight spires.

Go on. You are omitting something obvious.

Oh, right. There is a naked woman in the foreground. She is holding two urns and is pouring water out of each of them; one flows into a pond and the other onto the land. She has one foot in the water and is kneeling on the earth so her other foot is dry.

What is this imagery reminiscent of?

It is similar to the Temperance card, which shows an angel pouring water from one cup into another. The angel has one foot in the water and the other on land as well.

Precisely. Notice that while Temperance is number XIV, we can arrive at fourteen via 2×7. So both Temperance and The Star relate to the number seven. Rest assured,

XIV

we'll be speaking to you in greater length about Temperance another time. For now, we wish to focus on the eight as constructed by one and seven.

The number seven is an essential undertaking for the initiate. Monasteries, cloisters, abbeys, and the like were all erected to support this purpose. But what do the men and women who live within these walls hope to find? They seek connection...**communion**, and this is a significant meaning of eight! When you ask, it is given. When you seek, it shall be found. Seven is the asking and the seeking. Eight is that which is given and that which is found.

So the one and seven represents a way of being. It is the individual seeking to commune with the divine. As you were told already, he or she does this by reaching inward. These institutions serve, in part, by limiting external stimulus. Lessening the **noise** permits the internal voice of guidance to grow ever louder.

Recognize that on this Tarot card there are eight stars, not just one. The large star in the center represents the Higher Self, which **is** the greater aspect of guidance that is available to the one seeking. However, the Higher Self is not the only source of guidance. The additional stars represent guides, angels, healers, teachers, and loved ones. Innumerable masters have walked upon this dirt before you arrived. They have left behind instructions to help you on your way. There is never only one path to Source.

In basic numerology, where all is reduced to a single digit, eight represents the penultimate step—the second from last. All that remains is the nine: completion. And yet think of music. When playing a scale, each octave leads to the next. That is because completion only applies to the relative. There is no **real** completion. Life does not end, and thus creating does not end either. You can complete an endeavor, but you will never be finished.

We point this out because it is thinking that you must "get it right" that keeps many of you from venturing forward. Aspirations are wonderful...when they are stars of inspiration guiding you forward. But when unmet goals become equated to failures, one loses sight of the forest and sees only trees. The details of life do have meaning. There is information everywhere you look. You ask many questions and thus get many answers. But these are **not** the point of life. These are not the **purpose** of life. **Living** is the purpose of life.

Ask your questions. Listen for answers. Read the cards and consult the stars. Seek guidance in the myriad ways provided to you. But do not make the asking and the seeking the only aspects of life. Remember that conscious, intentional manifestation is merely the second realm of existence. The Magician is wise, but not omniscient. That is why he is number I. The Fool lives outside of reason, and is thus not limited to one realm of creating. His journey begins with the Magician, but moves on from there.

There are times in life when the best you can do is simply live life to the fullest right here and right now. Perpetual asking and seeking keeps you focused on the future, and then the present never seems to measure up. The future is as useful as the past, which is to say that it is not all that useful. It is still nothing but thoughts and ideas. True happiness and joy can only be found in the present, which is neither in the past nor in the future. There is always more to come, but if you are decidedly looking only to the future, you'll miss it when it arrives and then only have vague memories to look back upon.

You, John, have traversed what is likely to be the last of the more difficult passages of your life. The past is gone. The pain you have endured is over. Revisiting it or recreating it will serve no additional benefit. You have accessed the root of your misguided beliefs, and in reaching the core you have encountered your self.

What you do not realize is that you came here—to this beautiful country of Spain—for that reason alone. You have not only released pain and suffering accumulated in this lifetime, but have also worked through karma carried forward from lifetimes of old spent on the Iberian Peninsula. You have freed yourself of the bulk of it and can now travel forth a new man.

Go now. Choose and create with new eyes and see! The 17/8 is not merely a process; it is a state of being. It need not be only a tool, but can become a philosophy of life. Glance over all that you have seen today. You have come to visit a monastery, but is this a structure that was erected for visitors? Was it not built for men to live and in a specific way?

And yet, life imbued with the 17/8 need not be sequestered or subject to abstinence. One can retain the 17/8 among the masses. In fact this is preferred, for in this way one becomes a brightly lit star guiding others forward.

The monastic life resonates strongly with the seven, but within 17/8, the one is paired with the seven to create eight. Seven is hidden, but eight is visible for all to see. We invite you to embrace the one that you are, and to keep the seven always within reach, thus experiencing the eight over and over again—every day seeing, learning, creating, and experiencing—every day witnessing miracles. That is the way of the 17/8 and that is what beckons you forward.

John stopped writing. His eyes blurred with tears and his pencil dropped. He could feel the profundity of the information. He now realized his life was disjoint and that he operated within two discrete modes. When he was open, he connected with life around him. When he was hurt or scared, he isolated himself from everything and everyone. It didn't matter whether he was alone or surrounded by others; he simply vacillated between the one extreme and the other.

"I need to adopt a more holistic approach—akin to the 17/8," he said to himself optimistically as he climbed into bed. A serene meditative calm blanketed him and he quickly drifted off to sleep.

Huit – Otto – Ocho – Acht

J ohn met with Bernard and Micheline midmorning and together they enjoyed a leisure stroll to the museum. Along the path, they passed as many monks as visitors. *El Museu de Montserrat* would be John's first Spanish museum. Given the experiences of the day before: the visions at the monastery and the channeled message in the evening, John kept wondering if someone or something would spark familiarity. After wandering through a number of rooms, he soon forgot all about it.

The three had agreed to let each follow his or her own rhythm. The first few rooms featured classical paintings and murals, Micheline's favorite. John, who preferred sculpture, wandered ahead.

A few rooms later, John happened upon an artifact that was specifically appealing, mostly because it was the only piece he was allowed to touch. A fully functioning mosaic globe was crafted from inlaid stones of varying colors. John spun the globe, admiring the array of colors and textures. He also thought of all of the places he'd visited and those he would likely never see—*at least not in this lifetime*—he thought wondering how many lifetimes he'd lived so far.

"Hey John! What are studying over there?" Bernard caught up to John and saw him intently perusing something on the brightly colored orb.

John rotated the sphere positioning the Pacific Ocean toward Bernard. He then pointed to a symbol etched near the equator that resembled an elongated figure eight.

"Oh…that's called an analemma." Bernard said prosaically.

"Analemma? What is it?" The fact that it resembled the number eight had piqued John's interest.

"From what I understand, it encodes information about the earth's movement relative to the sun. Before it was understood, it was observed."

"Observed? What do you mean? Where? How?" John excitedly fired off his questions.

Bernard organized his thoughts for a moment, then said, "You know how the sun is lower in the sky in winter and higher in summer, like I was saying yesterday?"

"Yeah."

"Well, if you were to follow the movement of the sun from one day to the next for an entire year, by observing its position in the sky at precisely the same time each day, its path would look like this figure eight."

"How did anyone ever do that? How did they mark its position in the sky?"

"More than likely by tracking its shadow. Let's say you have a post, or better yet, a pole. On sunny days, the shadow of the pole forms a clear outline. To track the change from day to day, one could place a pebble at the tip of the shadow at the same time each day, for example 2:00 in the afternoon. You want to make sure it's a time of the day when the sun is above the horizon at all times of year. Early morning or late afternoon would not work. If you do this every day, or every few days, your pebbles will form the shape of an analemma on the ground. That's probably how it was done in the early days."

"Wow! That's fascinating. So you said it encodes information. What kind of information?"

"There are the causes and the effects. The causes relate to the shape of earth's orbit around the sun, the tilt of the earth, and the relationship between the rate of spin of the earth and its velocity along its orbit. The effects relate to time and climate as we experience it: the length of a day and the number of days in a year; the change of seasons and the varying ratio of sunlight to nighttime; even where the sun sets along the horizon throughout the year. From what I understand, every planet in the solar system has its own unique analemma, and thus its own seasonal pattern."

"Even the number of seasons?"

"Yes! In theory, a planet could have one season, two, or four. I'm not sure if other combinations have ever been observed, but who knows?"

"All of that from a simple little curve? Who would have ever expected that? I'd seen that shape on globes before, I just never knew what it meant."

"Well, now you know," Bernard said with a pat to John's back. He then rejoined Micheline, who had entered the room.

John continued to examine the globe and the analemma until he felt a tap on his shoulder.

"*Señor…perdón.* I couldn't help but overhear you. I thought you might like to know…" The monk paused to look around as if not wanting their conversation overheard. "There's an analemma calendar at the top of the mountain just like the one your friend described…except instead of a pole, it is constructed around an obelisk."

John raised an eyebrow and the monk took notice.

"At specific times of the year, a number of us from the monastery hike to the top of the mountain to observe key points along the curve. The summer solstice approaches and so we are now working on a plan for our next expedition." The monk looked around a second time, and then fished by saying, "There is only a small group of us that go…or even that know about these expeditions. They are not, shall we say, a part of the Benedictine Order. The ceremonies are private, but sometimes an individual outside of the order is invited to join. If you are interested, I can tell you where and when we will meet to discuss our next expedition, which is in less than a week."

"Are you saying that I am invited to go with you?"

"If it is pleasing to you, yes. Unfortunately, I cannot extend the invitation to your friends. I hope you understand."

John remained silent, unsure what to do…or think. He was completely intrigued by the idea of joining the expedition. At the same time, the man's tone told John that the invitation was for something much greater than a simple hike to the top of the mountain.

"*Señor,*" the monk went on, "I do not expect you to make such a decision in mere seconds. Think about it as you peruse the museum. I will make myself available to you as you exit. You can tell me of your decision then. Of course, you can find me here at the museum tomorrow morning as well, should you need more time."

"Thank you, uh…"

"Brother Miguel. Pleased to meet you." Brother Miguel bowed slightly, disregarding the hand that John extended. He then slipped away as silently as he had approached.

John watched Brother Miguel walk away while his mind raced. He needed time to think, but not to decide. He **was** going to accept the monk's offer; he just wasn't sure how to break the news to Bernard and Micheline or even how much to tell them. He questioned whether he was supposed to be discreet about the expedition and ceremony since the monk appeared to have been.

The monk returned to his post and observed John from across the room. He nodded his head subtly as if reacting to John's thoughts.

Feeling a bit self-conscious, John rejoined the others.

Micheline, who had been observing John with interest ever since they met, knew that something had happened. She could see it in John's face and in the way he held his head. She was curious, but kept quiet. She had also witnessed the tail end of the interaction between John and the monk, and figured that had everything to do with it. Not wanting to give away her spying, Micheline waited to see what John would divulge.

Despite the weight of the matter, John said nothing. He stayed with Bernard and Micheline, but was distant.

Micheline continued to contemplate the situation until she convinced herself that she had it all figured out. *John must have been invited to stay at the Monastery longer*—she reasoned. She then guessed that what troubled him was how to break the news to her and Bernard…as if it would be letting them down. After some contemplation, Micheline thought of a tactful way to get the conversation started.

"So John," she interjected. "We never did ask you. What are your plans for the rest of your time here in Spain? As you know, Bernard and I will be heading back to France in a couple of days.

You do not have to leave any time soon, right? Is there other places in Spain you wish to visit?"

The shift in John's face told her that her plan was working.

"Well," John said tentatively. "I'm considering staying here a bit longer and…maybe heading further west before returning to Barcelona."

Before Bernard could protest, Micheline responded encouragingly. "John, that's a splendid idea! The Spanish countryside, as you can see already, is very different than the city. It would be a shame for you not to experience more of it while you are here. We, of course, will miss you, but I'm confident you'll make it back to Lyon to visit us some day. We'll see you again, I'm sure."

John felt relieved, but Bernard was confused. He hadn't a clue as to what had just happened and was unsettled because suddenly things had changed and in ways he had not foreseen.

A couple of hours later, as they neared the exit of the museum, Micheline caught sight of the monk waiting for John at the door.

"John, Bernard and I will meet you outside in a few minutes. There is one piece of art that I simply have to visit one last time before we leave. Bernard, come with me." She then dragged her husband into the next room, giving John a bit of privacy.

John watched Micheline and Bernard walk away and then headed for the exit. Only then did he notice Brother Miguel waiting for him.

"*Señor*, have you come to a decision?"

"Yes, I have. I would like to meet the others in your group and will travel with you to visit the analemma calendar."

"I am so happy you have decided to join us. I am sure the others will be pleased to make your acquaintance. Tomorrow at 4:00 we will meet in the courtyard in front of the printing press. Do you know where that is?"

"Yes. We visited the press yesterday."

"Excellent. Are you staying here at the visitors' inn?"

"Yes."

"Why don't you check out of your room tomorrow and plan on staying with me until the expedition. That way I can more adequately prepare you for the trip. Bring your belongings with you tomorrow afternoon. I'll take you to my room after the meeting. Is this acceptable to you?"

"Yes, that's great!"

"Brother John, have a pleasant evening and enjoy the remainder of your time with your friends. Until tomorrow…"

"Thank you Brother Miguel. Until then…"

The monk slipped away quickly and only then did it occur to John how he had addressed him. *I never told him my name*—he thought—*and…**Brother** John?*

Huit – Otto – Ocho – Acht

Micheline, Bernard, and John took a circuitous route back to the inn to enjoy their last afternoon together. It was bittersweet.

The next morning, when it was time to say good-bye, all shed tears…even Bernard. John watched Micheline and Bernard's coach travel through the monastery gate and descend out of view. More tears streamed down his face, but the dry air evaporated them quickly. Separations always seemed to come too quickly for him.

"It is once again time for me to divert my attention toward something new," he told himself. "In a few hours, I will meet the members of the expedition."

The meeting, as it turned out, was less informative than John had hoped. The group discussed the logistics of the trek to the top of the mountain, but nothing else.

There has to be something more to this—he thought.

The whole affair felt clandestine and he could not shake the feeling that they were about to break some rule…or already had. This added a bit of excitement to his eight days in the monastery, but also induced anxiety.

Brother Miguel, however, offered no words of warning. He did not tell John to be cautious or discreet; he simply invited him to roam the monastery at will and to make himself at home.

Over the course of that week, John learned, first hand, what monastic life was really like. He did, however, gain no further insight on forthcoming events.

Huit – Otto – Ocho – Acht

T he day before the earliest sunrise of the year, John was woken well before dawn. He could hear Brother Miguel moving around the room, but he could not see a thing. He squinted, trying to focus in the dark. Before his eyes adjusted, light appeared.

Normally, Brother Miguel would gather up his belongings in the dark, since he had a clear mental image of the layout of his room. This morning he lit a candle for John's sake, and also because he didn't want them to be late. They had to leave before sunrise in order to reach the analemma calendar before sunset.

The candlelight cast long shadows, but was better than complete darkness. John put on his travel clothes, which he had set aside the night before. He stretched to wake himself more fully, picked up his satchel and a second bag allotted to him, and followed Brother Miguel out the door.

En route to the meeting place, John considered how long it had been since he last backpacked. He felt a bit out of shape and was nervous about keeping up. He voiced his concerns, but Brother Miguel immediately dismissed them.

"Most monks live a contemplative, sedentary lifestyle," he said. "You and I are the youngest in the group; you needn't worry. Our pace will be moderate. To us, life is never about the destination and always about the journey. A full day provides ample time to reach the analemma calendar with plenty of rests along the way."

Brother Miguel then went on to say that they primarily started early to perform the majority of the climb in the cooler morning hours. "By midday," he explained, "we will be able to see the obelisk in the distance—at the same elevation, but across a rocky plain. It will still take some time to get there, but the trek will not be laborious. The nearly treeless landscape, however, provides little shade, so even the easiest jaunt conjures up a sweat. Some of the elders typically require frequent breaks to cool off."

Huit – Otto – Ocho – Acht

E ight days after entering France, Johannes and his men reached the outskirts of Montpelier. They were nearly a full day behind what Johannes had hoped.

Johannes turned to his driver. "Do we have associates in the area?" he asked.

"Yes, Sir," the driver replied.

"We can swap horses then, and drive on through..." Johannes said this more as a statement than a question.

His driver nodded, just in case Johannes meant it as a question.

"And the ranch that is near," Johannes added, "are you certain my father would stop there...regardless?"

"As certain as I can be, Sir. I have driven this way with Herr Müller a number of times and we have always stopped in Montpelier. Sometimes we swap horses and sometimes we stay the night."

"Splendid." Johannes said this cheerfully, hiding some of his concern. He never expected them to cross the whole of France without encountering his father. They hadn't yet, but they were getting close.

As he ascended the coach once more, he silently hoped the rancher would have something to report.

Huit – Otto – Ocho – Acht

S hortly before sunset, the group arrived at the base of the obelisk. On the ground adjacent to it was the elongated figure eight that John had seen on the globe. A short distance away, nearly a dozen tents had been erected.

Most of the monks, being familiar with the routine, proceeded directly to their assigned tent. John and a few of the younger monks awaited direction. When John was shown to his tent, which he would share with three others, he was surprised that Brother Miguel wasn't among them. John placed his belongings on his cot and sought after his friend.

"Brother John," Brother Miguel called from the distance. "Come with me. We have a task to complete before dark."

Before John had a chance to ask any questions, Brother Miguel shot off toward another tent. Once Brother Miguel gathered the young monks together, he addressed them: "My Brothers, each of you have been assigned to a tent with three elders. We never anticipate a problem, but many within the group are well along in their years. If you hear something unusual during the night, do not hesitate to fetch me. I am not here for sleep, so you will not be disturbing me. I will check in with each of you before we retire."

Two of the young men turned as if to return to their tents, but then Brother Miguel's words stopped them. "Before you go, we have one task left to do. Being the youngest...and the most capable, it is our responsibility to fetch water for the others." Brother Miguel then led them to the well.

John carried what felt like enough water for the entire assemblage, and was surprised when they left for a second trip. He then saw that everyone was bathing and realized a couple more trips were forthcoming. The hike up the mountain was well within his capability, but two more trips for water were sure to tire him out completely.

I will sleep well tonight!—he thought to himself.

After the young men had collected enough water, Brother Miguel nodded with appreciation to the others and said, "Thank you. Sleep well, my Brothers. See you at dawn."

Huit – Otto – Ocho – Acht

A fter a brief conversation with the rancher, Johannes was torn. His father **had** passed through on his way to Spain, but that was weeks earlier. No word had been heard from him since.

Chances are, Klaus is still in Spain—Johannes reasoned—*but there is always the possibility that he neglected to stop on his way back to Germany.*

Johannes endeavored to keep his trepidation to a minimum for the majority of the trip. With each day traveled, that grew more difficult. Furthermore, he was the only one concerned. All of his men thought the trip was unwarranted; he could see it in their facial expressions. They never complained; they simply questioned the purpose.

Johannes began to question it as well.

"Driver, what do you think? Should we spend the night, or exchange our horses and push on through to Narbonne?"

"Sir?" The driver, unaccustomed to a query like that, looked at Johannes questioningly. After a longer than usual pause, he said, "I require rest, Sir, but there is another who could take over the driving if you wish to continue traveling."

Johannes, still uncertain what to do, decided a night of rest might do them all some good.

"That won't be necessary," he said to the driver. "Let's spend the night. Once we reach Narbonne, I will need to decide which route to take into Spain: the coast, or through the Pyrenees."

"Herr Müller has gone each way at different times," the driver offered.

"I know," Johannes said looking down at his hands. "I know."

Huit – Otto – Ocho – Acht

J ohn fell asleep quickly and slept through the night. As with the day before, he was roused before sunrise. This time, the sky was already aglow within the earlier stages of dawn.

John learned that two ceremonies were to be performed that day. The first, at daybreak, welcomed the earliest sunrise of the year. It would occur near the calendar, but not using it. The second, which did use the calendar, had to be performed precisely at its calibrated time—in this case: 9:00 am.

John dressed and then stretched. His legs were stiff from the hike up the mountain, and his arms were sore from carrying heavy jugs of water. He moved around to loosen up his muscles and to shake off some of the morning chill. The elders in his tent began exiting one after the other and John followed.

As the group gathered along the northeastern side the solar calendar, John made his way to Brother Miguel's side. He opened his mouth to greet him, but then hesitated. Since no one else had yet uttered a word, he simply nodded to his friend and smiled.

Brother Miguel looked John directly in the eyes and nodded slightly. His expression conveyed multiple sentiments, which left John feeling assured, but also curious. He then guided John to his allotted position and quickly moved into his own.

The group of men settled into place. They stood shoulder-to-shoulder in a semi-circular formation that faced away from the obelisk and toward the brightest section of the horizon. The eldest monk stood in the center of the arc while the younger men, including John and Brother Miguel, flanked out to either end.

From John's position, he could watch all of the others without turning his head. He scanned the group, anticipating what would happen next.

For a few moments, the group remained silent. All eyes were on the eldest, awaiting his lead.

The eldest monk studied the horizon to discern the proper moment to begin. Nearby, birds began to sing, breaking the silence. He turned to acknowledge all on his left and all on his right. Then, in unison, the monks clasped their hands in front of them, closed their eyes, and bowed.

John followed along, but peeked through his half-closed eyes.

The eldest lifted his head, studied the horizon for a moment, and then began chanting—softly at first, but quickly growing louder. After finishing the opening phrase, the group opened their eyes, raised their heads, and recited their version of the phrase in response.

The chant progressed and grew more sophisticated. John noticed that the men in the middle had the deepest voices, or at least were able to resonate within the lowest tones. He was also impressed with how long each could hold a note before needing to breathe. There were always at least two men carrying the same note and they somehow managed to stagger their inbreathing thus maintaining the note continuously.

Once all were toning and chanting, John was tempted to join in, but refrained since he knew not what would happen next. He could easily harmonize with them, but was afraid he would be caught off guard if the melody changed suddenly. In lieu of anything voiced, John decided to hum. In this way, he felt the vibration inside his body, but didn't add to the sound of the group.

As the sun pierced the horizon, the tune shifted—the constant tones giving way to flowing melodies. The richness and body of the music seemed to grow as more of the sun inched across the horizon. To John, it seemed as if their voices were actually lifting the sun higher into the sky.

When the sun rose completely above the horizon, the music grew even more complex. It morphed into a fugue of at least four voices. The elders led, and the younger monks followed. The quality of the music—a cappella—was so impressive that John sprouted goose bumps all over his body. He had long stopped humming and just listened and enjoyed.

The fugue then ended and only a pedal point remained; the note was deep, resonating, and constant. As the pedal point droned, Brother Miguel stepped out of formation and walked across the arc toward John. John watched as Brother Miguel reached for his hand, guided him to the focus of the curve, and then turned him to face the eldest before returning to his original place in line.

The pedal point continued, uninterrupted, but was joined with chanted melodies in the highest ranges of the group. Slowly, the chanting moved from the edges of the semicircle toward the middle, growing lower in tone and volume as it did. When it reached the center of the curve, all went silent and the eldest stepped forward to approach John.

The monk looked deeply into John's eyes, bowed slightly, and then placed his hands on John's shoulders, guiding John down to his knees. He covered John's crown with his palms and recited a few phrases in Latin. The others responded in kind.

Instinctively, John bowed his head deeply.

The chanting resumed and two others guided John into a standing position. They each kept a hand on one of John's shoulders. The elder then reached for John's hands and brought them together into the common mudra of prayer. He imitated the mudra, surrounding John's hands with his own. In a final gesture as the music waned, the old man lifted John's hands and kissed them lightly welcoming him into the group and completing the ceremony.

Once the music ended completely, the men dispersed and before John could react, Brother Miguel walked over to him, faced him squarely, and hugged him warmly. "Welcome to the Order," he said. "We are grateful that you chose to join us on this special day. Now, let us break bread and sate our hunger."

After the meal, John seized an opportunity with his friend.

"Brother Miguel, I have a question for you. Today is not the summer solstice, right?"

"Yes, that is correct. The summer solstice is next week."

"And the summer solstice is the day with the longest amount of sunlight, correct?"

"Yes."

"Then why is today the earliest sunrise and not then?"

"That is an excellent question. Come. Follow me. I will show you."

Brother Miguel rose from the table and headed toward the analemma calendar. John quietly followed.

"Brother John, notice that the analemma for Planet Earth is a figure eight. It is obvious to many that the sun is higher in the sky in the summer than it is in the winter. And everyone living in the more temperate regions knows that days are longer when the sun is high, and shorter when the sun is low. When you look at the analemma, the **length** of the figure eight illustrates this. The tip closest to the pole is the summer solstice; the sun is highest and thus the shadow is shortest. At the winter solstice, when the sun is lowest, the shadow is longest and thus the other end of the curve is reached.

"Now notice that at the bottom and top of the curve, the movement is from one side to the other. The day is not lengthening or shortening noticeably at those times, but it is shifting: towards the evening now, and towards the morning near the Winter Solstice. As a result, the earliest sunrise precedes the Solstice by about a week, and the latest sunset follows it by about the same. Do you understand?"

"I think so, but I need to think about it a while longer."

"Well, you'll have **plenty** of time to do that later. It is almost nine o'clock. The obelisk's pointy shadow is nearing the curve. See?" Brother Miguel pointed to the shadow on the ground. He then looked up and said, "And here come the others."

Brother Miguel told John where to sit, closest to the analemma curve and just in front of the spot where the obelisk's pointed shadow drifted. As the newest member of the group, he was afforded the closest view of the event. Brother Miguel then sat on his left. The others sat more or less where they pleased, circumscribing the entire figure.

Other than the fact that they were sitting around the analemma instead of standing, this ceremony resembled the earlier one. John could hardly tell the music apart and was happy to be hearing the tones and melodies once again.

As the nine o'clock hour struck, the melodies gave way to the pedal point. All watched as the shadow pointed directly to the part of the curve Brother Miguel had indicated earlier. Even though John knew it would happen, he shivered with excitement nonetheless.

When the shadow moved visibly off of the analemma curve, the chanting waned into silence, completing the ceremony.

Huit – Otto – Ocho – Acht

S ofia rapped at her mother's door and listened for sounds coming from inside. As soon as she heard the latch unlock, she said, "Hello Mama," through the opening door.

Tomasina hugged Sofia firmly and kissed each cheek twice. "Baby Girl! Come in," She said as she shut the door and escorted her daughter into the kitchen.

"Do you want something to eat? I was just about to fix myself a sandwich."

"You go ahead, Mama. I'm not hungry." Sofia sat at the breakfast table and looked out the window.

Tomasina pulled items out of the refrigerator and the cupboard and began making sandwiches. She made one for Sofia, just in case. She knew her daughter was upset, but said nothing. She was stalling, giving herself time to think.

"So…how is little Notte?" Tomasina asked over her shoulder.

Sofia sat up a little. "Notte is an angel! Of course, his halo is held up by a pair of horns." Sofia smiled for a moment, but then the somber expression returned.

Tomasina placed the sandwiches on the table and poured *limonata* for both of them. She then sat next to her daughter and placed a hand on Sofia's arm.

"How are you doing, Baby Girl? Have you receive word from Johannes?" *Best to just get it all out into the open*—Tomasina reasoned.

"I did! A letter arrived yesterday afternoon. Johannes made it to Heidelberg, but his father was not there. Apparently, Klaus is in Spain or maybe on his way back to Germany. Johannes decided to go in search of him."

"Well, you heard from Johannes…and he arrived safely. That has to make you feel better…doesn't it?"

"It does, Mama, but this is hard. It's hard being patient, waiting for him…not knowing when he'll return. He's gone off after his father…well…because it gives him something to **do**! I know it would drive him crazy to sit and wait for his father to return. Yet, here I am doing just that! And it is driving **me** crazy!"

"Baby Girl, sometimes patience is not about time."

Sofia's expression shifted. She looked at her mother, tilted her head slightly, and asked, "What do you mean, Mama?"

Tomasina took a deep breath, and went on. "Let me tell you a story:

Two men, traveling separately, arrive at an inn simultaneously. Each dismounts his horse and ties it to a post.

The first man says to the second, "I have been traveling all day. I am hungry and I am tired. I cannot wait to have a meal and go to sleep."

The second man says in return, "I have been on horseback all day as well. It feels great simply having my feet on the ground!"

The two men approach the front door one after the other. The first man attempts to open it, but it is locked.

"Don't tell me the inn is closed!" he says as he looks around, frustrated.

The second man looks around as well and notices a sign in the window. Pointing to it, he says, "The innkeeper must have gone out for moment. Look. It says he'll be back in 15 minutes."

The second man decides to use the time to attend to his horse. He pulls out some oats, fills the feedbag, and places it on his horse's face. While the horse eats, he brushes him, checks his hoofs, and whispers to him softly.

The first man, sits on a bench for a moment, then stands. He paces back and forth across the porch, and then looks into the window and taps on it. "Just my luck," he says, mostly to himself. "I've been traveling all day, and arrive **right** when the innkeeper is away." He then walks over to the sign and retorts, "I hate signs like this. If we don't know when he left, we can't know when he'll return. It should say something like: 'Back at 7:00'."

The second man finishes tending to his horse and starts unbuckling his bags from the saddle. "Where are you traveling from?" he says to the first.

"From the west," the first man replies. "Been traveling for three days now."

"How much further are you going?" the second asks.

"Two more days," the first man says as he looks into the window again and taps...a bit louder this time. "I can't wait for it to be over."

The second man considers sharing details of his own journey, but decides to remain quiet. *I'm sure he's not interested*—he thinks to himself. He then returns his focus to organizing his belongings.

The first man reinstates his pacing, sighing intermittently.

A few minutes later, they both hear the clink of the deadbolt.

The innkeeper opens the front door, greeting the men and welcoming them inside.

Tomasina finished her story by asking, "So, which man waited longer for the innkeeper to return?"

Sofia, knowing it was a trick question, said nothing.

"Clearly the men arrived at the same time," Tomasina concluded, "and therefore waited the same amount of time. However, don't you think those 15 minutes lasted a lot longer for the first man than the second?"

"You're right, Mama. Notte was a great distraction, but I guess I need to stop waiting, and start living my life again."

"One day at a time, Baby Girl. That's all it takes."

Huit – Otto – Ocho – Acht

T he afternoon resembled a typical day of monastic life… minus the monastery itself. The biggest exception was that everyone seemed to be eating more than usual. John first thought the feast was because of the ceremony and celebration, but he then questioned himself. The quantity of food consumed was greater, but didn't feel celebratory per se. Instead, it felt…intentional…and purposeful. Once John was able to get Brother Miguel's attention, he posed his next question.

"Brother Miguel, is something about to happen that I am unaware of? It feels as if we are here for more than simply the two ceremonies."

"You are astute Brother John. Something is **indeed** about to happen and is the greater purpose of the trip. Many will be embarking on a vision quest."

"Vision quest? What's that?"

"Well, my friend, I've intentionally kept details from you so as not to intimidate you ahead of time. A vision quest sounds challenging, but needn't be."

"Now you're scaring me," John said, half joking.

"None of that," Brother Miguel smiled. "A vision quest is simply an extended meditation and best done in nature."

"For how long?"

"Three or four days."

"**Days!** Three or four **hours** would be a challenge!"

"You will be surprised what you can do. The part that typically intimidates people more is fasting for the duration of the quest."

"Oh. That's why everyone is eating as much as they can today."

"It is probably best not to over do it. Eat well, but not excessively. The whole point is that as your digestive system empties, your visions enhance. By day three, you will be completely unaware of hunger, and possibly unaware of this physical plane."

"Isn't this dangerous. It's not like many of these men are young."

"Well, in this part of the expedition, the elders take care of the youngest. The elders no longer need what vision quests bring. They will stay lucid and watch over us. The beauty of this part of the mountain is that from that perch over there, they will be able to see all of us as we wander over here." Brother Miguel pointed as he spoke.

"We won't all be together?"

"Precisely. Your vision quest is yours alone. No one can go with you, so they needn't be near you either. Each person will select a spot to their liking and must remain near to it the whole time they are awake. Typically, all wandering will cease as each falls into trance. At that time, some will appear to be sleeping, while others will be demonstrably engaged within their visions.

"The elders will intermittently walk around, check on us, and refill water jugs as needed. That is why we had to fetch so much water last night and will top off our supply this evening. Our rations must last until the end of the quest.

"You needn't worry. Your body will take care of itself. It will drink only as much as it needs while your consciousness wanders."

"I guess that doesn't sound so bad."

"**You** are going to love it, I'm sure. Oh, there is one more thing. You must take paper and pencils to continue your writing. There is information forthcoming."

"You know about the writings?" John asked.

"I have observed your writing sessions over the past week, but I knew of them in any case."

"How…"

"Never mind," Brother Miguel interrupted. "Surely you didn't think you were selected at random, did you?"

"I guess I didn't think about it." John said, looking down.

"Your book is almost complete," Brother Miguel said proudly.

"So you know the writings are supposed to be published." John half said, half asked.

Brother Miguel just smiled.

"Do you know what the writings are about?" John asked him.

"No. That much I have not been told. And while I've been tempted to peek at the pages on your desk, I have been asked to be patient."

"As far as I'm concerned, you are welcome to read as much as you like. Everything is in my satchel. Are you doing a quest as well?"

"Hmm. I guess not. Intuitively, I am guided to begin reading your earlier chapters while you write the last of them. I am looking forward to it!"

"Well, now I feel a little self conscious...but then again, I'm not the author, just the scribe."

"No need to worry. I am confident the book will be most inspiring! Now let's join the others. Today is a day of feast and rest!"

Huit – Otto – Ocho – Acht

A fter an additional day of travel, Johannes and his men reached Narbonne. Still unsure whether to head into Spain via the coastal route or through the mountains, Johannes instead decided to stay put for a few days.

One last time, he considered the distances. *We have traveled 800 kilometers since leaving Germany, which places us about 100 kilometers from Spain. It is so interesting how the numbers keep working out.*

"Men, I have decided to remain here in Narbonne for the next three days at the least. Feel free to take this time for rest and leisure. Do whatever you please and report back in 72 hours." As

Johannes walked into the inn, his home for the next four nights, he added to himself—*and I do hope Klaus shows himself before I have to decide on my next course of action.*

9 – *Nine* – IX

Neuf – Nove – Nueve – Neun

The start of John's vision quest was reminiscent of the first days with his Guru in Nepal. Focusing was difficult. The hunger pangs did not help. The heat made it worse. He found himself restless and frustrated. He paced in an attempt to calm himself down…and then heard:

Recognize. Release. Return-to-Center.

"Who said that?" John asked, looking up. But no one was near.

John looked around and noticed that the others in the distance were pacing just as he was. *OK, I can do better than this*—he coaxed himself. *I'll sit here and lean against this tree…and concentrate.*

Soon John was able to meditate, but only for brief periods. And nothing significant resulted. Stillness seeped in, but without images or insights.

Much later, when John again took inventory of the others, he questioned what he was seeing. One monk appeared to be lying on a cot. *But where did that come from?* And another was…*up in a tree? Wait—I thought there were only nine of us on a quest today. Where did all of the others come from?*

John looked toward the sun, trying to ascertain the time of day, but couldn't remember which direction was west. "Is the sun approaching the horizon or leaving it?" he asked himself. "I can't tell if it is morning or evening."

He then asked himself a question that really struck him: "What day is it?" He could not seem to figure out if he'd been on a quest for one day or three.

Recognize. Release. Return-to-Center.

"Who's there?" John had distinctly heard the voice come from behind him. He spun around to see who it was and almost lost his balance.

"John, it's me. Here, let me help you." He put a hand on John's shoulder to steady him. "You look thirsty. Take a swig of this."

"Johannes! The last time you said that, I got drunk."

Johannes laughed. "You can trust me. Besides, you're already hallucinating. You don't need any help."

"Oh. Well, that's good to know. I thought I was going crazy."

While John drank, Johannes kept a hand on the canteen to help him. After a long enough pause, Johannes said, "Are you done? We need to go."

"We do? Where are we going?" John grew excited at the thought of a new journey.

"To the top of the mountain."

John furrowed his brow as he said, "I thought we were already at the top."

"No. Look! We're going up there." Johannes pointed to the jagged peak, which was more than a hundred yards above them. "Come on. The view is much better from there."

John turned to inspect the view. He could see down the mountain, across the valley, and all the way to the ocean. The water was orange and the sky was a color purple he had never seen before. He then turned back toward Johannes, but Johannes was already way ahead of him. He started to run, shouting, "Johannes! Wait for me!"

"Hurry!" Johannes yelled back. "You're going to be late."

"Late?" John paused, trying to remember what he must have forgotten. "Late for what?"

"We said we'd meet at the top of the mountain precisely at sunset. Look! The sun is already nearing the horizon."

John, still confused, said, "Johannes, why is the sky purple and the water orange?" He pointed down the mountain, but this time, the water was pink and the sky yellow.

Above him, Johannes laughed.

"Never mind." John turned to face the west, but suddenly the mountaintop was underneath him instead of above him; and Johannes stood next to him.

"Sorry. I couldn't wait any longer," Johannes confessed.

"Johannes, what are you doing here anyway? I thought you were in Italy?"

"I am actually in France right now. How did you know I was in Italy? Where are you? You're not still in Egypt, are you?"

"No. I'm..." John looked up, trying to remember. Thinking out loud, he said, "Let's see...we left Egypt, stopped in Italy, and then set sail again, so I'm..." He looked around at the scenery for clues, but that didn't help. He then turned to Johannes and said, "How do you **not** know where I am? You're standing right next to me." He then said, more to himself, "How do **I** not know where I am?"

"Wait a minute," Johannes interjected. "Backup. **You** were in **Italy**? When? Where?" For the first time in the conversation, Johannes was the one surprised.

"I was in Rome...for six days."

After John said this, the scene below them morphed from the Spanish countryside to the Seven Hills of Rome. John could see all of the places he had visited and grew nostalgic.

Johannes could see the scene as well and said, "It's beautiful. I want to go to Rome!"

"You should!" John encouraged him. "It's an amazing city. There are lots of obelisks there too. Oh...right...now I remember. I'm in Spain!"

"What brought you to Spain?" Johannes asked.

"I met a woman named Maria," John replied.

"That sounds like a song." Johannes chuckled. "I met a woman too! Her name is Sofia! That's why I'm here actually."

"I heard." John's voice dipped. He put his head down, slumped his shoulders, and sat on the ground.

Johannes sat down next to him and said, "You heard...what... exactly?"

Without looking up, John said, "I heard that you're getting married."

Johannes had been keenly observing John, but then looked away and said, "Do I even want to ask how you heard **that**?"

"It's a long story." Clearly, John did not want to discuss it.

Johannes eyed John again and asked, "So…what do you…think?" He was being cautious, but could not hide his excitement. He wanted John to be excited too and nudged him to get a response.

John looked at Johannes, but remained quiet. He actually didn't know what he thought about it.

Unsure how to interpret the silence, Johannes then said, "Maybe I should ask—how do you **feel** about it?"

John hesitated. He, at first, took the question literally and looked down at his hands. It then hit him what Johannes meant. "I'm OK. I'm happy for you." His tone was convincing, which surprised both of them.

"You are?" Johannes asked him. "Good. I just wanted to make sure. I thought you might be upset about it."

"Oh…I was," John assured him. "But Johannes, I don't understand. What's going on?"

"You'll understand soon. We just switched things up—you and me—decided that this way would be more…productive."

"How come you know all of this and I don't?" John asked, eying Johannes suspiciously.

Johannes shrugged his shoulders. "I don't know. You don't remember?"

"No. I don't. I don't remember agreeing to any of this."

"Agree to it?" Johannes said, taken aback. "It was **your** idea! **You** decided to speed things up and thought the best way was to take on karma for both of us. That's why I found love so quickly. You told me to go on and you'd catch up."

"Oh." John said, matter-of-factly. He then said, "Well…I miss you."

"Now you're being silly. I'm right here." Johannes leaned his shoulder up against John's.

John turned and looked at him. "I mean, I miss seeing you."

"Don't they have mirrors in Spain? Ha ha!"

"That's not the same." John stood up and looked away for a moment. When he looked back, Johannes was standing as well.

"Well come visit me!" Johannes implored.

John looked down at his feet and noticed he was not wearing shoes. He failed to notice that there was nothing beneath his feet.

"You left and I've been lost without you," he said.

"You don't look lost to me." Johannes waved his hand across the scene. "Look at all you've accomplished on your own!"

"You mean the writings?" John asked.

"I mean everything! Furthermore, you're almost done. Look, come to Venice. It's a beautiful city and I want you to meet Sofia. You two are going to love each other, I just know it!"

John remained quiet.

"Besides, you should be happy! After all, **we're** getting married!"

"Johannes—**you're** getting married." John quickly looked away because he had begun to cry and he didn't want Johannes to see. After he composed himself, he turned back, but Johannes was gone.

"Johannes! Where'd you go? Don't leave! I can't do this alone!"

From a distance, John heard, "You can. You have. You will. You **are**!" But this did not make him feel better. He broke down and cried heartily. The tears streamed down his cheeks and soaked his shirt, which was already damp with sweat.

Recognize. Release. Return-to-Center.

The words and the soothing timbre of the voice calmed John. His tears dried quickly and he felt...centered.

Recognize. Release. Return-to-Center. **This** is an exercise in completion.

We hinted at this before and now state it outright: nine is the number of **completion**.

As you move along the path of evolution, it is natural to repeat old patterns—to fall back to old ways. That is expected. In fact, it is necessary. It does not mean regression; it is simply the way things work...in time. Time is cyclical more than it is linear. Notice how, in the middle of summer, it is easier to remember summers from long ago than it is to remember the previous winter.

So, **recognize** when something old and unwanted comes back. **Release** your reaction to it. **Release** your self-judgment about it. And **release** your emotions surrounding it. Then, consciously, and in whatever way you choose, **return-to-center**.

After a brief pause, the oration in John's head continued, except now in a decidedly feminine voice.

Your time with Maria and now in Barcelona has exposed you to the languages of Spain. At times, you have mistaken one word for another. For example, consider how similar these three words are—in both sound and appearance: *nueve, nuevo,* and *huevo.* These words translate to nine, new, and egg. In French, the word *neuf* means nine, but also means new, as in brand-new. And the word for egg, as you know, is *oeuf.* We mustn't, of course, forget the Italian versions: *nove, nuovo,* and *uovo.*

One way to relate all of these words is thusly: **nine** months after a human **egg** is fertilized a **new** person is born.

Allow me to introduce myself. I am the Roman goddess *Nona.* I am often thought of with my sisters *Decima* and *Morta.* Together, we comprise the *Parcae*—the Fates, as you would call us in English.

Parcae comes from the Latin word *parere,* which means to create or to give birth. I am the goddess of pregnancy. My sister *Decima* is the goddess of birth, and *Morta* is the goddess of death. In a way, we are related to the three stages of a woman's life: maiden, mother, and crone.

My name *Nona* is the Latin word meaning ninth. *Decima,* means tenth, which is that which follows, and *Morta* means death—the completion of every life. Roman women would most often pray to me in their ninth month of pregnancy and then pray to my sister when in labor.

Frequently, much pain is experienced during birth and death. And, as many women know, a pregnancy can be rough at times. My sisters and I are here to bring as much comfort as we can to help humanity within these painfully profound experiences.

One meaning of nine is **completion**, such as the completion of a journey. A pregnancy is a journey indeed, both for the mother and the fetus. And, as with nine, the end of one journey is the beginning of another.

A more significant meaning of nine is **embodiment**. The nine-month gestation is literally that which is needed for the embodiment of a soul. It is not merely about the development of the body. Your spirit—your soul—is so vast and energetic, it takes nine months to step it down into the slow, viscous reality of the physical realm. As you know, it then takes years more to master rudimentary tasks such as walking, talking, reading, and writing.

Esoteric journeys follow a similar pattern. When you embody what you learn, you **become** it. As you were told before, in third density, you've been given self-awareness and commissioned to learn about love. Through the journey of nine, which you walk over and over again, you **become** love. You **are** love already, so what you are really doing is **embodying** love. You are coming to experience yourself as a physical depiction of love.

In one perspective, you are **creating** a physical model of love...namely your human body and the circumstances of your life. In another view, you are **experiencing** the physical sensations of love in all of its abundant varieties.

The three special numbers are three, six, and nine. 3+6=9. Embodying requires creating and experiencing—sending out and receiving in.

In your journeying, you first crave love. You then attract love. Eventually, you experience love: loving and being loved. Often, you experience giving love and receiving love separately before you are able to bring them together.

In the end, you will realize that you **are** love. And through this revelation, you will be born to fourth density. Once you gain your footing there, all of third density will be likened to your time *in utero*.

It takes nine months to go from an egg to a new life; ninety years are often spanned between birth and death; and it can take nine hundred lifetimes to learn enough in third density to ascend into fourth.

Within those last statements, John caught glimpses of the distant past and distant future. The sensation was nearly overwhelming. *Nona*, sensing John's apprehension, pulled backed her energy and quietly observed.

Once John regained his balance, the discourse restarted, but again in a different voice.

A final meaning of nine is **perfection**. The misunderstanding of this, however, beguiles many a seeker. You see, you cannot create perfection, only experience it.

The one who sets out to create perfection fails in two ways. First, he or she neglects to see that perfection is, always is, and is never missing. Second, he or she then judges all of his or her creations as lacking—as less than perfect—as not measuring up.

The journey of creation changes you...or rather, it changes how you see and experience yourself. By the time you have completed the creation of a thing or event, you have already come to know yourself as greater than that thing or event. Your creations therefore appear less than complete, less than perfect, and become less than satisfying.

Your awareness expands and thus, in looking back on anything you have done, you see flaws. In other words, you see ways to make it better! Even if you like the creation, you will soon want more...and want better.

Stop trying to **create** perfection. Instead, **see** the perfection that is.

Your job is never to improve the Universe. You cannot improve on perfection. All you can do is to create and experience (three and six) more of what you love and desire. This is not an improvement (from the perspective of the Universe) because perfection is and always will be. All desires manifest vibrationally **instantly**, so turning them into physical experience is not an improvement in the absolute (the Universe), merely an improvement in the relative (your experience of it).

The conditions of your life can improve. Your experiences can improve. You can gain understanding, awareness, and proficiency. But, in the eyes of God, you cannot become better than the perfect specimen that you are.

As John listened, he realized that the deep resonating voice was familiar.

"Ra? Is that you?" he asked. "Are you here?"

"Yes. I am Ra and I am here."

"But why are you here? This is Spain—not Egypt."

"Just because the Egyptians revered me," Ra explained, "does not mean I exist only for them. Are **you** here...in Spain?"

"Yes."

"Then I am here in Spain as well."

John thought about this for a moment and felt that there was more than one meaning to Ra's words. "What do you mean by that?" he asked.

Ra smiled proudly and said, "My boy, you have come a long way! You **are** gaining awareness! I am here in Spain **for** you and **with** you. However, it is also simply your physical presence in Spain that places me in Spain as well. Not just because I am here with you, but because you and I are one."

"As in: 'We are all one'?"

"That too, but that is not how I meant it."

"How did you mean it, then?" John asked.

"John, you and I are one because I am your Higher Self. You will...become me, just as I will become another."

"You are my Higher Self?" John asked, surprised and excited at the same time. "How come you never told me that before?"

"Because it was not time for you to know."

John thought for a moment and then said, "And what do you mean I will become you?"

"I am your Higher Self, which also means I am your **future** self —space and time. Remember?"

"Oh, I get it!"

"When you journeyed to Egypt, you sought after me, but since you and I are one, you also went in search of yourself. Furthermore, I am Johannes' Higher Self too, so when you found Johannes on top of that pyramid, you found a piece of yourself again. It works like this:

I am a river. My experiences are the waters that flow through me. As time passes, they shift and change me; much the way flowing water causes a river to change course. You and Johannes are tributaries. You are not different than I am, only smaller parts of me. Because you are **my** tributaries, your experiences flow through me just as a tributary's water flows into the river it feeds.

The place where this analogy falls short is that you are not along side of me; your experiences don't flow through you **and then** through me. I experience what you experience in the very same moment! We are not separated by time or space. One part of the river is you, and another part is Johannes. One cannot always separate the water that is yours from the water that is his. And the **entire** river is me, so **everything** that is yours or his is mine.

Because I have awareness beyond the linear flow of time, I can see the entire river as it flows. If you could see the way that I see, then you would never have felt as if you lost Johannes because a part of you is

266

always with him: on top of the pyramid, walking the dessert, and sharing a bed. These are memories to you, but they are ever happening inside of me! And I thank you for them. They are some of my fondest experiences in human form. Oh the joy of finding myself, guiding myself, and loving myself.

So, now that I have you before me, my boy, let us continue your instruction. You have journeyed to reach me and as always, there is reward. This forthcoming body of knowledge, wisdom, and awareness is that reward. Shall we go on then?

John nodded excitedly.

The Perfect Nine

Completion is the **relative** meaning of nine. Perfection is the **absolute** meaning of nine. So the next time you rate a performance, don't call it a perfect ten; call it a perfect nine!

Many moons ago, we alluded to the three special numbers. You now know that they are the three, the six, and the nine. Within our introduction to the eight, we illustrated how basic numbers are formed from the combination of other numbers. Now, behold what happens with a sequence created by adding nine.

This:

$$9, 18, 27, 36, 45, 54, 63, 72, 81...$$

produces this:

$$\underline{9}, 9, 9, 9, 9, 9, 9, 9, 9...$$

What this shows is first, that any number of nines added together will always produce nine, and next, the **products** of nine reveal all of the **paths** to nine:

$$18: 1+8=9$$
$$27: 2+7=9$$
$$36: 3+6=9$$
$$45: 4+5=9$$

Each of these paths illustrates an alchemical recipe for completion. Allow us to put them into words, giving examples of how they can manifest in human existence.

The **a-ha moment**—the eight—is the vibrational indication that the **individual** experiencing it has reached completion within a given endeavor. This is the 18/9. He or she is now ready to move up to the next level and will soon begin a new cycle.

When two individuals seek **deep** within themselves and **connect** to each other from that place, the greatest intimacy is experienced. There is nothing they cannot accomplish with the 27/9.

The purpose of life is to **create**, and the purpose of life is to **experience**. Thus the most complete picture of life's purpose is the 36/9.

Lastly, when there is **stagnation** (too much stasis), seek **movement**, and when there is **chaos** (too much change), seek **stability**. The 45/9 thus illustrates the proper balance for progression, healing, growth, and evolution.

The cycle of nine can be described like this:

ONE: Every journey starts with one, and every being was created in the image and likeness of THE ONE.

TWO: An observer, in seeing that which is observed, grows curious. It is only natural for the one observing to then seek further experience through another, through relationship—through partnerships and oppositions.

THREE: Keep in mind, however, that you are the creator of your own reality. Thus, when you enter into relationship with another, you are the sole creator of your experience of them, just as they are the sole creator of their experience of you. To be happy in relationship is solely up to you. It is how you choose to experience the other that holds all of the power, not what they choose to do in your presence. So one's experience of another is really just his or her experience of his or her self reflected in the other. Creation is ever present. You are always creating, even if you are not **consciously** creating.

FOUR: Physical reality is the result of creation. Everything that is physical now was thought into being. Yet, no matter how solid an atom may seem, it is nothing more than energy occupying space for a period of time as directed by consciousness. So while things may appear stable, solid, and hard, their days are numbered.

FIVE: Stability can seem to last eons of time, but change will always prevail. This is because change is vibration, and vibration is what the Universe is actually made of. You can direct change, but you cannot prevent change. Change will eventually carry you along to the next wave of growth.

SIX: The three dimensions of space are experienced as six directions from within it. You create in an instant, then experience what you created some **time** later. You are meant to experience; it is a part of your purpose. But you are also meant to move on from there.

SEVEN: From a deeper perspective, you are one experiencing the projected reality of your own making. You are thus hidden inside of everything that you experience. When you bump up against something, you bump against a part of yourself. Eventually, you will stop looking out there for the answers. When you seek inward, transformation begins.

EIGHT: As you seek, so shall you find. Thus come your discoveries: the peak experiences, the quantum leaps, and the ah-ha moments.

NINE: The completion of an endeavor can require iterations. You're not just learning, you are embodying. Soon you will realize that you cannot create perfection, merely behold the perfection that is.

TEN/ONE: And when one journey ends, another begins.

Perfection is. One cannot improve on perfection. Numerology shows us this: adding to nine does not result in a great number. Furthermore, the journey of nine brings every number back to itself. Look:

$$1+9 = 10/1$$
$$2+9 = 11/2$$
$$3+9 = 12/3$$
$$4+9 = 13/4$$
$$5+9 = 14/5$$
$$6+9 = 15/6$$
$$7+9 = 16/7$$
$$8+9 = 17/8$$
$$9+9 = 18/9$$

The message here is that every journey brings **you** back to **yourself**. It brings you home...to **where** you really are...to **who** you really are. It does this bit-by-bit. Each fractal journey enables you to embody a little bit more of the whole that you are. When the dust settles, only you remain.

The cycle goes full circle—in all directions. That is why the geometric shape that represents nine is a sphere. All of the corners have been filed down. All of the faces merge into one. The sphere has a single continuous surface that remains equidistant from its center point. The sphere is the most efficient solid, and thus forms naturally all around you. Bubbles of air encased in a film of soap, the cells in your body, droplets of rain—these are not perfect spheres, but are resemblant of them.

You walk on a spherical planet, though its surface feels flat to you. You look up at spherical stars that appear to be mere points of light. The spherical sun and the spherical moon are but circles in your sky. The sphere is everywhere, yet often goes unnoticed.

Vibrationally, nine is about completion and perfection and yet both of these concepts are more commonly associated with ten. Ten is what follows nine and forms the gateway to a new cycle of counting. We will thus follow this pattern as well and begin the discussion of ten.

10 – *Ten* – X

Dix – Dieci – Diez – Zehn

In Roman notation, as you have surely noticed, ten is a digit in and of itself and is represented by X. In the Tarot, of which you are familiar, ten is the gateway between the nine of one cycle and the one of the next. Humans have ten fingers, and thus in Arabia ten **digits** (0-9) were created in a decimal (base 10) number system.

In basic numerology, we do not treat ten as a special number; its significance to man makes it significant nonetheless. We have chosen to use the Tarot's meaning of ten and thus in this discussion we will look both forward and backward, after all, that is what a gateway is for. It is a time to review the past while simultaneously preparing for the future.

It is natural for men and women to pause when in a gateway. You celebrate your transitions: birthdays, anniversaries, changes in residences and seasons. You look back on a prior endeavor before diving into the next adventure. You celebrate the completions and the beginnings together. And thus ten represents a **rite of passage**.

To get the most out of a rite of passage, look back with **appreciation** at all that you have gained, and look ahead with **anticipation** for all that is yet to come. This is a high art of manifestation. We recommend that you practice it frequently.

Within our discourse of numbers, the gateway of ten sits between the basic numerology of the one to nine and the higher **applications** of numerology.

The Channel

We define channeling as the conveying of information from one realm to another. The channel—or scribe—is therefore another type of gateway. You essentially have a foot in each realm.

You, however, do not perceive it that way. The information seems to be delivered to you. You simply experience yourself as an ordinary third-density being, who—magically—hears messages from the fourth, fifth, and sixth.

This is, in fact, appropriate. If you became aware of your higher density presence, you would too quickly shift into those realms...and shift out of yours.

Now watch as we play for a moment. We will illustrate channeling via the number ten written as 10. The one—you—is the channel; zero is the absolute, the non-physical, that which is the source of all information. When you are you, you are 1, and when you are channeling—writing or speaking—you are 10.

But note that there is no difference. Ten **is** one! That is why we write it as 10/1. The zero changes it not.

You are not separate from those of us you speak and write for. The greater you—the larger one—is continually in our presence. If you were truly separated from us, you would not be able to hear our words. And yet, even in this very moment that you witness this information, you do not fully accept what we say.

Again, this is appropriate. If you were to accept these sentiments fully, your vibration would accelerate too quickly to fulfill your purpose as a channel. Those in third density would no longer have access to you. Thus, although we shower you with great wisdom, do not expect yourself to assimilate it immediately. That is not what we ask of you. Be simply the one that you are and those aspects of being that you choose. Be the

I **and** the 10, for in that is the perfection of the purpose you have selected for yourself.

The Numerology of Words

Throughout our discussions, we've used words to describe the meanings of numbers. Now we'd like to show you the opposite. We will now use numbers to illustrate the hidden vibration of words.

Consider the following table (for English), which shows the number assigned to each letter:

1	2	3	4	5	6	7	8	9
A	B	C	D	E	F	G	H	I
J	K	L	M	N	O	P	Q	R
S	T	U	V	W	X	Y	Z	

From this, we can then calculate the vibration hidden within names and words. Take for example the word **begin**. Analyzing it, we find the following:

```
B E G I N
2+5+7+9+5 = 28/10/1
```

How interesting! The number one means to begin, and **begin** holds the vibration of one! But notice that the word **being** contains the very same letters in a slightly different order.

```
B E I N G
2+5+9+5+7 = 28/10/1
```

A **being** is an individual and is thus another meaning of one. It, of course, adds up to one as well!

Let us try a few more words:

```
L  O  V  E
3+6+4+5  =  18/9
```

Love is perfect (9). Love is complete (9). From love, only love is created. **Love** is spelled l-o-v-e and thus within love are: creation (3), harmony (6), stability (4), and change (5). Love creates harmony and has the power to both move mountains and hold them together!

Now let us look at the opposite of love:

```
F  E  A  R
6+5+1+9  =  21/3
```

The opposite of love is fear. With fear, harmony (6) is shifted (5) away from resulting in a separation (1) that is accepted completely (9) and thus contains an emotional charge. In total, fear is a three because it is creative. Our fears are the creators of all unwanted experience.

From the perspective of the non-physical, fear is a necessary part of creation, for without fear, there is no separation, and without separation the physical realm could not exist.

Also notice that with fear, the 2 is in front of the 1. It is 21/3, not 12/3. That is because fear exists when an individual pays more attention to what is outside of him or her (2), rather than what is inside (1). When the one comes first, the creation is deliberate. When the two comes first, it is unintentional.

Let us compare three words that are similar:

```
H A P P I N E S S
8+1+7+7+9+5+5+1+1 = 44[8]

J O Y
1+6+7 = 14/5

B L I S S
2+3+9+1+1 = 16/7
```

Happiness is an 8; it is an ideal. It is sought frequently and is experienced often, even if for brief moments. It is a 44[8] because it is felt in the heart (4) and there is a bit of stability (4) to it. You can experience extended feelings of happiness by remaining in your heart.

Joy is an expression. You don't just feel joy; you **express** joy. It starts in the heart (4), but is then expressed outward. It is therefore a five because it has a greater ability to affect those around you. Emanate joy and watch how those in the room shift! But notice how some will be affected negatively (with envy perhaps), while others will be affected positively (as your joy activates theirs). The choice lies with them. Joy, as a five, is harder to maintain than happiness and thus tends to be experienced for briefer periods (albeit more intensely).

Lastly, bliss is a 16/7 because it is only achieved through a deep connection to the beauty (6) that is within you. You can be happy through the observation of pleasant circumstances around you, but you can only reach bliss by truly connecting with your Higher Self. True bliss is felt right down to your core and not just in your heart.

Numerological analysis does not merely apply to words. It applies to phrases as well. For example, consider the following:

```
I   C A N
9 + 3+1+5 = 18/9

I   D O
9 + 4+6 = 19/1

I   W I L L
9 + 5+9+3+3 = 29/11[2]

I   A M
9 + 1+4 = 14/5
```

When you say, "I can," you state your **ability** to complete (9) whatever follows. However, the statement alone does not put the creation into action, it merely paves the way forward. There is a completeness in this because in knowing you can, you need not prove it through action. The knowledge itself is enough.

When you say, "I do," you describe an aspect of self. You often identify (1) yourself by what you do: your jobs, your careers, and your accomplishments.

When you say, "I will," you are stating your intention, which establishes a goal and direction (2). The journey then ensues from there.

And when you say, "I am," that is when you create change (5), for you have acknowledged an absolute point of power within yourself. "I am," is a statement of being, in the present moment, here and now, and has the power to shift any experience into a new experience.

How about this one:

```
G  O  D
7+6+4  =  17/8
```

What does this bring to mind?

It reminds me of our discussion on The Star—card XVII in the Tarot.

Precisely. One need do nothing more than connect with the one inside to experience God (THE ONE)!

And what, I ask, is a way you can do this?

```
P  R  A  Y  E  R
7+9+1+7+5+9  =  38/11[2]
```

So prayer is a 2 because it is when one asks blessings from someone/something perceived to be outside of them. But notice that it is really an 11. Eleven is a Master Number and thus stands on its own. (We'll discuss Master Numbers more in a moment.)

For the sake of comparison, let us look at another way to connect with All-That-Is.

```
M  E  D  I  T  A  T  I  O  N
4+5+4+9+2+1+2+9+6+5  =  47/11[2]
```

It too is an 11[2]! Prayer and meditation—two slightly different ways to experience connection via the eleven.

Since we have reached the first of our Master Numbers, let us now discuss the number eleven.

11 – *Eleven* – XI

Onze – Undici – Once – Elf

Eleven is the first of our Master Numbers, which are defined as two digit numbers where both digits are the same. However, before we discuss anything further, let us analyze the words **master** and **mastery**.

```
M A S T E R
4+1+1+2+5+9 = 22[4]

M A S T E R Y
4+1+1+2+5+9+7 = 29/11[2]
```

Is there any surprise that both of these result in Master Numbers? Master Numbers have special meanings; they contain a higher vibration than the numbers they would otherwise reduce to. We thus use a slightly different notation for them. While ten is written as 10/1; eleven is written as 11[2].

Illumination

Eleven, as a Master Number, has more significance than two. However, eleven doesn't simply **add** meaning to the number two, it **raises** the meaning of two to a higher vibration. For example, when we describe the meaning of two, we use words like: connection, communication, and direction. Watch as we start with these words and reach higher.

Consider a scenario where an individual is seeking information from another. The one, in encountering the other, makes a connection (2). He or she then asks a question, initiating communication (2). And let us say in this case the second is able to answer the question thus providing direction (2). So far, what we are describing is a human experience that is classically two in its vibration.

Now let us take this to the next level. Instead of simply asking (2), the first person is now seeking (7). One who asks receives knowledge, but what happens when one seeks? We would say that he or she receives illumination (11)! Illumination is not just information (knowledge), but also inspiration (energy). It is a bathing of light. Light is information, but also sound...energy...**love**. You **see** light, **hear** sound, and **feel** love. From our perspective, they are merely different frequencies of vibration; light **is** love and love **is** light. During the daytime, half of your planet is bathed in the light of the sun and is thus **illuminated** by it. The sun is the **source** of that light. Thus illumination always has a source. That is why we often refer to THE ONE (God/Goddess/All-That-Is) as **Source!**

What is less obvious is that with illumination, one is moved into a higher vibration; one is affected and shifted. When a particle is illuminated with energy, it becomes excited. When a person is illuminated with love, he or she becomes excited. **Illumination** is not merely a two experience, it is an eleven! In fact, we are illuminating you right now. We are providing you information, but also light, unseen or otherwise.

Earlier we showed you how the number two in Roman notation is written as II, which closely resembles 11, the higher vibration of two. This is illustrated on The High Priestess, Tarot card number II, which is intimately related to the 11. In fetching this card, you will see that the High Priestess sits between two pillars—one dark and the other light.

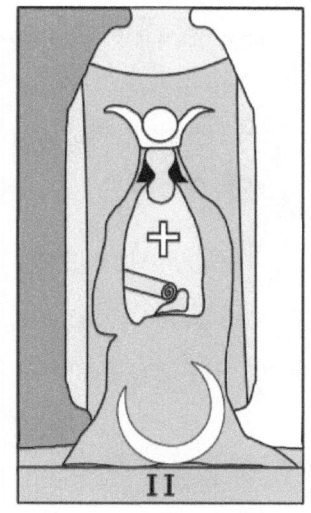

Eleven may be a higher vibration of two, but it is still dualistic. In other words, it contains two meanings. On the one hand there is illumination; on the other hand there i s **disillusionment**. The High Priestess is aware of this and thus resides between the two. You cannot have illumination without disillusionment. They are not opposites; they are the very same. With illumination, light reveals truth, but that is the very same process as when light dispels darkness. Disillusionment is when false ideas are revealed for what they are, and through this process the truth is unveiled.

Really, the only difference between illumination and disillusionment is one's perspective. When inside the gateway of ten, you are free to look backward or forward. When inside the gateway of eleven, you can look toward disillusionment or toward illumination. It is your choice (2). We of course, invite you to sit, as the High Priestess does, in between the two in full acknowledgement and acceptance of both—and thus inside of eleven where both paths are seen simultaneously.

And now here is something you can behold and enjoy—a visual mnemonic to help you remember the significance of what eleven brings. The Roman number II resembles 11, but so does the double el—'ll'. Now watch as we reveal words and phrases resonant with eleven:

We already told you of the two pi__ll__ars of eleven: i__ll__umination and disi__ll__usionment. These pillars do not cross like the X; they are para__ll__el. Thus the difference between two and eleven is alignment. But illumination is also a process, an ongoing process, and one that will continue infinitely. If there is anything that you wish to know, be patient, because

283

time will tell all. Anything false will fade away revealing truth eventually. Allow this, and you will grow wise well in advance of others. And thus you will experience fulfillment and wellbeing and continually move beyond the walls of illusion.

Master Numbers

The last thing we wish to show you is how the eleven reveals all of the other Master Numbers.

11, 22, 33, 44, 55, 66, 77, 88, 99

Someday we will walk you through each of these.

12 – *Twelve* – XII

Douze – Dodici – Doce – Zwölf

In our discussion of fear, we shared with you the difference between the 21/3 and the 12/3. With the number twelve, the one comes first. Twelve represents a higher form of creation, one that is intentional, personal, and thus purposeful.

What might you say is the greatest manifestation created in this manner? We would say: physical reality! As such, we associate the number twelve with the physical realm. We will now show you how the physical realm is imbued with the number twelve.

Furthermore, because we have commissioned you to write a book on the meaning of numbers, we are now going to guide you through a process that will create a key. This key, however, is not for you. Through you, it will make its way into the hands of the ones who seek it.

We, again, are going to walk you through the creation of a mathematical sequence, which is widely known as the Fibonacci sequence. It is a bit more complex than the others. Each number in this sequence is calculated as the sum of the previous two numbers. We start with the number 1. The second number is thus [0]+1, which is again 1. The third number, the sum of the previous two, is thus 1+1, which is 2. And the fourth number is thus 1+2, which is 3.

Carrying out this sequence through 26 positions thus yields:

1, 1, 2, 3, 5, 8, 13, 21, 34, 55, 89, 144, 233, 377, 610, 987, 1597, 2584, 4181, 6765, 10946, 17711, 28657, 46368, 75025, 121393

The Fibonacci sequence is very special and illustrates the Golden Mean.

If we reducing each position numerologically to a single digit, we obtain this:

1, 1, 2, 3, 5, 8, 4, 3, 7, 1, 8, 9, 8, 8, 7, 6, 4, 1, 5, 6, 2, 8, 1, 9, 1, 1

Now, let us create a slightly different sequence. This time, we will calculate each position as the sum of the previous two **reduced** values:

1, 1, 2, 3, 5, 8, 13, 12, 7, 10, 8, 9, 17, 17, 16, 15, 13, 10, 5, 6, 11, 8, 10, 9, 10, 10

When we reduced these values, we arrive here:

1, 1, 2, 3, 5, 8, 4, 3, 7, 1, 8, 9, 8, 8, 7, 6, 4, 1, 5, 6, 2, 8, 1, 9, 1, 1

The first thing this exercise shows you is that the first method produces the same results as the second. That is because reduction is based on addition just as the Fibonacci sequence is. Whether you add then reduce or reduce then add matters not.

Because the first method gives the same results as the second, we can then see that the pattern of reduced values repeats after 24 positions. We started with 1 then 1 and we ended with 1 then 1. Hidden within the Fibonacci sequence is a numerological cycle of 24.

The Cycle of 24 and the Cycle of 12

As a cycle of 24, no matter where you start, it will repeat after 24 iterations. We can therefore draw the 24 values around a **clock,** like so:

Notice that there are 24 values in our Golden Mean cycle, and 24 hours in a day. Intriguing coincidence, wouldn't you say?

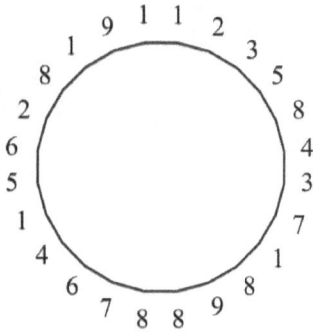

Now notice that at the top of our clock is 1-1, and at the bottom of our clock is 8-8. These are the only two places were a digit repeats within the sequence. They are balanced within the cycle. If we divide our clock in half, one side moves from 1 to 8 and the other from 8 back to 1.

So let us explore this further. Just as you count your 24-hour day as 12 hours *ante meridiem* and 12 hours *post meridiem,* let us redraw our clock with the first twelve numbers on an inner circle and the last twelve on the outer circle. We'll start at the 1:00 position and go from there.

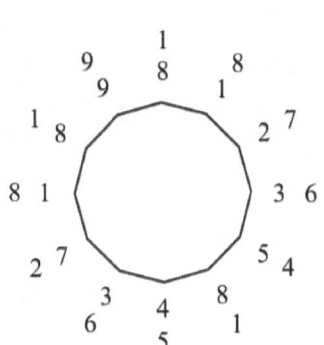

Notice that at the 11:00 position, we have the same number twice, namely nine. However, also consider this, which is not as immediately obvious: The sum at every position is numerologically the same, and again nine!

The numerological reduction of the Fibonacci sequence is a cycle of 24, that when layered as two cycles of 12 reveals the 9, once again displaying our three special numbers: 12/3, 24/6, and 9.

Lastly, to illustrate this further, look what happens when we highlight the location of the threes, the sixes, and the nines. Lo and behold, we find the hexagon and equilateral triangle:

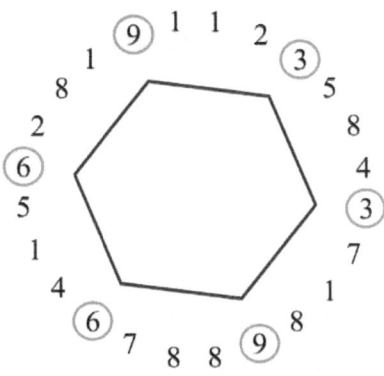

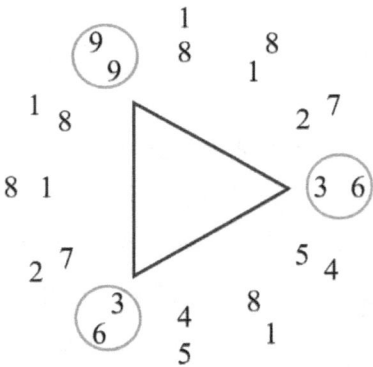

13 – *Thirteen* – **XIII**

Treize – Tredici – Trece – Dreizehn

As much as twelve is the perfect number for the physical realm that you live in, thirteen is the perfect number for the non-physical realm that surrounds, contains, and supports it. Recall our seven circles and how we drew the tetrahedron and hexahedron with them. Now watch what we can do when we add six more.

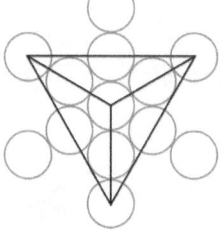

This is a thirteen created from seven and six. Since our seven was itself crated from a six and a one, we can view this as six, six, and one, which could also be thought of as twelve and one. Now watch what we can do with these thirteen circles.

First, we once again can create the tetrahedron...

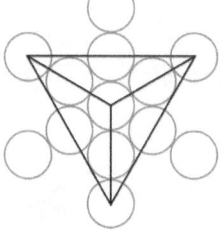
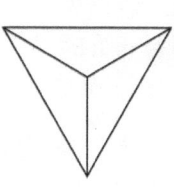

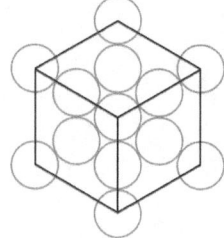
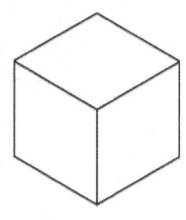

...and the cube.

These are simply larger versions of what was drawn before.

We can now also draw the Merkaba (which is also called a star tetrahedron)...

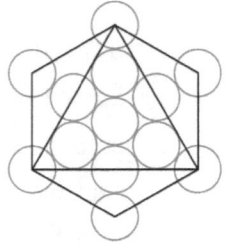 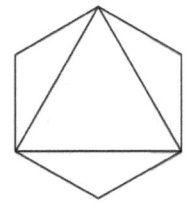

...and the octahedron.

Are these not elegant shapes to behold?

There is more. Watch what happens when we place thirteen smaller circles inside of each larger one, thus multiplying 13×13. Thirteen squared equals 169, which reduces to 16/7.

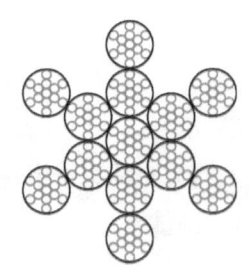

From this, we can now draw the icosahedron with its 20 identical triangular faces.

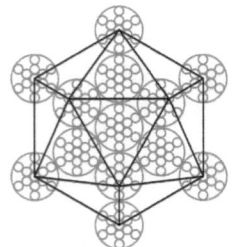 

Finally, to draw the penultimate of the perfect solids, we need to fill in the empty space. This object is called a dodecahedron and contains 12 identical pentagonal faces.

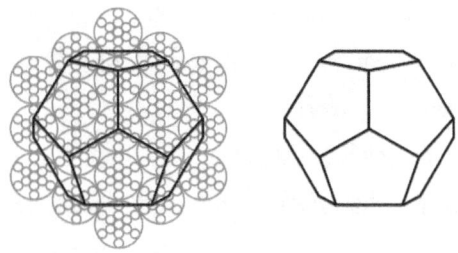

It may not be obvious, but these last two solids are related. In the icosahedron each face is an equilateral triangle and each point is the intersection of five of them. If you look squarely at an apex, you will see a pentagon. Similarly, with the dodecahedron, each face is a pentagon and each apex joins three of them. Does this not remind you of the eight formed from three and five?

The icosahedron and dodecahedron nest one within the other the same way the hexahedron and octahedron do. They are yet another set of twin flames!

Consider this: thirteen is really 13/4—a four formed from one and three. We can interpret 13/4 as **THE ONE (1) creating (3) physical reality (4)**. This also illustrates to us that physical matter (4) is created by the non-physical (13)!

All and all, if you start with one circle, and add six more around it, add another six, and then place thirteen in each, fill in the space and draw each of our perfect solids, you will have visualized the constituents of what is known as **Metatron's Cube.**

From our perspective, we can see it all together. We can see it in two dimensions **and** three. We can see it straight on and from every angle simultaneously. We can see it motionless and rotating. And we can see each piece separated yet joined with the others. Metatron is the master of 4, and Metatron's Cube is the 13/4!

From within the higher densities, one can see the reality of twelve and the realm of thirteen in these same ways: ever flowing, ever becoming, full of potential, and perfect. It is like hearing an entire song at once, while it is being played. All points in time and all points in space accessed simultaneously.

Now do you understand why we never fret? We never fear failure, end, or defeat. We cannot perceive stagnation without also seeing motion. We know that you can only perceive the pieces and parts individually, but we do not. You experience moments of loneliness, fear, sadness, and pain, and yet we can never view those without also seeing connection, harmony, happiness, and bliss. You can only hold yourself apart for so long.

Look at it this way: you can perceive yourself **apart** from the rest of All-That-Is, but you are always **a part** of All-That-It. You were never truly separated to begin with. Within your journeying, you may feel as if you are far **away** from that which you seek, yet you will ever and always find **a way** there, because you are connected to everything.

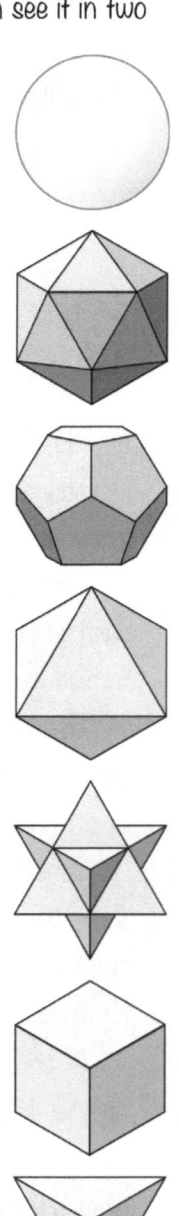

14 – *Fourteen* – XIV

Quatorze – Quattordici – Catorce – Vierzehn

John woke…in his tent and alone. He sat up and looked out of the opening. The sun was high; shadows were nearly non-existent. He wondered why he had been allowed to sleep so late, but then realized that he had no memory of retiring the night before.

Slowly, aspects of the vision quest seeped in. The morning of the first day was clear; the rest remained a blur.

John stood, stretched, and moved around. He felt light. He placed his hands on his stomach and could tell the difference. *Of course, I haven't eaten in days!* Yet, even after thinking this, his stomach did not growl. He was in no a hurry to eat; he was enjoying the clean, clear sensation in his body.

He then wondered where everyone was. He could not hear noise outside of his tent so he figured no one was near. Curiosity egged him on and propelled him out into the bright afternoon sun. In the distance, John saw a small collection of monks standing around talking. Brother Miguel was among them.

Brother Miguel caught sight of John and held up a finger. When he finished his conversation with the others, he excused himself and headed in John's direction. He carried a stack of papers with him.

"Brother John! Good afternoon. I am surprised that you are awake. Most of the others are still sleeping."

"I feel rested and light. I wish my body always felt like this."

"There are ways to reach this state within your body without having to go on a vision quest, you know. I'll tell you of them, if you wish, when we have the time."

John eyed the papers in Brother Miguel's hands, but did not say anything about them. Instead, he asked, "So, how did the quest go, over all? Everyone's all right, I assume."

"Yes. Everyone is well and I would have to say the quest was a success for everyone. We have not interviewed anyone, as of yet, but judging from appearances…"

John eyed the papers once again, and this time recognized his handwriting. "I see you have some of my writings with you," he said.

"Yes! I hope you don't mind, I've read them all…twice!"

"I already told you that you were welcome to read them."

"Oh, these are not the pages you gave me before the quest. These are the pages you gave me **afterward**!"

"I wrote all of **that** during the quest?" John said with shock on his face.

"Indeed!" the monk replied with a broad smile. "I'm guessing you don't remember any of it though, do you?"

"No," John said, shaking his head slowly while trying to conjure a memory.

"And you don't remember giving me permission to read all of this?"

"No. My memory is fuzzy. Is it…good?"

"Good?!? It is downright impressive! The others and I were just discussing some of the…mathematics."

"Mathematics?" John said furrowing his brow.

"Here," Brother Miguel handed John the stack of paper. "Why don't you sit down and read for a bit? I'll fetch you something to eat."

Quatorze – Quattordici – Catorce – Vierzehn

Three days in Narbonne rejuvenated Johannes' body, but did not quell his concerns.

The time is nigh—he thought to himself. *I must decide my next course of action.*

All of his men had returned and were ready to recommence the journey. He could not forestall things any longer.

I need five minutes to myself, and then, ready or not, I will join them.

Before five minutes passed, Johannes heard a knock. He composed himself, took a deep breath, and opened the door. He greeted his guard as pleasantly as possible: "My fine man, I was just on my way down."

"Sir, forgive me. I wouldn't have disturbed you, but I thought you would want to know: Herr Müller and his expedition have just arrived."

"What splendid news!" This time Johannes didn't have to feign his excitement.

The guard went on. "I informed him that you are here. He is on his way up…in fact, here he comes now." The guard stepped back, allowing Klaus Müller to enter Johannes' room. He bowed slightly and departed.

"Johannes, what a pleasant surprise!" the older Müller said. "What brings you to the far corner of France?"

"I came in search of you, Father."

"'Father?!'" Klaus tilted his head to the side "You never call me 'Father'." He then looked at his son out of the corner of his eye and said, "Are you…OK, Son?"

Johannes chuckled, realizing it had been some years since he last called Klaus 'Father'. A moment later, they were both laughing heartily. A tear escaped Johannes' eye and took with it the last of the pent up tension that had lingered within him.

Going with the joy of the moment, Johannes threw his arms around his father and hugged him firmly.

"I'm happy to see you…Klaus," Johannes said, beaming brightly.

Klaus held his son's shoulders and said, "I am happy to see you as well, Son." He then guided them into the room and said, "Tell me, how are things in Italy? For that matter, how was Egypt…and Crete before that? It's been too long. We have much to catch up on."

"Business is good in Italy. You've received my correspondences, yes?"

"Indeed. But I do not want to discuss business. I want to discuss **you**! Alas, we have plenty of time to catch up. We have all of

France to cross. Are you coming back to Germany with me or are you returning to Venice?"

"Actually, how would you feel about traveling to Italy with **me**? There is someone I would like you to meet."

"Oh?" Klaus said, raising an eyebrow.

"Her name is Sofia. She is my…fiancée."

"I guess there's more to catch up on than I expected. How exciting! Do you and your men need to rest? Or are you fit for travel?"

"We are ready to travel," Johannes said. *An understatement, for sure*—he added mentally.

"Then we'll head out as soon as we fill our stomachs. We mustn't keep my future daughter-in-law waiting." Klaus winked, having already warmed up to the idea of her.

"Excellent! I'll write to her immediately so she'll be expecting us!"

Quatorze – Quattordici – Catorce – Vierzehn

D uring the trek back to the monastery, John and Brother Miguel lagged behind the others because Brother Miguel wished to discuss the writings. By that point, he had read all of them three times over and everything was fresh in his mind. John had read the new material only once. He, of course, also wrote them; however in this case, having written the pages gave no advantage. In fact, it surprised him how often Brother Miguel recited a passage that he did not recall at all.

When they got back to their room at the monastery, John began unpacking his belongings. He pulled out the Tarot cards buried deep in his satchel, sat on his bed, and shuffled them. Shuffling cards relaxed him. It gave his hands something to do while his mind drifted. He did not intend to do a reading. In fact, he wasn't paying attention to anything he did.

A moment later, a card jumped out of the deck and landed on the floor. John reached down to pick it up, then hesitated. He admired the angel drawn upon the card and, for a second, swore she smiled back at him.

John examined the card and the number upon it: XIV. *Isn't that the last number for the book?* John, of course, only knew this because Brother Miguel had said that to him.

"When is the last chapter coming?" Brother Miguel had asked.

"I don't understand what you mean?" John had replied.

"When I first fetched you at the end of your quest, you said the last chapter, Chapter 14, was forthcoming."

"I did?"

"Trust me, my friend. That is what you said."

John picked up the card and placed it on the desk. *Temperance. Didn't they say there was more to come about Temperance?* John wanted to ask Brother Miguel, but he had left the room shortly after they arrived. And he had taken all of the pages with him. *I guess I'll have to ask him when he gets back, unless...*

John looked at the deck of cards in his hands and then was struck with an idea. The inclination was strong, so he shuffled a bit more, pulled cards one-by-one, and placed them on the desk. He didn't follow any specific layout he'd used before; he simply placed each card where he felt it belonged. He kept the Temperance card on the side, and arranged the other six in a pattern. When the image felt complete, the urge to write washed over him.

Temperance

My dear boy, I am Archangel Gabriel and I am here to share with you the blessings of Temperance. You were indeed told that more on this virtue was forthcoming. Through your journeying and your efforts, you have arrived.

Fourteen, in the grand scheme of things, seems not so special a number, and yet it is half of a lunar orbit and a full fortnight of days. The first and third quarter moons are exactly halfway between the full moon and the new moon; they are exemplary of Temperance herself. It is for this reason that waiting a fortnight before venturing headstrong into action can be such a powerful exercise in Temperance.

What makes the number fourteen special is the total of its numerological properties. Written as 14/5, we see a five comprised of a one and a four. One is represented by a point, and four is represented by a square. Fourteen can thus be drawn as a point within a square.

This image can symbolize the lunar cycle—each side representing a week. The four corners mark the significant phases of the moon: new moon, first quarter, full moon, and third quarter.

When you travel around a circle, you are always the same distance from the center. When you travel around a square, you move closer in, then further out over and over again. Doesn't that remind you of life? Have you not had times when life got easier and easier, and then times when it got harder and harder? Have you not had moments when, in reaching a corner, your life suddenly made a sharp turn, sometimes for the better, sometimes seemingly for the worse?

The circle is an ideal, but the square is closer to the way many of you experience reality. And yet there **are** ways to temper the extremes. Employing what we call **The Middle Way**, you can begin guiding your square into a circle.

Tempering oneself can be a tricky thing. If by tempering, one merely stifles the emotions within, they actually accentuate the corners rather than smoothing them. Anger repressed long enough becomes rage—years of coerced calm can thus give way to a violent storm.

The truer way of Temperance is to follow one's natural rhythms with freedom and authenticity. If your life resembles a square, walk the square. By expressing what you feel in the moment, you can more quickly round the corner and move back toward the center.

But then what? After one Recognizes, Releases, and Returns to Center (the RRR or the 999), will one naturally remain centered?

Cycles exist within cycles, so stasis is not the answer. Staying fixedly at the center is not the goal. However, there are ways to more proficiently return to center, with ease and grace: and that brings us to Temperance and the 14/5.

Let us revisit our square and point. This time we will connect the four corners to the center of the square, but in such a way as to highlight a pair of triangles: one point up and the other pointing down.

Being Centered

Now, let us study the spread of cards you have laid out:

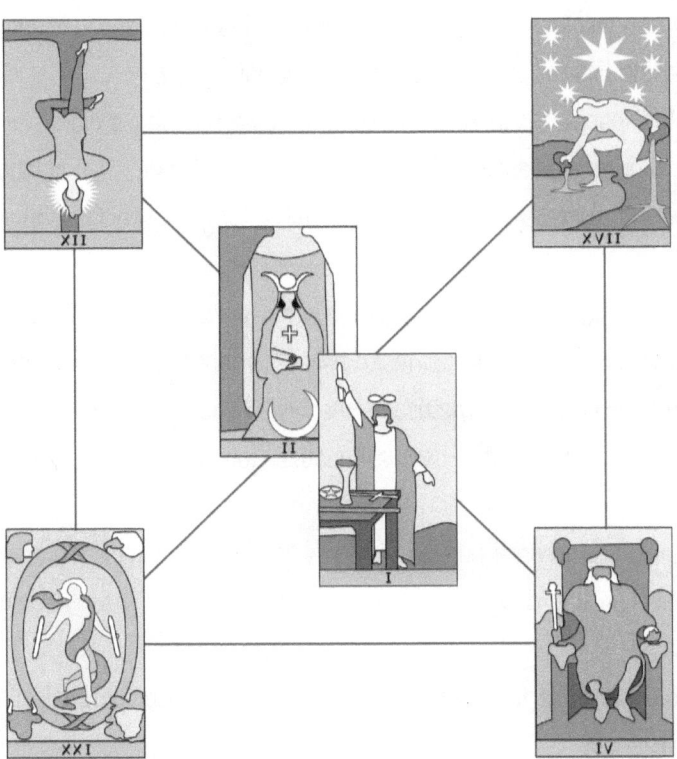

Notice that it resembles both of the diagrams we have drawn for you. Four cards form the corners of a square and a pair sits at the center.

Before we go on, examine the card in the lower left corner. Notice that this card, XXI - The World, itself resembles our diagram. There is a symbolic image at each corner and a woman in the middle. The symbols along the circumference of the wreath represent the four fixed signs of the Zodiac: Taurus (the bull), Leo (the lion), Scorpio (the eagle), and Aquarius (the man).

If we model one of your years as a square, we have a season for each side. The corners would thus indicate the solstices and the equinoxes. Divided this way, each side/season is comprised of three signs. The sign in the middle of each season is a fixed sign. Surely you have noticed that each season is most stable during the fixed signs. Early Aries can feel like winter, and late Gemini often feels like mid-summer, but during the time of Taurus, we are most certainly in spring.

Most people visualize the passing of time the way a clock turns—in other words clockwise. When looking at The World, the symbols are shown in reverse order—counterclockwise. Why do you think that would be?

Well, in part because the world is a **reflection** of your thoughts. It is an aberration; it is made-up, make-believe, a fabrication...it is a **creation**. Pay attention to the words used—made-up because you are making it up as you go along—make-believe because you are creating it with your beliefs.

The World is card number XXI—a 21/3. The numbers are reversed as well. The World is not a true 21/3, like the word **fear**, it only **looks** that way!

Now, we shall focus on subsets of the whole. Let us begin with the lower triangle.

At the top of the lower triangle, we have The Magician. Moving clockwise, we find The Emperor and then The World. The Magician is the archetypal teacher of **manifestation**. He teaches us how to create the physical world through use of the four elements and the Law of Attraction.

The Emperor represents **proficiency** within the physical realm. He is respected because of his mastery. We can surmise his history—how he came to be seated on the throne, but that matters not. What does matter is that, at present, he **sits** on his throne. He thus exhibits **inaction**. He is ready, willing, and able to act, but remains confident and calm until action is needed. He is a symbol of **empowerment**.

The Emperor, card number IV, embodies the vibration of four: tenacity, stability, and support.

Notice that the number 14 in Temperance contains 1, The Magician and 4, The Emperor.

The bottom triangle represents physical life and learning on a planet like Earth. The Magician guides and instructs The Emperor, who then creates The World as a refection of himself.

Now let us inspect the top triangle.

In the upper left corner, we have The Hanged Man. The Hanged Man is a human suspended—in time and space. He has withdrawn from the world of **doing** in order to connect to the realm of **being**. His inaction resembles The Emperor in the opposite corner, but has more intention and purpose.

When we consider the clockwise motion along the outside of the square, The Hanged Man takes us away from The World and toward The Star. He sacrifices experience in outer reality to focus on inner reality.

The Hanged Man is number XII, which is a 12/3. His sacrifice is thus creative. It is his intention to create something more or something better than he has already created in the world, which causes him to retreat and seek guidance from the stars.

So The Hanged Man represents a human, who pauses with purpose and the **process** he moves into is exactly the next card moving clockwise. The Star, as we've discussed before, **is** the process of seeking inward. It is number XVII because it is a one and a seven: 17/8. The Hanged Man thus sacrifices time in the mundane in order to connect with the astral. The Hanged Man understands that it is important to dream. By spending time in his imagination **first**, he is better able to create life in the world **afterward**.

But where does The Hanged Man learn of this wisdom? The High Priestess teaches him, of course. Just as The Magician is here to teach us all about the physical realm, The High Priestess is here to teach us all about the non-physical realm. His forte is the twelve; her forte is the thirteen.

The woman on The World holds two batons, one from The Magician and one from The Emperor. The same woman on The Star pours from two urns, one from The High Priestess (into the pond) and one from The Hanged Man (onto the land).

Let us analyze the numerology.

Within The Magician, there are four objects on his table representing the four elements. Above him is an infinity symbol (∞), a sideways eight. 4+8=12. The eight symbolizes The Star, which is the card above him; the four symbolizes The Emperor, which is the card below him. Notice that the Magician directs energy from the upper triangle down toward The Emperor; look at his hands!

The High Priestess is card number 11. Recall that she sits between two columns, resembling the Roman number II and the Arabic number 11, which is the higher vibration of two. II+2=I3. The thirteen represents the unknown, the unseen, the non-physical. Eleven—illumination—sheds light on the unseen so that it can be seen...and eventually understood. The High Priestess, as two, uses illumination to help reveal the unknown. She is the path and thus shows us the way from the eleven to the thirteen.

We said a moment ago that The Hanged Man focuses on the astral plane, the dream state. If you look at that word *astral*, it literally means "pertaining to stars," and has come to mean "pertaining to the non-physical." So The Hanged Man is the most representative, characteristic, and accomplished student of The High Priestess in the same way that The Emperor is the most representative, characteristic, and accomplished student of The Magician. From two great teachers—and two great teachings—we find two paths to proficiency, success, and accomplishment, each within its respective realm.

Before we go forward, I would like for you to fetch one more card from the deck. Seek and set out the Wheel of Fortune. Lay it down next to The World.

Now compare these two cards. The same four symbols are shown along the outer four corners. The Wheel of Fortune highlights the four fixed signs of the Zodiac just as The World does. Another way to interpret this imagery is the cycle of time. Time is ever flowing. You cannot stop time just like you cannot stop the spinning of your planet. The Wheel of Fortune also reminds us that we cannot turn off the cycles of karma.

So in moving from the Wheel of Fortune to The World, what has changed? Along the outer rim, nothing! At the Wheel of Fortune, you are at the mercy of time, karma, and physical circumstance. But at The World, all of those external conditions still apply. And yet, what we see on The World is a beautiful woman in peace, joy, and bliss for no reason. She doesn't reach these pleasurable emotions as a result of good fortune, she finds them within herself, at the center of her being, in spite of everything that is happening around her. The only difference between the Wheel of Fortune and The World is how you look at it and what you see!

This entire reading illustrates **a way** to achieve that perspective... namely, via the **middle** way!

Temperance offers a way of living that enables you to center yourself more proficiently. Temperance—XIV, lies along the journey from the Wheel of Fortune—X to The World—XXI. And notice there are eleven steps to reach The World from the Wheel of Fortune. 10+11=21.

The outer square contains The Hanged Man (above) and The Emperor (below). The Hanged Man is our time in the Astral—be it dreaming, contemplating, or meditating. The Emperor is our time in the World: "As above, so below." How we spend our time in the astral affects how our time in the world goes.

This reading tells us that by balancing ourselves between the two realms, spending time in both places appropriately, we can synergistically improve our entire experience.

The Magician and The High Priestess together represent the center point. You (in ultimate reality) are male **and** female. You are simultaneously children of the earth **and** children of the stars. You are physical **and** non-physical, human **and** spirit. When you seek inward, you find both teachers readily available to aid you within your journey.

Now let us look at some more numerology. The World is a 21/3. The Hanged Man is a 12/3. [Notice that The World is reversed: left-right and The Hanged Man is reversed: up-down.] In the center, we have The Magician and The High Priestess, which together are 1+2=3. On the right, we have The Star above and The Emperor below: 8+4=12/3, the same numerology we already saw on The Magician itself.

Summing the outer ring we have: 21+12+17+4, which totals 54/9. The inner 3 thus creates the outer 9. This is the purpose of life. By taking advantage of your center (your Higher Self), your outer life experience flourishes.

The imagery of Temperance as 14—a point within a square—is a diagram of mastery (4), inside of which is you (1)!

One: You are one, but also THE ONE. You appear separate and unique, yet are connected to the whole.

Two: You are two in that you are male and female, physical and non-physical. Everything you see and everything you seek is a reflection of your thoughts—your actions and your reactions.

Three: You are here to create and you do create in every moment, consciously or otherwise. Your combination of I-Magician and II-High Priestess endows you with the ability to create because you were made in the image and likeness of your creator.

Four: While here, you occupy a physical body, and live in a physical realm. Each morning, all appears roughly as it did the night before. This stability brings continuity to your existence in time.

Five: As you attain mastery in any endeavor, the winds of change will come and carry you to new challenges, contrasts, and conquests—propelling you further into evolution.

Six: Your yearning for perfection, beauty, and harmony molds your experience of the reality surrounding you. The hexahedral illusion can be fascinating to behold, but do not lose yourself within it.

Seven: Remember that who you really are is at the root of all experience. Seek deep within yourself to find truth.

Eight: You may be asked to jump into the void, but that is the only way to make a quantum leap. Time is an illusion, so all advancement and everything obtained, all insight and understanding, can be achieved in an instantaneous a-ha moment.

Nine: Perfection is. Completion is not. There is no true goal and thus no possibility for failure. Your reality seems real to you, and that is by design. You often think that this is all there is. Let us assure you: there is so much more than you currently see. In time, your awareness grows. There is no hurry, and yet there is no reason for you to wait. Life is everlasting.

There are no good numbers or bad numbers. There are no higher numbers or lower numbers. In ultimate reality, there is no good or evil. There is THE ONE, the absolute, with no beginning and no end.

And then, at the same time, there is infinite perspective, where each quantum of space and each quantum of time can be examined individually and in infinite detail.

You are the center of your own universe, at the core of your own creation. Paint the world with the hues of your heart and choose wisely.

Look first...then see. Know where you are...and know where you want to be. Then take the first step.

Look for love to find love, but know that there is nowhere to go and no one to be to achieve this. Love is the most abundant substance in the universe. There is no point in time or space where love isn't.

B rother Miguel, noticing what John was doing, crept into the room to not disturb him. He watched John write, wipe tears from his eyes, and then write some more. He knew and felt it in his heart that John was writing the last chapter of the book.

The next afternoon, John placed the final pages into the eager and awaiting hands of Brother Miguel. Brother Miguel beamed with anticipation, which added to the joy and accomplishment that John felt.

With the last chapter in his clasp, Brother Miguel told John the course of action going forward. A team of monks had already been collected, who would read and edit the material, adding any finishing touches that were needed. Once they were done, they would deliver the completed manuscript to the printing press so that a handful of proofs could be made. Once everyone agreed on its readiness, numerous copies would be produced and distributed.

John's part was done; yet he wasn't ready to leave. He felt that there was something still left to do or maybe something he was waiting for. Furthermore, there was a part of his vision quest he hadn't fully figured out, which distracted him.

At times, John would remember bits and pieces of his interactions with Ra, above and beyond what was written. But he knew there was something more just beyond his reach. It was like feeling around in a dark room, finding a door, but not being able to open it. Something on the other side called out to him, but he could not unlock the door to get to it.

This was what he could not yet remember:

"Ra. Can you show me what you look like?" John asked. Up to that point, John had only heard Ra, but had never seen him.

"How about I do something better? Instead of showing you what **I** look like through **your** eyes, I will show you what it looks like through **my** eyes."

The scene before John began to morph. Soon, nothing remained except a single white egg. As John examined the egg, a crack appeared and then grew across the surface. Additional cracks formed, fanning out from the center. Within them, John saw a pattern that he never noticed before.

A moment later, a small hole opened up. The tip of a tiny yellow beak could be seen poking through the hole. The being inside began eagerly chipping away at the hole, making it ever larger. Motivated by the fresh air, her efforts redoubled and soon the shell split in half and broke open.

John watched with awe as the fuzzy chick shook the rest of the shell loose and took her first steps. She blinked and looked around. In seeing John, she tilted her head and stared questioningly.

John consciousness shifted. He now looked out of her eyes instead of into them. Green grass, blue sky, yellow sun, and brown dirt—all seen for the first time…and **felt**.

His left wing quivered, drawing his focus from his surroundings to his little yellow body. *There it is again*—a trembling, except this time on the right. The pattern continued and grew stronger: shudder…tremble…calm.

His body expanded, spreading out across the blue sky. Before each tremble now came a flash of lightning. Below him, wide-open fields of green, gold, and brown extended all the way to the horizon. Not as much as a hill could be seen for miles. Rain precipitated within him and fell to the earth.

Crack…rumble…silence…crack…

John's cloud body gently began to rotate. His galactic arms, stretching out from his eye, lagged behind in graceful arcs. Cells of light glowed within the wispy, whirling motion of his body. Far in the distance, dotting the sea of blackness, floated similarly shaped rotating clusters.

The darkness intrigued John, lured his attention, and drew him in. There was darkness outside of him, and darkness at the center of him. He felt a force pulling on all parts of his body, accelerating him further into the void. Soon, not a speck of light could be seen, and yet John felt himself moving faster and faster.

With a pop, all went still. John's consciousness searched the abyss for understanding, but at first found nothing. Then a faint glow in the distance caught his attention. The glow leaked out from behind a rectangle. John felt himself float toward the light following two silhouetted figures.

Johannes opened the door and he and John stumbled into the room. The men staggered, partly from intoxication and partly from exhaustion. They fell onto the bed, sideways and side-by-side. John's auric consciousness watched as the men slept. The sky grew brighter with the approaching dawn. The first ray of sunlight raced across the hills, entered, and then lit up the room. It caressed the faces of the men lying on the bed.

John squinted his eyes against the light of the sun. He was, however, blind to all of the other frequencies that poured into the room. He groggily lifted himself off of the bed, pulled the drapes closed, and returned to Johannes' side. The observing consciousness now saw an outpouring of love emanating from John, blanking the beautiful, sleeping shape of Johannes.

Something about the glistening pulled at his consciousness, the same way the darkness had. Drifting and then racing, the observing John flowed into the river of love-light—becoming the love itself. He felt all the way into John's heart in one direction, and every inch of Johannes' body in the other. The current caught hold of him, surging out of John and streaming into Johannes.

…Rumble…rumble…rumble…crack…

With a start, he woke and opened his eyes. He felt hands caressing his chest, fingers tracing the lines in his stomach. The soft, smooth strokes were pleasant, soothing, and stimulating. His body felt utterly relaxed from the full night of activity within the full week of festivity.

As Johannes emerged further into wakefulness, the consciousness of John inside of him grew increasingly aware. He felt the vibrations of love radiating from John's hands. And he felt a complete absences of inhibition within Johannes. He watched as Johannes reached for John's hand encouraging him to explore further. He could feel Johannes' heart began to beat faster, and then heard Johannes' thoughts as his body became aroused by John's loving touch. *Keep going. This feels really good.*

Johannes' body craved more touch and more of the outpouring of love—that dear, sweet love, which was uniquely John. And now the visiting consciousness of John **knew** what it felt like to be loved by John.

...Rumble...rumble...rumble...crack...

With a start, he was scared. *Whose fear is this?* He couldn't tell. In fact, he could no longer separate John's experience from Johannes' experience. He was loving and being loved, touching and being touched, simultaneously aroused and scared.

At times, his conscious fell into the ecstasy of the moment, but then reemerged inside of Johannes' body—feeling John's touch, encouraging John's exploration, growing increasingly aroused, and wanting more. The fear evacuated, having been chased away by the pleasure.

More! More! Don't stop!

...Rumble...rumble...rumble...crack!

Violent tremors shook Johannes' body, John's body—**Ra's body**. A bolt of lightning snapped out of him and struck a tree.

...Flash...crack...rumble...rumble...rumble...

The chick, now a fully-grown hen, stood, stepped sideways, turned, and then gazed at the eggs she'd been sitting on. She had heard the crack and felt the rumble. As she investigated, she focused on the center-most egg, evidence etched across its surface. She watched...anticipated—more cracking...then the tip of a tiny beak. She stared and her eyes grew wide.

And then she caught sight of her, the fluffy, yellow, newborn chick. She could no longer restrain the love that poured out of her.

I love you, my little baby. I love you. She doesn't think this in words, because she doesn't even know words, but she thinks it— and feels it—nevertheless.

I love you. I love you. I love you. To me, you are the most beautiful creature in the entire universe. You are my child! I love you. I love you. I love you...

15 – *Fifteen* – XV

Quinze – Quindici – Quince – Fünfzehn

15/6: Harmony (6) results when one (1) embraces change (5).

Quinze – Quindici – Quince – Fünfzehn

O ne day, as John meandered the monastery grounds, he spotted a particularly handsome tourist. The man with dark hair and bright, blue eyes was well dressed and donned a meticulously groomed beard.

The tourist spotted John; he held up a finger and said, *"Scusi, Signore. Non*—hablo—*spagnolo*—pero… busco un…"

"Che cosa cerchi? Dove vuoi andare?" John interrupted the handsome Italian man, saving him from further struggle within his feeble attempt to speak Spanish.

"Amico mio! Parli italiano? Fantastico! Ti amo! Come ti chiami? Mi chiamo Emanuele…" The man spoke rapidly and enthusiastically.

"Emanuele, good to meet you. I'm John."

"Gianni, the pleasure is all mine! I have been in this country for five days now, and you are the first person I've met that speaks my language! I should have studied more Spanish before coming here…"

"Where in Italy are you from?"

"Bella Venezia! La conosci?"

"Funny you should ask. I've never been to Venice, but was considering traveling there next. I have a…friend that lives there."

"Well, now you have two! I have one more day in this country and then I am heading home myself. We should travel together! It is always nice to have a companion on the road. You know what they say: 'When two legs become four, twice the distance is covered in half the time.' Besides, you can be my translator! You wouldn't happen to speak French too, now would you?"

"In fact, I do!"

"Baciami, Madonna mia! Today is my lucky day! Maybe this time I'll actually **enjoy** the journey…"

"Do you have any interest in spending a few days in Lyon? I have friends there too. It is almost precisely half way between here and Venice, or so I'm told."

"Amico mio, with you along, we can go all the way to *Parigi* if you like!"

Paris? Now that's an idea! John considered the thought for a moment, then let it pass. He was genuinely excited to visit Lyon again and visit Venice for the first time. *Besides*—he found himself thinking—*something tells me it will be an entertaining journey with Emanuele along…*

Quinze – Quindici – Quince – Fünfzehn

M ama! Mama!" Sofia knocked rapidly as she called through the door.

Tomasina, hearing the clamoring, hurried herself across the house. "Oh dear," she whispered, "What has happened now?" She took a deep breath, and opened the door. "Baby Girl, what is it?"

"Mama, I have great news! Johannes found his father…and is bringing him here…to meet me! *Mama,* I'm so excited!"

"I'm happy for you, Baby Girl."

Relief washed over Tomasina. *Everything* ***is*** *going to work out after all*—she thought to herself

"Baby Girl, I have an idea." Tomasina said this without thinking it.

"What is it, *Mama?* "

"How about we throw you an engagement party while Johannes' father is here? It's Klaus, right? I'll invite the cousins and make sure Lorita brings Feliciano. As you know, there are not very many men in the family, so I want to make sure Klaus has a peer to talk to. You know how men are…"

Sofia's tears doubled. Without voicing a response, she threw her arms around her mother and hugged her firmly.

"*Mama,* I am the luckiest girl in the world!" she said.

#   #   #

About the Author

David P. Tangredi is an intuitive guide. He employs archetypal tools such as Tarot, Astrology, and Numerology to bolster, assist, and inspire. Foundationally, he utilizes healing energies and the Akashic Records within all of his work.

David first achieved success as a Software Engineer and Architect. In 2005, he began the transition from technology to philosophy, from physics to metaphysics. Instead of writing code and technical specs, he now writes a blog and books. His core goals remain the same. He continues to combine logical, problem solving skills with creativity, intuition, and intention to help individuals accomplish their ambitions.

In recent years, David founded **A Fool's Inclination**. We are all fools on this journey called life. Guidance is always available, but often appears as subtle inclinations. The archetypal Fool teaches through his example. He shows us the joy and bliss that can be experienced by living in the present moment. He reminds us that the courageous are not fearless and that through increased awareness everything becomes easier.

David divides his time between writing and working with clients in private sessions, group workshops, and seminars. He is based in Austin, Texas, where the city slogan is "Keep Austin Weird." Can you think of a better place for a Fool?

Visit afoolsinclination.com to learn more.

www.ingramcontent.com/pod-product-compliance
Lightning Source LLC
Chambersburg PA
CBHW030930260626
47169CB00002B/433